THE GAMBLE

BOOK TWO: THE LOSS OF CERTAINTY SERIES

THE GAMBLE

For Sherrie Cotter,
With affection

T. P. JONES

T.P. "Tom" Jones

Synergy Books

The Gamble
Book Two: The Loss of Certainty Series
Published by Synergy Books
P.O. Box 80107
Austin, Texas 78758

For more information about our books, please write to us, call 512.478.2028, or visit our website at www.synergybooks.net.

Publisher's Cataloging-in-Publication
(Provided by Quality Books, Inc.)

Jones, T. P., 1941-
   The gamble / T.P. Jones.
   p. cm. -- (The loss of certainty series ; bk. 2)
   LCCN 2009931881
   ISBN-13: 978-0-9840760-2-4
   ISBN-10: 0-9840760-2-6

   1. United States--Race relations--Fiction. 2. Whites
--Race identity--Fiction. 3. African Americans--Race
identity--Fiction. 4. City and town life--Iowa--
Fiction. 5. Local government--Iowa--Fiction. 6. Iowa--
Social conditions--Fiction. 7. Iowa--Economic
conditions--Fiction. 8. Iowa--Fiction.   I. Title.
II. Series: Jones, T. P., 1941- Loss of certainty series
; bk. 2.

   PS3610.O6298G36 2010   813'.6
                        QBI09-600118

This is a work of fiction. Many of the scenes in this as well as the later volumes are written from the points of view of people who are technically trained. The author has attempted to be as accurate as possible in his portrayal of these professions, but if any errors have managed to slip through, they are the author's responsibility entirely. Furthermore, the characters themselves are fictitious. Any resemblance to actual people is purely coincidental.

10 9 8 7 6 5 4 3 2 1

In memory of my parents,
Thomas P. Jones Jr. and Eleanor R.B. Jones.

Author's Note

~

In the 1980s, I spent two years as a participant-observer in a number of city departments in Dubuque, Iowa, intending to write a novel describing how a city on a major river prepares for and fights a massive flood. I expected to spend, all told, four years on the project. But no matter how I stretched and twisted and knotted my simple linear narrative, I could not make it encompass the complexities of life in a place such as Dubuque. The four years became eighteen, the political novel became a novel about business and race and religion, as well, and the single book I originally envisioned grew into a trilogy.

Jackson, the first volume, told the story of an attempt to save a large local meatpacker, threatened with bankruptcy, by selling it to its employees and at the same time breaking down the barriers that have traditionally separated management from rank-and-file employees. *The Gamble*, the second volume, takes up the matter of race, that universal human problem of "the other," of groups of people who have been defined as different in some fundamental and demeaning way by the dominant group within their community or nation, whether it be Gypsies in Europe or Untouchables in India or African-Americans in the United States. Of course, American blacks have made considerable progress in recent decades, but they are still not easily accepted in many places. In *The Gamble*, an attempt is made to answer the following question: What do you do after all of the laws are in place but the racism still remains?

~

Part I

~

Late December

Chapter 1

~

Ned Pickett drove one of the early cars, providing overlap between the second and third shifts. The lineup would be recorded, and later he could stop back at the law enforcement center for the tape and listen to it as he patrolled.

As he did before each tour of duty, he checked the squad car, beginning with a walk around it, looking for dings. Next, the trunk—first aid kit, Ambu bag, couple of blankets, flares, tape measure, traffic vest, pry bar, tire chains. He felt under the back seat for drugs or anything else ditched by the bozos picked up by the second shift. Lights and flashers okay. PA, siren, top lights. In the glove compartment—forms and envelopes, a couple of rounds of number six birdshot for varmints. He noted with satisfaction the several repair links for the tire chains. Big storm on the way. He checked the Remington 870 12-gauge (a loaded four-round magazine), then used his tuning forks to verify the radar gun's calibration. Everything being shipshape, he notified the comm center he was beginning his tour of duty.

He drove out to Five Corners, where the early downtown car would sit during the shift change unless something happened, and parked in plain sight. From his vantage at the edge of the Super Drug's parking lot, he had a straight shot down Twelfth Street as far as St. Luke's. He could see a couple hundred yards along Colter and Brennan, less of Railroad and Anne. The restaurant on the opposite corner, the pharmacy and supermarket behind him, all closed for the night. Not much traffic. A typical Thursday.

One of the street lamps on Colter had failed, and he made a note to contact the city. Despite the cold, he opened the driver's side window. With the window up, Ned felt duller, slightly anesthetized. He preferred summer, when he could keep it down all the time. Now, the cold air quickly filled the squad, wrapping itself around him with a kind of frigid intimacy.

He waited. The minutes ticked by.

A car approached the stop sign on Anne Street, a dark sedan, drifting steadily along, not fast, but at a speed that suggested a certain insolence, or so it seemed, for Ned knew with his cop's instinct that the driver had no intention of stopping.

And the fellow didn't, merely slowing briefly at the stop sign, the genuflection of an unbeliever, and then continuing placidly onward, directly across Ned's line of sight.

Ned started the squad and put it in gear but didn't pull out. As he watched the taillights receding—both lights functioning properly, he noted—he concentrated not on them so much as the cascade of his own thoughts—the way his mind worked in the presence of some trivial violation like this. First, the slight letdown feeling, very brief, like the flicker of a strobe light, so quick the inner eye might miss it entirely. Then the impulse to take the matter personally, as if the guy running the stop sign had been flipping Ned the bird. Anger came next, and when younger, he would often act on this. But not now. Now he simply readjusted his thinking, telling himself that most likely it had nothing to do with him, and anyway it was a trivial thing, not worth making a federal case over.

He removed his foot from the gas pedal and watched the taillights disappear. The whole sequence had taken only a few moments, but he felt a certain satisfaction, as a person does at the completion of a successful transaction, however minor and hidden from the world.

He settled back and resumed his wait for the other third-shift people to begin their tours. Then he drove down to the law enforcement center to get the lineup tape.

~

At one a.m., when Moocher Cole, who was running the game, came back with beer and smokes, he also brought the news that he could no longer see the stars.

"Storm's movin' in."

Moocher would sit in if they were short a player, but otherwise he ran errands and kibitzed.

Deuce Goetzinger threw his hand in and stared up into the dim ceiling joists, beyond which he imagined the now-starless sky. Since he'd arrived, after finishing the second shift at the water plant, he hadn't been able to buy a card. On nights like this, he dumped his busted hands early and never lost much, only the time spent twiddling his thumbs and listening to the chatter, hardly worth the price of admission given this bunch of lumberheads. Might as well be back at the plant watching the gauges.

Moocher passed around the beer, giving the latest weather report—freezing rain first, then the snow.

"I never worry about ice," Ed Byner announced. Byner couldn't open his mouth without annoying Deuce.

"You're a great ice man, are you, Ed?"

"I know how to handle a car. No brag. Always been a good driver, that's all. Taught myself." The button was in front of Byner, and with each card, he dealt another nugget of the grandeur which was himself. "My dad couldn't drive for shit. Mom was even worse. Whenever we went anywhere, I was the one drove, even before I got my license."

"Ed Byner, the child prodigy," Deuce said.

This little exchange, the irritation of it, revived Deuce's interest in the game for the moment, although it didn't do anything to improve his cards. He dumped more hands and listened to more chatter and tried to remember what it felt like to enjoy playing.

The conversation meandered from one subject to another in its faintly logical way, from driving on ice to ice hockey to rollerblades to the best way to cripple an attacker to medical costs to proctology and finally alighted on the worst job any of them had ever held down.

"That's easy," Deuce said as he tossed away another worthless hand, "farm work. Go clean pig shit out of a confinement building once, you want a good time."

"Pretty crummy, all right," Norm Pfohl agreed, "but I'll tell you what you couldn't get me to do, not in a million years—work on skyscrapers." Pfohl, a tight player, stared intently at his cards as he spoke. "I see pictures of guys strolling along an itty-bitty beam a hundred stories up, it gives me the creeps."

"It's some Indian tribe does it," Ed Byner chimed in.

"Mohawks." This came from Moocher, who knew odd shit like that. He had settled down at a nearby card table and begun to play solitaire.

"Mohawks, Apaches, whatever," Byner said. "They got no fear of heights. They're too dumb to be afraid or something. You take the fear away, why hell, the job's easy as pie."

The conversation having been opened to shitty work in general, other candidates followed: coroner, miner, migrant farm worker. Moocher even nominated prostitutes. "Think of the scumbags those girls got to do it to."

Deuce ignored this byplay, his mind drawn back to his life on the farm. His childhood, the unremitting misery. The old man on his case every other friggin' minute. Like living under a goddamn vow, his father as pious about farmwork as any abbot had ever been about the life in a monkery.

Another hand was dealt. Byner, with a little pair showing, raised the bet. Deuce had a king in the hole, nothing showing, but he stayed, playing carelessly, his thoughts still on the farm—the recent past, barely two months ago, when his mother had left a message on his answering machine, begging him to come back and run out the upper fields, his father too busy to harvest the corn.

"Do it for me," his mother had pleaded, knowing full well that he'd never do it for the old man. Deuce could still hear the pain in her voice, and he knew how much she hated having to shame him into doing it.

The next card didn't help. He had a possible inside straight, but he thought what the fuck and raised the ante anyway, something he never did.

A couple of the others, who obviously didn't hold much, had folded as soon as they saw Deuce raise. He was tempted to stay, just for the hell of it, and try to drive everybody else out on the basis of his reputation. But Byner was still in, which meant he had something, maybe not a lot, but something, and when Byner got a few beers in him, he couldn't be bluffed. He lost for other reasons. Anyway, Deuce didn't feel bored enough to do something really stupid, so he tossed his own hand in.

He leaned back and returned to his recollections; his mind's eye now scanned the horizon, the long curve of Iowa prairie above the farm, for on that day two months ago, he had done what his mother wanted—he had harvested the corn, for her and because of the tone in her voice. How strange it had felt, perched up in the picker again after so many years, counting the rows as he swung the machine onto each new set, flushing pheasants and rabbits, watching a massive rainstorm advancing from the west. After the droughty summer, the harvest was meager, but still he could look back with satisfaction at the clean-picked fields when he was through, a satisfaction he never remembered experiencing as a youth. He remembered only his resentment. His father had taken his labor. Even that wasn't his.

Byner won the hand. As he raked in his winnings, he said to Deuce, "Guess this ain't your night." Byner fancied himself a crackerjack poker player, and his smile suggested that maybe the forces for justice in the universe had finally been properly aligned and Deuce's seven-year run of luck come to an end.

Perhaps not quite yet. On the next hand, he caught two pair. On the draw, everyone else took three cards, and he didn't take any. He won the hand on the pat bluff, although he took no pleasure in it.

~

By two a.m., Ned Pickett had parked the squad car on Freight Street. Before him rose the massive, somber brick walls of the packinghouse, where the next day the final round of layoffs would begin.

Not much had been happening on the shift. A night of windshield inspections. No domestic calls. In cold weather like this, everybody kept their doors and windows closed, so the neighbors had less to complain about.

The lineup tape hadn't contained anything interesting, either. Talk about the blizzard coming in. Ice first, looked like. If it hit before the morning commute, Ned would probably end up with some overtime. That was okay.

Streetlights weakly speckled the flanks of the antiquated packing company building, grown too large to survive. In just a few hours, many of the employees would begin their last shift, the kill floor people first. He remembered the summer he worked there as a kid and how much he hated it.

The end of the company had been a long time coming, decades depending on who told the tale, and though Ned was a loyal union man, hated to see any union people lose their jobs, no matter how shitty, his sympathies had been worn down over the chronic struggle to save the place.

Restlessly, he put the squad back in gear and moved out from beneath the shadow of the old plant, his thoughts returning full circle, to the men soon to be laid off, many of them of his generation, many, he knew, probably too old to catch on anywhere else. How would he have felt, he wondered, if this had been his final shift on the force?

Ned was fifty-two, a cop for nineteen years, a patrolman all that time except for a brief stint as sergeant, until he made them bust him back to doughboy. When the time came and they forced him to retire, he'd do security work, he supposed. After that, who knows? With luck, he'd already be dead.

Uptown, he made a slow pass along Central Avenue. He drove at a crawl by the pool hall, closed hours ago, but a faint glow still visible from within, spilling over the partition in the back of the main room. Moocher Cole would be running one of his poker games. Illegal, of course, although Ned wasn't averse to sitting in on a game himself from time to time. A faint impulse arose to put the arm on Moocher and his friends, even fainter than the impulse earlier to give a traffic ticket to the guy who ran the stop sign. Occasionally, the cops busted a game, but only if they'd been getting complaints. It wasn't, as far as Ned was concerned, real police work.

He let the squad continue to inch along, past the empty storefront next door and then the title company next to that.

~

The button had come around to Deuce again. Out of his irritation, he chose Kansas City lowball, a game the others didn't much like. But he'd been pulling crappy cards all night, so he might as well take advantage of the fact. Sure enough, he dealt himself nothing but crabs and ice water.

Ed Byner had gotten off on one of his pet peeves.

"Here you got all these people at the Pack about to lose their jobs," he was bitching, "and the niggers get everything handed to them on a silver platter."

"They're not self-made men like you, is that right, Ed?"

"Who the hell built this country, Goetzinger?" Byner demanded. "Wha'd'ya suppose Daniel Boone would think of this shit?"

These were not questions Deuce cared to explore. Byner looked at him with satisfaction.

The conversation continued. Everybody had a theory. Deuce forgot about himself for a moment and sat back and listened. Since almost no blacks lived in the city, none of these clowns knew jack shit, just what they saw on TV or heard from their dumb friends.

On the other hand, he wondered why there were any blacks at all in Jackson. Why would they choose to live where so many people hated them? But then again, what was the option, living in Cabrini-Green or one of them other Chicago projects? That had to be it—damned if you do, damned if you don't.

"Hey, Deuce, you gonna bet or what?"

Deuce didn't move. So, okay, Jackson wasn't a decent place for a black man. What about a white guy? What about himself? What the hell was he doing there? Work, poker, chickies—that was his life. Pathetic. He supposed he could get married. The women he took out were each year a year older and more desperate to settle down and start raising a family. But if he did get married, it would just be to please his mother, and what kind of fucking reason was that? Deuce had no interest in children. The world had too many goddamn people in it already.

"He's gone to sleep."

Probably he should quit his job and become a poker hustler. That's what he should do. Go out and live on the edge. At least there'd be some juice then. His mother would disapprove. Her disapproval would be bottomless. But what the fuck, anything was better than what he was doing now.

He threw his hand in, waving after it in disgust. "You can cash me out."

"What? It ain't even 3:30 yet," Filer said. "The night's hardly begun."

"I'm through. That's it for me" was all Deuce said.

"Let the bastard go," Byner told the others.

Deuce gave him a big, false smile. "Thanks, Ed. I knew you'd understand."

"Fuck you."

Deuce took his money and went home.

❧

Two hours later and still no sign of the storm, Ned Pickett had parked the squad car at Ice Harbor Place, pointed toward the bluffs.

In the distance, across a sheaf of railroad tracks, shadowy factory and warehouse buildings were backlit by the downtown streetlights, the tracks mostly unused now, the buildings abandoned.

This late, it wasn't worth it even to work traffic. Nothing had happened the whole shift and nothing was likely to, not now, so Ned's attention had flagged a little and he failed to spot the three figures until they had reached the far side of the tracks and were already disappearing into an alley between two buildings.

He put the squad in gear and stepped on the gas but didn't hit the lights or siren. The car bucked across the tracks, then did a one-eighty on the loose gravel as he circled to the far end of the alley and braked. Nobody.

He panned the scene—filled with deep shadows—and gently depressed the accelerator and began prowling around the old industrial buildings, his lights still off.

Ned didn't care if he actually apprehended anybody. That might involve a foot chase, and over the years he'd put on a few pounds. He just wanted to get a good look. All the local police characters were well known. One good look was all it'd take. Then, if need be, the bozos could be picked up at leisure.

He cruised slowly among the old buildings, trolling as patiently as a fisherman. He rolled down the window again, as he had earlier, the frigid air crackling in his ears.

Like a boat in a current, the car drifted. Waiting, waiting…but still, nothing.

Finally, disappointed, he returned to Ice Harbor Place and began searching for any sign of a break-in. He started with the commercial buildings, driving at first, playing the squad's spotlight off the doors and windows, and when that didn't turn up anything, he took his flashlight and began checking on foot. Like other old-timers on the third shift, Ned took pride in doing this kind of work thoroughly.

But still he couldn't find anything. When he had seen the three figures, they appeared to be loping away from the old railroad station now being used by the historical museum, and so Ned finally turned his attention to this building. He couldn't imagine there was much worth stealing. But, he reminded himself, the mind of your average deviant worked in wondrous ways.

The main entrance remained securely locked. He slowly circled the building, checking each window in turn. In back, grunting, he climbed up onto the station platform. Wooden shelters had been erected, forming a walkway from the station to a Pullman coach being used as part of an exhibit. One of the plywood sheets stood askew, as if it had been removed and then rapidly replaced. Ned approached cautiously, playing his light up and down the loose edge of the board.

He pulled the sheet out a little and shined his light behind it. The door to the station had been forced. He pulled the plywood out far enough so he could squeeze behind it. As he approached the building, he smelled something. At the door, he stopped dead in his tracks.

CHAPTER 2

~

Walter Plowman's emergency radio had switched on automatically when the National Weather Service upgraded the winter storm watch to a warning, and now he sat wolfing down his breakfast before rushing off to the TV station.

His wife El had taken her bowl of bran flakes into the dining room, where she could stare out at a yard as drab as her mood. The vista from the kitchen was identical, but Walter, as usual, kept the blinds drawn, unwilling to think about the weather while he was eating his bacon and eggs. He'd been a TV weatherman since forever and loved his job the way other men love sports, but still he would not look at the sky until he had finished eating. El preferred the daylight.

At the moment, however, the sky, an intense, woolly gray, promised little, and through the French doors, she sadly contemplated her cherished old roses. The canvas tarps that used to protect them in the winter had become stiff and frayed and discolored with age, the wooden frames holding them up as spraddle-legged and rickety as old men. She should do something, she really should, if only she had the time.

In the kitchen, Walter picked up a rasher of bacon and inspected it, then bit off an end and savored the sweet saltiness. He was recalling a mud daubers' nest he had found several months earlier, constructed high in the rafters of an old abandoned cabin next to the Mississippi. Of course, he reminded himself, the idea that wasps could predict spring floods was nothing but an old wives' tale and no doubt he would have forgotten all about it except for the fact that other, more reputable precursors of high water had tracked across the Upper Midwest since—heavy fall rains, extreme cold—and now this, the first winter storm, a big one. Ice, then snow. And yet, none of this, not the wasps' nest certainly or any of the rest, made a big spring flood inevitable. Or, for that matter, even likely.

Something caught his eye, a glint of color, a Post-it note on the fridge, grape purple, recalling the crayons he had used as a child. For a moment, the anticipation of the storm and the taste of the bacon and the Crayola color formed a single complex but pleasant sensation. Then, remembering that he was in a rush, he swallowed and went quickly on to the next bite.

In the other room, the gray light surrounded El and vaguely touched the Victorian furniture and seemed to grow darker. She thought once more that she really ought to do something about the roses, the idea obsessing her, pushed away only to return, another symptom, this obsessing over minor problems, of her depression. Too late, not enough time even if she hadn't had so many other things to do. She sighed, conscious of how much effort life required. And to get away from these thoughts, if not herself, she picked up her cereal and wandered back into the kitchen and sat down opposite Walter and watched him organizing his food on his plate with quick movements, as a child might cut shapes out of construction paper.

The phone began to ring. Or rather, the phones. El had had them installed all over the house, the one in the kitchen higher-toned and a splinter of a second before the dining room, like a grace note. Burdened at the moment by her sense of all that needed to be done, she didn't answer immediately.

Walter listened to the braying chorus. El got half a dozen calls for every one of his...although, he supposed, with the storm bearing down on them, someone might be trying to reach him. He had half a mind to answer it himself. But even as he considered this radical possibility, El rose heavily from her chair.

She picked up the receiver, then fell silent and listened for several long moments. No doubt something to do with one of her myriad of organizations, the city council most likely. He waited, mildly wishing that he possessed his wife's ferret-like interest in many things rather than his own elephantine one in the weather.

"What?" she said, her voice rising. Again she listened, but not for long. "Don't tell me that." And finally, after an even briefer gap, "I'll be right there."

El hung up, thinking that it was true what people said, no matter how bad things were, they could always get worse. She grabbed her unfinished cereal. "Gotta go!"

"What happened?"

"That was Reiny. Somebody vandalized the exhibit." The bowl and cup clattered as she dumped them into the sink.

"The exhibit?" On non-weather matters, Walter's mind didn't always engage at once. He looked up complacently, his fork raised halfway to his mouth, his hair, which had gone white, flopping down over his unlined forehead.

El stopped long enough to cast a testy look at him and reply sarcastically, "The black history exhibit?"

"Oh," he said meekly, and then, making a weak attempt to rise to the occasion, added, "dear me."

"Right," she said as she threw on her coat on, "dear me." She hurried through the mudroom and down the back steps.

"Be careful," she heard him call, coming after her. "Don't forget the storm." When she didn't slow down or acknowledge that she'd heard, he yelled, "Stop! Councilwoman Plowman!"

She paused and turned halfway around, looking back at him over her shoulder. "I heard you." He stood holding the door open with one hand and his napkin with the other, his white bangs snapping in the wind.

He paused. That was something else about Walter that could irritate. It took him time to gather his thoughts, and, once gathered, there turned out to be too many of them. But now all he said was, "Ice!"

"What about it?"

"Freezing rain before the snow. Freezing rain, then sleet."

"Okay. Fine." She waved and continued toward her car. More troubles, always more troubles.

Walter watched her disappear into the garage and an instant later heard the whirr of the electric motor as the door folded up. He was irritated, too, but his irritation didn't resemble his wife's, arising not from impatience but rather its opposite, patience violated. He watched the maroon-colored Buick backing quickly down the drive. El always drove too fast, forward, backward, it made no difference.

Before he went inside, he surveyed the sky. Clouds scudded overhead. A wind had come up, bitter. He judged the direction, southerly, beginning, he imagined, to swing around more to the east.

In the kitchen, he called down to the station to make sure they had heard about the attack on the museum. By the time he got back to his breakfast, he'd all but lost his appetite, still filled with the vision of El, coattails flying, tote bag clutched under one arm, jog-walking toward her car as if she'd already put the storm out of her mind.

He deposited his own dishes in the sink and headed at once for the station.

~

Police tape had been stretched across the door to the museum. El ducked under, into the former stationmaster's office where tickets to the exhibit were sold and audio cassettes rented for the self-guided tours. The vandals had turned drawers upside down and disemboweled the booklets describing the exhibit and unspooled the cassette reels, flinging the tapes into a mare's nest on the floor.

Even as El inspected the mess, which could be put to rights easily enough, her thoughts lay elsewhere, in the next room where putting things to rights was not likely to be such a simple matter. Reluctantly she moved through the door into what had been the station's waiting room, where the exhibit proper began, a mock-up of the Mississippi Delta. She could hear muffled voices from behind the far wall.

The murals had been slashed, flaps of canvas folded over on themselves and racist slogans spray-painted. In the scene before the general store, the three mannequins representing black men now hung from the rafter ends, while the mannequin representing the white overseer, its foot raised on the front end of a Packard automobile, had not been touched. El advanced farther into the room, her shock quickly replaced by outrage. Smelling feces, she glanced into the keepsake trunk on the porch of the shotgun house and backed away at once.

She stared around herself at the devastation and remembered the day the exhibit had opened, Hiram and Pearl Johnson touring it, the old Pullman porter so pleased and proud at this evocation of his Southern youth, stepping jauntily along and twirling the tip of his cane as he went, his bright eyes alighting on object after object, recalling incidents and sharing them with El and the other officials clustered around. How perfect the moment had been, how wonderful the pleasure she herself had felt, both personally and as the head of the museum board, that they could so honor this decent old man.

Back in the anteroom El righted a chair and collapsed into it, unwilling for the moment to see the rest. So many people, so much effort. And now this! "Why?" she asked aloud. Why would anyone do something as vicious as this? Although, in truth, she knew very well why.

Others came in, ignoring the police tape. Rachel Brandeis, the *Tribune* reporter, arrived and tried to question her.

"Go see for yourself," El told her.

Finally she got up again and walked back into the Delta room. One of the museum staffers had materialized and was standing idly, making no attempt to begin cleaning up the mess.

"Cut down those mannequins, Joyce," El told her.

"Reiny told me not to, El. He said to make sure nobody touches anything." Joyce seemed about to cry. El's first impulse was to countermand the order but changed her mind. Perhaps it had something to do with the police. She embraced Joyce and told her okay and not to worry, they were going to remount the exhibit, as good as new, better, although right at that moment El had no idea how.

Somehow! Her anger came in waves. This was not acceptable. This was an outrage! She made her way through the rest of the ruined exhibit, forcing herself to take in the damage as she went, but moving quickly. Outside, she found graffiti painted on the side of the Pullman sleeper, but the car itself remained locked. Apparently the vandals hadn't been able to get inside. That was something, at least. For a moment, she dared to hope that they hadn't gotten into the other half of the exhibit, either: the old baggage room that had been converted into a display of the Johnsons' life in Jackson. As soon as she reached the large sliding door to the room, she realized the hope was forlorn. Everywhere she looked, she saw more devastation.

A number of people were in the room, several police officers and a couple of media people besides Rachel Brandeis. Reiny Kopp's wife, Kate Sullivan, wandered disconsolately around, the camera she carried hanging limply at her side as if she couldn't bring herself to raise it and record the scene. The museum director himself stood with Brandeis and a police sergeant before the frame which held the quilt Pearl Johnson had sewn especially for the exhibit.

As El paused at the door, another person passed her carrying camera equipment, and she recognized the police photographer. He went immediately over to Reiny and the sergeant, and by the time El reached them, he was explaining his normal procedure for Reiny's benefit.

"I provide a free set of prints to the police. I sell others to interested parties."

"I'll want several."

"No problem."

"I want pictures of everything, close-ups, the works," Reiny told him. "I'm looking for stuff I can blow up and get good resolution."

"You got her." Immediately the photographer set about his work.

El shook hands with the grave and businesslike sergeant, then turned to Reiny. "This is obscene. I hate to think what this is going to do to the Johnsons. And you, too. All the work, all the work. And now this." It had been one of his best efforts. He nodded curtly, dismissively. Work meant nothing. Work could be put in again.

She turned her attention to the police officer, who was nodding. "Very nasty business," he said.

El had her back to the quilt, putting off the moment when she would have to confront it. "Reiny said that Ned Pickett made the discovery."

Pickett stood several paces away, talking to another cop. The sergeant called him over, and the heavyset patrolman approached deliberately.

El knew Pickett. An old-timer on the force, although El's contact with him had mostly been in his role as president of the police association. His ancestors had been union activists for generations, although so far as El knew, Ned was the first cop in the lineage.

She shook hands with him, and he told her what he knew. After he described the scene—his fruitless pursuit of the vandals, his search for evidence of a break-in—El said merely, "I'm sorry you didn't get a good look at them."

He jutted out his chin and scratched it. "So am I." He spoke in the inflectionless way she associated with cops.

The sergeant assured her that all the local police characters would be hauled in and grilled.

"What are the chances some of them did it?"

"Possible."

"Maybe," Pickett observed deliberately. He stood gazing thoughtfully over El's shoulder toward the quilt. She took a deep breath and turned to look herself.

For an instant, she thought the large patchwork coverlet remained undamaged. But only for an instant. Then she saw. Some of the patches had been left as is, but others had been entirely spray painted out. The logic quickly became apparent. Only the squares depicting African Americans, mostly members of Hiram and Pearl Johnson's family, had been obliterated, while other, city scenes, had been spared, just as in the other room the mannequin representing the white overseer hadn't been touched.

"Such viciousness," she said. "Such ignorance."

"Is that what you think?" Reiny asked. "Ignorance?" He stood, thin and bony, with a kind of ugly good looks, like a half-starved rock star. His expression betrayed little, only his usual calculation. When El didn't respond, he said, "These assholes knew exactly what they were doing."

"It *is* ignorance," El persisted.

Other reporters had been steadily arriving and joining the little group she stood among, including a fellow with a TV cameraman from Walter's station.

"At the level you're talking about," Reiny sniffed disdainfully, "we're all ignorant."

"Maybe it didn't have anything to do with race," Ned Pickett suggested. "A personal grudge, maybe. Made to look like something else."

El found Pickett's cool cop's detachment, his willingness to consider all the possibilities, as distasteful as Reiny's cocksureness.

"At the moment," she said, "it doesn't make any difference. It's happened. I hope you can find out who did it."

"Do you have a list of known local racists?" Rachel Brandeis asked. The cops shook their heads. Reiny merely laughed.

The reporter persisted. "Before I moved here last summer, I read about an incident involving a group of blacks passing through town. What about the people involved in that?"

El looked at her with misgivings. Despite the provocation, this was not the kind of publicity she wanted. Brandeis, the sharp New Yorker, on her way up in the journalist's trade, to whom Jackson was nothing more than a stopover, could be counted on to make the most of this opportunity.

Where, El wondered, was Johnny Pond? As the one black newsman in the city, why wasn't he there? Could it be possible that he hadn't yet heard? Didn't he have a police scanner like everybody else?

El and Reiny and the two cops talked some more and answered the reporters' questions. El gave Brandeis a quote and did an on-camera interview for Walter's station. After a time, people began to drift off. Reiny left to see how the police photographer was coming along. Brandeis walked from one devastated display to another, jotting down notes. El went over to hug Kate Sullivan, who stared sadly at each poor ruined object before reluctantly raising her camera to record it.

Finally El couldn't wait around any longer. She had something to do and do quickly. She caught up with Reiny and told him about Walter's weather forecast and ordered him to send the museum staffers home and seal the building as soon as the police were through and he had his pictures.

Outside, spotting Johnny Pond backing his car out and about to drive away, she called to him. He stopped and rolled his window down.

"I wondered where you were," she said. "Did you go inside?"

"I did." He filled the driver's seat to overflowing, the sedan too small for his bulky frame.

"Did you see everything?" El asked. "It's terrible. Did you see what they did to the quilt?"

"Saw enough. Vandalism's all the same."

His habitual demeanor, at once distant and intimate, had deserted him, replaced by a steely, shuttered look.

"It's simply awful, Johnny. I can't tell you how badly I feel. How angry!"

"Yeah."

"Do you have a few minutes?"

"Why?" The question was hostile.

"Come with me up to Hiram and Pearl's. I don't want them to hear about this on the news."

He looked off in the distance, his lips pressed tightly together. He was a reporter. Even a story he absolutely despised was still a story, and he'd want to get it on the air before anybody else. His gaze swung back around to El.

"I'll meet you there."

"Thank you."

El watched him drive off. A light, cold rain had begun to fall, and when she got to her car, she saw that a thin veneer of ice already covered the windshield. Walter had been right. Too impatient to get the scraper out, she took off her glove and pounded the glass with the base of her hand and picked the ice fragments off, feeling the cold like small knife points inserted under her fingernails. Then she got in and followed Johnny Pond.

CHAPTER 3

∾

The blizzard set in quickly. Soon sleet and finally snow began to fall, but by then, ice gleamed from trees and power lines and streets. With sharp reports rising above the keening of the storm, tree limbs failed and plunged into yards and streets, the ice that encased them shattering as they hit. Electrical lines yawed in the wind, tugging at their moorings until they pulled free in an explosion of sparks, lashing the ground. A firestorm of sirens spread across the city.

J.J. Dusterhoft, driving one of the city trucks, backed up the hills to spread his salt, weaving around abandoned and disabled vehicles. J.J. worked the hills because he had a reputation as the best driver in the street department, although J.J. himself would have opined that talking was his real forte, with other activities tacked on, something to keep his hands busy, as it were. At the moment, his hands were very busy. But he didn't stop talking. He cajoled his truck. He warned off the idiots still out on the road, their vehicles sashaying all around him. He considered other career choices. And he waited for something to go wrong with his truck, as it always did during the first big storm of the winter.

He worked the arterial streets, leaving the secondaries for later, probably a lot later. It took only one or two passes to reach the top of most of the hills, but the long, steep grade on University was a different kettle of fish. Several times, he backed as far up as he could, the truck gradually losing its momentum. "Come on, baby, come on, come on, come on!" he urged her, having finally made it around the big curve next to Leaky's Tap, the brow of the bluff just up ahead, but the truck just couldn't...quite...make it.

On the next try, halfway back up, with enough speed to make it to the top this time, he heard something snap. The spreader stopped throwing salt. "Figures," he said, and pulled over. From the sound of it, he guessed that probably the chain driving the augur had broken. He got out, hoping to field-fix it, but the chain seemed okay, and he couldn't find anything else the matter. Finally, he gave up and drove down to the garage to let one of the mechanics have a look-see.

He had to get in line, several of the other drivers already there with ailments of one sort or another: split hoses, welds that didn't hold, broken drive chains. As they waited, they lounged around and drank coffee and groused. The trashing of the museum had come up, and they were having what J.J. called their "Negro discussion." The word "Negro" was long out of date, but down at the garage, it was still in use, the fellows in the street department not being slaves to current fashion.

He said, "I think I would've made a good black man."

Jerry Caan looked up from the euchre game he was playing while he waited for a hydraulic hose to be replaced. "As a white guy, Dusterhoft, you ain't such great shakes. Don't expect it'd be much of an improvement just because you got a paint job."

J.J. ignored this jibe. "I could have risen above my condition," he said loftily. "Now you, Jerry, I hate to say it, but if you had been black, you'd probably be dead by now, not having the gift for fitting in."

"If you were colored, Dusterhoft, it'd give prejudice a good name." "Colored" was another word still au courant among the street elite.

They went on like this until Hank Kraft, their boss, stuck his head out the door of his office. "Don't you fellows have some work to do?"

"Yes, we do, and if the city'd give us decent equipment, we'd be out there doing it, you bet," J.J. assured him. And so they started to rag on Kraft.

The fix finally accomplished, J.J. went back out. He still had a partial load of salt, but decided he'd better pick up some more. In weather like this, you needed traction. The more weight in the box, the better. Snow fell thickly now, covering the ice—*like a hunter scattering leaves over his snare*, J.J. thought. The analogy pleased him.

Down at the AgriComp terminal, he drove onto the scales and weighed in, then swung behind the main building, a long, gable-shaped storage shed, and stopped at the salt pile. An end loader scooped up buckets of salt and dropped them into the box, the truck shuddering. The operator gave him a thumbs-up, and J.J. drove back to the terminal office, weighed in again, and went inside to sign the load ticket.

"Pretty bad out there?" the clerk behind the counter asked as he tore off J.J.'s copy of the ticket.

"Demolition derby."

"People out in weather like this don't have the sense they were born with."

"Well," J.J. said, "I guess you're right. I'm out in it, and I'm not feeling particularly bright at the moment."

Back on the road, he jockeyed the truck along, heading back to University to finish what he'd started.

Halfway up the hill this time, however, a small red Mazda blocked the way. It appeared to have spun out and hit a parked car, coming to rest at right angles to the line of travel.

"Well, what have we here?" J.J. said to himself, for he recognized the driver, who was out inspecting the damage. J.J. set the brake, got out himself, and gingerly made his way up the slope.

"Must have a big game somewhere, Deuce, to be out in widow-maker weather like this." J.J. had been known to sit in on a poker game from time to time. Not high-stakes games, though, and not with the likes of Deuce Goetzinger.

"Cards?" Deuce said. "No chance. It's my goddamn old man."

"What about him?"

"You're not going to believe this. The son-of-a-bitch is out harvesting corn."

J.J. shook his head. "Well, that's certainly what I'd wanna be doing if I didn't have to drive this darn truck around."

"Right."

J.J. couldn't help but laugh. "Like they say, all farmers are a bale shy of a full load. Don't see why your daddy should be any different." Fritz Goetzinger might not be your average farmer, but he had the attitude.

Hearing tires spinning, J.J. looked around. A car had come up behind the salt truck and tried to pass. Upon moving out of the lee of the truck, it immediately hit a patch of unsalted ice.

He turned back toward Deuce. "Guess this ain't the time to psychoanalyze Fritz. Let's see if we can get you on your way, so you can go do whatever the hell it is you got in mind."

One of the tires of the sports car was suspended above the pavement where the front bumper had gotten hooked over the fender of the bulky old Chevy that Goetzinger had hit.

"Took some fancy driving to do that," J.J. observed.

"Don't ask."

"Maybe we can bounce her off."

Deuce went around so that he could work from the front, while J.J. grabbed the crescent-shaped panel above the wheel.

"Be careful," Deuce warned.

"Don't worry, my friend."

After an uncertain start, they synchronized the lifts, each time the corner of the little red car rising a bit higher. Suddenly, it came free. Feeling the pressure against his legs as the nose swung around, J.J. managed to scramble onto the hood, where he clung momentarily as the car slid slowly downward. He clambered off, doing a sort of jig while he tried simultaneously to remain upright and stop the Mazda, succeeding in doing neither, his legs shooting out from under him and the car continuing its slow descent, finally coming to rest against the corner of the salt truck. Deuce, hanging on to the other side, had been dragged along facedown.

J.J. stood up, rubbing the sore spot where his butt had kissed the ice. The front of Deuce's jacket and trousers were coated with snow.

"Just like we planned it," J.J. observed.

They inspected the car. It appeared undamaged.

"Sure you don't wanna just go home and leave your old man to the fates?"

"I don't give a shit about him," Deuce said. "Can you get me to the top of this damn hill?"

"Expect so. Best go down and start over."

J.J. waved the other car back. Deuce got in his little red car and edged around the truck, and then J.J. climbed back into his cab, drove down to the base of the hill and started backing up once more, leading the others, Pied Piper-fashion.

He thought about Deuce's last remark about his father. Fritz Goetzinger—farmer, former Pack worker, current mayor of Jackson, and all-around hard case. Fritz being famously contrary, it made perfectly good sense that he'd do something as loony as harvesting corn in the middle of a blizzard. But that didn't explain why Deuce was concerning himself with the matter, since he professed not to give a shit.

Of course, J.J. had often noted the unusual relationships between what people said and what they did. But he'd always considered Deuce a sensible fellow, seriously into the business of separating nincompoops from their money—even something of a student of human behavior, as J.J. fancied himself, although unlike J.J., Deuce kept what he knew to himself. A small mystery, then, that Deuce should be off to rescue his father, the man he professed to think so little of.

But then again, J.J. thought, arguing with himself, we were talking about family matters here. And when it comes to families, even the wisest of us are fools.

CHAPTER 4

~

Deuce's elbow and hip ached from where he had fallen on the ice as he raced from his apartment. He flexed his arm but didn't dare take his other hand off the steering wheel to rub it because the RX-7 felt queasy beneath him, and the next time he lost control, there'd be no J.J. to help out.

Snow rushed up at the windshield, and the car shook as the wind pounded it, first from one direction, then another. The storm flung the glare of his headlights back into his face.

He peered ahead for traces of the familiar and crept from street to street. If he couldn't feel the skid before it began, it'd be too late. In the rearview mirror, vision improved, the way behind him pure white but clearer, the snow in retreat. But in front, nothing, a kind of blindness, the storm battering him. He stopped at a cross street, got out to read the signs, and found that somehow he'd arrived at Ridge Road, which led out toward the farm.

He got back into his car and turned onto Ridge, skirting the prairie fringe. He couldn't see anything, didn't even know which side of the road he drove on, yet he had the impression of the landscape opening around him.

When he imagined he must be near the farm, he got out of the car at mailboxes and rubbed the snow off them to read the names. Finally, he found "Goetzinger."

At the top of the driveway, parked by the back door, he slumped back in the seat for a few moments, relieved to be stopped.

On the porch, he found Teddy pulling his galoshes on. That meant their parents hadn't returned.

"Where do you think you're going?" Deuce asked him.

"With you."

"Not hardly. You haven't heard anything? Ma hasn't called?"

Teddy shook his head, still getting ready to go outside. He seemed calmer now, at least. On the phone, he'd been so hyped that he'd had to repeat his message several times before Deuce understood that their idiot father was trying to run the lower field on out and Ma had left in the old Plymouth to go down and fetch him home.

"Take your boots off, Teddy," Deuce ordered him.

But Teddy wouldn't, determined in his fourteen-year-old's way to go with Deuce.

"Take the damn boots off," Deuce repeated. "Look, I've got something more important for you to do. If I'm not back in an hour, I need you to call nine-one-one."

"Why don't we call now?"

Shit, Deuce thought. "No," he told his brother sharply, then softened his tone. "You think Dad would want us doing that, running off for help, the first sign of trouble? Look, this ain't a big deal. I'll be back with them way sooner than an hour. But we've gotta have a backup plan. That's you. It's stupid not to have a backup. Okay?"

Reluctantly, Teddy saw the logic. His shoulders sagged, and for a moment Deuce felt sorry that he had to deny his brother this adventure. Teddy leaned over and began moodily to unsnap his boots. Deuce told him what he should report to the people at the emergency center. And then, on second thought, since communication between his brother and strangers often faltered, Deuce went into the kitchen and wrote out exactly what he wanted him to do and say.

Teddy, boots still on and flapping around his ankles, trailed him back out to the Mazda. Deuce got in and rolled down the window long enough to say to the forlorn figure, "Don't worry. Ma's sensible, she'll be okay. She and the old man have taken cover somewheres. We'll be back in no time."

Then he began the hazardous drive back off the bluffs, down Brick Kiln Road. He could have driven directly out to the field from his apartment after his brother had called, but he was determined to retrace the route his mother had taken, just in case. She was the one he was worried about.

It pissed him off no end. If somebody had to go rescue the old man from his folly, it should've been him. He could guess why she hadn't called. She knew how he would have reacted to yet another demonstration of his father's goddamn obsessive behavior. She'd pestered Deuce so many times before, she wouldn't pester him anymore.

He inched along, looking for her car, straining to see. Nobody else on the road, the pavement unplowed and trackless, the whiteout into which he stared seeming to leech away his eyesight, leaving bright splotches and streaks in his field of vision.

Several times the RX-7 began to skid and he barely managed to keep it from sliding off the road's steep embankment. Each time, he gentled her back onto the roadway and continued down the hill, using his poker player's ability to concentrate on the moment, blinking away the mirages which rose, peering through the storm for any sign of the Plymouth.

When he reached the foot of the bluff, he still hadn't found her. He continued to creep along, looking to either side of the road, expecting to come upon her car at any moment. He drove through pockets of calm, when for a moment the landscape opened up around him and he could scan the roadsides fifty or a hundred yards ahead. But the storm would quickly spring on him again, buffeting the little car and causing him to inadvertently recoil from the blast of white sweeping over the hood.

His mother was such a timid driver that he couldn't imagine she would have pressed on through weather like this. Hard on the heels of this thought, however, came another: her loyalty to his father.

He turned on the gravel access road leading to the field. Normally, it only took a couple minutes to reach the end of the gravel, but now he drove at a snail's pace, imagining he could make out tire tracks in the snow.

Suddenly, the tailgate of a pickup loomed out of the storm, just a few feet away. He jumped on the brake. The RX-7 fishtailed into the truck. He felt only a nudge as it hit, and he backed away and stared at the vehicle—his father's. And still no Plymouth.

The cornfield was just a few yards away, but he couldn't see a thing. He got out, ducking his head as the wind and sleety snow hit him. "Damn!"

The truck sat empty, no key in the ignition. On the far side stood the grain wagons and ancient tractor. Corn, a bright, almost eerie yellow in the blizzard, had been piled high in one of the wagons. Deuce wondered how his father had managed to get all this equipment down to the field.

He went back to the RX-7, where he sat and considered the situation. Unlike the old man, his mother had some sense. So she'd probably gone for help. He wondered if she'd maybe gotten all the way down there and picked up his father. No, they would've taken the pickup and abandoned the Plymouth.

But that meant his father was still nearby. Deuce stared toward the field until the storm eased briefly and he could see several rows of corn stubble. He strained to make out the picker. Nothing.

He started the car, thinking he'd go back and try again to find his mother.

But he didn't put it in gear, merely continued staring out at the field. In the next pause in the storm, he was shown exactly what he had seen the first time. Again, he thought he would leave, and again he didn't move.

No way, he thought, could he get back up the hill, no way in hell.

He could go for help...but it would be hours before a search party could be organized, probably not until the storm was over. And his mother would never forgive him if he simply deserted the old man.

He looked out at the snow slashing across the field. Did he hate his father enough to abandon him? The temptation tugged at him. *How appropriate*, he thought, *if the old man should die while he worked at some hopeless task.*

But his mother would never forgive him.

In the small ways in which he had, from time to time, taken his revenge on his father, he had hurt his mother as well. And because he never wanted to hurt her, he had felt the pain, too. A thousand times, he had told himself to move the hell away from Jackson, away from all this—his father, his mother's disapproval because he hadn't made something out of himself, the constant reminders of his childhood. But he hadn't; he'd diddled and diddled and now this, his mother lost, who knows where, and his father out in the middle of a blizzard because the old man was a respecter of nothing, not storms, not people, only the demons that drove him.

Deuce turned off the engine and climbed back out of the car and stood with his head ducked down into the collar of his coat. He strained to hear the motor of the corn harvester. Nothing, just the blast of the snow whipping across his vision, and the ominous moaning of the storm overhead. Deuce remembered stories his father had told of Dakota winters during his boyhood, where blizzards were so violent that a farmer could get lost and perish going from house to barn.

The wind appeared to be coming up the valley, and he thought he might use it to orient himself. Since a low embankment edged much of the field, staying close to this at first and working around the perimeter made sense. If he could find the edge of the unharvested corn, he could find the picker.

He slipped down the bank. Bending his head into the wind, he began to walk. When Teddy had called, Deuce had been getting ready to go to work, and he had left without taking the time to change into outdoor clothing. Now his low work shoes quickly filled with snow, the cold seeping beneath the cuffs of his trousers and up his calves. Every few steps he halted and peered toward the field and called out and listened.

From time to time, he cursed the old man, just to make himself feel a little better. Eventually, the ground in front of him began to slope upwards. Judging he had reached the end of the field, he turned right. Walking across the headlands, however, with its gentler rise, he found it harder to keep his bearings. The wind turned out to be no help. It blew stiffly one way, only to suddenly pause, then swing around and blast at him from a different direction, like a fighter throwing combinations.

The wind and cold probed every tiny pore in his thin clothing. Why hadn't he taken the time to change? Idiot! He was as dumb as the old man. The snow seeped under his collar, and he could feel meltwater trickling down his back and chest.

"This is insane!" he yelled, and the wind, as if it had heard, eased. The snow for a few moments fell straight from the sky. The white shroud enveloping him had turned the gray of long unwashed sheets, and he realized that night approached and soon he wouldn't be able to see a thing. Even if he found the old man, who the hell would save the two of them?

He didn't know what to do. As a kid, he'd spent much time down there, escaping from his father. He'd explored the old lead mines that honeycombed the bluffs. He'd bow-hunted and fished and tried without luck to trap muskrats. That other life, so long forgotten, now came back to him, and he stood for a minute in a reverie which gradually turned into a longing and then self-pity before he managed to pull himself out of it and look at the whiteness whistling all around.

The wind had returned. Snow swirled into his eyes. The strange, ominous noise the storm made overhead stalked him as he stumbled onward. In his heart rose a wild desire to start running, but he stopped and held himself steady until the wailing of the storm eased and he could think clearly.

Then he set off again, trying only to move in a straight line, first between the rows of corn stubble, then at right angles. In this way, he found the edge between the harvested and unharvested sections of the field.

His feet slipped this way and that on the ice as he made his way along the boundary of the corn stalks, listening for the approach of the picker. But after a time, the ground began to rise and he realized he had come to one of the headlands. At the top of the bank stood a thicket of willow saplings. He'd been walking the wrong way; the picker must be behind him.

He turned around and was about to start back along the edge of the standing corn when in a fissure through the slanting snow, he spotted something. He couldn't be sure and moved toward it, walking nearly past before he looked back and saw the dark shape again, plastered with snow, standing stock still. His father.

All Deuce's anger at once returned. He grabbed him and yelled, "What the fuck, are you crazy?!" His father didn't speak but merely twisted free and brushed past.

"Shit!" Deuce shouted, then grabbed him by the sleeve and half dragged him back up on the headlands.

"Where's the picker?!"

"Back there! Stalled out!"

Shit, Deuce thought. He shouted, "Okay, follow me!"

His father showed no surprise at Deuce's sudden appearance. Or interest. *The bastard*, Deuce thought.

He turned and began to walk across the harvested field, trying to keep in a straight line, galvanized by his anger. He looked behind, half expecting his father to have disappeared back into the storm. But the old man trudged silently in Deuce's footsteps.

Deuce concentrated on what he was doing, but he quickly became disoriented again. He kept on walking, but long after he thought they should have reached the edge of the field where the RX-7 was parked, the corn stubble still stretched away on all sides. His sense of purposefulness vanished. His father still trailing along, leaning into the storm, stopping when Deuce stopped, starting when he started.

Finally they entered a stand of trees. Deuce halted. Before cards, before women, these woods had been his passion. He'd known, in fact, every scrap of landscape from the hanging valleys to the sloughs. Now he recognized nothing.

He started out again, thinking to keep to the edge of the woods, going in the direction where he imagined the car to be waiting.

This didn't work, either. After a time, trees and bushes and brush surrounded them, hedged them in, blocked their way and grabbed at their clothing. Deuce had no idea which direction to take. Nothing had worked, and so finally he surrendered himself to the simple act of walking. In the woods, the storm was less intense, but it had grown darker, one kind of blindness becoming another.

He trudged on, wondering how long a person could survive under such conditions, noticing that he wasn't afraid. His feet were no longer cold.

It got darker. The ground became steeper. They must be on the ridge, although there was some high ground beyond the far northern end of the field. He hadn't exercised in years and so had to stop often and take a blow.

They should dig a nest for themselves in the undergrowth, Deuce told himself, but he went on, driving himself up the slope.

Finally, out of the grayness ahead, a massive tree rose before them. In his youth, the ancient oaks, which had grown when the land still remained open prairie, served as his sentinels, benevolent giants, each with its own personality. He approached this one, running his hand over the rough bulwark of its trunk and looking up into the maze of black limbs disappearing into the storm. He thought he could remember…he thought he could, but the once beloved place, silent and black beneath the howling wind, offered no comfort to its long-lost companion.

"Follow me!" he called to his father and moved quickly past the tree.

A short way up the slope, he stopped at a ragged abutment of limestone. The outcropping had become so choked with brush that he still couldn't be sure he recognized the place. He pulled the branches apart and felt his way down, crawling deeper and deeper until his hands grasped an odd-shaped cleft in the rock. *Yes*, he thought, *yes*.

"Down here!" he yelled to the eerily silent figure behind him. "It's a tight squeeze for a few feet, but then it opens up."

He wondered what animals might be hibernating below, but then thought, *What the fuck!* and plunged downward, into the blackness, wriggling through the opening, feeling the pattern of ridges and hollows in the rock, the sudden resurrection of memory.

Behind him, he heard his father grunting as he tried to fit through the narrow space, and he reached back to help. Finally, they were both through.

"Don't try to stand up," Deuce warned. "There's not enough headroom."

"Where we at?"

The old man's voice was filled with irritation. Deuce felt only elation. The moist, earthy odor filled his nostrils as it had half a lifetime ago. He was sixteen again. He whooped.

"We're in one of the old lead mines—Whistler Number Two."

His father said nothing. Deuce crouched and duckwalked several steps forward, then sat with his back against the adit wall.

"Come in some more," he called back to his father, "away from the entrance."

He took off his shoes and shook the snow out of them. He felt almost hot. "Fifty degrees," he said. He peeled his socks off and set about rubbing some warmth back into his feet.

"What?" The old man hadn't moved closer.

"It's fifty degrees down here. All the time it's fifty—the average year-round temperature outside." Facts he hadn't thought about since he was a teenager now came tumbling back to him, as fresh as the first time he'd learned them. For the moment, his anger at his father eased and he talked readily. "If you reach out, you can feel the old wooden tracks the miners used." Deuce rubbed his own hand across the dirt until he located them, nothing more than narrow boards imbedded in the floor of the mine. "Animals use these old mines as dens sometimes." He listened but could hear nothing. He visualized the place. "There are seams in the ceiling where bats roost. If we had a light, we could see 'em hibernating." He wondered if any of his old camping gear might be left after all this time, and moved carefully deeper into the shaft, but could find nothing. "I used to have a sleeping bag down here, a Coleman stove, an old miner's hat, canned goods, that sort of stuff. Remember when I used to disappear? This was where I came." Sometimes he'd spent days living in the mine, exploring the woods, hiding from his father. When he went home, there'd be hell to pay, but it had been worth it. "Funny, ain't it? Now we're both here."

To this recollection, all the old man had to say was, "You worried your mother."

At her mention, the pleasant memories of Deuce's youth evaporated, replaced by images of his search for her in the storm. "I've got news for you, buster," he told his father, "at the moment, you're the one she's worried about." He recounted the events of the day beginning with Teddy's call. "Drove down from the farm, didn't see any sign of her. She musta gone for help."

"Nobody'll come out until after the storm," his father said.

"No kidding, Einstein." Having summoned his normal irritation with the old man, Deuce said, "So, tell me, what the hell were you thinking, trying to run the field on out in the middle of a friggin' blizzard? Nobody in his right mind would be pickin' on a day like this."

He didn't expect an answer and didn't get one.

"Real smart," he said.

They sat silently in the blackness. Deuce listened to his own breathing and, faintly in the distance, concussions of the storm. The white blindness outside had been replaced by a darkness even more intense. A trickle of snowmelt dribbled into the corner of one eye and he rubbed it away.

He heard the rustling of clothing and thought for an instant that his father was finally moving deeper into the mine. But the sound didn't come closer. Deuce listened. What was he doing?

Suddenly, he realized and scrambled toward the entrance, where he managed to grab his father's leg. The leg was jerked out of his grasp.

"Going to find your mother," his father grunted as he tried to squeeze back up through the entrance.

Deuce grabbed him again. "In this weather? No fucking chance."

His father shook free, but Deuce clambered after and seized him around the waist. His father cuffed him on the side of his head, but Deuce just gritted his teeth and hung on.

"Let go!"

"Like hell! You've done enough stupid things for one day."

"Damn you!"

Deuce felt another blow, harder, but he still hung on, the side of his face stinging. They struggled now in silence. His father got a knee up in his chest, but Deuce managed to slide off it. They had little room to maneuver. Another blow glanced off the back of Deuce's head. He ducked his chin against his father's side, wrapped himself around him, and waited.

Finally, the old man stopped trying to squirm free.

"When the damn storm's over, you can go to hell for all I care," Deuce said.

At these words, his father struggled free again and Deuce had to grab and wrestle with him once more. They struggled only briefly this time.

"Leave it go," Deuce panted when it was over. "Forget it. If we had a chance in hell of finding her, I'd be out there. No way. No fucking way."

Deuce half expected the struggle to resume, but his father stayed put this time, all the fight gone out of him. Deuce, however, taking no chances, lingered nearby. Hot and sweaty, his sore elbow throbbing, he waited a long time before gradually moving a few feet back into the mine, listening for any suspicious sounds, determined to keep his father in the mine, whatever it took. That much he would do for his mother.

His breathing slowly returned to normal. He rubbed his elbow and carefully flexed his arm. The heat suffusing him quickly disappeared, leaving him cold, his socks and trousers clammy.

They probably wouldn't be there long enough for hypothermia to become a problem, not at fifty degrees, so all he had to do, he told himself, was make sure the old man stayed put until the storm blew over.

And so he settled down to wait.

As time passed, his fear for his mother's safety grew. He tried to take comfort in the fact that he hadn't found her as he drove down from the farm. Chances were, she'd gone for help, he told himself. She was the Goetzinger that had some sense. One way or another, all the men in the family were brain-dead. But not her. As soon as she got out in the storm, she would've realized that the idea of trying to fetch the old man back was a nonstarter. She'd have gone for help. That was the only thing that made any sense.

He tried to construct a plausible scenario. Probably she stopped somewheres and called the cops first. The corn field was outside the city limits, so they'd transfer her to the sheriff's department, or even more likely, the country rescue squad. Would those guys come out in the middle of the storm? Maybe. They loved to John Wayne it. And Deuce might think his father was a worthless piece of shit, but the fact that he was the mayor of Jackson counted for something. Maybe if Deuce had just hung around his car, some of the county rescue guys would have shown up in their four-wheel drives, hauling their snowmobiles with them.

Beginning to shiver, he swung his arms against his body to warm up and then leaned his head back against the wall and closed his eyes. He wished his mother had called him. Why would she consider, even for a moment, driving in such weather? He felt this as a personal rejection, as if she, like his father, had at long last written him off. As elated as he'd felt upon finding the old mine, now he felt like shit. He tried to make his mind a blank. When that didn't work, he focused on the cold gradually working its way deeper into his flesh. He curled up his legs and crossed his arms tightly around his knees.

He remembered that you lose a sense of the passage of time in a mine. He tried to estimate how long they'd been there, perhaps an hour. Double the time you think it is, that was the rule of thumb. Two hours, then.

As his mind wandered this way and that, he heard a strange sound, very low at first. He remembered his original worry that animals might be using the place as a den. But the noise came from toward the entrance. Not his father trying to leave this time, something else. He concentrated, thinking that perhaps the wind outside had changed direction and was soughing around the opening. He remembered the name of the mine, Whistler Number Two, but couldn't recall ever hearing it make such a noise. Low, uneven, mournful. Human.

Never in Deuce's thirty-three years had he heard his father cry. The old man was incapable.

He slid farther away from the noise, deeper into the adit.

Finally, after the awful sound had died away, the two of them sat for a very long time in dead silence. And when they did finally speak to each other, both still awake and listening to the endless blows of the storm, they talked about nothing important.

Soon after dawn, the snow let up, and by the time they descended out of the woods, wading up to their thighs, they encountered the searchers who had come to look for them. In the middle of the field, the red picker stood, its corn head buried, snow drifting all the way up to the cab. The field gleamed brilliantly in the morning sunlight.

Only later in the day was the Plymouth found, far off the road where it had skidded, apparently when Deuce's mother lost control while trying to turn. The car was empty. It took them two days to find her body.

CHAPTER 5

～

Not much had fallen yet, just a scattering of flakes, point men for the new storm. No ice forecast this time, just more snow, a lot of it. The midmorning darkness continued to intensify.

"They're lucky they found her when they did," Chuck Fellows, the acting public works director, said as he turned away from the window. "Twenty-four hours from now, might as well have waited 'til spring."

City councilwoman El Plowman had cleared off a chair and sat down. Chuck's office being occupied at the moment, the assistant city engineer subbing for Chuck at another meeting, the two of them were using Mark O'Banion's for this impromptu session. Since Mark's death, Chuck had let the city foist his old job off on him, public works now heaped on top of his own duties as city engineer, but he wouldn't move into Mark's old digs. Joyce, the department secretary, had begun to store stuff in the unused room, dumping it unceremoniously on Mark's desk and the chairs and the floor, a stack of draft budgets, another of EIRs, others of who-knows-what. The fuggy odor of paper beginning to combust filled Chuck's nostrils.

Rather than turning the lights on, he had simply raised the blinds on the two windows. A meager patch of the grayness entered the room, barely reaching El in her cleared-off chair. She sat, stolid and unhappy, her overcoat folded over her knees.

"What a terrible way to die," she said.

Chuck had been powerfully affected when Mark had died two months earlier, but this new death meant little to him. He propped himself against the corner of the desk and crossed his arms. "There are a helluva lot worse." As far as he was concerned, death in the snow had much to recommend it. He could easily imagine himself in the far north, walking into white wastes, following a longitudinal line toward the pole, ending his life on his own terms.

El took a breath and resettled herself on the chair.

"To be alone like that."

Chuck didn't respond. His thoughts lingered on the image of himself tracking northward, to where compasses were no longer of any use. He'd always told people he'd be dead before thirty-five. Here he was, forty-four years old and still around, still dealing with all the bullshit. He sniffed, thrust this reflection aside, and turned his attention back to El.

"What's on your mind?" He knew perfectly well—Sam Turner. She wanted to know how Turner had been faring up in the drafting room. Were they race-baiting him? Had he been given more than make-work to do?

She leaned forward, bringing her face farther into the light, which covered her like a dusting of frost. The shoulder pads of her suit jacket bunched up, reminding him of epaulets.

"About Sam…," she began. Chuck smiled to himself.

Nobody had been bitching, he told her, not Sam, not any of the other draftsmen, either. As for the work, he was being given what he could handle, which wasn't much. He'd been out of school too long. He had no experience.

She frowned as she listened to this curt recitation. "Still, you *are* keeping tabs on him?"

"I go upstairs when I've got something to go up there for."

"Which means?"

"I don't go up to babysit him."

El became still, regarding Chuck carefully. Her tone of voice lingered between them. "My understanding was that Mark planned to bring him along," she said at last, her manner now firmer. "There *is* such a thing as on-the-job training, you know."

"I'm not Mark O'Banion. I go up to give an assignment or get information or deal with a problem. Period."

Mark had gotten along with the city council members. He even seemed to like some of them.

"Are others helping him?" El asked.

"I told them to spend enough time to make sure he knows how to operate the instruments properly."

"Will that be enough?"

"We'll have to wait and see. I can't afford to take men off their own work just to train Sam Turner. If he wants to make it, he's going to have to show some initiative."

She obviously didn't care for his brusqueness. She shifted again in the chair and resettled the coat on her lap.

Chuck didn't pretend to understand a woman like Plowman. She seemed to imagine that she could make the world a better place. Mark O'Banion had a lot of the do-gooder in him, too, but at least he acted out of his personal commitment to his own behavior, not because he had any illusions that he might have some wonderful effect.

Remembering his old boss, Chuck regretted bringing Plowman into the room. Mark had covered the walls with his pictures and citations, and after his death, his wife had come and taken the ones she wanted, leaving a gap-toothed effect. Still, the room reminded Chuck too much of him, of the conversations they would never enjoy again, the momentary exchanges when Chuck stuck his head in the door on the way by, or the more leisurely discussions at the end of a workday. Since Mark's death, Chuck's confrontations had been mostly like this one, with people who were trying to arrange the world to their own satisfaction and didn't mind wasting his time to do it.

When she continued, El had lowered her sights. "He's been coming to work? Getting here on time? That's not a problem at least?"

"Sam always comes to work. On time, too." Sometimes hung over, Chuck might have added, but he didn't. Actually, he rather liked Turner, although he couldn't have said exactly why. Certainly not because the guy was a fireball.

"So you have no idea how he's doing," Plowman said.

"We could go up and ask him, I suppose." Chuck immediately regretted these words. "We could, but it wouldn't be a helluva bright idea. Sam's gotta succeed, or fail, on his own. We go up there, we make matters worse."

El had sat back in her chair, sinking into the gloom. She suffered from bouts of depression, or so he understood. She seemed morose enough, but according to his understanding, depressives were supposed to lack self-confidence. Perhaps she did, but she was sure as hell persistent.

Finally, she said, "Tell me, do you happen to know how he's taken the vandalism?"

"Turner?"

"Yes."

He hesitated, surprised at this abrupt shift and at something in her tone, suggesting that this question had been at the back of her mind all along, everything else merely preliminary to its asking.

"You mean, does he blame himself?"

"I suppose so, yes."

Everyone knew why the exhibit was trashed. The assholes didn't leave a manifesto, but if it hadn't been for the Sam Turner business—forcing the city to promote him at the same time so many people were losing their jobs at the Pack… A small thing, perhaps, but sometimes it didn't take much.

"I don't know," he told El.

"But you haven't heard anything," she pressed him.

He shook his head. "Makes no difference. Nothing you can do about it. You insisted on promoting Turner. This is what you get."

"So it doesn't bother you, what happened?"

Plowman and the others were reaping what they had sown, that was all. Chuck hadn't gone down to the museum to look at the damage—he wasn't a rubberneck—but he'd seen the pictures in the paper and felt outrage on behalf of the family the city had been trying to honor, the only innocents in this clusterfuck. Chuck didn't let himself entirely off the hook, either. Even if he hadn't foreseen the outcome, he'd known they shouldn't promote Turner. He could have put up more of a fight. But he hadn't. After he'd bitched about it, he'd followed orders. That's what he believed; you followed orders. The orders might be for shit, made no difference, you followed them. Now he had witnessed the entire trajectory of this sorry business, and he accepted his part in it. To Plowman he said, "Whoever trashed the museum should be hung up by his balls, okay? Is that it? Can I go back to my meeting?"

She said yes, and Chuck left the room at once.

⌒

Upstairs, on the top floor of city hall, Sam Turner had gone to the lavatory to clean his pen again, and out of the porthole window he watched the snowflakes settling through the air, falling with little hesitations. Each flake had a style all its own, separating itself from the gray sky and jigging like a solitary dancer past Sam, only to become lost in the confusion below.

Sam had gone to clean his pen so often that he figured the others thought he was a cokehead or something. Wasn't true. He never did cocaine but once. Used to be, when he was a kid, he got nosebleeds all the time. Had his nose cauterized, and that helped some, but he still got them. Never knew when one was coming. He'd blow his nose and it would start to bleed. Or maybe he'd just be sitting around, doing nothing, and it would start up. Or he'd wake up in the middle of the night and have to rush into the bathroom, cupping his hand under his nose to catch the drippings. No way he was ever going to be a cokehead. Have a nosebleed twenty-four/seven then.

Anyway, nobody said anything about him going to the shitter so often. Mostly they didn't say anything to him about anything.

He had turned away from the window and set about drying the pen. He worked slowly, winding the paper towel into a coil and stuffing it tightly into the barrel and turning it with a screwing motion. Then he pulled it out and held the instrument up to the lightbulb. "Still got some water in ya?" He could see none, but dried it again anyway.

Since he was there, he took a leak, and then washed his hands and checked them out, front and back, and imagined he could make out ghosts of the filth from the dredge. One thing about drafting work, he got to keep his hands clean…although, if they'd given him his choice, he wouldn't have minded being back on the dredge.

He tilted his head up to inspect himself in the mirror, a small rectangle of glass hung off a hook above the sink. He admired his shaved head, the angles and curves of it, then forced himself to stare into the eyes looking back at him. He didn't know why that made him so uncomfortable. When other eyes were looking at you, there was always the chance they might be wrong, maybe that was it.

He walked out into the high-ceilinged room running the length of the top floor of city hall—no longer used for balls and mass meetings and such—and moved toward the end that had been sectioned off for the draftsmen. He pushed through the double doors.

Nobody glanced up. When he'd been doing other stuff—hauling trash for the city or working on the dredge—he'd forgotten how quiet it could be in a drafting room. The people were working with their backs to each other, hunched over their drawing boards, taking up and putting down their implements like surgeons. The lights suspended above each board made little islands of brightness in the gloom.

At lunchtime, there might be some chatter, but people mostly scattered. One guy ate at his board, reading the newspaper. Sam didn't know what the rest did. They all left him alone. At first, he thought they were giving him the cold shoulder. Maybe they were, but they didn't seem to have much to do with each other, either, as if working alone at their drawing boards spilled over into eating alone and maybe, for all Sam knew, spending all their free time by themselves, too.

When people were gone, he would walk around and look at their work—a site plan for a public toilet at one of the city parks, cross sections for the reconstruction of a residential street, the elevations for a well. In one corner hung the pin map on which all the vehicular accidents in the city during the year were located, already a lot because of the ice storm, even though the year had barely begun. He located the pin on Brick Kiln Road where the mayor's wife had gone into the ditch.

That morning, the other draftsmen had been talking about finding her body, and he'd gotten into the conversation for a little bit. Used to be, there were lots of famous stories about people getting lost in storms, back before cars and good roads and whatnot. Mostly the stories were about women getting lost, too, just like Edna Goetzinger there, sometimes women and children.

The other draftsmen listened to him, but they didn't have much to say about it. The guys he used to haul trash with would have been more interested. More than once it had occurred to Sam that draftsmen weren't as much fun as garbage collectors.

Now he went over and sat back down at his own board and watched his hands putting the pen back together. He began lettering again, using the guide, adding names to the street outlines he had already drawn. He worked slowly and carefully, so that when he stopped and checked out what he'd accomplished so far, he could take some pride in it.

He was doing okay, he judged, even if the work wasn't much. He'd done okay in drafting school, too, but it was true, he'd always worked along at his own pace. Nobody hassled him, mostly probably because they were afraid of being called racists. His mind wandered. He would imagine scenes with the other draftsmen, scenes where perhaps he made friends with them or, more often, where he came in and found them talking about him, talking about the nigger, and then he'd go ahead and say something, and they'd say something back, and the anger would keep on building up, like that. Sam got into a lot more racist shit inside his head than he ever did in real life. Didn't mean nothing, just his thoughts going off on their own. Sam knew that people—real people, that is, not all the ones lived inside his head—mostly liked to avoid trouble. And these boys weren't any different by the look of it.

The silence in that room felt like the kind that could go on forever. He worked for a short time, until his thoughts got in the way and he stopped. Some days, he was conscious of light changing in the room, but today, it being so dark outside, only the steady glow from the hanging fixture lay across his drawing board.

Come right down to it, he wished he was back on the dredge. Or still collecting trash. Yeah, collecting trash, that's the way it should have been, back to the beginning. Then none of this would have happened. His head dipped down until he was staring at nothing, just the edge of the drafting board. That's the way it should have been.

CHAPTER 6

~

When El Plowman arrived at Pearl and Hiram Johnson's, she found several cars pulled up outside the brick bungalow. She got out and surveyed the vehicles with displeasure, recognizing only the ancient, battered Chevy Suburban driven by the museum's director Reiny Kopp. Reiny's she expected. As for the rest…

She walked up to the front door through the light snow and rang the bell. Neither Pearl nor Hiram answered, but rather May Daniels, director of the Locust Street Opportunity Center. El greeted her, and May nodded and said a couple of words, holding the door open. As El entered the living room from the tiny foyer, the scene unfolded, more people, the black lawyer Roy Singleton and then the AME minister Henry Russell Tipton, talking to Singleton, and then Johnny Pond, the KJAX radio newsman and personality, much younger than the rest. Pearl Johnson sat by herself on the love seat, the room being too small for a conventional sofa.

That explained the cars outside, one mystery merely replaced with another, however. The meeting had been scheduled so that El and Reiny and the Johnsons could hash out the remounting of the vandalized museum exhibit. Nothing had been said about including these other people. Why were they there? And where was Hiram? There was no sign of him.

"Hello, everyone," El said, uncertain for the moment how to proceed.

Singleton and Tipton merely glanced toward her, nodding perfunctorily before returning in an intense and hurried way to their conversation. Johnny Pond stood, a silent sentinel near the love seat, where May Daniels had gone to sit beside Pearl.

"I'm sorry," El said to Pearl, "I'm a little late."

Reiny had taken up a position slightly removed, his back to one of the windows. He was smiling slightly, which usually meant something had gone awry.

Well, El decided, even if it had, she'd better try to make the best of it. So she said, "I'm glad you're all here. The more, the better."

At once, the minister broke off his conversation with the lawyer and turned toward her. "Please," he said. He indicated a chair, his hands opening up in a florid gesture, as disconcerting as his curt nod had been moments earlier.

As El seated herself, she asked after Hiram.

"Taking his nap," Pearl informed her. Hiram's chair, a hybrid easy chair and rocker, remained empty, like a throne in the king's absence, with the bronzed stand next to it, on top of which his pipes, resembling the points of a crown, protruded from the ruby-colored ashtray. An aroma of cherry tobacco lingered in the air.

"Is he well?" El asked.

Pearl nodded, a single brisk, dismissive movement. She had gotten dressed for the occasion. Add a hat, and she would have been ready to go to church. In fact, everyone except Reiny was turned out, certainly more carefully than a group of whites would have been in a similar situation…whatever the situation might be. Reiny wore his normal out-in-the-world outfit, cowboy boots and blue jeans below his dress shirt, tie, and jacket, as if he was one of the on-camera talent at Walter's TV station, visible only from the waist up. Behind him, the little stained glass picture hanging in the window, so bright and cheerful on a sunlit day, shone dully before the grayness of the storm.

No one was speaking at the moment, everyone waiting, it seemed, for someone else to begin. El shifted forward, perching on the very lip of the chair. Sitting had been a mistake, putting her at a disadvantage to the men, who were all still standing. Hiram's absence seemed ominous. It was barely ten o'clock in the morning, surely too early for a nap. And he'd always insisted on being involved before. The exhibit, after all, had been created to honor his long career as a Pullman porter. No coffee or fruit juice or snacks had been put out, either. Pearl had always been a scrupulous, if somewhat reserved, hostess.

El addressed her. "There's snow on the way. Perhaps, under the circumstances, it would be best if we got right down to the exhibit."

Pearl laid her hands quietly in her lap. "That would be all right," she said.

Tipton broke in, "Sister Pearl has been telling us about it," and his tone made it clear at once that he, and not Pearl, was to take the lead here.

El still had no idea what was going on. She shifted her position so that she could look directly at the minister. "There's a lot of work to be done to accomplish the remounting. Of course," she assured him at once, "Reiny and the museum staff will take care of most of it. But we were hoping that the Johnsons—perhaps all of you, since you're here—might help us with some of the more personal items. We also hope Pearl will be willing to make another quilt." At the edge of her field of vision, Reiny had begun to stir.

"Hmm," the minister said.

"We realize it's a lot to ask…after what happened to the first one."

Tipton ignored this last comment. "So that's what you got in mind, repair the old exhibit, just like it was?" On the day of the vandalism, she had phoned him about this matter, but he spoke now as if hearing it for the first time.

"We're also considering the possibility of adding a photo display, perhaps blowups of the vandalism…," she told him. "Of course, that depends on Pearl and Hiram—"

Reiny interrupted. "I'll tell you what we *should* do. I say, to hell with repairing it. Leave it as is. Let the vandalism be the new exhibit."

The room grew quieter. He had already broached this possibility to El. It was typical. Pure Reiny. And totally impossible. "We came," El admonished him quietly, "to hear what the Johnsons want."

"No, no," Tipton interposed, "let him say what he's a mind to."

Reiny had stuffed his hands in his jean pockets, standing with all his gaunt intensity, bony shoulders hitched up, arms ramrod straight, welded to his side. The stance was unlike him, his usual juggler's ease gone, and El understood that even he—even the irrepressible Reiny—felt somewhat constrained in this roomful of black faces. But he doggedly went on and made his case.

"We prepare new tapes. But not the *Reader's Digest* version this time. This time we blow the cover off, show the racism in this city for what it is."

The silence in the room appeared to be a wall raised against him, but Reiny ignored it, glaring resolutely from one person to another. He lowered his voice, which reduced the excitement in his words but raised the tension.

"I've been talking to Hiram. He's told me some of the shit goes on. You people know a lot more. Together we could put on a real exhibit. No more damn pussyfooting around. No more making nicey-nice. Let the damn racists in this town see themselves in the mirror for once."

"This is not possible," El said.

Tipton held up a restraining hand. He wanted Reiny to finish. He seemed interested, and so another interpretation of the mood of the blacks occurred to El. Perhaps they actually liked Reiny's scheme, or at least were tempted by it.

Reiny had continued. As he talked, El settled back for the moment and studied the others, particularly Henry Tipton. Given his large, somber features and his heavy but soft-looking shoulders, his high chest but meager legs, he gave the impression of a dignified but precarious balance. He listened with his hands clasped behind his back, staring at the floor, rocking slightly backward and forward.

Finally Reiny finished. Tipton unclasped his hands and pulled at the points of his vest and cleared his throat. "This *is* a most serious matter." He might have meant the vandalism or Reiny's proposal for an all-out response to it. He spoke to El. "Impossible, you say?"

Reiny answered for her, "No. We can do it. We should do it." He understood perfectly well all of El's reservations—and not just hers—but he didn't care. That wasn't Reiny's nature. He would storm them all with his certainties.

When he started to add to this blunt assessment, El cut him off. "That's enough." He continued, and she repeated herself, more forcefully, and he finally shut up.

She turned to Tipton. "I've spoken to members of the museum board, and the consensus is to remount to old exhibit. Contrary to Reiny, the feeling is that the vandals would like nothing better than to have their handiwork left up. Anyway, we want to show them we won't be intimidated. We think the best way is to repair the exhibit...assuming the Johnsons agree."

The minister nodded gravely as he listened to her. "That's what the board thinks, Henry," El continued. "What do you think?" She still had no idea why Tipton and the others were there.

Tipton nodded slowly. "Most likely you're correct. Best do the repairs."

Good, El thought. That made matters simpler.

"However…," Tipton started and then paused. He cleared his throat again and pursed his lips, then dipped his large head slightly so that he regarded her from beneath his dark brows, his eyes ringed with a deeper shade of black than the rest of his complexion, suggesting long, sleepless nights. "The feeling is that you've been putting a good deal of pressure on Hiram. He's not a young man anymore."

"I can assure you that hasn't been our intention," El responded at once, but Reiny *had* been pestering Hiram for more and more anecdotes. And even though Hiram hadn't minded, his wife apparently was another matter.

Pearl sat perfectly straight next to May Daniels. "Hiram really doesn't need to do anything else," El assured her. "But we do hope you'll continue to help." Pearl was considerably younger than her husband, a still-vigorous woman in her early seventies. And the quilt had been the centerpiece of the exhibit, the traditional folk art a perfect way of symbolizing the melding of the Johnsons' lives into the life of the community. It would be a shame not to have another one in its place.

Pearl looked down at her hands, lying motionless in her lap. Her passive reaction reminded El once more of the mysterious presence of these others, except for Tipton all of them as silent as witnesses at some legal proceeding. Whatever was going on, they hadn't come to deliberate. Reiny stood now silent as well, looking at nothing in particular and half smiling in the way he had.

El wasn't sure what to do. She looked at Johnny Pond, much younger than the rest, only in the city in the years since he had come to play football at the U., an outsider really. He must have been invited because of his high visibility in the community—Jackson's window black, if the truth be told. He also happened to be the one El knew the best, the one who might be expected to help her out a little here. But apparently not.

She looked around impatiently. "If I may ask, why are you all here? If Pearl thought we were putting undue pressure on Hiram, all she needed to do was say so." She turned and addressed Pearl directly. "That's all."

Pearl didn't respond, but Tipton did. "I'm sure, El, you'll agree that there comes a time when, everything considered, enough is enough."

"Enough is enough?" El continued to speak to Pearl. "Does that mean it's not just Hiram? You don't want to be involved anymore, either?"

Pearl finally spoke. "That's right."

She had never been as enthusiastic about the project as her husband. El had understood almost from the beginning that her cooperation, even the sewing of the quilt, had come in a grudging way, done solely for her husband's sake. Now, it appeared, she had decided to do something for herself.

"We're not to have the quilt then?" she asked softly, looking straight at Pearl, as if the two of them were in the room by themselves.

"I think Pearl has decided not to make another quilt," Tipton said. "Is that right, sister?"

"Yes, that's right."

"We do intend to have security this time," El explained. "A guard, twenty-four hours."

"That's all well and good," Tipton told her, meaning it made no difference.

El continued to look only at Pearl. "You could have told me. You didn't need to—"

"I just wanted you to know," Pearl said. She sat resolutely on the love seat, dressed for the occasion, stout and immovable, her skin of a lustrous black which had always reminded El of glazed ceramics, and so much darker than her husband's parsnip-colored complexion. The absent Hiram.

"What about the photos?" El asked, speaking now to Tipton. "Do you object to them?"

"If that's what you've a mind to do, I suppose it would be all right," Tipton said.

"But if it was you, you wouldn't?"

When he didn't answer right away, Roy Singleton, the lawyer, began, "In the absence of a clear purpose to be accomplished…," and left the thought hanging.

Her annoyance getting the better of her for a moment, El said, "Perhaps we should forget about remounting the exhibit at all…if what we're to have is a shoddy replica of the first."

"No, no," Tipton countered once more. "Got to remount the exhibit, we all know that." His tone softened somewhat, forgoing for the moment his irritating ministerial gravity. "Surely, El, you've got enough material to work with. Maybe it won't be quite so good. That would be too bad, but I'm sure you'd agree the most important thing is to repair the exhibit as best you can."

"And what about the rest of you?" El asked. "What help are you prepared to give?"

Tipton made a vague gesture and said, "That's something we'll have to talk about."

"I see."

Reiny said nothing. Even the suggestion that a poor copy of the original exhibit might be good enough didn't set him off again, although such an idea would be beneath his contempt.

Tipton continued to reassure El that the exhibit was surely needed and nobody meant to suggest otherwise. She listened, getting even more annoyed. Pearl could have simply told her she wasn't going to make another quilt. She didn't need all this backup. But there they were, half of the black leadership in the city. Their presence suggested a further possibility, something even more disheartening.

"You know," she reminded Tipton and the others, "that we've reactivated the integration task force. Some of you are on it with me. One more time we're going to talk about how few blacks we have in Jackson. One more time we're going to try and figure a way to have a real impact, how we can make Jackson a place where others like yourselves will feel comfortable coming to live. One more time. And I hardly need remind you the vandalism doesn't help. It made me physically ill, it really did, and I think Reiny's right, it's an opportunity to get people off their bottoms and thinking seriously about the situation we've got here. Maybe not his way, but *some* way...Or at least it should be." She looked inquiringly around. "Are you suggesting that these efforts ought to be...I don't know...that we should just go through the motions?"

El watched the glances shared around the room. The question was either expected or unexpected, but either way, it touched a nerve.

Nevertheless, Tipton gave her a threadbare response. "These are matters best left to another time. Right now, we're concerned about the Johnsons. This business has put a strain on them that's something terrible, something terrible. Hiram's eighty-seven years old. He's too old a man to have to put up with all this foolishness.

He's had a lifetime of it, and sometimes a man's got to be able to rest, you got to leave him be."

"Amen," said May Daniels.

El continued to look around, meeting eyes and receiving nods. She said, "So we're on our own, then."

Reiny stood behind the others, hands in pockets, perfectly still except for the slight movement where he jiggled his change or keys.

The room itself, which he had reproduced so faithfully as part of the exhibit and which unlike its counterpart remained undamaged, might have soothed El except that obviously changes had been wreaked there, too, and all the more damaging for their invisibility.

El, sick at heart, wanted only to leave as quickly as she could.

≈

The thin sheet of snow that had fallen since she entered the house felt mealy underneath as she and Reiny hurried down the walk. He said derisively, "What a bunch of fucking cowards." He didn't seem surprised, his tone suggesting a kind of humorless amusement, for even when dead serious, Reiny's mind didn't lie far from mocking laughter.

As for Pearl and the others, El didn't know what to think. She had attended a couple of the services at the local black church, the only white present, and experienced an odd, displaced feeling, but she'd been fascinated, too, as when a familiar scene is unexpectedly glimpsed from a new point of view. Today it was more as if she had stumbled onto something new and perhaps interesting, only to discover that she had been mistaken and that another angle revealed merely calculation and self-interest.

Were Pearl and the others simply frightened, was that it? Their livelihoods depended to a considerable extent on the goodwill of local whites. Did they imagine that at risk? She almost wished that they had, after all, been in favor of Reiny's scheme to leave the vandalism in place. That would have set up a clash with the museum board, but anything was better than this.

She and Reiny had stopped beside his ancient Suburban. The snow fell thickly, enveloping them and making a small private space in which to talk.

"It's our baby then," he said. "If they don't want to help, fuck 'em. We'll do it our way." By which he meant his way.

"We'll remount the exhibit," she told him.

"And that's it? You're gonna knuckle under, just like that?" He acted as if the blacks' views didn't matter. As if the museum board didn't exist.

"We'll remount the exhibit," El told him, "and we'll use the pictures of the vandalism, we'll do that, too."

"Big deal. As if that'll accomplish anything."

"It might. Anyway, that's what we're going to do."

Reiny did El the honor of fighting with her. If he didn't respect someone, he'd ignore them and do what he damn well pleased and to hell with the consequences. But not with El. With her, he tried to make his case. And she was tempted, a little. What had happened at the museum was an outrage, didn't it deserve an outraged response? Except, of course, there was the museum board to consider. She'd have to convince them. And she simply wasn't up to it, not at the moment. Maybe if she'd felt better. "With or without the Johnsons' help, Reiny," she told him, "we remount the old exhibit."

CHAPTER 7

~

The snow got heavier, and Chuck Fellows, the city's public works director, switched from the city vehicle to his own 4x4 as he drove between meetings, crisscrossing from one side of town to the other, watching to see which streets had been plowed and how cleanly the plows were picking up the snow. He was glad to have a few minutes alone, although these brief trips felt like longer journeys interrupted.

From the wastewater treatment plant, where the utilities director proposed another harebrained scheme for dealing with the loss of organics now that the local meatpacker had closed, Chuck went back uptown for the weekly contractors' meeting at the dog track construction site on Apple Island.

As he drove, his thoughts returned to the earlier conversation with El Plowman over the issue of Sam Turner and the potential for trouble up in the drafting room. Chuck hadn't changed his mind. The man was on his own, at least until something happened. He'd been given some instruction. Perhaps that would be enough. Chuck hoped so. Even as he thought this, he realized its unworthiness. Hope, for him, was nothing but a straw emotion, which people used to beg from the world what they were too cowardly or lazy or incompetent to take responsibility for themselves.

On the north side of town, he drove along the inside of the levee, then turned through it and over the short bridge onto the island. In the distance rose a second bridge, much longer, arching across the main channel of the Mississippi to Wisconsin. He didn't drive toward this, however, but immediately turned onto the access road leading to the construction site on the north side of the island. A pair of fifty-ton cranes had finally begun to fly the steel, making ghostly transits through the storm as they lifted columns and beams up onto the deck of the dog track's grandstand.

Inside the smoke-clogged construction trailer, a dozen men stood or sat, joking and bitching, nobody in a rush to go back out into the weather. At the far end of the long, low-ceilinged space sat Jack Kelley, the construction manager, the only man in the room wearing a tie. With him were the secretary who took meeting notes and the raw recruit he'd hired from a nearby engineering school as an acolyte when his original field manager went AWOL. The three of them, Kelley and the secretary and the kid, clustered around the one desk in the place, as serious as if they were about to take a deposition. Chuck numbered the construction manager among the people he had managed to annoy.

The meeting finally got under way, Kelley running it in his usual long-winded fashion. Given contractors' expertise in posturing and ass covering and general bullshit, Chuck's patience wore thinner as the status of shop drawings and pending cost proposals and change orders and all the other standard agenda items were slowly jawed to death.

Kelley's gaze moved around the room, coming to rest on Chuck and lingering several beats. Apparently he hadn't given up all hope that Chuck might be a nice guy after all. The dog track being a city project and Kelley as CM representing the city's interest, he and Chuck had every reason to make common cause, right?

Kelley looked like a tough Irish street kid, his face wide and flat and invulnerable, his eyes bright with the possibility of taking offense, but Chuck had quickly learned that whatever might once have been the case, now Jack was strictly a company man, his bright eyes signifying nothing more than calculated manipulation as he attempted to finish the project on time, on budget, and according to the specs.

Chuck wasn't totally disinterested. Building a dog track in midwinter held some allure, the difficulty of it at least. So did the attempt to beat all the other cities in the region to the punch, have the first track up and running, make a few extra bucks. Why the hell not? What Chuck had no patience with was the idea that the project might have any deeper significance.

Finally, meeting done, he left before Kelley had the chance to corner him. Outside, he sucked in the clean, cold air, and his mood brightened slightly.

He drove down off the platform of sand that had been dredged from the river bottom to bring the construction site up to the level of the city's floodwall and levee system. On the far side of the rough, frozen hardpan where the sand for the parking lots had yet to be pumped, he turned along the dredge's pipeline, which he followed out to the eastern shore and under the approach to the Wisconsin bridge. The dredge itself, formerly operated by the city's dock board but commandeered by Chuck six weeks earlier, jutted at an angle into the Mississippi River. He pulled in next to a half dozen parked cars covered by several inches of snow.

Ice capped the river, a distant bluish-white suggestion in the storm. The harbor tug Chuck had hired to keep the water open in the area to be dredged, patrolled at the edge of the ice, the little boat's backwash churning. Snow fell thickly, melting on the large rectangle of water.

He walked out along the planking laid across the section of floating line and found his crew in the dredge's machine room, clustered around the prime mover.

Bud Pregler, the foreman, prowled impatiently while Sid Furlong, the acknowledged whizbang at machine troubleshooting in the group, stood stock still with one hand on the cylinder head of the large diesel and his eyes half closed, as if divining the situation through his fingertips.

The motor and the pump linked to it, heart of the system, sat silently amidships, the only noise in the dim, musty, chilly space coming from the corner where the generator which drove the electrical system and hydraulics thumped away.

"What's the problem now?" Chuck asked Pregler, for taking over the dredge had been one thing, actually making it work something else entirely.

The foreman pursed his lips for a moment before answering. "No problem. Won't start is all."

"You sure you got fuel?" Chuck asked, just to bust his chops. "Battery okay?"

Pregler said nothing, merely casting a baleful sidelong glance toward Chuck as he stalked by.

Chuck was again surprised by how small the man was. When Chuck had gone into the bowels of the packing plant, during the last days of the company, trying to recruit the maintenance people for his dredge operation, a fellow with a huge black beard who turned out to be Pregler had peppered him with skeptical questions. The beard being enormous, Chuck had just naturally assumed the man behind it was enormous, too. Turned out not to be true. Pregler was all beard. His hair stood out like an animal that bristles in the presence of a predator. But gnome or not, he showed all the signs of being as arbitrary and one-way as Chuck himself. Chuck liked him.

Furlong had removed the hand that had been palpating the cylinder head and begun to slowly circle the machine.

Diesels being balky in cold weather, the maintenance people had patched the holes in the dilapidated room and added some insulation and space heaters. Place still wasn't a sauna. Along the far wall, a workbench stretched, one end a mare's nest, the other neatly arranged, the boundary that lay between marking the moment when Chuck had been forced to move Sam Turner up to the drafting room.

Chuck turned his attention back to the others. "Suppose there's no reason for me to stick around."

"Suppose not," Pregler agreed.

Chuck lingered a couple of minutes, anyway, thinking about what he'd gotten himself into. Probably he shouldn't have taken the dredge away from the dock board. Probably he should have let them shut the operation down for the winter and start up in the spring again. Probably a lot of things, but Chuck liked the idea of doing what everybody said was impossible, dredging in midwinter with a bunch of guys who didn't know diddly about the work. That was the sort of thing made life endurable.

"Let me know when you're ready to pump," he told Pregler.

"Umm."

From the dredge, he drove back up to city hall, where he futzed around with a revision of the engineering budget over the lunch hour. He had given up lunches. For a couple of weeks after saddling himself with Mark O'Banion's old job as PW head, he'd eaten everything in sight, drunk more, too, socking down the beers late at night. Nothing but self-pity, he decided, and so he cut it out.

At one o'clock, he drove over to the Jackson Building for another of the weekly dog track meetings, this one with the consultants, yet more people that he'd managed to annoy. No cigarette smoke this time, nice architect's office decor, too.

The next bid packet was being put together—the interior systems contract among others. The project had fallen behind schedule. The weather had turned against them. With interest and polite disbelief, they asked how his winter dredging project was coming along, and he had to admit that so far it had been a bust.

Back in his office, sifting through his messages, he found one from Bud Pregler.

"When did this come in?" he asked Joyce.

"Few minutes ago."

"See if you can raise him."

Joyce got on the two-way, and soon Chuck was talking to Pregler and listening to the machine clatter in the background.

"You got a mind to see this, boss, better get your fanny on down here!"

"I'm on my way. Give me ten."

Chuck rejiggered his schedule on the spot and in a few minutes was swinging the 4x4 into the makeshift parking lot at the shoreline.

A section of the floating line had been removed for the purpose of the trial run—before they tried to pump sand from the river bottom to the job site, they'd see if they could pump water from one end of the dredge to the other—and so he could no longer walk out, but even as he set the parking brake and opened the door, one of the dredge crew had already launched the workboat and started toward shore to fetch him.

Back on board, they tied off next to the fuel barge and joined the others in the machine house, where the diesel engine throbbed as Sid Furlong, wearing earmuffs, poked around it, making adjustments. Yelling to make himself heard over the din, he told Chuck that the problem had had nothing to do with the cold, as he'd thought at first. The air flaps on the emergency shut-down device had been tripped, he didn't know why. He spoke with the satisfaction of a man who had solved a simple but not obvious mystery.

Chuck walked over and stood with Phil, the pump repairman, and watched as Furlong continued to tinker and the prime mover alternately roared and groaned. On the floor nearby, where snow had been tracked, a small puddle of meltwater shimmered. Only the pump, with its volute curved like an enormous seashell, had not been engaged and still sat quietly at the vortex of the racket raised by the other equipment.

"As bad as the rock and roll my goddamn kid plays all the time!" Phil leaned over to yell in Chuck's ear.

"Sounds okay to me!" After all the silence, it couldn't get too noisy to suit Chuck.

Finally, Furlong took a step back and rubbed his hands on a rag as he surveyed his work, then came gravely over.

"I hope you're not lookin' for a warranty or nothing! Without you rebore the head, ain't much more you can do!"

"She runs, that's all I care!"

Furlong gave Chuck a no-warranty look.

Chuck's old boss Mark O'Banion, being a reformed drunk, used to talk about living life one day at a time. Chuck patted the casing of the gearbox between the diesel and pump. *Okay*, he thought.

"Now it's your turn," he said to Phil.

The pump repairman nodded.

Chuck turned to Bud Pregler. "You ready to take this baby for a spin?!"

The little man with the big black beard frowned fiercely. "Let's do her!"

Leaving Sid and Phil to tend to their charges, Chuck and the rest of his crew climbed up into the lever room.

Pregler settled himself among the gauges and controls, took a deep breath, and flipped the switch to activate the forward winch motor. Next he grasped the handle on the winch's rheostat and slowly pushed it forward. At the bow of the dredge, the ladder and cutter—the thirty-foot nozzle of what was, in effect, a huge vacuum cleaner, with its basket of blades to loosen the sand on the bottom of the river and its pipe to suck the sand up—swung through the thickly falling snow toward the water, the cables playing out over the sheaves.

Chuck, who had spent many hours on the dredge before he found his crew, could almost feel against his palm the worn, smooth brass handle of the rheostat as Pregler pushed it forward. The basket of blades disappeared into the river with barely a ripple. To stop its descent well off the bottom—since for this trial run they were only going to pump water—Pregler pulled back on the rheostat, then quickly set the winch's brake, a waist-high lever like those used on old pickup trucks, which he leaned all his insignificant weight against as the ladder inched to a stop. Chuck watched these movements with satisfaction, feeling vicariously the tension of them.

Next Pregler started the small compressor used to prime the pump and yelled back down to Phil in the machine room that the cutter was in the water, the primer on.

Thinking, despite himself, of Murphy's Law, Chuck climbed partway down the gangway and ducked his head so he could watch as Phil moved to the gearbox and engaged the pump, adding one final noise to the rest, barely audible in the dim, the accelerating vanes of the impeller inside the seashell-shaped pump housing.

The dredge lurched slightly. Chuck stood up and looked forward. Out toward the bow, the ladder cables jumped, then became still.

"Vacuum?!" he yelled at Pregler.

Pregler looked at the gauge. "Coming up! Ten, still rising!"

Excited, Chuck leaped down the stairs.

"Look okay, Phil?!"

Phil nodded.

"Good!" Chuck yelled.

He rested his hand on the pipe leading into the stone box and felt, through the cold metal, the moving water. He paused at the intricate coupling which connected the pump to the prime mover that drove it—no sign of leaking.

"Okay, Sid?!"

"So far!"

Followed by a couple of the others, Chuck headed for the stern. At first nothing seemed to be discharging, and Chuck swore. But then he noticed water leaking out of one of the couplings between the floating sections of the line. At the end of the run of pipe, where a section had been removed, a thin stream began to spill into the river. Suddenly water came ejaculating in spurts from the pipe and almost at once settled into a strong, steady flow, arcing back into the river after its short trip from the cutter head at the bow.

The others let out a whoop, but Chuck stood quietly. He watched the opened vein of the pipeline spill its fluid back into the river and thought, *Okay, not much, but something. A start.* The experts he'd contacted, none of them willing to lend a hand, had warned him that dredging was a skill only mastered after a long apprenticeship. They thought that working in midwinter was completely nutso, too. "Well," Chuck said softly under his breath, "fuck 'em."

He turned his attention back to the problems at hand.

Only a few feet from where they were standing at the stern, water hissed from the swivel elbow, as it might from a faulty garden hose, the joint allowing the dredge to swing back and forth as it vacuumed sand off the bottom. Chuck could feel the freezing mist.

Out along the line of pontoon sections—which carried not only the discharge line, but also the walkway onto the dredge—the clamps on several of the rubber sleeves linking pontoon to pontoon leaked as well, water fizzing from them onto the walkway. Those leaks could be patched, or ice might form a natural seal, but the swivel el was another matter. Chuck regretted he didn't have Sam Turner on the dredge anymore, someone he could put on ice detail.

"We're gonna have to abandon the walkway," he told the men who had come aft with him. "I don't want some idiot ending up in the drink." Chuck told them to dismantle both ends of it.

Everybody would now have to be ferried back and forth. A pain in the ass, but nothing to be done about it. It would, at least, keep sightseers off the dredge.

Back up in the lever room, he looked at the gauge readings, then thumped Pregler on the shoulder and told him to shut her down, and go home. On Monday, they'd begin pumping sand.

Five minutes later, having been deposited back on shore, Chuck watched the launch as it returned toward the dredge, disappearing into the storm. The elation he had experienced while standing at the stern and feeling the icy mist and watching water spill from the pipeline had already eroded away. Another man, he supposed, would have felt better than he did.

In the intensity of the snowfall, the dredge had been reduced to nothing more than a dim outline. It occurred to him that both storm and dredge could be thought of as phases of hydrologic cycles, one man-made, the other natural. In a moment, he had discarded the idea, for true or not, the comparison seemed shabby. What was pumping water when matched against the great and subtle wheel of the weather?

Chuck's own interest in nature had nothing to do with its complexity or beauty or any of the other attributes that had led to the endless platitudes spouted by people Chuck had no use for. The storm's indifference drew his attention. Not even that, for to call the storm indifferent was to invest it with human emotions, and no word could express the separation between him and it. Chuck noticed this, and for a few moments his mind lay quiet, and nothing more.

CHAPTER 8

~

Walking the half block from where she had parked, El Plowman barely noticed the storm, her attention taken up by troubling recollections of the encounter that morning at Pearl and Hiram Johnson's, alighting first on one participant and then another—the words of the Rev. Tipton so carefully chosen, his calculated leaving of things up in the air; Pearl Johnson's evident grim satisfaction at doing her own bidding for once; Reiny's scorn; the silent witness of Johnny Pond and the others.

She had assumed the city's black community would rally behind the remounting of the exhibit. Apparently, she'd assumed too much.

Should she act on her own, then, perhaps even give Reiny his head? That temptation—impossible, of course—still lingered. The desire to act. Knowing more sometimes helped, and sometimes it didn't. To pay attention to everybody's sensibilities was to do nothing. And depressed or not, El had never been a woman to do nothing.

She mounted the KJAX steps and entered the warm, humid air of the radio station's reception area.

Pond appeared almost at once, coat on, and said, "Let's go for a walk," and El found herself back outside again. He started to go one way, then changed his mind and set off in the other direction.

The streetlights had been turned on.

"Growing up in the projects, I used to love the snow," he said after they passed over the intersection of Bluff and Commercial and he'd turned down Commercial, where city workers were taking down Christmas decorations. He kicked his way along. "Liked to play in it—what kid doesn't? But mostly I liked the look of it. Made the place look kind of, I don't know, magical. Took some doing, making the Robert Taylor Homes look magical." After his silence at the meeting, he had reverted to his usual chatty self.

They arrived at the Three Annes Café, and he suggested they go in for something to drink.

He went straight to a table in the back, where he grabbed the lapels of his coat and shook the snow off and then sat down, legs spread, without taking the coat off, suggesting both that he was settling himself comfortably and planned to leave almost at once, just as their arrival at the café itself had seemed both spontaneous and planned. The coat was long and ample, like a military greatcoat, of a mulberry color, and it draped from his huge shoulders and completely hid the chair he sat in. Underneath, he wore the rather conservative suit he had had on that morning, so despite his chattiness and Johnny-like gestures, he still didn't seem quite himself.

"The usual," he said to the waitress.

"Nothing for me," El told her.

Pond sat relaxed in his chair, his hands in his lap, tapping the tips of his fingers together as he regarded her cannily.

"An interesting meeting this morning," El said.

He continued to study her with calculation. "Been waiting for you to come see me."

"Oh?"

"Been waiting a couple months now."

"Is that right?"

He nodded.

El knew what he was talking about—the public fuss over the promotion of Sam Turner. An odd time to bring the matter up. "I knew you planted the stories, if that's what you mean," she said. It had been immediately clear where they'd come from, Johnny using Rachel Brandeis, the *Trib* reporter, as his stalking horse.

"I was surprised you didn't break the story yourself," she said.

Pond frowned, not unpleasantly, but didn't offer a comment.

"Although," El said, "after the performance this morning, perhaps I shouldn't have been." As she spoke, she remembered her anger. "You could have helped me out a little, you know." She leaned toward him and spoke low, so she wouldn't be heard all over the room. "I don't appreciate getting hung out to dry like that."

Unperturbed, Pond said, "Had nothing to do with you. Nothing personal. Or me, either, for that matter."

"Oh, is that right? Then why were you there, pray tell?" She leaned back in her chair and crossed her arms and waited for him to try and justify himself.

Pond stared off into space, then slowly back at El. When he spoke, he ignored what had happened at the Johnsons'. He wasn't through with the Sam Turner business.

"Sam had the qualifications. You could have kept the whole thing in-house, if you'd a mind to."

Assigning blame, of course, consisted of the art of identifying a first cause, and El saw at once the fruitlessness of such an exercise here.

"Perhaps. Anyway, there's nothing to be done. Except support Sam as best we can." She remembered the unhappy exchange with Chuck Fellows that had begun this unhappy day. "At the moment, I'm more interested in Pearl and Hiram."

He nodded slowly and stopped to taste his drink, sipping it gingerly, a man who would take the time to make a judgment.

"What is that?" she asked. She had given up coffee before all the fancy drinks started to get popular.

"Austrian. They make it with dried figs." Satisfied, he took another sip. "Of course, a purist always drinks his coffee black. Black is best. A good Ethiopian roast."

"But not you."

He settled back. "Not me."

The drink, in its dainty cup and with its topping of whipped cream and what looked like cinnamon, seemed hardly the sort of thing Pond would have chosen.

El studied him closely. "What *did* happen at Pearl and Hiram's, Johnny?"

He touched the handle of the coffee cup but did not pick it up, then tapped the table top several times, then clasped his hands together and looked at her intently.

"Wasn't about you…"

"You already said that. Reiny, then?"

"You're highly regarded," he finished the first thought.

"But?"

He leaned far to the side in the chair, the greatcoat pulled taut, and stared at her, making a judgment, as he had after sipping the coffee. With his large round head and body to match, he looked every inch the football player he had once been, but El imagined his gridiron success had less to do with his massive body than the way he would have gotten inside his opponents' heads. She could see him carrying on casual conversations with them between plays, casual conversations being inimical to success on the gridiron for people unlike himself.

Now he said, "What you got to understand, El, is this exhibit got nothing to do with the Johnsons. From the beginning."

"I beg your pardon."

"They were okay with it."

"Hiram was more than okay with it."

He paused a beat and then continued with his own line of reasoning. "Perhaps. But they didn't need to feel better about themselves or anything like that. They mostly did it as a favor to the city. Help you folks out because you've got a problem."

"*We've* got a problem?"

He nodded deliberately.

"It's your problem, too," she told him.

Pond thought about that and countered, "It's our burden. We've had it laid upon us, been carrying it around for a good long time. Don't expect to put it down anytime soon, neither."

El found this distancing on his part extremely irritating. "Frankly, Johnny, I'm not interested in bantering words back and forth. It's our burden, too."

"Some people get to carry a lighter load."

"You don't think I know that?"

He didn't answer the question. Instead he asked one of his own. "Tell me, El, why you so het up about this thing? City's had these sorts of racist flare-ups before. Wait a couple months, it'll blow over, people go back in their holes."

Given her annoyance, she said at once, "As the chair of the museum board, I don't like it when one of my exhibits is trashed."

"Is that all?"

"All?" She slowed herself down before continuing. "No, that's not all...As a matter of fact, while we were building the exhibit, I had the chance to work with a number of blacks. As you well know, since you were one of them. I'm grateful for that. I learned a lot." She leaned intently forward. "I don't pretend to understand everything—how could I?—but believe it or not, Johnny, I think I do have some sense of what you've been through. And that, frankly, is why I find the attitude of the people this morning so odd...and troubling."

He pressed his lips firmly together and continued to regard her intently.

"I do believe it," he said at last. "I do believe you're more sensitive than a lot of other folk. Trouble is, you had the experience. These others?" He shook his head. "See what I'm saying? You got the benefit. But the rest, why, they're just as ignorant as they've always been. Ain't they? And I'll tell you what, El, you go ahead with the idea you can accomplish something here, improve the situation somehow, you're gonna make matters worse, guaranteed…" Pond was the second person who had told her that today, a reprise of Chuck Fellows's claim earlier that she'd make matters worse if she insisted on going up to the drafting room to see how Sam Turner was getting along. "Suppose," Pond continued, "we let Reiny Kopp do what he wants to do. Who benefits? The whites, the ones who need to hear the message, why, they don't go near the exhibit. You know that. Even if they did, they'd think it was meant for somebody else. So who benefits? I'll tell you. Nobody."

"I don't know what you mean by 'improve the situation,'" she said. "I want to remount the exhibit, that's all. But if Pearl won't make another quilt…Without the help of the black community, Johnny, all we'll end up with is a shabby copy of the original."

He revolved his coffee cup in its saucer, staring into it.

"What if this had been you?" she asked. "What if it had been your family?" She couldn't imagine Johnny was the kind of person who would back away from such a situation.

"Then it would have been personal."

"And this isn't?" If El had been black and someone had done this, she certainly would have felt violated.

"I tell you what," he said, "I'm against capital punishment, okay, but you ask me how I'd react if one of my little girls was murdered… Sometimes you got to get some distance from the emotion of a thing to see what ought to be done."

The spirit of this conversation, so different from the night two months earlier when he'd suddenly shown up on her doorstep and browbeat her about promoting Sam Turner, left El wondering if Pond knew his own mind.

"I suppose we can just go through the motions," she said. "That's what you want me to do, right? Go through the motions?"

"Up to you."

With one elbow propped on the table, he leaned his forehead against his large hand, fingers splayed, his genius for contradiction expressed in this pose, both perplexed and cagey.

"It's up to me, huh?"

"Do what you think you should," he said. "Why do you need my approval?"

Stung, El said, "I'm not looking for approval."

He nodded. "Good."

∾

She drove down to the museum to give Reiny his marching orders, to repeat them, to leave no doubt in his mind. She'd have to contact the other museum board members to bring them up to date and schedule another emergency meeting if they wanted one. Probably unnecessary.

She remembered the series of newspaper articles Rachel Brandeis was projecting on race relations in the city. In the absence of some sort of concerted effort, such stories would have little impact. People didn't have to read what they didn't want to, any more than they had to go to the exhibit, and they were sick to death of hearing about the troubles of blacks.

El supposed that Johnny Pond had been right. If she was honest with herself, she really had been looking for "approval," as he put it. Without her old confidence, unable to envision the course of events, she'd be a fool to do anything but the minimum. The safe choice seemed more or less pointless, but at least required little energy. Repair the exhibit as best they could, with or without help. Reopen it, this time with a twenty-four-hour guard. And hope matters didn't get any worse. Matters could always get worse.

Nearing the museum, her thoughts turned to the problem of Reiny Kopp. She remembered Ned Pickett's suggestion that perhaps the vandalism involved nothing more than a personal grudge someone had had against the Johnsons. El didn't believe it for a moment, but she could think of another possibility. An eye had to be kept on Reiny. He still possessed the soul of an activist, the so-called prankster he'd been in the sixties, and it had occurred to El that he might have vandalized the exhibit himself, or arranged to have it done. From the beginning, he'd wanted to mount an aggressive, lay-it-all-on-the-line display. He'd been thwarted. What better way to turn people around than arrange for something as ugly as this to happen?

Did he? She wasn't prepared to believe it. Anyway, if he had, it didn't work. Like it or not, he was going to remount the old exhibit. He could make a small display of the vandalism photos, but nothing more.

He wouldn't like it, he wouldn't be graceful about it, but El knew that usually, in his own sweet time, Reiny reached some sort of private accommodation with his habitual moral outrage and did what he was told. She trusted he would this time, too. Nevertheless, she cautioned herself to be absolutely unequivocal with him, to leave no small opening for creative interpretation. That would save the need for undoing later.

She parked in the museum lot and went inside through the snow.

CHAPTER 9

~

S am Turner woke up at four thirty the next morning—same time
he used to get up to go collect garbage. He lay still, the silence
plugging his ears. Storm must've ended. He rolled over, propped
himself on his elbow, and peeled back the lower edge of the window shade.

Cool air from the glass made his eyes smart. With his head,
he held the shade away from the window as he tried to raise the
sash, but it had frozen shut. Snow mounted the ledge outside. He
touched the frost built up on the inside of the pane, cold and sticky,
then raised himself higher, the shade rubbing against the back of
his head, and watched the snow's herky-jerky passage through the
glow of the nearby streetlight. Storm wasn't over. He listened carefully and could hear the soft cuffs it made. Satisfied, he flopped
back onto the mattress and closed his eyes.

When he woke up again, the room was filled with light the
color of brown sugar. Throwing off the covers, he knelt on his
bed. A flick of the wrist released the shade, which rolled all the
way up with a snap, the glare of the sun flooding in and drowning
the brown sugar light. He squinted at the outdoor world. Over
the housetops, a solid blue sky. Down in the unplowed street,
great humps of snow thrown over cars sparked like electricity in
the sunlight.

After a minute or two, he turned around and sat hunched on
the edge of the bed. He wanted to go back to sleep and wanted
to rush outside, couldn't decide which. So instead he picked up
the fantasy novel he'd taken out of the library the day before and
began to read it. He read a few lines and then decided he wasn't in
the mood for Glandroks and Morbs and tossed the book aside and
stood up. His small drawing board and T-square, the box holding
his instruments, the rolled up drawings he'd borrowed from the

city—all these lay on the card table in the corner, organized, as orderly as if somebody had died.

Good day to practice drawing. Cold winter's day. And he felt good, didn't have a hangover. He made up his mind. He'd do it, just like he'd been saying he would.

But first…

He went down the hall and washed up, the house quiet. His roomies were still asleep, or maybe they hadn't come home last night. Next, he took a load of dirty clothes down to the basement and threw it in the washing machine. Felt good not to have a hangover. Back upstairs, he decided to make the bed. It'd improve his concentration when he was working if the room didn't look like a motherfucking pigsty. Smelling the sour, filthy sheets, he changed his mind and stripped the bed instead. In the linen closet, on the shelf he'd marked with his name, using masking tape and his drafts-man's lettering, he found a pair of sheets, raggedy but clean, and he remade the bed, tucking the blanket so tight that the mattress curled. He stowed the books strewn around the room in the make-shift bookcase, except for the one he was reading, which he laid first on the card table but then, thinking it would be too much of a temptation, on one of the arms of the director's chair in the other corner. Having done this, he looked around, satisfied that here was a place where a man might get something done. He'd never gotten around to putting up pictures, which would have meant picking some out for himself. Sam had always lived in rooms with other people's pictures.

He took the dirty sheets down to the laundry for the next load.

After he ate his cereal and drank a second cup of coffee and cleaned the kitchen, he found he still wasn't quite ready to tackle the drawings. Once he got going, he'd be okay. Just got to get going. He wished he had a newspaper and thought about turning on the radio but didn't.

In the distance, he heard a scraping noise, and this reminded him of the snow. He wondered how much had fallen. If he didn't go outside now, he'd miss it while it was still nice and clean. He looked at his watch. Early yet. Plenty of time to do his work upstairs.

With his old trash-collecting clothes on, he donned his shades and then the wool cap with its ear flaps, which ruined the effect of the glasses, making him look like a doofus trying to be cool. Kept him warm, that was what counted.

He stepped out the back door, into the brilliant day. His roomies' cars were gone.

Down the street, a solitary figure shoveled, the sound of scraping reaching Sam an instant after he saw the man's arms move, the snow swirling off his shovel, like the northern lights or solar flares or something.

He looked behind himself, at the snow shovel propped beside the back door. Where the sun touched the snow clutching the porch railing, water droplets had formed and frozen and others hung, still liquid, the beginnings of icicles. A whiff of wood smoke came to him, and, with the shovel now in hand, he looked up to see birds fluttering around the top of the chimney next door. "Keepin' warm, are ya?" he said to them.

He shoveled out toward the street first and then along the sidewalk. When he was through, he'd scatter some rock salt, just to be on the safe side. In the summer, he cut the grass and trimmed the bushes and pulled weeds and stood around jawing with the guy next door, talking the shit neighbors talked. He got along with people on the street, just like he got along with the guys in the drafting room or on the trash crew. He wasn't about making his life any more difficult than it already was.

He had stopped shoveling, his eyes drifting across the white landscape as he wondered why he found it so much easier to shovel snow than go upstairs and practice drawing. Maybe he should go in and grab himself a sketch pad and draw a picture of the snowy landscape or something. That would be constructive.

The garage door had opened across the street, and he could see the guy starting up his riding tractor. Wasn't gonna be nice and quiet anymore. From the cave of the garage, the machine howled and reverberated, but as the guy drove outside, the noise died down some. Not enough. Sam gave up the idea of a sketch. Who could draw with that kind of racket going on? Sam waved, and the guy, looking to either side as the John Deere began to rifle snow as far as his neighbor's yard, gave him half a wave back. The man surely did love his John Deere. Had the seeder attachment to use in the spring, mower for summer, leaf mulcher for fall—never a day he couldn't find some excuse for riding around on that sucker.

Sam was shoveling again, the first shovelful taken without realizing what he was doing and then the next while he wondered at the first and the third and fourth and fifth until he had his rhythm again, like he'd reappeared in time, that's what it seemed. Slowly, he cleared the walkways, cutting perfect cliffs of white on either side. He portioned out neat blocks and tossed them first one way, then the other.

It was easier to think when he wasn't shoveling, and the next time he stopped to rest, he again remembered the drafting work waiting for him upstairs. Other people didn't have trouble getting motivated, or they didn't give a shit, which amounted to pretty much the same thing. Sam floated, that was the thing of it, and whatever he did, it seemed like it wasn't quite him who was doing it. That's what he thought anyway.

He began shoveling again, working longer without stopping. After the sidewalk along the street, he cleared the walk to the front porch, which nobody used, and then out to the end of the driveway even though it'd just be filled up again soon as the plow came. He worked steadily but slowly, feeling the sweat forming beneath his layers of clothing.

The guy across the street had finished and driven his Deere back into the garage, and it was quiet again.

Sam turned and made a path to his thirdhand blue 1974 Toyota hatchback with the 200,000 miles on it. He brushed the snow off, feeling restless now, feeling the pressure. Needed to go in and sit down at the drafting board, that's what he needed to do. Once he got going, he'd be okay. Go inside and put on some clean clothes, make another pot of coffee, and he'd be ready.

As he shoveled his way back down the driveway, a car approached through the unplowed street. Sam checked it out, a big black sport utility vehicle, slowing down. Looked like it was coming to his house. He turned away and went back to shoveling, listening to the crump of the tires die away and a door open and slam shut.

Out of the corner of his eye, he watched a guy he'd never seen before come walking up the path he'd cleared—white, wearing a Russian hat, making a beeline for Sam. Sam continued shoveling, checking the guy out on the sly. What did this mother want?

"Excuse me!" the newcomer called out as he neared.

Continuing to ladle snow away from the driveway, Sam tilted his head toward the approaching figure.

"You Sam Turner?"

Sam sent one more shovelful into the yard and then stood up.

The fellow required no answer to his question. "You're a hard man to find, Mr. Turner." He pushed his Russian hat back as if it had been a visor and looked around. "Your house?" he asked.

This guy trouble? Sam wondered.

"My name's St. John, Miller St. John." He removed a glove and held out his hand to shake. "I'm with the *New York Times*."

Chapter 10

~

"A gain?"

As the funeral director spoke, he studied Deuce Goetzinger with what might have been renewed interest. The one-word question seemed more recognition than inquiry. "It's awfully late. We're about to move her."

Deuce didn't respond, and the other man, as he led the way briskly past the silent parlors, faintly scented with the flowers of past bereavements, repeated, "There's not much time."

The casket lay not in one of the public rooms but on a dolly in an anteroom in the back, a place clean but spartan. As they entered, a door on the side was hurriedly closed, Deuce catching a glimpse of the office beyond, computers and the other paraphernalia of modern business life.

"Shall I?"

"Yes."

He stood a couple of paces away as the lid rose, the outline of his mother's face revealed, now familiar in death, surrounded by white satin. The satin reminded him of the inside of a water moccasin's mouth.

"I've softened the makeup as you requested." The other man's tone of voice, which Deuce didn't like, hinted at a special understanding between the two of them. "But I was wondering…Perhaps just a touch more color."

Deuce moved a step closer. His mother looked almost exactly as she had on the day they found her frozen in the fetal position beneath a bower of evergreens.

"No."

"As you wish."

Unlike the day before, when the undertaker had gone away at once, leaving Deuce alone in one of the formal front rooms, he now lingered, neither of them speaking. Deuce stared at his mother's icy complexion, her head resting in the terrible whiteness. Her profile had become sharper, her brow stronger, her eyes closed over what she no longer chose to see, her long nose with the familiar bump in the middle more resolute, as if in death her sense of what was right had been fixed even more firmly.

The other man finally spoke. "I just want to say, I am *truly* sorry." The annoying hint of a special understanding remained, but Deuce heard genuine empathy in the words, too. It occurred to him that such a man would have many opportunities to judge people unworthy.

Now, requiring no response, he retreated. Deuce listened to the soft closing of the door. From a nested stack stored in the far corner, he lifted a straight-backed chair and placed it where he couldn't see his mother and sat down. Abandoning his rigidly aloof manner, he slumped, one leg slung carelessly over the other.

He almost hadn't come back. His emotions had been filed down during the search and over the long, tedious preparations for the funeral Mass, but this dulling only exposed more starkly the disgust and self-loathing lying beneath. He thought about the respect the funeral director had shown him. What a joke.

He looked around although there wasn't much to see. Wainscoting and moldings had been installed, as if at one time the place had had some more important function, since abandoned. Now nothing but a waiting room for corpses.

He was there, he supposed, because his father was not. He didn't want to witness the old man's grief anymore, just as he hadn't wanted to hear him cry in Whistler Number Two. It was too late for that sort of crap. He wished to be shut of the old bastard.

He *was* shut of him, but he didn't have any delusions about his own behavior. Before he left the cave, he'd known in his heart that his mother was dead. He hated his father and blamed him, but he blamed himself, too. He'd always had it in his power to divert events by a degree or two, just enough so that when she wanted to fetch the old man home, she would have called him instead of trying to do it herself. He had let her drive down that hill as surely as the old man had.

He allowed these thoughts to dissolve, unslung his leg, and slouched deeper in the chair.

After a while, a vehicle drew up outside, the motor murmuring quietly, followed by the sound of a door opening but not closing. Through a dusty sidelight next to the entrance, the corner of a hearse was now visible, parked under a covered entryway. The undertaker would be back any moment, and Deuce felt rushed even though he was doing nothing.

He hadn't believed in God or the afterlife since he was ten years old. His mother was dead, period, that was what he believed. The distress lodged in the center of his chest would in time disappear, leaving only a residue, like the ashes of a fire. That would be what was left of his mother, the residue at the center of his chest. And then he would die, and memories of her would die with him, and finally nothing would be left of her.

Or of Deuce. Or anyone. A million years from now or ten million or a hundred million, humans would be nothing but fossils in rock strata. Rock strata everywhere, there had been so fucking many of them. In a few billion more, the sun would bloat and consume the earth, and the solar system itself would die, nothing but cinders drifting in the void. Deuce had been raised in the Church, but this was what he believed. And he hadn't come to the funeral home yesterday and again today to say good-bye to his mother; she was already gone. He didn't know why he'd come. He just had.

Finally, the funeral director returned. He seemed not surprised to find Deuce way on the other side of the room. It was time to go. Deuce nodded, and as the lid on the elaborate coffin was closed, he imagined the shadow crossing the horrible white satin and then her face.

Several more men came in the room and lifted the coffin and carried it outside, giving each other instructions and moving quickly and efficiently, these not being the official pallbearers and so not required to observe the strict solemnity of the occasion. For them, it was just a job. Finding the everydayness of this fact a small comfort, Deuce watched them go, and then followed.

Chapter 11

❧

Before she went down to the small room at the other end of the hall for the bargaining session, Aggie Klauer, the city's personnel director and union negotiator, closed the door to her office for a few minutes and did some stretching exercises. A limber body made for a limber mind. At least, that was the theory.

She pulled her shoulders back, feeling the blades pinching together, sucked in a lungful of air, held it, then exhaled, her chest collapsing like a deflating balloon. She did this several times, until her vision wavered slightly, a hint of the onset of hyperventilation. Then she began rotating her shoulders in a kayak-paddling fashion.

Across the room, on the top shelf of the built-in bookcase, souvenirs of the latest employee enrichment program jockeyed for position—SPIRIT mugs and SPIRIT pens and SPIRIT caps and SPIRIT tote bags, as if she were a booster for some seminary football team. Paul Cutler, having proposed, left her to dispose. In the strata of papers piled on her shelves and in her drawers, an archaeologist would have found plenty of evidence of the city manager's earlier enthusiasms: role playing, team building, and so forth.

Aggie wiggled her hips back and forth and then bent over and touched her toes, knees straight.

And now this! They'd never done anything like it before. No way would the seed she was about to plant grow into anything but the rankest of weeds. The soil hadn't been tilled, herbicides and fertilizer applied. For whatever good it would have done. She took a deep breath, and stretched and twisted for all she was worth, and listened to her joints cracking. Finally, she shook herself like a dog coming out of the water, and began to collect the documents she'd need, hustling now because she had made herself late.

The material clutched unceremoniously under her arm, she marched down the broad hallway past permits, past the city clerk, past finance, until she arrived at the tiny conference room tucked in the northwest corner of the first floor. The door stood open.

As she entered, her eye moved along the row of upturned union faces, seeking out J.J. Dusterhoft, the union's negotiator. Not finding him, she looked again, as she might make a second pass along a bookshelf in search of a favorite volume.

"Where's J.J.?"

In his accustomed place sat Barbara Amos, the members of the union's negotiating team ranged on either side.

"Out on his truck," she told Aggie.

Aggie glanced through the window. Hardly any snow had fallen, although the day certainly looked ominous enough, a pall of gray, expectant air engulfing the buildings and trees and passing cars. When she had been outside earlier, Aggie didn't remember seeing any city trucks, but now, as if Amos had conjured it, one drove by, its plow raised. Aggie couldn't make out the driver.

She turned back toward Barb, not her favorite person in the world, and considered calling off the session on the grounds that the union's chief negotiator wasn't present. Then she told herself, *Don't be a wuss, Ag, it doesn't matter.* She was just there to plant the seed. The real unpleasantness would come later.

On Aggie's side of the table, an empty chair had been left between the city's finance director and the steno. She greeted everyone, dropped the sheaf of new city proposals on the table, and settled herself into the empty chair as if perfectly at ease.

For a minute or two, she chatted about whatever came into her head. Then, there being no reason to put off the inevitable, she handed the proposals around.

She thought about drawing their attention to the article on wages, but decided they'd find it soon enough on their own and so waited silently, the only sound the crinkling of pages being turned. Barbara Amos, as she read, smiled and shook her head, which didn't necessarily mean anything.

Aggie's disappointment at J.J.'s absence would have been noted. A moment of unprofessionalism. She must make a point of not being caught unawares like that in the future.

She felt deserted, the room a little gloomier. J.J. was a man to like. He went through life as if visiting the place for the first time and never seemed to have anything more important to do than whatever he happened to be doing at the moment. He'd inject into a conversation any matter that caught his fancy, so that all sorts of oddments had, over the years, been included, by reference, in their negotiations: how to perform a tracheotomy, whether women make better cops than men, the decline of letter writing, the virtues of ice fishing…In the midst of all this, the union contracts somehow always managed to get settled.

Amos and her companions continued reading. The union had emptied its hope chest into its initial proposal, which was helpful since it made it easy for Aggie to counter with the city's. Some items in the union wish list—dental plan, making birthdays holidays, unlimited accrual of unused sick leave—were put in year after year, and Aggie, year after year, would counter with proposals to delete the requirement that the city pay for uniforms, that layoffs be based on competence rather than seniority, and so forth. The union had a nice long list; Aggie had a nice long list. Into the proposals these items would go, and out they would come again.

As Barb Amos read, she glanced up occasionally, pinning Aggie in place. Amos always wore black and white, today a white blouse beneath a black tunic. A heart-shaped silver brooch added a hint of sentimentality. Her hair, worn too long for her squarish face, had the orderliness of a wig. Her hazel eyes were mismatched as well, one slightly larger than the other, but alert and a little fearful, too, as if brought along against their will.

Since most of the changes proposed by the city were hoary with age, Barb might have rushed through them and arrived quickly at the crux of the matter, but not being used to sitting in the negotiator's seat perhaps and, of course, distrustful, she picked her way along like a soldier through a minefield. Aggie watched her eyes drop line by line. Her companions, moving more briskly, came to the zinger first. One of them pointed it out to her.

"Where?" she said beneath her breath, leaning over and looking at his copy of the document and then leafing ahead in hers.

At first, she seemed less angry than confused. She looked across the table. "There's a typo here. This can't be right."

"That's our proposal," Aggie said, speaking as blandly as she could under the circumstances.

"A giveback?"

"That's right. Ten percent."

"You're kidding."

Aggie shook her head. "Not about something like that."

The city had never pleaded poor before. The employees had never been asked to take a pay cut. They'd always gotten at least nothing, and most of the time a little more and occasionally even something above the CPI, catching the brass ring for a change in their unending chase after their confreres in the private sector.

Amos was turning to the other members of the union's negotiating team and pointing out the page. "Can you believe this?"

Aggie remained passive. She wished J.J. were there. She didn't like negotiating with women. Women, unable to appreciate the game-playing aspect of the business, rode in on their moral high horses. Barb was no different, her horse, if anything, higher than most. Her bad case of nerves didn't change that. Still, she seemed unable to settle on any response other than incredulity.

She turned back to Aggie. "So what do we get in exchange?" she demanded. Surely, there must be something in exchange. "No layoffs?"

"Of course we don't want to lay anybody off," Aggie assured her, but lest Amos in her current state misconstrue this, Aggie added, "However, I can't make any guarantees."

"So we get nothing?"

At this point, the city manager, had he been there, would have launched into some variation of his SPIRIT speech, and he and Barb gotten into a high noon shoot-out. Well, actually, it couldn't have conceivably happened, because Paul would never put himself in that situation, and even if he had, he wouldn't have demeaned himself by arguing with Barb. He left those tasks to Aggie. She was the one following him along with her pooper-scooper.

All she said now was, "Given the shortfall, Barb, we'd like to avoid cutting services." She toyed briefly with the idea of adding, "They affect everybody," but decided no. Keep it simple. This wasn't about *everybody*.

It made no difference. Amos had already latched onto a version of the same thought. She sat back in her chair. Her nervousness remained, but she had begun to get a grip on herself. She even managed to say something with a whiff of strategy about it. "Tell me, please, is this for all the employees?" She waved at the document. "Does everybody take a cut? What about you and Paul Cutler?"

J.J. wouldn't have asked Aggie such a thing, but it was just what she'd expect out of Amos's mouth.

"Not a matter for discussion at this table," Aggie told her.

"It's just a question."

Aggie said nothing.

"I thought so."

Amos nodded at the perverse logic of it all. Her mouth was partially open, a frown exposing a bottom row of uneven teeth. She didn't seem to know what she wanted to say next.

So Aggie suggested, "Unless you have any other points that you want clarified..."

Amos went back to where she had been in the proposal and began to read again and turn pages furiously. "Is there anything else?" she asked angrily.

"Nothing you haven't seen before."

"Okay," she said and slammed the document shut.

"Okay," Aggie said.

And as abruptly as that, the session was over.

Aggie, relieved, nodded good-bye to the finance director and steno and was the first person out the door. The deed had been done; now it was up to the union. And, Aggie thought, as much as she disliked asking for givebacks, as much as she wouldn't look forward to negotiating over them, at least in the future she wouldn't be dealing with Barb Amos. As she marched smartly back down the hall, she made a mental note to check the weather forecast before scheduling future sessions.

CHAPTER 12

~

D euce couldn't park without blocking somebody, so he pulled in behind his sister's car. He turned the motor off but didn't get out.

After leaving the church, he'd driven aimlessly around. Neighborhoods slid by, the yards as empty as no-man's-lands. His thoughts were scattered, broken off, abandoned, the only constant the silent judging observer behind them.

During the funeral—which the priest called a celebration— Deuce had listened to the eulogies without interest. He didn't give one himself. Everything he said to other people about his mother seemed false. His father didn't get up either. Among the family only his sister Elaine spoke. She told anecdotes, like the one about the first time their mother sold a boar to a commercial hog farmer. Buying a boar from a woman violated the fellow's chauvinistic pride, but he wouldn't admit it, and so she argued him into a corner until there was nothing he could do but buy the animal. What Deuce remembered most about the incident was the delight his mother had taken in retelling the story herself.

Elaine had been after Deuce to come back up to the farm for the reception. She badgered him before the service, and she badgered him after.

"You're becoming a pill," he said, "you know that?"

"I've always been a pill. You've just never noticed. You've been too busy being mad at Daddy."

He scoffed pleasantly at the notion that she'd been flying under his radar all these years. "You think just because you're the only woman left in the family, you can tell everybody else what to do."

"Baloney. You're the only one I'm trying to tell what to do. Come up to the farm. Pleeeease."

He frowned. The idea turned his stomach. But he didn't want to disappoint her. Close up, he could see how tired she was, her grief all but swamped by the exhaustion of the many funeral preparations, taken completely into her own hands because the Goetzinger men were such a hopeless lot.

"And you really ought to patch it up with Daddy," she persisted. "He wants to, you know."

"No," Deuce said sharply, the playfulness in his tone gone in an instant.

Elaine recoiled, but she had the Goetzinger determination and wouldn't just let the matter drop. "What about Mother? She'd want it, too."

This mother-would-want ploy was exactly the wrong thing to say. "Cut it out, Sis." He meant business. "Don't bring Ma into this. The old man tried to pull that kind of shit on me all the time."

"All right," she apologized quickly. "All right, I'm sorry. But do come back to the farm." Pain had come into her face. The world hadn't changed. "Please."

Deuce reached up and touched her cheek with his fingertips. "Okay," he told her. "For you." He dropped his hand. "Just keep the old man away from me." As if she could.

And so he had driven around, thinking he'd go back on his word, and finally hadn't. He drove up Brick Kiln Road, past the spot where his mother's car had gone off into the woods, and nearing the farm, he felt as if he was drawing farther away from her. Now he sat in the Mazda in the midst of the farm buildings and all the cars that had arrived before him.

He stared at the trunk of Elaine's car, where, fearful of what their father might do, she had gotten her husband to stash the old man's gun. Snowflakes slipped one by one down the slick paint job.

The last time, he decided. With his mother dead, he had no reason to come up to the farm anymore. The old man could go rot in hell.

He got out of the car and went inside.

The place was crowded, and he thought he might hide himself among so many people, but Elaine was at his side in a second.

"I knew you'd come. Good." She dragged his coat off him. "Try to be pleasant, dear. You can do it," she whispered, as if she were a coach and he some underachieving player being sent into the big game. She did everything but pat him on the ass.

In the living room, he found somebody he liked well enough and chatted with him. Then he found somebody else and did the same. He kept a weather eye out for the old man and made a special note of the long-familiar objects in the room, hardly any of them changed since his childhood, merely more out-of-date and faded and patched.

Followed by his two young cousins, Teddy wove back and forth among the adults, holding a platter of food up for them with his usual mixture of vagueness and diffidence and intensity. Deuce's imitation of conviviality faltered slightly at the sight of his young brother, eyes still red from where he'd been crying earlier. Deuce respected Teddy's emotions. They went all the way down.

And Deuce realized that if he never came up there again, he'd never see his brother. Nothing to be done, he wasn't coming back. When Teddy got old enough, he could come downtown and visit.

The kitchen table was covered with dishes brought by neighbors and family friends. Elaine had used a Crock-Pot to cook a sausage stew and brought up some of their mother's sauerkraut from the basement. Deuce wasn't hungry, but he got a paper plate and forked a brat and some kraut onto it. One taste of the kraut was all he could take, and he put the rest down untouched.

"Hello," someone said at his back. He turned to find Father Mike Daugherty, the pastor of St. Columbkille's, inspecting the food with interest, leaning over the table, hands clasped behind his back, like a judge in a cooking contest.

The priest shook Deuce's hand. "I thought it was a lovely service," he said, plunging right in. "You must have fond memories of your mother. She *was* a most wonderful woman." He spoke with the assurance of a man who always had the words to match the occasion.

Deuce, irritated by the smooth countenance smiling expertly at him and by the smoother words, wondered what he could say to offend. "I'm sure she was useful."

Daugherty's expression changed slightly. "We all try to be useful." He talked about Edna's service to the church, visiting shut-ins and baking German dishes for parish functions, his praise as slick as his officiating at the funeral Mass had been.

Deuce knew a little bit about him. He wasn't that much older than Deuce himself, late thirties maybe, his face mostly remarkable because of the intensity with which he listened, as if he tried to curb a natural self-absorption by this exaggerated focus on others. He'd "grown" the parish, that's what people liked to say of him. Built a new school, brought young families back into the church or poached them from other parishes. Gave hot shit homilies. Deuce wondered what was wrong with him. Nobody became a priest anymore.

"Your mother thought very highly of you," Daugherty said suddenly. He had taken up a paper plate and begun a finicky sampling of the dishes. Deuce could imagine what his mother had told him. He waited for Daugherty to complete the thought, but the priest surprised him.

"They call you Deuce, don't they?"

"Not around here." Not unless you counted Elaine's occasional, playful, nettling "Deucey."

"I understand you're very good." Daugherty turned over a cube of potato in a salad, like a man looking under a rock, then scooped a tiny portion onto his plate.

"At cards? Not particularly."

"Oh? That's not what I hear." The priest was now inspecting a casserole of uncertain manufacture. "I hear you're very good indeed."

Deuce resisted the temptation to be flattered. He didn't trust it. Maybe the priest was a voyeur, fascinated by life among the heathens, where to be good meant something so different from what it did in his line of work. Or, on the other hand, maybe he just liked to begin with praise...

"Frankly, Father, there's nobody in this town knows enough to tell if I'm any good."

"Ah." The priest paused. He had passed up the casserole and was now considering a beef and noodle dish. "Yes, I see how that could be." He took even a smaller portion of the beef and noodles. "Perhaps we can get together sometime." He stopped his food sampling long enough to turn his head and regard Deuce, his gaze mild but precise. He apparently always saw what he looked at; Deuce gave him that much credit at least. "Perhaps a friendly little game."

"It depends on what you mean."

"Well, of course, I'm just a poor cleric."

Even when there was a good deal of money on the table, Deuce's blood barely moved through his veins anymore.

"I don't play 'friendly little games,'" he told the priest.

"No, of course you don't," the priest agreed at once, ignoring the hostile intent of the remark. "Perhaps you could offer some tips, then, help spruce up my own game." He took a slightly larger sample of tossed salad.

"I don't give lessons."

"No?" Daugherty said, cocking an eye toward him as if surprised, then as quickly changing his tone, "No, of course. You don't do that either."

"Tell me, Father, what do you suppose my mother would think of this, you and me shooting the shit about poker? You think she'd approve?"

Daugherty smiled. "I don't suppose she would."

"Then perhaps we should leave it go."

"Perhaps we should."

Deuce said nothing more, and the priest finally folded his busted hand. His expression became severe and he nodded farewell and left the kitchen without a further glance at the food, his plate still half empty. Friendliness came once again into his voice as he greeted someone in the next room.

Having had enough of people for the moment, Deuce moved in the seams between conversations. Shoved behind the porch swing in the sunroom, he found the small metal garbage bucket his mother had used for birdseed. He folded down the bail and lifted the cover. Nearly full. A partition separated sunflower seeds from millet, the coffee can she used as a scoop half buried in the millet.

Out in the side yard, the snow had drifted thigh-high in places and crusted over. With karate chops, he broke the crust and waded past the lilac and ceanothus bushes she'd planted to attract butterflies. At the head-high feeder he paused, conscious of the absence of birdsong. The snow continued to fall in individual flakes from the solid gray overcast. With his forearm, he swept the mound of frozen snow from the feeder, then filled it with a couple of cans of sunflower seed and one of millet. He scattered three more of the millet across the snow for the ground feeding birds. The tiny gray and white pellets made a watery sound as they cascaded down and skittered over the icy surface.

The cold air soaked into him. He listened to the silence and to the memory of the watery sound and let the cold seep deeper. But something was not quite right. Almost as if by reflex, as if caught and twisted in a magnetic field, he turned and looked back toward the house.

In one of the windows stood his father. Bits of landscape and farm buildings, reflected in the glass, partly obscured him. Their eyes met.

Once, calculation and judgment had animated his father's entire face, but now he had withdrawn inside himself and only his mouth betrayed the old dissatisfactions. The glass removed everything inessential from his expression, leaving the lopsided patches of white hair, the furrows like scars on his forehead, the severe mouth.

Deuce held his father's gaze long enough not to give him any advantage. Then he turned away and, head down, retraced the trail he had broken until he was no longer visible from the window. The jagged crusts on either side of the path formed thin shelves beneath which the softer snow had collapsed in small avalanches.

At the back door, rather than go inside again, he put the pail down and walked toward the farrowing house. People were beginning to leave, cars pulling out.

His mother's sun hat still hung from a peg inside the door. The building, a dilapidated mobile home with the walls on two sides broken out and sheds added on, was warm and humid, filled with the odors of hogs and wood shavings and animal waste. Beneath the intensity of these smells, Deuce had always imagined he could detect a tinge of milk, too. He walked from crate to crate, the piglets looking up at him, momentarily interested, the sows massive and self-absorbed, with an air that their lives could have been different. Unlike the abandoned bird feeder, here everything remained in order. The old man would never neglect the farm. Deuce held that against him, too.

As he watched the runt of a litter trying to wedge between its siblings and get hold of a teat, its little trotters slip-sliding on the floor of the crate, Deuce remembered a scene from two months earlier, after he'd run the upper fields on out and gone looking for his mother, finding her right there, almost exactly where he now stood. It was to be the next to last time he saw her alive.

He drifted deeper into the shed, leaned against a railing, and stared into an empty crate.

When he got back to the house, most of the people had left. His sister, as soon as she spotted him, came briskly across the room.

"I've been looking for you."

"I'm going."

"No, no, not yet. We've got something to discuss."

"What?"

"Not here."

She grabbed him by the sleeve and he let himself be conducted toward the dining room. If they'd been by themselves, she would have pushed him from behind like a bulky piece of furniture, just as she'd been doing since she was four and he six.

Their path brought them near their father and Elaine said to him, "You, too. We've got something to talk about."

Seeing that the old man was to be involved, Deuce pulled free.

Elaine spun on the two of them. She'd obviously been working herself up to this encounter. She moved very close so no one else would hear. "Look, this is something the three of us have to decide. If we don't do it now, it won't get done."

In the presence of his father, Deuce could feel the muscles of his back and jaw cinch up. But he thought, *What the hell.* Something else he'd do for his sister, one last thing. The old man made whatever accommodation he had to, as well, and the three of them went into the deserted dining room. Deuce and his father watched but made no offer to help as Elaine struggled to close the sliding door, which probably hadn't been shut in years. Frustrated, she abandoned her effort, half finished, and turned back to them, dusting off her hands.

"What are we going to do about Teddy?"

Deuce didn't know what she was talking about.

"Is he to stay here with Daddy?" She said this to Deuce, and then, turning to the old man, added, "Or should he come live with me and Bill?"

The answer to these questions seemed pretty damn obvious. Teddy loved the farm. He loved the old man, too, go figure. Deuce wondered why his sister even bothered to bring the thing up.

Still, their father remained mute, and so Deuce suggested, "Why doesn't he come live with me?"

For a moment, this comment annoyed Elaine, but then she saw the humor in it and half smiled. "I'm sure he could get quite an education." She moved over and took her father's arm, still speaking to Deuce. "You could teach him all the finer points of Texas Hold'em."

"What do you know about Texas Hold'em?" Deuce asked. So far as he was aware, she'd never played a hand of cards in her life.

"You'd be surprised," she said.

Before they could expand on this topic, their father spoke up. "What does the boy want?"

"I don't know," Elaine admitted, turning her attention to the old man and becoming serious. "I saw him playing with my kids—you know how much they adore him—and I just thought it was something we should talk about." Like a chameleon, his sister resembled her father when she was standing next to him just as she used to look like her mother in her presence, although Deuce didn't think his parents looked anything alike.

Elaine was now holding the old man's arm with both hands and looking intently into his face.

"Can you give him the attention he needs, Daddy?"

At that moment, Teddy himself appeared in the imperfectly-closed door.

"Speak of the devil," Deuce said. The boy had a look of single-minded concentration.

"The lady's come," he said to his father.

"Has she? Good."

"What lady?" Elaine asked, but without a word of explanation the old man extracted himself from her grasp and left the room, resting his hand briefly on the top of Teddy's head as he passed. The boy followed.

Suddenly by themselves, Elaine looked at Deuce. "What lady?"

"Got me."

She went to find out what lady. Deuce, not interested, stayed put.

He looked around. They almost never used the dining room, but it had been there where he'd seen his mother the final time. She had been clearing the Christmas dinner, dividing the food into human leftovers and slops for the hogs. She wasted nothing. Eight days later, she would be dead. The dinner hadn't gone well, and she wasn't happy, and she blamed Deuce. She blamed him because she believed him capable of change. Everybody else she accepted as they were.

"I'm going," he had told her.

"Go," she had said.

The last words spoken between them had been in anger.

He stood bleakly among the old-fashioned furniture, moving his eye from object to object. Only the chairs around the massive oak dining table meant anything to him. They were straight-backed and miserably uncomfortable, but when he'd been a little kid, he used to upend and throw sheets over them to make tunnels where he could get lost.

He walked back toward the kitchen through the pantry, trying to avoid the others. His father and Elaine and Teddy were nowhere to be seen. Someone was climbing the back stairs. He could see the priest in the sunroom, talking to a couple who were leaving. Beyond, the storm seemed to have intensified.

As Deuce grabbed his coat, the footsteps on the stairs hesitated, then suddenly reversed and came clattering back down, not one set now but several. Elaine appeared and then a woman and then his father. The woman, whom Deuce recognized as a reporter with the *Jackson Tribune*, looked uncomfortable.

"What is it?" his sister asked, hurrying along beside the other two. The reporter glanced in Elaine's direction but said nothing, instead turning, notebook in hand, to tell the old man thank you as she neared the door. Father Daugherty and the others parted to let her go by.

"What is it, Daddy?" Elaine asked. The old man had come to a halt several paces from the others, his back to Deuce so that it wasn't possible to read the expression on his face.

"Daddy?!"

Deuce's father said something inaudible. Whatever it was, it didn't satisfy his sister.

Thwarted, Elaine looked around and spotted Deuce and came hustling over.

"Don't look at me, Sis." He had no idea what was happening.

"Do you know her?" Elaine demanded.

"Met her a couple times."

"Who is she?"

"Name's Brandeis. Works for the paper. When the Pack was in trouble, she wrote most of the stories."

"Talk to her. Find out what's going on."

It might be nothing that was going on, of course, but Elaine had a sixth sense where trouble was concerned. All the Goetzinger kids did.

When Deuce didn't snap to, Elaine pressed him, "Hurry up, before she gets away." One more thing he could do for her on this day of last things.

By the time he got outside, Brandeis was already backing out, and he had to jog next to her car and rap on the passenger side window. She stopped and lowered the window.

"Hi," he said. He crouched down so he could look her in the eye. "How ya doin'?"

She nodded.

"The old man invited you up here, did he? You didn't just crash the party?"

"Of course not," she said.

"Is there something the family needs to know?" he asked. And then more directly, "What did he want?"

"Perhaps you should ask him."

"We're not on speaking terms."

She took in this comment with her reporter's interest. Although young—still in her twenties, Deuce judged—she possessed the settled expression of an older woman.

Deuce briefly considered a tit-for-tat, you show me yours and I'll show you mine, then discarded the idea. "The old man swear you to secrecy, did he?"

"No."

"What's the problem, then?"

She considered. Deuce crouched, holding on to the bottom of the window frame, feeling the line that the upper edge of the glass made across his palms.

"I suppose there's no reason not to tell you," she decided. She paused for a couple more beats, a moment to change her mind, and then said, "Your father is resigning as mayor."

Deuce stared at her. "Really?" He was shocked. The old man resign? Never. "You sure he wasn't pulling your leg?"

"A funny kind of a joke."

Damn strange. Amazing. "He tell you why?"

She shook her head. "Just that it was a decision he'd made. After all that's happened..." Deuce heard a crunching sound behind him and glanced back to see Elaine approaching, one step at a time, coatless, anxious, and hugging herself. Teddy trailed behind her and behind him, his two little cousins. Father Daugherty stood outside the back door with the couple leaving. Everyone looked toward Deuce and the car.

He turned back to the reporter. "That's about right, I suppose," he told her. "The old man doesn't need a reason." He might have left it at that, but the exchange had been frank enough for him to say something that he would not have said a minute earlier. "He does what he wants. The rest of the world be damned. Otherwise, my mother would be alive today."

Deuce gripped the window tighter and swung up to a standing position and backed away as the car started down the driveway, the window sliding shut.

Elaine was immediately at his side. "What is it?"

He told her what Brandeis had said.

"I don't believe it." She hugged herself and shivered violently. "What will he do, then?"

"Go inside, Sis. You're freezing."

"We've got to stop him."

Deuce was zipping up his jacket. "Let me know what you decide about Teddy."

"Junior!" Elaine implored, reverting to his old family nickname.

He flipped up the collar of his jacket.

"If you don't get me," he told her, "leave a message on my machine."

CHAPTER 13

～

Jerry Caan glanced up from the euchre game he was playing in the locker room at the city garage. "Barb Amos been looking for you."

J.J. Dusterhoft, who had come back to gas up and take a leak and stretch his legs—these twelve-hour shifts were beginning to get to him—continued his placid progress toward the john. He was not prepared to think about Barbara Amos on a full bladder.

At the urinal, he unzipped and tilted his chin up, eyes closed, and waited. Finally, the urine started to flow, in grudging little bursts. He could remember a time when taking a piss had been one of life's small pleasures.

As he returned to the locker room, Caan jerked his head in the general direction of J.J.'s locker, then went back to his game, gathering in a fresh hand and tapping the cards twice sharply on the table before fanning them out. "She was pissed. City's out to screw us again."

J.J. sighed. Barb's marching orders had been explicit enough: go to the meeting with Aggie, collect the city's counteroffer, nothing more. A get-together of the negotiating team had already been set up. Whatever had happened, it could wait.

"She say why?" J.J. asked as he memorized the telephone number penciled on his locker.

"Nope." Caan never pumped anyone for information. He was a transponder, not a recorder.

J.J. went up front where, the street commissioner having taken a personal day, he could use the phone in his office and have some privacy. He called the number and listened as Barb Amos told him she was pissed and the city was out to screw them again. She laid out her bills of particulars, the centerpiece a sudden demand for a huge pay cut.

Having delivered herself of the facts of the case, she ended with an editorial. "Aggie Klauer was smug as hell. Paul Cutler's little gopher. I don't know what you see in her, J.J." Barb spoke with pristine determination, as if she hadn't said the same thing numberless times before, the words always meant to censure him as much as Aggie. Since he couldn't say anything that might conceivably appease her, he probably should have kept his mouth shut, but hell, what fun was that?

"Of course, Barb, you're right about the city manager. He's a bounder and ought to be dealt with. But Aggie's a sweetheart, she really is. You've just got to get past what she does for a living."

This pronouncement gave birth to an ominous silence on the other end of the line.

J.J. and Aggie had had a good time negotiating contracts, and the union had always got pretty much what there was to get. Made no difference. Barb Amos never was satisfied. A fringe benefit that should have been demanded, a few extra pennies left on the table, a work rule they had failed to liberalize—these were her siren songs. She didn't bow to the realities or give style points. J.J. could only shake his head.

"This isn't funny, J.J.," Amos said at the end of the ominous silence, her voice rather calmer than he would have expected.

"Of course it isn't, my dear," he acceded, "of course, it isn't." He might have added that nothing was funny unless you made it so, but figured he better not.

After reaffirming the arrangement to meet with the negotiating team to strategize, he hung up and, musing, went back out to his truck.

The storm had tapered off again, uncovering the meager daylight, the snow coming now at a walking pace, just enough to keep him out on the road.

He drove down to AgriComp for another load of salt, pulling around the storage shed, which reminded him of the longhouse of some Indian tribe sunk into the ground up to its eaves. Behind the shed, he cozied up to the salt pile.

The truck settled more firmly over the drive wheels with each bucketful from the end loader. In the last few minutes, the storm had picked up again. It couldn't seem to make up its mind. He gauged the severity of a blow by whether he could see the other side of the Mississippi. At the moment, he wasn't quite sure. A low-lying mass seemed to be sweeping down the river at the far edge of his field of vision. It might have been the storm, or it might only have been the bluffs on the Wisconsin side.

He mentioned this to the clerk in the office after weighing the load. "Hear they're really getting pasted up north."

"Ah, yes, Minnesota. Wonderful place."

J.J. went fishing around the Lake of the Woods in the fall, between the black fly season and winter, the week or so during the year that the place was fit for human habitation. "Well," he observed, "the Scandahoovians are really proud of their bad weather, so I guess we should be glad for them."

He drove back uptown and worked the bluff streets for a time. The storm once more backed off a notch and then another and finally almost stopped entirely. When he judged the arteries could take care of themselves for a few minutes, he decided a little detour was in order.

It was nearly five and the last bit of daylight gone as he pulled into a conveniently vacant loading zone next to city hall and got out. Inside, he didn't walk down the corridor to billing, where he would have found Barb Amos, but turned instead into the small suite of personnel offices, nodded at Aggie Klauer's assistant, and stuck his head in the door to the inner sanctum.

For a few moments, Aggie wasn't aware of his presence, her head tilted to one side, the paradiddle of her pen on the desk pad the only sound. She was thinking.

"The woman contemplates the havoc she has wrought," he said.

Calmly, she turned. "Ah. You." She made a show of dropping the pen back on the desk, as if it had been released from the belly of a bomber. "We missed you this afternoon."

"Barb is not amused."

"So it appeared." Aggie gestured to the chair across from the desk and reached into a folder, extracting a thin document. "This will be no surprise, then."

As he paged through the city's counter to the union, he said distractedly, "No. But it's always nice to see the corpus delicti for myself. You never can tell…"

His perusal complete and the worst confirmed, he folded the offer and put it in his pocket. "Tell me, has the city ever asked for wage concessions before?"

"Not that I know of, not since the unions were formed, anyway."

He nodded. "Interesting. I suppose this is what they mean when they say government ought to be run more like a business."

"We don't have any stock we can offer in exchange, I'm afraid."

At this reference to the doomed attempt to sell the packing company to its employees, they fell silent.

Given the nature of city-union negotiations, the end was always implied in the beginning. Probably now, too, although this innovation on the city's part made the finish line a little fuzzy. J.J. tried without much luck to read the expression on his friend's face.

Aggie sat expectant, her hair short and curling like generous shavings of cherry wood, her skin a little too pale, perhaps, but vividly framing her keen blue eyes and waiting-to-smile lips. The pictures he had seen of her had all been terrible, like a wonderful product with bad advertising, for which he was almost grateful since it made her seem rather like his private discovery. He had always liked the fact that she wasn't married, the possibilities it suggested if only he could do something about his own marriage…and his age and his ugly puss.

The business of the moment had been transacted and he really did need to get back out on his snow route, but he couldn't let the occasion pass without a word or two of a nonessential nature.

"How's Lucille?" he asked.

"She's discovered chat rooms."

"Is that good?"

"Briefly."

And so they contemplated for five minutes the great burden of Aggie's life, her mother.

When he came out of the personnel offices, J.J. noticed three women coming down the corridor. Only after he had turned away, his mind for the moment split between the conversation just finished and the snow awaiting him, did he realize that one of them had been Barb Amos.

Oh, dear.

He considered continuing on his way, perhaps even speeding up to create the illusion of great haste. No, no, no, that would not do. To leave would be interpreted as flight, haste as guilt.

He stopped and turned back.

"Why, Barb!"

Amos and the other two women, a couple of her cronies from finance, had their coats on.

"Is it five o'clock already?" he wondered aloud and watched as Amos's surprise at seeing him quickly turned inward, settling into something like resignation. J.J. tapped the pocket of his jacket. "Got a copy of the city's counter."

"I could have given you one," she said, and as earlier, when he had heard a note of unaccustomed calmness in her voice during the phone call, now he heard something else un-Barb-like, a hint of sorrow.

"I was interested in what Aggie would have to say for herself."

"I'm sure you were. And what *did* she?"

"City's never asked for givebacks before."

"I told you that."

"Yes, you did." As always in her presence, J.J. felt the air beginning to congeal between them.

The other women looked on without expression, no doubt already briefed as to the situation. Without a doubt, as well, Amos would be on the phone that night, and not just to other members of the negotiating team. J.J. felt a faint stirring of irritation and considered how easy it would be to goad her.

The four of them stood awkwardly in the middle of the hallway, an island in the stream, as the building emptied out around them.

J.J. made a stab at mollifying his unhappy fellow unionist. "Probably the city's bluffing, Barb. Probably doesn't mean a thing."

"But 10 percent?!" The words were barely audible, but spoken intensely. "This was supposed to be a catch-up year."

Yes, it was, he thought, *but did we ever really believe it? And now the Pack has closed and two thousand people are out on the street...* To Amos, he said simply, "Yes, it was."

If he added up the union's proposal for a 6 percent raise and the city's counter and divided by two, he came up with a two percent giveback. That probably meant the city was determined to get some sort of concession, however modest. But a token decrease or a whopper, the membership could be counted on to get into a monumental snit.

They most assuredly would, and this was obviously the moment to mollify Barb, to close ranks, to utter a battle cry. If only she didn't take words...the way she took them.

"You girls might be heading on home," he told them, "but I've gotta saddle up again." He added, speaking only to Amos and in a tone meant to suggest the impropriety of carrying on in public like this, "We'll talk about it when the team gets together." Amos said nothing. She was eyeing him unhappily, her winter pallor so different from Aggie's paleness, so much part of Barb's burden in some way. J.J. was not unsympathetic. He *did* understand what drove her, that pervasive sense of injustice of hers. Of being in a world not really made for her and which she was powerless to change. No, no, he was not entirely unsympathetic. If only…

Outside, the storm had intensified once more. Glad of it, he hurried back to his truck.

CHAPTER 14

~

Three days later, as Deuce Goetzinger arrived back in the lab at the water plant with his six a.m. samples, who should be sitting there but Ned Pickett? Pickett, as usual, was stuffed into his uniform as tight as braunschweiger.

The cop nodded. "How you?"

Deuce put the samples down.

"Been a while."

"Saw you a couple of times during the search for your mother. Guess you didn't notice."

"You were out there?" Deuce remembered many faces from the search, but there had been hundreds more, spread in skirmish lines through the woods. "Appreciate it," he said.

Pickett nodded. "Glad to help. Wish it turned out different."

"Yeah."

"Nobody had anything but good to say about Edna."

Deuce didn't intend to talk about his mother. "You just comin' off, Ned, or going on?"

"Off. Still on the third shift. You can do real police work on the third." Deuce remembered that about Pickett, a man who had found his niche. "What about you," the cop asked, "still rotating?"

"Yeah."

Pickett snorted and shook his head. "All right for a single man, I guess."

"I don't mind." Deuce made it a point of not minding. "Day shift's the worst."

"After another hard night at the gaming table? Still cleaning everybody out, are you?" There was a tone to these questions that seemed to suggest some sort of extra meaning.

In a counterfeit of ease, Pickett had tilted back precariously in the ancient office chair, his head so far forward that his jowls bulged out. Deuce turned away, toward the lab table, and set about testing his samples.

"You here just to pass the time of day?" he asked over his shoulder.

"On a mission."

"Oh, yeah?" Something to do with him? Deuce couldn't imagine what.

He poured part of the first sample into a graduated cylinder and got rid of the excess with practiced little flicks of the wrist.

He and Pickett were not quite friends, not quite anything at all. It might be said they hardly knew each other. Pickett was, by all accounts, a good cop. Deuce knew his job, too, so they had that in common, the brotherhood of the competent, although operators at the water plant didn't get to strut their stuff like cops.

Pickett said, "It's a shitty time, I know, after what happened."

"You're right, Ned, it's a shitty time." Deuce squinted at the markings on the cylinder.

"Yeah, right, well…" The cop hesitated, and Deuce thought, *Here it comes.* "You've heard about the city's latest offer to the unions?"

Everybody had, so an answer was unnecessary.

"Cutler reckons to balance his budget on our backs."

Again Deuce didn't react. What did this have to do with him? A few bucks taken out of his pay every couple of weeks? So what? One night at the poker table and he'd more than cover it.

"You still the head of the police association?" he asked the cop.

"Yup."

"Lifetime job, is it?" Pickett had been head of the police union since Neanderthal times, so far as Deuce could tell. Pickett was a true believer.

"Whatever's done," the other said, ignoring the gibe, "got to be a concerted effort. I've been talking to fire, I've been talking to transit, I've been talking to everybody."

"If you're talking to me, you're damn well talking to everybody. I'm not even in the friggin' union."

"That's easily remedied."

"You came all the way up here to tell me to join the union?"

"That's part of it."

"What's the rest?"

"J.J. Dusterhoft, you know him?"

At the mention of Dusterhoft, Deuce's mind immediately went back to the night of the storm, when J.J. had come along in his salt truck and helped Deuce free his car, and even as they were doing it, already too late, his mother already gone off the road and begun wandering in the woods. He should've gone straight up Brick Kiln Road, instead of wasting all that time creeping around the city. Violently, he flung the excess water from the graduated cylinder.

"What was that, Ned? What'd you say?"

"You know Dusterhoft?" the cop asked again. "Negotiator for the big union."

"Yeah, sure. Why?"

"Barb Amos caught him the other day coming out of Aggie Klauer's office. First thing, he finds out about the city's offer, he runs to Klauer."

"So?"

"Barb figures he and Aggie decide things between themselves. The negotiations are nothing but playacting, the fix already in. That's what she thinks."

"What do you think?"

"Probably she's right. Dusterhoft and Klauer are big buddies."

Would J.J. do that? Deuce didn't know. Probably didn't make much difference one way or the other.

"We figure it's time for new leadership in the big union," Pickett said.

"You want my recommendations?" Deuce asked incredulously.

"No, but your name did come up."

They didn't want his recommendations, but his name had come up? What did that mean? The only other possibility made no sense at all.

"You can't be serious."

"I'm dead serious."

"Me? You want me to negotiate with the city?"

"Maybe." The cop paused. Deuce negotiate? How fucking demented was that? When Pickett continued, he acknowledged that Deuce's name had hardly been at the top of the list of candidates. "Problem is, you look at the other people who might take over the job and what you got is a pretty damn sorry lot." He ticked off names and deficiencies. "As for you, well, who knows? We figure you're your old man's kid, that much at least."

"You figure wrong."

"Anyway, true or not, that's what interests the others. That's why they'd give you a tumble. Is it true, by the way? Is Fritz really gonna resign?"

Anyone who knew his father at all knew the answer to that one. "The old man's never run a bluff in his life."

"Yeah, I guess that's right," the cop agreed and then fell silent for a time before going back to the original subject. "The way I see it, the question facing the union is—do they want some mediocrity who knows the ropes or somebody with a little native wit who's gotta do some catching up?"

"There has to be somebody else, Ned. Not everybody in the union's a dimwit."

"True. Might be there's somebody else. But negotiating takes a particular set of skills."

This was all bullshit, Deuce told himself, but his curiosity aroused, he said, "And you think I've got 'em?"

"You seem to forget that I've seen you at the poker table."

"So what?"

"The union doesn't need a screamer now. They've got screamers. They've got people who could just go in there and stonewall, too, tell the city to go fuck itself and force the thing to arbitration and then hope the hell the arbitrator sees it our way. Any moron could do that. No, what we need is somebody with the smarts to really take Cutler on. Somebody who can bring something new to the table."

"But I don't give a shit, Ned. What about that?" Deuce watched the pill of the magnetic stirrer whirring madly in the bottom of his beaker of raw water. The whole scheme was just too goddamn bizarre. Pickett couldn't believe what he was saying.

But he apparently he did. "You got tons of unused ability, my friend. It's time to stop dicking around with the cards and get serious."

Clean up his language and the son-of-a-bitch sounded just like Deuce's mother. As if he needed somebody else complaining because he was a world-class underachiever.

"I do my job, Ned. But that's it. I don't own a white horse."

"This isn't a job for a guy on a white horse," the cop countered. "What the big union needs is a coldhearted bastard who's got some imagination and knows how to play head games."

"Since you put it that way...Tell me, Ned, you're a great union man—why don't you get the cops to lead your crusade? Forget about the big union."

Pickett snorted. "If we can get something done here, it'll be all I can do to keep my people from breaking ranks."

That was right. The police association had its own agenda, which was to get one buck more than the firefighters got. That done, nothing on heaven or earth could move them a single step farther.

"So you want me to do the dirty work?"

"The big union represents employees from a whole bunch of different departments. It's the natural group to spearhead the thing. And you're the man to make it happen, or at least, you could be if you'd get off your ass."

Ned's logic might be gonzo, but the way he was talking it seemed almost as if logic was beside the point, as if he'd taken this idea into his head and in his persistent cop's way was determined to make it happen.

Deuce stopped what he was doing and looked back at him. "How come you're the one came up here? It isn't your fucking union. If these other guys are so hot that I should represent them, why aren't they here on bended knee?"

"Nobody likes to get sneered at."

Deuce smiled. "You don't seem to mind." He turned back to his work, sticking the probe of his pH meter into the beaker and waiting for the digital readout to stabilize. "I still say, why me? I ain't that smart."

"I disagree. Negotiating ought to be right down your alley."

Deuce wondered why the idea held so little appeal. But then again, reasons were not hard to come by. He preferred poker. Poker had at least a certain precision, a certain...clarity. It wasn't like life. But Pickett would never buy the distinction, so to him Deuce said something else, also true.

"I'll tell you what, Ned, you people believe, in your heart of hearts, that the city holds all the cards. Basically, for me, the union's chickenshit. Maybe not you, I'll grant you that. But you don't speak for the rank and file...And, frankly, I just don't like penny-ante games."

"We're looking to play hardball with Cutler this time."

The readout finally stabilized and Deuce took his measurement, then tossed the first sample into the sink. "I been telling them they need a new probe, but nobody listens. These things are only made to last a year. What was that you said?"

"I said, this year's different."

"Sure it is. Every year's different." Deuce continued to talk with his back to the cop. "But then, after you've settled or taken some piddly-assed little issue to arbitration, somehow it all ends up the same."

This shut Pickett up for a few moments.

"I must say, Deuce, you really are one helluva cynical fucker."

From the cylinder with the second sample, Deuce flipped the excess water with the same expert little flicks of the wrist as the first time. "No, Ned," he said, "not any more than you are." As he had continued to fence with the cop, Deuce's anger had grown, which surprised him, because this wasn't worth being mad over. "And I ain't such a great poker player, neither. But if there's nothing at stake, I'm not going to sit down at the table. That's just the way it is. And being as how your union friends are too gutless even to talk to me, where are they going to find the courage to ante up something has real value when they start trying to play tough with the city? I'll tell you. Nowhere. And that's a fact. And nothin' you can say is going to change it one friggin' iota. You're just tilting at windmills, Ned. There's nothin' for you here."

Deuce made a point of not looking at the cop as Pickett left.

But that didn't end it. He finished taking his readings and doing his calculations, then spent the rest of the shift in the base-ment of the plant, following the runs of pipe, the rows of tanks and controllers, the outmoded water treatment equipment that had never been hauled away and always reminded him of old aban-doned farm machinery, although, in fact, the resemblance was slight. Among these he wandered, furious and desolate.

～

At nine o'clock the next night, Barbara Amos arrived at the water plant, an L-shaped building next to a broad, low, capped structure she took to be a reservoir. She'd worked for the city for nearly twenty years, but never been inside the building. Light shone dimly through the tiers of glass bricks on one wing. Along the other, most of the windows remained black, except for a couple on the second story.

Filled with misgivings, she parked and got out into the cold. The weather had cleared, the temperature dropping well below zero, and the frigid air had something inhuman about it. She clutched her coat about her and hurried to the dark door, where despite the cold, she hesitated, wondering if she should knock. She craned her neck, looking up at the lighted windows, halfway down the building. At that extreme angle, she couldn't see the windows themselves, only their auras in the darkness.

She tried the door. Unlocked.

Inside she found a stairwell, silent and dim, just enough light spilling down to show her the stairs, which she mounted in hesitant little dashes, stopping to glance this way and that, as if she expected something to come crashing down upon her. All remained silent, the silence even deeper on the second floor, where she came out into a long hallway. Deuce Goetzinger hadn't told her where to find him. On the phone, his tone didn't give her much hope. If she hadn't been so crazy to get somebody to replace J.J., she wouldn't have come at all.

Near the head of the stairs, she found a large split-level room, the lower area with a fridge and coffee maker and refectory table, the upper filled with computer consoles and tall cabinets with gauges. No one there.

She went back into the hallway and toward the two rooms she had seen from below. Light spilled from their doorways across the spotless tiles. In the second, a laboratory, a man sat reading a newspaper.

"Goetzinger?" he said. "Around somewheres. If he ain't in the control room, he's out in the plant." She watched as he gave her the once over and then lost interest, going back to his paper.

She returned to the control room, but soon became restless and, feeling a little more relaxed and bolder, walked back along the hall, peering in at doorways. The corridor eventually turned right and left, and the light being better to the left, she went that way, into a room with a row of low, open tanks on either side. Some of the tanks had water in them and gave off a muted, shimmering light.

She paused in the cool air, tinged with a chlorine odor, the murmuring disturbed only by a machine noise in the distance, the noise muted but rising slowly as she went on, approaching the end of the room, where a door opened onto a platform and she found herself standing on a small balcony and staring down at an array of industrial-gray machines. The noise now battered against her, the coolness and chlorine odor gone, replaced by warmth and the scent of lubricating oils. She recognized the machines as pumps and generators. Her father had worked in the shops of the Milwaukee Railroad, and she was comfortable around large equipment.

"Yes?" a voice said at her elbow.

She flinched. Her hand flew up to her chest, and she turned as sharply as if hit.

He stood only a couple of paces away.

"You scared me."

"Sorry," he said, his tone unapologetic.

"Deuce?" He nodded slowly. A good-looking fellow. "Hi, I'm Barb."

His hand was soft in hers.

"You came," he said, as if surprised but not necessarily pleased.

Barb took a deep breath. "Yes." Since the reference was obvious, she added, "So, you can see I'm not a coward."

He half smiled at this but didn't appear to be much impressed. Listening to herself, Barb wasn't impressed either, her voice wavering in a higher register than normal. She felt skittish, pushed off center by the suddenness of the encounter. But still, determined to do what she'd come to do, she set about pulling herself together. She'd prepared a little speech.

"I'm sorry about what happened to your mom." He acknowledged this with a single blink of the eyes and imperceptible nod of the head. "I lost my dad last year. He was just sixty-three, still pretty young, you know, like your mom was." She felt at once the hastiness of her words, the rushing ahead before she was quite settled. She didn't know what else she could do, now that she'd started, but she listened to herself with a kind of foreboding. She paused briefly, to let him say something, but was too nervous not to continue when he didn't respond at once.

She had tried to figure how she might get through to Goetzinger, him so famous for being difficult. Finally she'd hit upon the idea of talking about when her father had been dying of cancer, which was different, she understood, from "losing your mom like you did, so sudden. But all the same..." She had to speak up to be heard above the machine noise. Goetzinger looked at her expressionlessly. He *was* good-looking; she could understand why girls would fall for him. He had that kind of sullen handsomeness that some go for. But not Barb. She found him a little scary.

She went on doggedly with what she'd prepared, talking about the emotions she felt when her father was dying and afterward. "You try to imagine what it'll be like, but you can't. Then my dad died. It was awful. It was, like…I don't know, words can't describe it. I'd see all the people around me going about their lives, you know, as if nothing had happened, and I could sorta remember what it was like to feel okay, but it was strange, too. It was like before he died I couldn't image what the pain would be like, and then afterwards I couldn't imagine anything else. Don't you think?"

Goetzinger seemed uninterested, a man who suffered in private. He threw a switch on the wall, and the room below them, filled with its machines, went black.

Barb followed him into the silence of the room with the tanks, saying, because being still nervous she couldn't seem to keep herself from talking, "Anyway, my dad was a union man. All his life. A good union man. I was born and raised union. Like some of the others work for the city, too. A few of us get together sometimes…at Labor Day picnics and such…so we know each other." Goetzinger stopped at one of the tanks and looked at the lectern-sized console with readouts and controls, and then down at the water. He gave no indication that he was listening to her, but Barb plunged on. "And something comes up, you know, like this giveback deal, we talk about it. We've been trying to figure out who we can get to negotiate for the big union. We need somebody new, that's for sure, and Ned Pickett seems to think you'd do a good job."

Goetzinger perked up a little, cocking his head toward her. "So this is all Ned's idea?"

"He suggested it."

This satisfied him for some reason.

"A couple of the others also thought it might be a good idea, given your reputation and all."

"But not you."

"I don't know you."

"No," he agreed, "you don't know me."

He continued on, moving at a thoughtful pace, and stopped at the next console.

"What are all these tanks?" she asked.

"Sand filters."

He checked the readings, as he had before, then leaned up against the railing and stared down at the water. Barb did, too, glad for the moment to be talking about something other than the reason for her visit.

"What's being filtered?"

"Water."

"I mean, out of the water."

"Suspended matter, before we put the finished water out in the system. Chemical precipitates, oxidized metals, microorganisms."

"So this is near the end of the process?"

"Pretty near. Still got a few things to do." Rather than clamming up, as she half expected him to do, since he wasn't a very forthcoming sort of person, he continued explaining, telling her in a very matter-of-fact way about the steps necessary to complete treatment. He still wasn't what she would have exactly called friendly, but at least he was talking a little. He wore a blue work shirt with a water symbol on the breast pocket, the shirt fitting him so trimly that it could have been custom-made. When he had finished his explanation, he fell silent again. She turned and leaned against the railing, and they both looked down into the tank, like a couple of buddies fishing off a bridge.

The surface of the water, filled with movement like stitches, made a gentle rustling sound. Barb could feel the cool air welling up from it.

She could now feel something else, as well, the substance of the man next to her. He didn't match her expectations—someone fiery and antagonistic—but instead had turned out to be gloomy and introspective. She had no clear vision of how the union negotiations might unfold in his hands, but something in his manner suggested that perhaps Ned Pickett had been right about him.

"Ned said you told him what we were doing wasn't important. I don't know how you can say that."

Goetzinger didn't respond, just stared down at the water in the brooding way he had.

Barb went on hesitantly, talking about the union, leaving spaces between her sentences for Goetzinger to interject whatever he had a mind to. He left the spaces unfilled. She repeated herself, struggling to say the same things in different words, as if that might make a difference. Finally, she stopped. Goetzinger remained silent. She watched him watching the reflections of light thrown off the water and washing across the brick walls and steel beams. She found his ability to remain silent unnerving.

"Your dad has always been a good union man."

"Best not bring my father into the conversation."

"I just meant—"

He turned toward her. "Tell me—Barbara, is it?—if you feel so strongly about the thing, why don't *you* negotiate?"

"Me?"

"Yeah. You're so damn mad, do it yourself."

She considered the possibility. "I think that's pretty much the problem. I mean, even if the fellows would let me do it, I just get so angry. The city never wants to give us anything. The idea that they negotiate in good faith is a joke. I just get…"—she leaned closer as if out of fear that somebody else might overhear—"so fucking mad!" She stopped and smiled a little sheepishly. "You see, I take everything too personal. If I was negotiating, it'd just be fighting, fighting, all the time. We'd never accomplish anything. I care too much."

"And I don't care at all."

"Perhaps you would."

He studied her carefully, but his gaze seemed to increase the distance between them. "I wouldn't count on it."

"If that's the way you feel, then I guess we can just forget about it." Yet something in the way he spoke encouraged her. "People say you're a playboy and cardsharp and all that. I don't know how the girls will feel." She meant the girls in finance and billing. "They'd be interested in hearing you out, though. I could set up a meeting…" Since he seemed barely willing to talk to her, she couldn't imagine what he'd have to say to the others. "There's lots of male insensitivity in the union hall. Sometimes the girls feel intimidated. They won't even come to meetings. Some of them have even quit paying dues. So, you know, you'll have to prove your position, not just words."

Why was she talking to him about the women in the union? Probably because of his reputation. Probably he'd be worse than the guys they were already having trouble with.

He stood next to the tank, still leaning on the railing, passive but alert. She could imagine him holding whatever position he was in for long periods, like maybe…she didn't know, maybe some animal of prey.

And maybe he was the right guy. But if he didn't care—if nothing she could say made any difference…

"I should think you'd like to do this. I mean, there's a lot more at stake here than in any ol' game of cards. This is about people's lives, their self-respect."

He smiled at this and shook his head slightly. Her words just bounced off him.

"And so you won't consider doing it?"

"Like I told Ned, it's strictly penny-ante."

"No, it's not."

He shrugged.

Well, Barb thought, okay, that was it, she'd tried.

"Anyway," she said, "thank you for your time. And…and I'm sorry about your mom, I really am. And I won't bother you anymore, okay?"

She began to leave. This exertion, feeling her body moving under her, brought her back to herself, almost like waking up. She increased her pace. She'd tried, what more could she do? This fellow might be smart and all that, but what did it matter?

All at once, however, as she neared the point where she would have turned right and disappeared down the corridor, a cry arose behind her.

"What's the matter?!" She turned quickly back around. "Are you all right?"

Goetzinger stood where she had left him. His arms hung limply at his sides. He stared at her, and his face was for a few moments so changed that she could not recognize it.

They stood mutely, staring at each other across the space separating them. Barb took a step back toward him. And then another.

PART II

CHAPTER 15

～

Aggie Klauer routed El Plowman out for their six a.m. walk. When El got into one of her depressions, she looked on exercise morosely but allowed Aggie to bully her. In the morning darkness, they mounted the bluffs toward Grandview Boulevard, Aggie's consciousness split between her own rather avian-like exertions and the more earthbound ones of her friend.

At Grandview, Aggie turned and, doing a jogging shuffle, waited for the dark figure to struggle the last few steps up to her, after which they set off, now on the flat, dodging around snowbanks.

Aggie had a question she was anxious to ask, but the moment didn't seem quite right. Night hadn't begun to lift yet. Tendrils of cold crept through the pores of her gloves, and the sharp predawn air seemed to remove layers of skin from her cheeks. She walked briskly, knees and arms pumping, exulting in the cold and her exertion. The headlights of passing vehicles slid along the embankment, which was topped by a veneer of new snowfall, like a bad wig barely covering the old discolored and dull snow beneath.

Some houses remained dark. Others showed lights in their upper stories, and Aggie glanced up at the bright but empty windows, which revealed perhaps a scrap of decoration or the bare angle between wall and ceiling. At these glimpses into the spaces where other lives were lived, she felt a pang of sadness.

El kept on falling behind, and Aggie would halt and do her soft-shoe routine until El caught up. Then on they'd go.

At a street corner, as they waited for an early-morning bus to pass, Aggie asked her question.

"Is it true, El? Are you to finish out Fritz's term as mayor?"

El stood with her hands on her hips, slightly hunched over. Aggie jogged in place, exhaling cold puffs of air and jiggling her hands.

The bus had passed and they had resumed their forced march when El said, "Some of the council members have been talking about it."

"That's wonderful!"

"The feeling is that somebody has to do it."

Aggie turned around and walked backwards. "You'll make a super mayor."

"There's just ten months left until the next election. And given the way things are going…" El words were as dogged as her steps.

Seeing this downward current in her friend's thinking, Aggie countered, "I think you're the perfect person for the job."

"You do, huh?"

"Of course."

Aggie turned back around and they continued; after a short distance, El said, "I'll tell you what I think. I think I'm just a convenient scapegoat, someone to load all the city's troubles onto and drive into the wilderness next November."

"Baloney. You're exactly what the city needs." Aggie said this, but she wondered if El might not be a little bit right about the intention of the others.

She set about convincing the two of them otherwise, talking about the myriad of local organizations El belonged to, her years of public service, throwing all this information back over her shoulder. "You've done more than anybody for Jackson."

Behind her, El grumbled, and at the next corner suddenly changed the subject.

"Edie's trying to talk her husband into moving back here."

"Edie? Really? I thought she swore she'd never come back. Didn't you tell me that?"

"That was before day care centers. She's gone through three of them. They're all staffed by child molesters. At least, so she says. You know Edie." Aggie did know Edie. She was rather like her mother, although, of course, El would never accuse anyone of child molesting, not without a good deal of evidence.

They crossed the street, El huffing along at Aggie's heels and speaking in spurt-like sentences, more interested in this subject for some reason than the prospect of becoming mayor. "Claims she can't find a reliable babysitter, either. And that the local Montessori schools are run by Mormons." The piling on of arguments, that was how daughter resembled mother.

Aggie asked over her shoulder, "Surely she doesn't think you're good babysitting material?" Such an idea was preposterous.

"Edie's cagey. Who knows what she's got up her sleeve?"

"What about her husband?" Aggie moderated her pace again and they continued this line of speculation with regard to El's youngest. El might be a grandmother, but for all her virtues, she was hardly grandmotherly. Aggie remembered with what relief El had nudged her daughters out the door and onto their own, being a woman with little patience for the niggling self-absorptions of normal lives, her kids' or anybody else's.

Finally she told Aggie, "I think the whole problem is that Phoenix, Arizona, isn't Jackson, Iowa. You know what she said? She said it over and over. 'Jackson's a good place to raise a family, Mom. It's safe. It's away from all the stuff that goes on everywhere else.'"

This platitude about the virtues of Jackson as a nursery might have been the motto on the city seal, it was repeated so often.

Aggie understood all at once exactly why El had brought the matter up in the first place. She stopped dead in her tracks. "Oh, dear!"

El brushed by her, saying, "Yes, right. Oh, dear," and Aggie had to start walking again to avoid getting left behind.

"The article," she said to El's back.

"That's right, the article. And now they want me to be mayor."

The conversation they had been having had nothing to do with amusing family anecdotes and daughters who change their minds. Aggie should have guessed that one way or another, they'd end up discussing the perfectly dreadful *New York Times* story—the *New York Times*, of all places, the front page!

In her agitation, El had accelerated, and Aggie had to pick up the pace to stay abreast of her friend.

"I didn't tell you something else that Edie said," El had gone on. "She said, 'It's creepy, Mom, being around all these blacks and Mexicans. I know I shouldn't feel that way, but I do.' My own daughter said that."

"Edie grew up here. She's uncomfortable around other races." Aggie was, too. And most of the people she knew. "That doesn't mean she's a racist."

"Doesn't it?"

"No, of course it doesn't," Aggie said, perhaps rather too quickly. She had read too much about racial matters not to understand the complexities. But, she admonished herself, this was no time for hair splitting. "Maybe people here aren't the most enlightened in the world, El, but most of them are decent. Hardly anybody would have done what happened at the museum."

"That's obviously not what Mr. Miller St. John thinks. And now, thanks to him, the rest of the country, too."

At this bleak assertion, Aggie fell silent.

They'd all been forewarned, known the story was coming. It had been a nasty shock, all the same, with its poisonous slant and smug tone. And the quotes from local whites! All of them of the Jackson-was-a-good-place-to-raise-children sort, all implying they wanted to keep it that way.

By the time the reporter had finished, the photos of the vandalized museum accompanying the story had mutated into portraits not of the haphazard acts of a few no-goodniks but the condemnation of an entire city.

"The story was ugly and untrue, El."

"Ugly, certainly. And certainly requiring a response."

Aggie reminded herself that she hadn't written her protest letter to the *Times* yet. "Most Jacksonians are decent people," she insisted.

"Yes," El agreed, "and you're right, they would never have vandalized the exhibit. But these decent people don't want blacks here, either, Aggie."

"Some do."

"A few."

They rounded a bend on Grandview and briefly were reflected in the plate glass window of Keefer's neighborhood market, El in her solid colors—suggesting to Aggie winter vegetables—and Aggie in her usual motley. El, much the larger, bent forward at the waist and moved with a heavy, slightly awkward determination, which Aggie found admirable. Aggie, on the other hand, her elbows and hat aflap—whatever she wore on her head flapped—reminded herself of some flightless bird that hadn't given up trying, and she had to resist the urge to slow down and walk like a normal human being.

"They will make me mayor, Aggie, so that I'm the one standing in front of the camera and trying to justify us to the world."

"You could refuse. Nobody can make you do it."

"No. I won't refuse."

They veered to the left and passed out of the range of the window, but the afterimage and the conversation and a sense of evils which she felt helpless to do anything about left their marks on Aggie. To establish some positive bedrock for whatever might come next, she said, "Okay, then, but the *New York Times* guy was still wrong."

"Makes no difference. The damage is done. The question is, what are we going to do about it? The letter writing campaign is not enough."

What *could* they do? In the four years Aggie had been head of personnel for the city, she had certainly learned, if she didn't know it already, that human beings weren't made out of clay but some less malleable stuff.

"Perhaps it would be better to sit tight," she suggested.

"And let Miller St. John make us the symbol of racism in America? Not if I have anything to say about it!" El was moving along with a will now, and didn't wait for an approaching car but forced it to slow down as she stormed across an intersection.

Scampering after her friend, Aggie asked, "What then?"

"I don't know. Something."

They were heading back down Grandview toward their starting point. Daylight struggled in beneath the solid cloud cover, the tail end of yet another storm.

"Something!" El repeated, and on they charged.

CHAPTER 16

~

Chuck Fellows liked his wife Diane most in the morning, during the breakfast rush, which she organized as if they were all on military maneuvers. Chuck was detailed to take care of himself, make sure the kids were dressed, feed and kennel the dogs. Diane, besides the elaborate ritual of getting herself ready to go to work, made sure Chuck had made sure the kids were dressed. She also fixed their breakfasts and packed their lunches, made necessary telephone calls and handled incoming, did the breakfast dishes, determined and announced the schedules for the day, and dealt with emergencies, of which there were many. As strack as any old-time drill sergeant, she operated on the edge of anger, except of course when dealing with three-year-old Grace. With Grace, she was never military. As for Chuck, well, at these moments, he imagined he might one day love his wife almost as much as he loved some of his old buddies from 'Nam.

"There's a winter rendezvous out at Mines of Spain," she announced this morning. "The kids and I are going. Will you have time, dear?" Her words were slightly rushed, timed to the haste with which she was making sandwiches, but beyond that betraying no hint of the answer she expected.

Chuck said nothing. Instead he thought about how much Diane had, despite the constancy of these early morning maneuvers, changed since he'd become acting public works director. She wasn't more attentive to his needs, as he supposed he had expected. She hadn't taken a contrary tack, either, and set about consolidating her victory. Instead, she had reached some private accommodation, not shared with him but suggested at moments like this, when her tone of voice lacked the hopefulness it would have had in the old days. Since she had hounded him into taking the job, the tone said, she would not turn around and start complaining because he no longer had any time to spend with his family.

"Would you check on the kids, please?" she asked. "I don't hear anything from upstairs."

The dogs followed him around as he performed this chore. Todd, just turned eight, had put on his buckskins and was monkeying with his new computer. Chuck turned the machine off and told him to change his clothes. Grace, half dressed, asked where Mommy was. He helped her finish and told her that Mommy had been kidnapped by the Balloon People, but she didn't believe him because he'd told her this before and it had turned out not to be true.

Back downstairs, the kitchen now filled with hyperactive kids and dogs, he shifted his chair and sat on the edge, downing the rest of his coffee before herding the dogs into the backyard.

Diane glanced up at him as she arranged Todd and Grace's bowls and poured out the cereals they were willing to eat. "It'll be rugged, you might like it."

"What about the kids? You think they're up to it?"

"Up to what?" Todd wanted to know.

"If it gets too bad, we'll come back in," Diane said.

This was not an exchange Chuck could win, but he said, "If it gets too bad, I actually *might* start to like it."

"Like what?" Todd asked.

Diane smiled to herself as she was turning away. "You could stay." She knew, of course, that he wouldn't, no matter how miserable it got, not given his contempt for the buckskinners and their half-assed version of frontier life.

He asked which weekend and told her he'd try to make it.

"I'm sewing capotes for me and the kids. Should I do one for you, too?"

"A what?"

"Capote. It's a blanket coat, very popular among buckskinners for winter wear."

"Yeah, Dad, get one, it'll be neat," enthused Todd, who had by now gotten with the program.

Chuck stared sourly at Diane as she took off the apron she put on to protect the outfit she wore to work, careful as she lifted the straps over her head so as not to muss her hair. Day after day, like clockwork, she led her blameless life. She never criticized him, or almost never, and did exactly what she had decided ought to be done. Chuck could have played rugby, if he wanted, or taken his long solo motorcycle rides or gone off in the woods by himself, and Diane wouldn't have said a word. Trouble was, he never had any time to play rugby or do any of those other things, so his willfulness didn't get him very far, just more unredeemed promises to himself.

"I'll wear my mackinaw."

"Aw," Todd said.

"Suit yourself," Diane said.

Outside, Chuck brooded as he stood next to his 4x4 and stared up at the thin layer of clouds. Light snow still fell, but directly overhead a perfect circle of pale sky had been cut out of the blue-gray overcast. He would have found Diane's attitude quite admirable if only she had happened to be married to somebody else. In her own way, she had become as uncompromising and one-way as Chuck himself. She'd learned to play him like a drum, too, and there wasn't a damn thing he could do about it. Nothing but say to hell with her and the kids, his job, everything, fuck it all, and get on his bike and just go. He slammed the door of the 4x4 shut. That was the thing of it. He *could* get his life back from Diane. But he'd have to steal it back; he could never get it back honestly.

He drove down the bluffs toward city hall, then at the bottom changed his mind and altered course.

In a couple of minutes, he'd parked on the street outside the Jackson Building. He would pay a visit to Walter Plowman. Walt would cheer him up.

He took the elevator up to the KJTV floor where Plowman worked as the lead weatherman. Since he gave the weathercasts later in the day, it occurred to Chuck that he might not be there. Then again, he might. After all, unlike Chuck, Walt was a man who had found his life's work.

The receptionist went to look for him.

As Chuck waited, he inspected the news photos covering the walls, and when Walt finally came out, was standing in front of a famous one taken in Vietnam, the young girl fleeing naked from a napalm attack, a picture he had seem many, many times but which never failed to stir a deep uneasiness in him.

Plowman didn't seem particularly pleased to see him. Anyway, he said, "Come on back," and led the way to his little cubicle, located at the geographical heart of the station and jammed with weather forecasting gear. The place looked about the same as the last time Chuck had seen it. Paper had scrolled out of the machines linked to weather services and curled down to the floor, the overnight accumulation.

"Sit down if you want." Walt gestured toward the single office chair on which, during Chuck's previous visits, the weatherman had scooted from one machine to another as he prepared his forecasts.

Chuck remained standing and asked what the problem was. This brought on a spontaneous tirade against TV station managers in general and the KJTV manager in particular. Chuck, who previously had only witnessed Plowman's friendliness and intense curiosity and desire to be helpful, stood rather amazed at this bitter outburst. Walt ticked off his grievances, then turned away as if done only to swing back and take another shot. Finally, he simply collapsed into the unoccupied chair, the fighter slumping in his corner at the end of a round in which he had gotten the worst of it.

And then, as quickly as it had come on, the squall had passed and Walt was his old self. With a little don't-mind-me wave of his hand, he said, "Long time, no see. I've been wondering how you were doing."

"Up to my eyeballs."

Plowman nodded several times in sympathy. Then he started. "Coffee! You want a cup?"

Chuck checked his watch. "No time." He had an 8:30. Stuff to do before that. "Just stopped to say hello. I've been thinking about you, too, and about you-know-what."

"Ah!" Plowman leaped up and started tearing the sheets off his machines. In a flurry, he sorted through them, pulling off perforated edges, discarding most with hardly a glance. "It's absolutely uncanny, isn't it?" He found what he wanted, a large sheet, curled nearly into a cylinder. He took a plastic squeeze bottle down from an overhead shelf and spritzed the brittle-looking grayish paper. Using the palms of hands, he smoothed it out and then impaled it on top of similar sheets hung on a cork bulletin board. A weather map of the U.S.

"Okay," he said, "here's where we're at…"

Watching and listening, Chuck felt a tension, which he had not actually been conscious off until that very moment, begin to uncoil inside him.

Walt talked, one of his hands gripping the top of his head while the other traced the weather patterns he described, his gestures swinging beyond the edges of the map, to the west where lay the spawning ground of storms in the Gulf of Alaska, to the south where moisture, drawn from the Caribbean, fed the storms as they reorganized on the plains east of the Rockies.

"The polar front's very well defined in this vicinity." His hand moved back and forth across northern Idaho and Montana. "A strong temperature gradient, perfect for storm development." He took the hand down from the top of his head. His white hair stood straight up in places, as if he'd had a terrific fright. "We're sitting ducks for a series of major storms, my friend."

"I see," Chuck said. He ticked off the precursors of a massive spring flood, a list which he'd learned from Walt hardly more than two months earlier and which had become a litany crouching in the back precincts of his consciousness. "We've had the fall rains, Walt, we've had the cold, now we're getting the snow."

Plowman nodded. "It's worse up north. Have you noticed?" That would be where the floodwater came from, of course. The snow that fell on Jackson might be a bitch to get rid of, might wreak havoc with Chuck's snow removal budget, but when spring arrived, it would be the responsibility of the people downstream. The snow Chuck would have to worry about come April lay at the moment on the plains of northern Wisconsin and Minnesota and the eastern Dakotas.

Chuck looked at Walt, and Walt looked back. "I remember how long you told me the odds were the first time we talked about this, Walt. What about now?"

The weatherman had turned on his computer, combing his hair with his fingers as he waited for the machine to run through its start-up routines. When he answered, he answered with care. "Still longer than you might think. Back in '73, it looked like we were in for a humdinger. It was even later in the winter than we are now. All the conditions were right. Deep frost, deeper snowpack. The Corps of Engineers geared up. The politicians found some extra money somewhere to reinforce levees and so forth. It was really quite interesting. Everybody says all the time how people never prepare for disasters. Well, not in '73. We were prepared and then some." He smiled over at Chuck. "Nothing happened, a piddly little flood, hardly worth mentioning. No spring rain to speak of.

The snowpack came off like a dream, a bit at a time. Stage in Jackson never topped eighteen feet.

"By the way, how's the dredging going?" Plowman asked, suddenly changing course, a new subject. Although, of course, it wasn't new at all, since the only reason Chuck had decided to attempt winter dredging in the first place had been the prospect of a spring flood. If he didn't pump the sand for the dog track construction now, he might not be able to do it then, either.

He shook his head. "Everything's taking longer than I thought. I wanted to be running around the clock by now."

Walt made a sympathetic noise.

"Too many damn stoppages," Chuck told him. "We get up and running and then, bam, we're down again."

"Ice?"

"No. We keep slugging the line, plugging it up. With sand first, when we were trying to pump too much, now with all kinds of other shit. The bottom of the river is lousy with it. A lot of staves for some reason, staves and other parts of barrels."

Walt stopped what he was doing with the computer and turned back around toward Chuck. "Interesting." His expression had changed. "Very interesting." Chuck looked at him suspiciously. This particular problem was not, as a matter of fact, very interesting, and Chuck didn't want it to get very interesting. The weatherman had folded his lower lip over his upper and was scratching his chin meditatively. "Tell me, is some of it burned?"

"Yes...why?"

Walter nodded. "Tierces," he said.

Tierces? Chuck remembered the capotes of earlier. Apparently this was his day to learn new vocabulary. "Tierces?"

"An old measure. Volume. I've never been exactly clear on how large. Smaller than a hogshead, I think."

Chuck didn't have any idea how big a hogshead was, much less a tierce, but he could connect enough of the dots to say, "So the debris I've been picking up is perhaps from tierces. And this means?"

"Well, among other things, I know a local historian who'd be interested in having a word or two with you."

Chuck stared at Plowman. Historian? "What are you talking about, Walt?"

"Pork packing."

"A packing plant? On Apple Island?"

"Not a modern one. Very old, nineteenth century. There was a cooperage, too, I think."

"Wonderful. How big?"

"By modern standards?" Plowman shook his head. "You'll want to ask my friend, but not big. Back then, packing was strictly a wintertime activity. Problem with spoilage. The tierces were used to store lard. Of course, the buildings got pretty much saturated with grease and whatnot. Burned down all the time. Real spectacular fires, too, they were." From beneath his generous eyebrows, Plowman looked up slyly at Chuck. His sourness of earlier might have dissipated, but what he'd had to say so far had done nothing to improve Chuck's mood. "The Apple Island site was abandoned long before the turn of the century. Then, what with floods and so forth, the location pretty much disappeared. People forgot about it. Didn't much care, I don't suppose. That is, until this fellow I know decided to do an historical geography of the city. Interesting idea, don't you think, an historical geography?" Walt nodded, agreeing with himself. "Pretty hard, too." He smiled up at Chuck. "But now, thanks to you, one of his problems might have been solved."

"Thanks to me, my foot," Chuck countered. He envisioned the dredge overrun by historians and archaeologists, cofferdams built, swarms of antiquarians sifting through the sand on the bottom of the river.

"You haven't saved any of the stuff you've dredged up by any chance, have you?" Walt asked.

"I don't know."

"My friend would be interested."

"Shit," Chuck said, but without any particular emphasis. "I don't know why I bother to come up here, Walt. Every time I do, you've got more bad news for me."

"Masochist, I guess."

Chuck snorted at such an idea, although, he had to admit, it would explain a lot.

"I'll tell you one thing," he said, "you think you know where your troubles are, but you're wrong. Here I've been assuming all along it was the dredge. Deal with that, the rest is cake."

Walt nodded thoughtfully at this bit of wisdom. "The rest is never cake. On the positive side, sometimes disasters don't pan out, either. These winter storms, they might never materialize."

Chuck nodded. "Or they could be even worse."

"Could." Plowman smiled. "It all depends."

But even if they were, bad weather didn't bother Chuck. Nothing the weather did ever bothered him. A flood wouldn't bother him, either. But the remains of a goddamn century-old packing plant...

"This guy I should talk to, Walt, what's his name?"

~

Back outside, the disk of pale blue had grown, covering half the sky, but light snow still fell out of this clearness. Chuck got back into his vehicle and drove over to city hall.

The rest of the day was not worth remembering. It took him until noon to free up enough time to go down to the dredge, where he passed along to Bud Pregler and his crew what Walt had told him about the former packing operation on the island. Since they had some open water to work with, they decided to begin moving the dredge around, see if they might find a place where they could pump without fouling their equipment.

Nothing was absolutely water-tight on the dilapidated craft, so sheets of clear ice lay across decks and up bulkheads. Ragged humps of white ice, like fenders, hung off the railings, and hundreds of icicles stepped down the rigging. Ice everywhere, ice where he couldn't imagine water would ever reach.

On his way off the island, Chuck stopped at the dog track construction site for a few minutes, with the idea of telling Jack Kelley about the potential for a lot more bad weather. Kelley, with his face of an Irish street fighter but soul of a company man, didn't take bad news well, so naturally Chuck liked giving it to him.

Unfortunately, Kelley wasn't there at the moment, just the kid he'd hired as a gopher when his original field man went AWOL. Chuck borrowed a hardhat and walked around for a few minutes. The sky had cleared, the snow finally stopped, and now the wind was picking up, the temperature quickly dropping. With respect, and even a little envy, he watched the ironworkers aloft in the grandstand, framing, bolting, and welding joists to beams and beams to columns.

At the end of the day, back in his office and just out of another meeting, he remembered the local historian that could perhaps tell him how serious his dredging problem was. He called the number

Walt had given him and reached the fellow, who was as delighted at the news as Walt had said he'd be and told Chuck he'd be happy to meet right away if Chuck wanted. Chuck said fine.

He looked at his watch. It was already pushing six, and he had a city council meeting at 7:30. He hated council meetings, hours wasted waiting on a few minutes. He called Diane and told her he wouldn't be home for dinner.

"Get here when you can. I'll keep something warm for you."

"Don't bother. No telling when I'll get back. Most likely after midnight."

"Okay," she said.

As Chuck hung up, he realized that that was another way Diane had changed. She no longer hounded him with her desire to perform good works.

She had become the perfect wife.

CHAPTER 17

~

After the city council meeting ended, El Plowman lingered in the council chambers. Despite everything, her depression, the suspect nature of the honor, the national obloquy to which the community was being subjected at the moment, she had been secretly pleased that the other council members wished to give her Fritz Goetzinger's old job. She had often imagined herself as mayor. For anyone who had dedicated her life to local public service, the mayoralty represented the end of a natural progression. She would be the first woman to hold the post. That pleased her, too.

The pleasure, however, had almost immediately begun to wear off, become more like a pleasure anticipated than anything which might be enjoyed in the performance.

During the meeting, as the rest of the council members took turns praising her, El idly fingered her copy of Fritz's letter of resignation: a single sentence, three-lines, handwritten. Heaven knows, she was no friend of the man, but that his long public life should end so abruptly and so bitterly and in the shadow of so much tragedy...

After the others had finished with their praising, it was her turn to say something, and she made a short speech, thanking Fritz in absentia for his service and then talking about her hopes for the future, calling for a new spirit of cooperation.

But the words sounded flat, like a thousand other political speeches, placeholders for what should be said. She noticed her own phrases reappearing from the last council meeting, when she had also spoken about the need for community renewal. Her ideas, ill-formed though they were, had already begun to harden.

And then, at the end of the meeting, she had lingered in the chamber. The others gradually drifted off until she sat by herself. It was well after midnight, another long, long day drawing to a close.

But she was in no rush to go home and to bed. It made no difference how tired she was, she wouldn't sleep.

The copy of Fritz's letter still lay in front of her, and her thoughts returned to him. Despite all the bad things that people had to say about him, the truth of the matter was that he had twice been elected mayor, and by significant majorities, and, when it came right down to it, by the very groups El would need to approach with her plea for renewal—the blue collar and the pink collar, the silent, the isolated, the indifferent, the cynical, the alienated. If Fritz withdrew, didn't all these people withdraw with him? How could she reach them? How could she reach people who viewed the very act of reaching with the greatest distrust?

She rubbed her hands slowly down over her face, and as her eyes opened again, she caught a movement in the rear of the room and started, realizing that she wasn't alone. Almost as if one of the painted figures in the faded WPA mural covering the back wall had suddenly come to life, a man arose and approached.

Oh, dear, she thought, for she recognized him at once and he was hardly the sort of person, at that moment of transition in her life, she would have most wanted to materialize out of nowhere. She had had dealings with Marion Dolan before.

"Bugs, you startled me!"

"Been watchin' you." Dolan, like the figures in the mural, wasn't quite life-size. He stood barely over five feet tall in the ancient work boots he habitually wore and, after a lifetime of riotous living, seemed to be wasting away to nothing.

Not a man to rest on ceremony, he sidled around to El's side of the council table, pulled a chair up close, sat down, leaned into her air space, and said, "Looks like you could use a friend."

An ominous remark. "I'm sure, as mayor, I'll have more friends than I want," she said.

"But friends are good."

Before she had given up realty work, El had had occasion to deal with Dolan, one of the larger contractors in the city despite the derelict look about him. Everybody in Jackson knew Bugs. What everybody thought about him, well, that was quite another matter. He was famous—for being short and ferrety, for cutting corners, for epic carousing. But no doubt he had voted for Fritz Goetzinger, no doubt he was one of the very people she hoped to reach, although in the flesh so much less attractive than in the abstract.

"Friends are many things," she said carefully.

"Friends help out friends."

It occurred to her that although she wasn't yet appointed, she was about to perform her first act as mayor.

"Perhaps, Bugs, but best you tell me what it is you've got in mind."

"Been listening. I figure you got a problem, the times being what they are. You can talk about community spirit all you want, don't mean nothing. It's just words."

She waited.

"Ya wanna do something? I mean, *really* do something?"

With his eyes, Bugs tested the material she wore and measured her for a new outfit. He smelled like somebody's attic.

"Might be, I can help." His smile hinted at secrets.

"Is that right?"

"Might be. Might be, this is your lucky day."

El shuddered and thought, *Heaven help us.* She waited for him to continue.

~

Late the next morning, she drove along the pipeline, snaking up onto the dog track construction site. Nothing was coming out of the end of the pipe. She wondered about that. Her car bumped over the frozen tracks left by construction equipment, then nosed up onto the sand platform atop which construction proceeded.

She parked and turned off the engine. Above the foundation of the grandstand, a webbing of steel beams and columns had begun to rise.

The others were already there: Jack Kelley, the construction manager; a second man whom she didn't know at all and assumed to be one of Kelley's people; and finally Chuck Fellows, whom she knew only too well. Arms folded, hardhats on, they stood outside the construction trailer, watching a crane swing its heavy load up onto the deck. Men in their element.

El took a deep breath and got out of her car. They weren't going to like what she had to say. Not that she liked it all that much herself. She had decided not to mention Bugs Dolan.

"Thank you for seeing me on such short notice, gentlemen," she told them as she came up to the little group.

"No problem," Kelley told her, although his gaze, both frank and quizzical, left open the possibility that El had brought trouble with her. "Go get the lady a hardhat, Sean," he told the fellow El didn't know.

Kelley stood with his legs apart, radiating a kind of bland good humor. He had a broad, canny face. Despite the cold, the lapels of his coat were thrown back. Beneath he wore khaki pants, checkered green shirt, a black tie, tweedy sport coat, no one item quite matching any other—a construction man who had been kicked upstairs. When he wasn't speaking, a trace of a smile remained, like a man politely listening to an old joke.

Chuck Fellows, not to be outdone, had the lapels of his coat thrown open, too.

Sean returned with the hardhat and then Kelley suggested that since El was there, what about a tour of the job site? And so they made a slow circuit of the buildings as they talked. The construction manager pointed out this and that: the piled-up materials for the grandstand, which had fallen three weeks behind schedule, the framed-in paddock building, the kennels where siding was beginning to go up.

Beneath absolutely clear skies—for this day in its own way was as extreme as all the other recent weather—a cold wind slashed diagonally across the sand, and El's eyes teared as she walked into the teeth of it, holding on to her hardhat, which felt about to fly off. The men didn't have that problem. Their hats looked like they'd been glued on.

"It's my understanding," she said to Kelley, "that plans and specifications are out for the last major package of bids."

Kelley nodded and took some moments to process this statement before responding. "Still got bid packs D and E later on, but you're right, they're pretty minor—painting and ceramic tile, seating, landscaping, closed-circuit TVs, last minute stuff."

The major contract to be let this time was for the interior systems, but El did not mention this since it was precisely the one of interest to Bugs Dolan.

"What are the chances," she asked, "that local guys will get some of this work?"

"Anybody can bid," Kelley replied evasively. And then he listed the successful bids already made by locals—grading, concrete, plumbing, electrical, HVAC.

"That's true, Jack, but it wasn't really my question."

Kelley stopped and gazed across the roughed-in oval of the track and pointed to the other side, where a slab-shaped edifice rose out of the landscape: the tote board, on which the odds and winners would eventually be posted but which was now only a long, unpainted box.

When he returned to the conversation, he mentioned a local contractor he thought might be contemplating a bid on the interior systems. Not Dolan. This was less obviously an evasion, and better yet it offered a possible alternative to Bugs.

"And do you expect him to be successful if he does?"

"Probably not. Probably, come right down to it, he won't bid. I doubt he's even got the bonding capacity." Kelley looked at her speculatively.

"Anybody else?" she asked. "Jackson's a city of sixty thousand. Surely, there are others who could do the work."

The construction manager had resumed his measured pace. Yes, he admitted, there were people who could do the work. However, the biggest local outfit was browned off because they hadn't been named general contractor for the entire project. And others no doubt looked at the time of year, the tight schedules, and thought thanks but no thanks.

"What about the penalty for nonperformance?" she asked. "Would that be a deterrent, too?"

He glanced aside at her, a quick glance, almost too fast to see. "Liquidated damages?"

"Yes." Liquidated damages, the money a contractor had to forfeit if he went past his deadline for completion. "It has been suggested," she told Kelley, "that if we eliminated liquidated damages, that would give more locals a shot at the work."

They had continued walking, rounding the northwest corner of the grandstand, which brought them nearly back to where they'd started.

A handful of columns and girders had risen from the west end of the grandstand deck, barely hinting at the sweep of steel webbing that would eventually form the framing for the large building. At the base of a column, a welder worked, leaning forward in an attitude of almost prayerful intensity, wearing a thick gray mask that reminded El of primitive African art. Bursts of white-hot sparks showered the base of the column, ricocheting and dying in the cold air.

"If you remove liquidated damages," Kelley said, "you're going against the advice the consultants gave you back when we started." The architect, the engineers...and, of course, Jack himself.

El took a deep breath, the sharp air stinging her lungs. "I have a major concern here, Jack—keeping work in the community. The situation has changed since we began."

He nodded. His words were coming a little more quickly now that he knew what this was all about. "The closing of the meatpacking plant."

"Precisely."

She talked about the sharp rise in unemployment. She talked about money leaving the city. She talked about the symbolic significance of the track project. Kelley listened, half turned away, staring up into the grandstand framing.

"Look up there," he told her when she reached a stopping place. "What do you see?"

She clamped a hand on top of her hardhat as she squinted upward, toward the morning sun. Guy wires stabilized the beams and columns already erected, the wires strings of reflected light, as if the structure was being held up by nothing more than sunshine.

"What am I supposed to see?"

"It's what you don't see. Ironworkers. It's five degrees out, and the wind chill's fifteen below. Time and again, my steel guy has sent his people aloft and time after time he's had to bring them back down again because of the conditions. Yesterday they were able to get a few hours in, until it got so cold their tools began to shatter. If we had another steel contractor on the site, I'd be worried. But not with this guy. He's good, he'll find a way." Kelley was looking intently at El now. "I need more people like him, El...people who, to be frank, don't give a damn whether we run the job with penalties or not."

"And what about you?" she asked Chuck Fellows, who had remained silent all this time. "What do you have to add to this?"

Fellows looked back and forth between El and Kelley, as if deciding whose side to take. Finally, he simply shrugged and said, "Liquidated damages are pretty much impossible to enforce."

El turned back to Kelley. "Jack?"

He smiled, a little painfully, she thought, but he conceded Fellows's point. "That's right. And normally it doesn't make much difference to me whether I run a job one way or the other. At the end of the day, it's true, you can always go after the penalties. Mostly, however, that's a pointless exercise. You put some marginal performer out of business, but that doesn't help you finish the job. No, if liquidated damages have any value, it's not that. It's who you keep off the job site in the first place. And that's what I'm concerned about here."

Bugs Dolan, of course, was the very definition of the marginal performer. "Yes, Jack, I see what you're saying. And believe me, I have no desire to put you in a more difficult position than you're already in."

"If the doggies aren't up and running by June 15, El, the city loses revenue. That's what you should be worried about."

"Of course. But, as you agreed, the Pack has gone out of business. The situation has changed. Our lives are a little harder now."

He nodded reluctantly, and in this way they achieved a kind of standoff. He understood and she understood and there you were.

Fellows seemed to be enjoying the situation, but then again, what else could you expect from a person like Chuck Fellows?

～

Only as she began to drive away, heading back uptown, did El realize just how rotten she really felt, and so she turned off and drove along the river until she reached the lock and dam at the north end of town, where the bluffs rose, a palisade pinching toward the river, leaving just enough room for railroad tracks arriving from the north and the Corps of Engineers buildings. She parked and got back out into the cold and stood at the fence separating the public area from the lock and dam.

A short distance upstream stood the Dixie Darlin', the large commercial towboat that had been pushing a load of barges south at the end of the navigation season and become trapped in the ice. Behind the snow-laden barges, the towboat rose several stories into the crystalline air and canted at a slight angle outward from the lock's guidewall in an impression of arrested motion. A path had been shoveled out to the marooned boat and worn ragged by the passage of many feet.

Why, El wondered, did she feel so lousy? The exchange with Jack Kelley had actually gone better than expected. He understood her situation. Or seemed to, at least. His apparent acquiescence might have been a sham. He might rush off and try to scuttle her effort to remove liquidated damages. Perhaps she'd offended him. Here she was, not even the mayor yet, and already trying to run things.

She didn't know. Anything might happen. She'd been party to enough machinations on the council over the years. As mayor, that sort of thing could only get worse.

Someone had come out onto the deck of the Dixie Darlin'. El turned away. Above the navigation dam, the frozen, wind-scoured backwater reached far to the north. Below the dam, for perhaps a hundred yards, lay open water and then the river ice began again and more people could be seen, fishermen who had drilled holes as near the edge as they dared. One had dragged a skiff out with him and sat next to it as he fished. El's gaze returned to the open water, where two eagles flew, tracing an intricate pattern in the air. At the dam, water rushed over two partially submerged gates, churning violently at the bottom. There was some sort of technical name for the churning. Walter would know it. If a boat got too close, it would be sucked into the gate and destroyed, drowning anyone unlucky enough to be on board.

She wished that Jack had asked who had been talking to her. That would have been better. Heaven knows, she had no earthly desire to be known as Bugs Dolan's standard-bearer. But still, she wished that Jack had asked.

CHAPTER 18

~

"Problem," Kelley had said over the phone. *So what else is new?* Chuck Fellows thought, and at five p.m. he drove down to the job site, dark except for the lights coming from the construction trailer. He hadn't been there since the meeting with El Plowman several days earlier. Her wacko idea of opening up the bidding to all the local lowlifes rather amused him, mostly because he enjoyed Kelley's discomfort. Chuck assumed, of course, that Kelley would try to lay off as much of the burden on him as he could, so his amusement was not untempered by annoyance.

He climbed out of his vehicle and paused to gaze up at the dome of the late afternoon sky, clear and cold and still, a scattering of high-magnitude stars already visible. The night sky was all that remained of his former solitary treks in the wilderness. He loved the vastness of it, the blue shroud of daytime gone, the universe revealing itself, whittling man down to size.

Inside the trailer, Kelley stood at the drawing board, going over plans. As soon as he saw Chuck, he abandoned them and walked back the length of the room, complaining that he had nobody but himself to do all the fine detail work, the job of a good field manager, if only he'd had one, if only the guy he'd hired hadn't gone missing two months into the job. That was one of the reasons Chuck had little use for Kelley—all this whining about his fate.

Kelley threw himself down at his desk. "You ever heard of Dexter Walcott?"

Chuck turned a chair around and sat with his arms folded across the back. "Nope."

"I've been calling around, checking the suppliers, the subs, the distributors, like I always do…" Kelley stopped. He had assumed a matter-of-fact pose, leaning on one elbow and stroking his jaw with thumb and forefinger.

"And?"

"Walcott's out of Waterloo. A contractor." He waited a few moments, as if this information was supposed to mean something to Chuck.

"What about him?"

"He's gonna put in a bid on the interior systems. Apparently he found out that the city plans to remove the penalties..." Kelley paused again and let the pause drag out this time, sitting motionless, bringing the full force of his attention on Chuck. "He's black."

"So?"

At this curt response, Kelley leaned back and became matter-of-fact once more.

"I'd heard of Walcott. But that's all he was, a name. So I thought I'd better vet the guy, very informally, you understand. In these matters, you've gotta be careful. Anyway, it seems that basically he makes a living going around to projects involving federal money, which require a certain percentage of minority participation."

"Gotta chase the money, Jack."

"Also, he's never done a job this big."

"How big?"

"His biggest contract? Four hundred."

"Not much smaller than this one." The construction manager's problem here was obvious, but it wasn't the one he was talking about. "You said yourself, Jack, yank the penalties and the floodgates open. People like Bugs Dolan, now this guy Walcott, what does it matter?"

"What does it matter? You're kidding." Kelley, who of course knew Chuck quite well by now, took a deep breath and continued. "Okay, I'll tell you. You mentioned Bugsy Dolan. I sure as hell don't want Dolan down here. I've already got one contractor who's a royal pain in the ass, I don't need another. But it comes to that, I can deal with Dolan. I can lay down the law to him, make the little runt perform. Dexter Walcott, however..." He paused again, but only long enough to lean far forward. "You put a bunch of blacks down here—and not only blacks but out-of-towners taking jobs away from the locals—this place is gonna be a war zone. You can kiss the project good-bye. We'll be lucky if we ever finish."

Interesting, Chuck thought. He got to his feet. "Let's save our-selves some time here, Jack. If you want me to do something on the basis of race, you've picked the wrong man. If this fellow Walcott puts in the low bid, so be it."

"Sit down," Kelley said.

Chuck remained standing.

"I'm not asking you to do anything based on race."

"Like hell."

"I'm saying he can't handle the work, period. He's too damn small. Race got nothing to do with it." Kelley had grabbed the arms of his chair in a stranglehold. "Frankly, Chuck, I don't give a shit what you think of me. Or my motives. Makes no difference. But I represent the owner, and so do you. We got the responsibility to finish this damn project. And if you put a black contractor down here…"

"Then convince the council to keep the liquidated damages."

"I've tried." Kelley shook his head.

Chuck wasn't surprised. The council members, being a bunch of your typical pols, wanted to have their cake and eat it, too.

"You said it yourself, Jack. Liquidated damages help keep yahoos off the job site. If the council removes them, then"—Chuck smiled at him—"shits and giggles."

"Shits and giggles? Is that right?" Kelley chewed on his lip as he regarded Chuck through lowered eyelids. He wasn't through. "Okay, put it this way. I'm saying you'll be derelict in your duty if you don't run a D and B on the guy. It's called due diligence. You've heard of that? Like it or not, it's your responsibility to check Walcott out. Maybe he's about to go into Chapter Eleven, maybe he's got pending litigation up the ying-yang, who the hell knows? You check and believe me, you're gonna find out he's not qualified to do the work. And you can think whatever the fuck you want, it's got nothing to do with race."

Dun and Bradstreet. Yeah, Chuck thought, if this Walcott fellow was strictly terra incognita, a credit check was called for, that much at least. Chuck's inclination was to continue busting Kelley's chops, but if he had a point, he had a point.

"Okay, Jack, okay. But that's as far as it goes. If it looks like Walcott is at least as upstanding as Bugsy Dolan, then we deal him in."

That Dolan had become the yardstick of competence showed just how far they'd fallen, but such was the hand that Plowman had dealt them.

Yet, as Chuck drove back uptown, he considered the consequences should blacks end up on the job site. After the trashing of the museum, it seemed like a little bit of poetic justice. But Jack was right; the whites wouldn't welcome them with open arms. It could get ugly. On the other hand, people better be ready to fight for what was rightfully theirs, that's what Chuck believed, and if the bloods were willing to waltz onto a project full of rednecks, more power to them. Didn't bother Chuck the least little bit. What he hated was hypocrisy.

With each passing block, the idea of the black contractor became more and more appealing. *In your face*, he thought. *You gotta love it.*

~

Chuck ran the D and B, which proved inconclusive and mostly just raised his curiosity about the man. He smiled as he thought about his old boss Mark O'Banion's reaction to such a situation. And, of course, there was the virtue of getting Kelley's goat after Jack had been so anxious to dump this problem in his lap. Yes, indeed.

But at this point in his reasoning, Chuck suddenly hesitated and asked himself, what if, as Jack claimed, Walcott really wasn't qualified? What if he was just some poor schmuck trying to make a buck and desperate enough to come where he wasn't wanted…and where he really couldn't perform?

Chuck called Walcott and requested a visit.

"There's a question whether you can handle the work."

Walcott, whose voice revealed little, paused for consideration. "Expect I can."

"Nobody over here knows you."

Walcott chuckled on the other end of the line. "Expect that's so."

"I'd like to see your shop."

Another contemplative silence. "Come on over."

Chuck spent the better part of an evening studying the specs and drawings for the interior systems. Kelley showed a surprising reluctance to tag along, suddenly all nervous about the way it would look.

"Suit yourself," Chuck said.

A half hour later, Kelley called back and said he'd changed his mind, and the next day the two of them drove west across the sunblasted winter landscape toward Waterloo.

~

Walcott was straight out of the forties, with processed hair and a thin mustache, a tall slight man, stooped, his skin faded looking, as if it had once been much darker. A hitch in his movements suggested some old injury, and Chuck, still troubled from time to time by his own wounds from Vietnam, felt an immediate kinship.

Kelley set about being unusually friendly, showing how goddamn unprejudiced he was, Chuck supposed.

They toured a couple of Walcott buildings—a residence, a two-story office complex on a commercial strip, his four-hundred-grand job. The workmanship appeared creditable.

Finally they toured Walcott's cabinetry workshop, a World War II Quonset hut around which were stored an endless profusion of scrap, and inside, rows of vintage woodworking machines, where young black men worked, ignoring the visitors. "These are good boys," Walcott said. "Trained 'em myself.

"I grew up in this shop, learned my trade on that radial saw over there. Build almost anything on that one tool, you know what you're about. Make my own jigs, too.

"I come from a long line of craftsmen, gentlemen, my daddy before me, his before him. Lumbermen, pattern makers, cabinetmakers, contractors. Mostly we used to work for black folks, building homes, mom-and-pop stores, churches, such like. I've branched out. Do metalwork, concrete, electrical, plumbing, you name it. Got to be versatile in this world today."

Walcott opened a loose-leaf binder with page after page of photos encased in plastic—a record of his progress on the commercial job they'd just toured. He turned the pages of the binder, one by one, his fingers pale, one finger missing, another severed down to the first joint.

Jack, after his initial palsy-walsy outburst, had become quiet and attentive. If he seemed open to the man, he showed reserve toward his work. He squinted at the details in the photographs and asked doubtful questions.

Since Walcott's woodworking experience was evident all around them, in the snapshots the contractor pointed out the metal studwork, the acoustical ceiling grids, the gypsum wallboard installations. "Do most of my fabrication on the job site." His mustache, magic marker thin, rose and fell across the valley and ridges of his upper lip, dancing as he touted his craftsmanship. To Chuck, it hinted at painstaking attention to detail. Patience. Order.

"I take it, Mr. Walcott," Jack said, tossing out an idea as if it had just occurred to him, "you heard that the Jackson city council is considering removing some of the damages when they let this contract."

"That's correct."

"And you understand the reason?"

Walcott responded, when he did, with, "Still expect you're after the lowest responsible bid, ain't that right?"

"What I'm after is to finish the job on time, on budget, and according to the specs."

Walcott nodded.

"I don't suppose," Kelley pressed on with his interrogation, "you planned to bid before you heard about damages being removed."

Another of the pauses that Chuck understood was typical of Walcott's style of speaking followed.

"Nope," he said finally.

"Do you mind my asking why?"

Walcott tapped his mustache with a forefinger.

"Thought of biddin' anyway. Could use the work, times being what they is…But if I got to work a job with white boys, Mr. Kelley, nothing personal, I got to worry about what might happen."

Kelley nodded sympathetically. "I know what you mean. We've had some troubles recently, as you've no doubt been reading about. Expect you'd just as soon avoid a situation like that."

Chuck watched as Walcott gave Jack a long, considered look. "Expect I would," the black man said. "Gotta work, though."

Chuck liked Walcott better all the time.

∽

"A nice fellow. Clearly not qualified," Jack said, as he and Chuck started back toward Jackson.

"Come on, Jack. Your mind was made up before we ever left Jackson."

Over the eastern Iowa fields, the divided highway loped, as straight as the surveyor's art could make it. The farmers had cleared the land, fencerow to fencerow, snow covering everything. They could have been crossing tundra.

"You know, Chuck, the whole reason for removing these damages is to give the locals a shot at the contracts. You end up with some marginal guy from another town, that just defeats the purpose of the thing."

"Life," Chuck said. "Ain't it a bitch?"

He didn't take his eyes off the road, but he could tell Kelley's expression had changed. "You're a real sweetheart."

"I'll tell you what, Jack, Walcott looked okay to me, a little old-fashioned maybe, but okay, a guy who knows how to make do." Something else Chuck liked about the man. "If he gets the contract, you're right, though, you've got yourself a situation. You'd get a lot more sympathy out of me if you stopped whining about it. But there's no way I'm gonna disqualify Walcott, certainly not just to make your life a little easier."

"This is no damn time for social engineering."

"What?"

"You heard me. Put a bunch of black guys down on the job site, and you better believe that's what you got."

Shit, Chuck thought. "There's another word for it, too, Jack—integration."

This, of course, pissed Kelley off all the more. "Do you really want to have to deal with a bunch of racial incidents, with—with—who the hell knows what? Fights, work stoppages, sabotage? That's what you'll get, you know!"

"Doesn't bother me a bit."

"Shit, I don't believe you." Kelley had up a head of steam now, and he kept at Chuck, but Chuck, satisfied, saw no reason to react.

Finally, Kelley gave up and they drove on in silence.

Chapter 19

~

The rest of the bids for Bid Pack C had been opened, leaving only the contract for interior systems. *Jack Kelley was right,* Chuck thought. Bad drives out good. When the locals discovered Bugs Dolan had joined the chase, their enthusiasm waned, and as Chuck stood in the council chambers, repeating the ground rules for the reps, only a handful of envelopes remained on the table before the city clerk—three from contractors who would have bid anyway, hoping that damages weren't removed, one from Dolan, and one from the black Waterloo builder, Dexter Walcott.

The rules of the road were familiar to everyone present, but Chuck stressed them anyway, mostly for Dolan's benefit—all bids to be accompanied by a satisfactory bid security and so forth.

Chuck's one small concession to the drama of the moment had been to align the bids so that Walcott's would be opened next to last, Dolan's last.

One by one, the city clerk peeled back the flaps from the first three and read off the figures. Then she handed the documents to Chuck so that he could glance over the contents—Richardson from Cedar Rapids the low man so far. A big regional operator, Richardson had already won and fulfilled the contract for foundational work at the track. He had the resources to handle the inside systems with ease, but he had a lot of overhead costs, too.

Chuck nodded and the clerk opened Walcott's bid. Four hundred eighty-eight thousand and change. A new low man. Chuck did a quick calculation. Twenty-one grand under Richardson's, assuming the penalties for late completion were removed. Chuck glanced over the documentation, sensing a faint restlessness in the room. The representatives of the contractors stood in a couple of small knots, men who had developed their professional relationships over the years, been to a drove of openings like this, won some, lost some, made their private little deals on the side from time to time, didn't for the most part worry overmuch about the fate of a single bid, for life went on and a month or two down the line they'd find themselves together someplace else and dance this dance one more time. Dolan had insinuated himself into one group. Dexter Walcott stood off to the side.

Chuck nodded again, and the last envelope was opened, Dolan's. The clerk read the figure in her usual monotone—four hundred and ten thousand. Not even close, seventy-eight grand under Walcott's bid, nearly a hundred under Richardson's.

Slowly, the silence dissipated and one of the reps whistled softly; another smiled and said something Chuck couldn't make out and the men around him laughed. Dolan strutted among them, his insignificant chest thrown out. Dexter Walcott, unsmiling, regarded him from a distance.

Chuck leafed through the attachments in case Dolan had fucked up the paperwork. Everything as it should be, including his bid security check. Chuck called the gathering back to order long enough to repeat the date at which the city council would take final action and to remind them that the council reserved the right to reject any and all bids.

And that concluded the brief ceremony.

⁓

Hardly had he gotten back to his office, however, before Dexter Walcott showed up and insisted on speaking with him.

"Let me guess," Chuck said as soon as the door was closed, "you think Dolan lowballed the job."

"And what about you, Mr. Fellows? What do you think?"

"Maybe."

"I don't believe there's any maybe 'bout it. Expect you're gonna see a mess of change orders out of that fellow." The classic trick used by unscrupulous contractors—bid low, then demand changes by claiming the plans and specs were inadequate.

Chuck motioned to a chair across from his desk, and the two of them sat down. The leather of Walcott's brown bomber jacket was cracked and in places faded almost to white. He sat with his legs slightly parted, his cap perched on his knee.

"You from around here, Mr. Fellows?"

"Chuck."

Walcott nodded. "You from around here, Chuck?"

"No."

"Then you maybe don't know the history."

"I know enough."

They sat silently regarding each other. Walcott's face lacked the liveliness it had during his workshop tour. His mustache no longer danced as he spoke.

"I bid that job tight, real tight. If you're willing to take the trouble, you'll find that Mr. Dolan there can't even cover his fixed costs, submitting a bid like what he done. Can't but lose money, and that's a fact."

In the words, Chuck heard not only a challenge but also doubt as to his own integrity. He wasn't offended. The fix might be in, so far as Walcott knew, and Chuck just another honky taking care of business.

"If what you say is true, Dex, then Bugsy's bought himself a peck of trouble."

The black man nodded parsimoniously.

"Might I take that to mean Mr. Dolan ain't necessarily gonna get the contract?"

"You might. But I'm not gonna sit here and guarantee anything. His bid is low. Probably the city council will go with him. As for what happens afterwards, well…"

Another parsimonious nod.

"Tell me, Dex…According to Jack Kelley, if you do get the work, there'll be a shit storm down on the job site. You ready for that?"

Walcott looked away and then back. "You ever heard of the dozens, Mr. Fellows…Chuck?"

"Yeah, it's an insult game they play in the ghetto."

"Right. My boys are good at the dozens…real good." He stopped and continued to regard Chuck frankly, but offered no more on the subject of the dozens. All he said was, "I'd be obliged if you let me know what happens, one way or t'other."

"I'll do that."

"Then I'll be expecting to hear from you."

Chuck nodded.

"You just remember what I said, Mr. Fellows. No way this bid is strictly on the up-and-up. You check it on out."

After he had finished and left, Chuck mulled over the conversation. Walcott had appeared neither surprised nor particularly pissed. What was this but an incident, a mere rivulet in the long history of black-white relations, emptying into a vast ocean? The challenge was Chuck's, no one else's. Of course, he could simply let the matter slide, approve the change orders that Dolan would probably submit, let him make his sleazy profit, leave sleeping dogs lie. He could.

Like hell.

He called Jack Kelley and gave him the bidding results. Kelley showed no more surprise than Walcott had, not even at just how low Dolan's bid had been.

"That's Bugsy," was all he said.

"Okay," Chuck countered, "that's Bugsy, but I'm telling you, Jack, don't bring me any change orders he can't damn well justify. If Dolan thinks he can lowball the city and get away with it, he's got another think coming. He's in the game now. It's house rules."

"Fair enough," Kelley agreed. "Of course, on accelerated projects like this, cost overruns and design changes happen all the time. Just because Dolan asks for a change doesn't mean he's sandbagging us."

Kelley's point, in another context, would have been straightforward enough, but Chuck didn't trust him. He could have gone to Dolan and made an arrangement on the side, anything to avoid racial problems on the job site.

Next, Kelley said, "I'll work with the guy. Maybe we can turn him around."

"Turn him around? If he's gonna lose his shirt, what's to turn around?"

"I didn't create the situation, Chuck. Blame El Plowman, not me. I've just got to pick up the pieces, and if that means working with Bugsy, so be it."

Chuck dropped his hand, the receiver hanging at his side. Did he want to get in Kelley's grill again? What was the point?

Kelley had continued to talk. Chuck couldn't distinguish the words, only the dead earnestness in the tone.

This conversation, he decided, had gone on long enough. He lifted the receiver. "I'll make the arrangements, Jack. I want Dolan in my office. If I'm gonna recommend the council accept his bid, I wanna make damn sure he knows what he's getting himself into."

Kelley hesitated and then said, "Sure, fine. Tell you what, Chuck, why don't you recommend the council disqualify Bugs and Walcott and give the contract to Richardson?"

That, of course, would solve all of Kelley's problems.

"We're gonna get Dolan in here," Chuck told him. "We'll deal with him first." And he hung up.

CHAPTER 20

~

Bugs Dolan was already late, but he took the time to finish his cigarette on the steps outside city hall, then stopped for a piss inside and inspected himself in the john mirror, or at least as much of himself as he could see. The world had not been designed for people the size of Bugs.

He liked what he saw. He was runty and ugly as sin. His nose particularly he was proud of, one of those oversized, oft-broken, large-pored, purplish jobs everybody noticed but nobody made reference to—at least not when they were sober—the nose of a man never got nothing for free.

And could smell trouble a mile off. For the truth of the matter was that Bugs felt deeply uneasy. This whole business with the dog track had begun to take on a very bad odor. When Jack Kelley had come to see him the first time, talking about the colored contractor from Waterloo and all, Bugsy just naturally assumed he and Kelley had an understanding. Not that they was exactly asshole buddies. But they was both sons of the old sod. That oughta count for something. So what happens? Suddenly, Kelley's all hot that Bugsy should justify his damn bid. Whatever happened to old-country loyalties? What was the world coming to?

Not that Bugs hadn't created part of the problem himself. He'd bid too goddamn low. Coulda added practically eighty grand and still been low man. That was stupid, but then again, how was he supposed to know? Bugsy had never thought much of the way they did the bidding thing anyway. It was the muckety-mucks' way, designed to put the screws to guys like Bugs. His idea was, tell him what the low bid was, he'd knock off a few bucks. That's the way it oughta be done. Or maybe like an auction, except in reverse, each guy putting in a lower bid until there was only one guy left. Or just sit down and negotiate the damn thing and forget all this who-

145

shot-John. Build better projects that way, too. Bugsy felt put-upon. He didn't like to lowball a bid any more than the next guy. Create an honest system and, hell, he'd be honest, too.

But what could he do? He'd put in his bid. Like it or not, he'd have to live with it.

He pulled himself together, puffed out his chest, and strutted upstairs, the Bugster off to do battle with the big boys once more.

∼

The three of them had gone up to the drafting room on the third floor, found an unoccupied table and laid out the plans and specs. Chuck Fellows started questioning him closely— how did he do his quantity takeoffs, who were his vendors, the whole schmear.

Bugsy didn't have much respect for the yokels in city hall. If they'd been any good, they'd be out in the private sector, making some real money. This Chuck Fellows character wasn't any different. A big son-of-a-bitch, not the kind of guy you'd like to tangle with in some back alley, maybe. Big and dumb, Bugsy decided. A guy you could get around. Or at least, Jack Kelley could get around. Or so Bugsy had assumed. Now he didn't know what to think, for Kelley was just standing back and letting Fellows whale away at him.

"How did you figure your labor costs?" Fellows demanded.

Bugs was ready for that one. "I ain't union, you know. And my boys need the work, what with it being winter and all. We're gonna get in there, get things done pronto, and get the hell out."

"Yeah," Fellows said, "right." Bugsy was used to such skepticism. Made no difference. Let 'em think what they liked.

Still, it just annoyed the hell out of him that he'd bid so low. He'd left a shitload of money on the table. He coulda made his figures look a helluva lot better.

"You think my bid ain't what it oughta be," he told Fellows hopefully, "what say we amend it." It was a little irregular, but what the hell, Bugsy was flexible.

"That's not the way it works, Bugs," Kelley told him. "You know that."

Maybe, Bugs thought, if he got mad, that'd work. "Hey, the new mayor's got a mind to accomplish something here, keep work in the city and such. I'm just trying to do my part. You guys might try to help out, too, instead of giving me such a goddamn hard time."

"Bugsy," Kelley told him good-humoredly, "you're full of crap." Fellows smiled and shook his head.

Bugsy decided that maybe he'd laid it on a bit thick, but he wasn't going to back down from this pair of garbanzo beans. One thing he did when estimating a job was look for mistakes, ambiguities, oversights, missing details—anything in the plans that might give him a little edge. Then he'd walk the job site and scope out the situation. He could always count on finding something somebody had screwed up. Generally he liked to keep all this to himself until the proper time. Given the circumstances, however, he decided to fire off a few salvos now, and he whipped through the plans until he found what he was looking for.

"See this, see this!" He was pointing at the details for a hand railing. "You want me to install this, you gotta have sleeves in the concrete topping. Tell you what, why don't you go out and take a look. Toppings been poured, where the hell are the sleeves? Ain't there." He didn't wait for a response but searched angrily through the plans until he'd found a particular detail in the metal studwork drawing—another error—and then in the joint between fascia and sheetrock, another.

"A piss-poor set of plans, I'd call 'em. I try to estimate the job the best I can, but wha'da'ya think I am, Swami Bugsy or something? I ain't no mind reader. You got some dumb architect never been on a job site in his life, what am I supposed to do?"

He knew what Fellows was gonna say when he finished, so he didn't finish, just kept on bitching about this flaw and that, thinking all the time, maybe bidding on public projects ain't such a swell idea after all. Maybe this Fellows guy is so dumb he don't know the left hand washes the right. Maybe he never heard of good enough.

Fellows kept staring at him, arms folded. *He was,* Bugsy thought again, *a mean looking son-of-a-bitch. Shit.*

~

Back out on the city hall steps with Kelley, Bugsy stopped and lit up a ciggy and inhaled deeply. "Don't you smoke no more, Jack?" When Bugs left the meeting, Kelley had invited himself along.

"No."

"You becoming a yuppie or what?"

"You got more important things to worry about, Bugs, than my social ambitions."

"That's right, Jack. I worry why you didn't give me some more help in there. I thought we had a deal."

"I didn't tell you to bid the job that low. What the hell were you thinking?"

"You said there'd be lots of change orders."

"And there will be. But you still gotta bid the documents." These words sent a chill through Bugs. "And how in God's name did you figure your labor costs? It's not 1950 anymore, you know."

"Yeah, but Jack, if the goddamn city council is gonna drop the damages, you don't want that spade from Waterloo getting the work. Now do ya?"

Kelley admitted as much by saying nothing.

"And, shit, Jack, everybody knows the colored will work for practically nothin'."

Kelley closed his eyes and shook his head. "Bugs, Bugs, what the hell am I going to do with you?"

"You gotta work with me, Jack. You gotta help me get around that turkey upstairs."

With a finger, Kelley punched Bugs in the chest. "And you, my friend, are gonna have to run an honest job."

"Man, I do the best I can."

Bugs didn't like the look in Kelley's eye. The construction manager leaned close and punched him in the chest again. "Trouble is, Bugsy, you just don't listen. Let me repeat myself. This will be a decent job—even if it puts you out of business."

"Yeah, yeah, yeah," Bugsy said, "but we still got a deal, right?" Kelley's tone of voice was just too damn sincere, as if he really meant what he was saying. "Deal?"

Kelley nodded deliberately. "Looks like, Bugs...but don't be surprised when your feet get held to the fire. No joke. We're not building some half-assed commercial warehouse. This project means a lot to the city. I'll help out the best I can, but if you think you can pull all your old shit, you're sadly mistaken...my friend."

All these words of warning, a goddamn truckload of 'em, shook Bugsy, and he went away troubled in his soul.

CHAPTER 21

~

Jack Kelley applauded politely with the others at the end of the brief swearing-in ceremony. El Plowman had officially become the mayor of Jackson, Iowa. She was outfitted for the occasion in a long, flowing maroon dress, her gray-streaked hair meticulously arranged, her lipstick bright red, a regular makeover. Some women, Jack thought, were better off not getting dressed up. Plowman was too big, too middle-aged, too round-faced, too midwinter pallid. She radiated seriousness and determination, admirable attributes, he supposed, if only she wouldn't meddle in affairs best left to the people who knew what the hell they were doing.

Jack had tried another ploy to keep the liquidated damages in place, a chat with his boss, Harry Steadman. Jack knew the construction community, but old Harry was the one in the firm plugged into the local power structure—and maybe Harry had been putting in some calls, but if so, they hadn't had any noticeable effect, and it looked as if, like it or not, Jack would have to be satisfied with Bugsy Dolan. If only the runt hadn't put in such a cockeyed bid.

Jack came forward to the podium to provide the regular report to the council on progress at the job site, normally Harry's job, but Harry was out of town at the moment. Jack was just as glad. It gave him one last chance to influence the letting…and for once to let the council know just how tough things were down on the job site. Harry always liked to put a positive spin on events. All problems were mere inconveniences, if you listened to Harry. But Harry seldom showed his face at the track site. He lived in cloud-cuckooland. Jack was determined to set the council straight.

He took his time, giving the precise status of each of the contracts, the problems caused by the abnormal cold, the problems caused by the abnormal snowfall, the human problems. "Overall, we're about three weeks behind schedule. It's got so I don't dare to watch the weather forecasts anymore."

"Walter will be sorry to hear that," Plowman interposed, and everybody had a good laugh.

After the noise died down, she added, smiling, "But I assume you're still committed to finishing the project by June 15, Mr. Kelley, even without my husband's cooperation."

"We're going to try." The mayor knew what Jack was angling to do and wasn't having any part of it. Nonetheless, he would say what he meant to say, a bit of ancient construction lore resurrected for the occasion. "What you have to understand, Mayor Plowman, is that it's tough as the dickens to make up, at the end of a project, time lost at the beginning."

She, in turn, came back with, "But it's certainly no secret that we're building in winter."

"Yes."

"And all projects have to deal with the unexpected."

"Of course."

"I appreciate your difficulties, Mr. Kelley, but this council is still determined that the June 15 deadline will be met."

"I understand," Jack said, "and we'll do our best." Since Plowman was being so bloody direct, he was tempted to come right out and make a plea—for God's sake, don't drop the damages—but he thought better of it. What he couldn't do in private, he sure as hell wasn't going to accomplish in public.

He sat back down, feeling defeated.

Bugsy had come to the meeting, apparently to make sure he got the bid. At the moment, however, he looked anything but cocky.

Fellows was there, too, of course, sitting in a clump of city staffers, looking disgruntled as usual. Jack didn't understand the man. Fellows seemed to have taken a dislike to Jack for no reason at all. And now this business with Bugsy and the guy from Waterloo… Fortunately, Dexter Walcott wasn't going to get the contract. Still, the whole business just bothered the hell out of Jack. People assumed you were a racist. It really pissed Jack off. And Fellows's general smugness pissed him off, too. Just thinking about it pissed him off all over again.

Jack listened as one council member after another solemnized over the situation. They spoke in code, for no one could openly admit that the real reason for removing damages wasn't to save money so much as to favor a local contractor. From what they said, Jack was able to more or less reconstruct the private conversations that had preceded the meeting: give Dolan the bid, but make him aware, in no uncertain terms, that he was to be held accountable, on pain of eternal civic damnation or some such. Nobody was mentioning Dolan, but they didn't have to. Jack almost felt sorry for the guy.

Finally, El Plowman spoke, adding her caveat to the others, taking the occasion to raise the banner under which her mayoralty would sally forth. She stared straight at Bugsy as she spoke, and little Dolan fidgeted in his seat, looking less like an adult than a schoolboy with an aging disease.

Undoubtedly, Plowman had strong-armed the other council members into going along with her. Well, she *was* determined, that's for sure. How else to explain her willingness to lay her spotless reputation on the line for the likes of Dolan? At the moment, her speech concluded, she was looking left and right toward the other council members, ready to call the question.

But she never had the chance.

Jack heard movement to his side and turned to see Bugsy rising from his chair and stumbling as he forced his way out to the aisle and up toward the podium. He grabbed the gooseneck of the microphone and yanked it down to his level.

Plowman's mouth was open to say something, but he beat her to it.

"This is rich, you know," he said, voice cracking. "Don't think I can't see what's going on here. Ever since I made my bid, you people been on my case. You, Mayor, and Kelley over there, Fellows, all you goddamn people. Givin' me all this crap about running a good job. I always run good jobs, ask anybody. But I know, I know what's going on. You better believe it. Bugsy Dolan wasn't born yesterday. Well, the hell with it!" He held his hands over his head and waved them forward in a gesture of dismissal. "You can keep your goddamn contract."

In the stunned silence which followed, Dolan looked around, as if surprised himself at the words that had come out of his mouth. Then he drew himself up to his full height, such as it was, and said with dignity, "Go ahead and give the work to somebody else, I don't give a shit. But you ain't gonna screw over Bugsy Dolan. No friggin' way."

And he slowly left the chambers, shoulders erect, head thrown back. The room was so quiet that Jack could hear the slight creak of the hinge as the heavy door swung shut. He thought, *What the...?* and leaped to his feet, catching up to Dolan just as he was about to get on the elevator.

"Bugs, are you crazy? What the hell do you think you're doing?"

"You heard me." Dolan seemed quite calm now.

"You can't withdraw your bid."

"Oh, yeah? Watch me."

"You'll lose the security. Can you afford to flush that much money down the toilet?"

Dolan shrugged. "Go ahead, Jack, take the money, fuck me over, put me outta business." The elevator door started to close until Dolan hit it with a forearm and it shuddered and reopened.

Someone else came into the hall: the city hall reporter for the newspaper.

"Yeah, go ahead," Dolan told Jack, "give the contract to the colored guy and put me outta business. That'll go over real big, Jack, real big." And he gave Kelley a smile. The elevator door tried to close again, and once more he nailed it with his forearm. "You want a quote?" he asked the reporter, and then with a flourish added, "Step into my office."

The elevator descended, taking Dolan and the reporter with it, leaving Jack alone. He stood there, the shock of the sudden change in events starting to wear off, leaving in its place...nothing, a feeling almost like in the old days when he had been a contractor himself and had put a lot of work into a bid and the bid had failed. A feeling of being disconnected.

Through the thick doors to the council chamber he could hear muted voices, a gentle murmuring sound.

He wondered why he hadn't seen it coming. Of course, he could see it all quite clearly now, now that it was too late. They'd hounded Bugsy, and at some point he'd started looking for a way out, any way. He was nothing if not crude. But he had a point. He'd probably get his security back, whatever happened. And he wouldn't lose his shirt trying to fulfill the contract, either.

When Jack walked back into the council chambers, Sister Jean, the other woman on the council, had the floor.

After further discussion, in which both Jack and Chuck Fellows took part, answering questions put to them by the various council members, the council voted to award the contract for the interior systems at the dog track to Dexter Walcott of Waterloo.

CHAPTER 22

~

In the sunlight, Hidden Slough lay silent, no bird calling in the distance, no wind ruffling the pine tops. Thickets of sandbar willows crowded the shorelines. A massive old cottonwood leaned far over the ice, snow uplifted on one side, forming a warren of cavities among its exposed roots. Midwinter lay like a truce in the elaborate give and take between river and forest, the sun, even at midday, canting in from the tree line, its muted glow more like shadow than light.

Far off to the north, a sound, a faint droning, insinuated itself into this quiet winter-locked scene. The disturbance, very soft, rising slowly, moved at an angle, nearing but still soft, still shielded by the forest, closer, now quiet and loud at once, closer, closer… suddenly exploding, bursting from behind a stand of trees! A boat skidded into view, driven by a large fan mounted at its stern. It hit a windrow of snow, barely moving through the wave of white as the racket of the engine wound ever higher, then accelerating as the odd craft breasted the low ridge and raced back onto bare ice. At mid-slough, the engine was suddenly cut, and the boat, sashaying, its runners cutting into the surface, abruptly slowed. In a few moments, it had come to a dead stop while its noise seemed to rush onward and disappear, ghostlike, downstream.

In the stern stood two men, one hunched up in his parka, the other casually tilting his cap back and surveying the scene until he noticed his companion and laughed.

"Enjoy the ride?" J.J. Dusterhoft spoke louder then necessary, his hearing still muffled from the noise of his airboat.

"F-f-fuck." Deuce Goetzinger tentatively pushed the hood of his parka back, a sliver of his face appearing.

J.J. laughed. "Nothing like a little fresh air."

The wind had burned Deuce's face red, J.J. noticed with approval. *Let the man suffer a little*, he thought, *do him good.*

J.J. hopped out onto the ice and began at once to haul tackle from the boat.

"This year we can use three tip-ups and two poles," he informed Deuce, who grunted and climbed stiffly over the gunwale. "Stay away from the places that are covered with snow." J.J. pointed at a bare but discolored patch. "And yellow ice, too. Springs. You think you're cold now…"

His old fishing holes had frozen shut, resembling the bottoms of thick tumblers.

"We're in business." He went back to the gear and handed Deuce a strainer.

"Wha's zis for?" Deuce mouthed. He was having some difficulty forming his words.

"You'll see."

Next, J.J. hauled his auger out, laid it on its side and pulled the starter cord sharply until the little gas motor caught, the motor tiny but very loud, the mechanical equivalent of a small yappy dog. He hoisted the thing upright and positioned it over the first of the old holes. The noise rose amid the spew of ice shavings.

Deuce yelled, "Fis'll be lon' gon'!"

"Naw! This time of year, they're all slugabeds! Need to roust them out! Once they're up, they'll just naturally start thinkin' about breakfast!"

After the hole had been reopened, J.J. pointed at the slush still in it and made a scooping motion.

Now Deuce knew what the strainer was for, but the information didn't seem to gladden his heart.

"You were the one wanted to talk, remember," J.J. reminded him.

"Didn't say anything about fishin'," Deuce countered gloomily. "Friggin' deranged." His mouth seemed to be getting back into working order.

J.J. laughed. "Ice fishing ain't for the masses, I'll grant you that."

Deuce squatted on his haunches and began flinging the slush aside.

They proceeded from hole to hole, J.J. reopening each, Deuce stiffly scooping out the slush ice.

Next, J.J. decided where he'd put his tip-ups. "The basic idea is, you cut a bunch of holes, hope you get lucky. This time of year they school." He was talking about panfish—crappies, bluegills, pumpkinseeds.

He fetched a hand drill from his toolbox and with it made two tiny holes on either side of one of the augered holes.

"Low tech," he told Deuce as he inserted a wicket. The wicket came from an old croquet set, the tip-up improvised from a coat hanger. The hanger—straightened, a loop in the middle, a tiny red flag on one end, a short fishing line on the other—rotated on the wicket.

J.J. had a sounding line he used to test the depth, then adjusted the line so the bait—minnows—would ride just above the bottom. The contraption was rigged flag down. If a fish took the bait, the tug on the line would cause the flag to flip upwards. He explained all this as he worked.

"Here, you do the next one."

He watched Deuce's hands redden in the cold air.

Once the tip-ups were set, they carried their poles and stools and bait bucket out to the last two holes.

Rigging the poles was a little trickier, so J.J. offered to do Deuce's.

"No chance," Deuce said. J.J. nodded his approval, then rigged his own line slowly enough so that Deuce could copy him.

Finally, they each picked a hole and settled down to fish. They were several yards apart, but in the still air hardly needed to raise their voices in order to converse.

"Don't get it," Deuce said after a time.

"What?"

"Never figured you for a fisherman."

"No? Why not?"

"Man likes to talk as much as you do."

"Ah, true enough, I do like a good conversation… Of course, fishing's no impediment to that. Enjoy the silence, too. Trouble with most people, you ask me, is they ain't any good at either."

Deuce snorted.

"Just listen," J.J. said, cocking his ear. "Nothing. No wind, no dog barking across the river. Nothing. Just the silence." He had let his voice gradually die away. Finally, he held his breath and it was as if time itself had paused.

They jigged their lines. Deuce wasn't inclined to comment, and so for a time they fished without speaking, Deuce obviously in no rush to reveal what was on his mind, the reason for this little get-together.

J.J. hadn't often played poker with him, the games being too rich for J.J.'s blood, but he'd sat in enough times to understand the power of patience in the man's approach to life. Essential in the good poker player, no doubt. But in Goetzinger, something else as well, something more fundamental in his makeup, like a man forever aware of the gap between himself and others.

J.J. gave his line a tug and felt the slight resistance of the bait. No bites yet. Probably the fish were elsewhere. Didn't make any difference.

Finally, he decided what the hell, he might as well take the lead himself, get this thing over with. He waited a skosh longer, to get a proper rhythm, then said casually, "You're planning to stage a palace coup, are you?"

Deuce roused himself. "You heard, then?"

"A rumor."

Deuce hunched back down over his line and gave it a couple of sharp jigs. "Barbara Amos approached me."

"So I understood. And who else have you talked to?"

"No one."

J.J. rearranged his thoughts, trying to recapture the sense of calm momentarily lost. Knowing what was coming, even bringing it up himself, hadn't been sufficient to avoid a feeling of violation. Barb Amos had been, of course, dissatisfied with J.J.'s style of negotiating for a long time.

"So…you talked to Amos, did you?" It was difficult to imagine her making any discernible impression on the likes of Deuce Goetzinger. "Barb's a little excitable." Deuce didn't react to this, so J.J. added, "Undoubtedly she thinks I'm not excitable enough. Why you, did she say?"

"Ned Pickett suggested me."

"Pickett, huh?" J.J. hadn't heard that Pickett was involved, but it made some sense. Barb knew Pickett and Pickett knew Deuce. "So Ned thinks you're the man for the job, does he?"

"I suppose he's got the impression I'm a hard-ass like my old man."

"Of course, you're just a cream puff."

"Of course." Deuce spoke without emphasis, still hunched up and staring morosely down at the hole into which his line disappeared.

J.J. chuckled. He considered why Amos might have taken Ned's advice and pursued Goetzinger. "Barb, I'm afraid, has a rather inflated opinion of the union's power."

"Said she was born and raised union."

"Yup, that's Barb. Union made." All the more reason, so J.J. thought, that she wasn't likely to make any impression on Deuce, him not being the kind of man to react well to enthusiasm.

After a pause, Deuce said, "She saw you coming out of Aggie Klauer's office."

"Ah, so that's it." Of course. J.J. remembered his premonition at the time. "As a matter of fact, I just went in to get the city's counter."

"She interpreted it different."

"I'm sure she did."

"She figured you'd rather switch than fight, so she's looking for somebody else."

J.J.'s equanimity back in place, this blunt assessment didn't much disturb him.

"And you're considering taking her up on the offer."

Deuce didn't say anything, but that had to mean yes.

"Why?" J.J. asked. "This ain't exactly your idea of a good time."

J.J. waited for an answer. Finally all Deuce volunteered was, "Nope."

J.J. thought about the recent sorrows in the Goetzinger family, and Deuce's gloomy reverie, and said, "Fair enough."

Having been forewarned, he had already given the possibility of Deuce taking over the negotiating some thought and found he wasn't totally averse to the idea. He remembered Deuce's insistence on rigging his own line. The man had, J.J. acknowledged, some character. And J.J. liked him well enough. He was bright, too. On the other hand, he seemed a little too cynical for the task at hand.

"And if I say no?" J.J. asked.

Deuce paused a long time before saying, "Then I suppose I'll have to do it the hard way."

J.J. heard these uncompromising words and said, "Expect you've got a little of your old man in you, after all."

"Not much."

"You'd better have *some* if you're serious about this thing… I got one more question for you. Why should I let you? Why shouldn't I fight?"

"It's your call."

J.J. caught a movement out of the corner of his eye and looked up just in time to see one of the tip-ups complete its graceful arc, the stiff little flag vibrating.

When he got over to it, however, the line was slack. He pulled it up, baited and reset it, then returned thoughtfully to his camp-stool.

"Suppose, just suppose, for the sake of argument, I go along with you. What you got in mind?" he asked.

Deuce shrugged. "Don't know. Something different."

"Different, huh? Like maybe trade some sort of wage cut for a guarantee of no layoffs."

"Yup. Gave that some thought."

"And?"

"It'd split the union."

Deuce was right. The old guys, who had longevity, didn't give a shit about layoffs. Not when push came to shove.

"Might be we could use it as a bargaining chip," J.J. suggested.

"Might be," Deuce agreed without enthusiasm. "Gotta be something better."

"If you say so."

They fell silent and considered what that ineffable something might be.

J.J. remembered the city's negotiator and his friend, Aggie Klauer, and was tempted to tell Deuce to go easy on her. He might like Deuce well enough, but he liked Aggie a helluva lot more. Did he really want to subject her to the ministrations of this fellow? Although, on the other hand, Aggie was the pro here, Goetzinger a rank amateur. That counted for something. A lot, in fact. But not quite everything. At the poker table, Goetzinger was a coldhearted son of a bitch. Would he be any different as a negotiator? And how much nastier would he get when his cardplayer's tricks didn't work on Aggie? Maybe, J.J. thought, what he should do was warn her. These possibilities ran quickly through his mind, and were as quickly dismissed. In thinking them, however, he realized that he had, indeed, made up his mind about the other matter.

"Well," he said, "expect this ain't the time to start fighting amongst ourselves."

Deuce accepted this concession in silence.

"Anyway," J.J. added, "always happy to have more time to fish."

"What makes you think you're gonna have more time to fish?"

"Oh?"

"Part of the deal is, you stay on the committee."

"Me?" Negotiating was all well and good, but sitting around while somebody else did the talking, now that was an entirely different kettle of fish. "I ain't the kind of rough rider you're looking for."

"Maybe not, but you got a sense of humor."

J.J. laughed. "And I intend to keep it."

Deuce craned around and gave him one of his cardplayer's looks.

J.J. sighed. *The true angler would never go fishing just to avoid trouble*, he thought, making up an aphorism on the spot. "You're asking a lot, you know."

Deuce nodded, dead serious.

"Okay," J.J. said finally, "but I'm gonna hold you to your promise."

"Promise?"

"'Something different,' you said."

At this, Deuce looked up and off into the distance, as if he had suddenly been struck by an idea. Then he turned his gaze back toward J.J. "But you like the silence, too, right?"

"Yup."

Deuce nodded again. "Fair enough."

He said no more, and they continued to fish, J.J. sitting on his stool and jigging his line and feeling a little guilty—about Aggie, not about the fate of his fellow unionists. He considered that and decided, yes, probably it was time for him to step aside.

CHAPTER 23

~

Walter wheezed next to El, like a man laboring up a hill. His head hit the pillow, he was asleep. She supposed it had something to do with his profession. As for El, she could climb into bed dog tired and began to fade off only to suddenly snap back awake, as if she had passed through some small antechamber and been shown the instruments of her release only to have them snatched away, leaving her in the great glaring hall where all her assorted problems patiently waited, confident of her speedy return.

Someone once told her you got 80 percent of the benefit of sleep by just lying there, so she did that. Perhaps, she imagined, a life could be lived without sleep, just intervals of lying down. In communication with your personal demons. She knew, at any rate, where the Catholics got their idea of purgatory.

Outside, she could hear the night sounds of the city, her city, the acceleration of cars climbing the bluff, an occasional siren, the tolling of the hours in Town Clock Plaza. From the pattern of the explosive rising and dying away of the diesels, she followed along as the trucks snaked through town, naming the streets to herself as they went.

A streetlight at the foot of the driveway cast its glow across the drawn curtains, mixed tonight with the slightly whiter light of a full moon, the room oppressively bright.

The luminous dial on the bedside clock read 1:30. The night had hardly begun. Her body ached. She shifted around, trying to get comfortable, but whatever position she tried, the aching returned almost immediately, and finally she just flopped onto her back and went limp and exhaled impatiently. Walter wheezed away, dreaming happily of floods or El Niño or blizzards or who knows what.

She tried not to go over for the umpteenth time the Bugsy Dolan fiasco, but since it was impossible not to think about *something*, she ran that tape again, torturing herself with how simple it would have been to avoid the whole sorry business. At the end of this act of contrition, she added the moral of the story: if you don't have a plan of your own, you're condemned to pursue the stratagems of others. Even of so sleazy a character as the infamous Bugsy.

What made the Dolan episode such bitter fruit was that El did have...well, not a plan exactly, more like a vision, although one locked securely inside...a sense of...she didn't know...not something so specific as a city ordinance, certainly...more the planting of seeds of empathy...a possibility to be grasped were she but clever enough, willing enough...but which she remained utterly powerless to describe to the people of Jackson except in silly ways...as if the truly good, like the name of God in the Old Testament, could not be uttered.

And now this petition that was supposed to be going around town...this new trouble on top of all the others.

Outside, a car with a faulty muffler climbed the hill past the house. Lights moved across the ceiling of the bedroom, which meant that the car had swung into the driveway. She thought it must intend to turn around, but the lights continued to shine on the ceiling, not steadily but shimmering, almost vibrating.

After a minute, she threw the covers off, padded across the cold floor, and parted the curtains enough to see out.

The headlights blinded her. She could make out nothing, only some sort of vehicle, idling, canted sharply upward because of the slope of the driveway. She withdrew slightly, letting the curtain swing back, but continued to look through the chink until her eyes adjusted to the glare and she could identify the silhouette of a pickup truck. The truck pulsed, its headlights jittering up and down. It seemed to ride high off the ground, as if elevated on heavy-duty shock absorbers, the way certain young men rigged their vehicles, called high riders or something like that, a sign of manhood.

Although she must have been seen when she opened the curtains, whoever it was made no move to leave. For one, two, three minutes, she and the truck remained where they were, in a kind of suspended animation as the unease she had felt at first passed over into irritation.

She couldn't make out the license plate, but wouldn't it be nice, she decided, to know just who it was. However, almost immediately after she had turned to go to the phone, she heard the engine revving, and by the time she returned to the window, the truck was backing out.

She watched as it climbed the hill with insolent deliberation and disappeared.

∼

Just over four hours later, El and Aggie Klauer went silently up toward the brow of the bluff, leaning into the slope, following the very course that El's night visitor had taken. For once, El took the lead, striding with great energy, head down, pumping her arms and legs. Soon she was panting, and Aggie, with her quick, light steps, pranced by.

The exertion didn't help. El didn't feel any better. Aggie, seeing her lagging behind, for once didn't bully her to keep up but slackened her own pace.

"I couldn't sleep," El told her, and then described the incident with the pickup truck.

When she had finished, Aggie said, "Maybe they were just talking or something. Maybe it didn't have anything to do with you."

El shook her head. "I've started to get letters, too."

"Letters?"

"Hate mail."

"About the Bugsy Dolan business?"

"That's part of it. You wouldn't believe what people are capable of saying."

"Threats?"

"A few. But mostly just people giving me what for."

"Have you gone to the police?"

"I have. But the actionable ones are never signed. Hardly any of them are signed." Even beyond any threat to herself, El found something so very dispiriting about such letters, people removing their public faces and giving her a glimpse of what lay below.

Aggie stopped them both long enough to give El a hug. "What can I do?"

El just shook her head and started off again. She wanted to keep moving.

Catching up, Aggie said, "It's not fair. You're not the reason that the black contractor got the dog track job."

Yes, El thought, *but*... "It's not just that. It's the promotion of Sam Turner, too. I was the one who forced that issue, remember? And the museum exhibit. I'm the chair of the board. And, of course, I'm also on the integration task force. Some people have put all these facts together and come to the obvious conclusion."

Aggie, a step ahead of El, was shaking her head. "I still say it's not you, El. You didn't start any of those things. You were just doing what had to be done."

"Makes no difference. Makes no earthly difference who started them or why. They're mine now. Maybe you're right about the pickup last night, maybe it didn't mean anything, but there's no mistaking the letters."

Aggie continued to shake her head in the determined little way she had when she had decided to be stubborn about something.

"But even if *you're* right about the truck, El—and everything else—these are just a few crumb-bums blowing off steam."

Which brought them back to the proposition that most Jacksonians were decent people who would never dream of doing such things—the conversation they had had a couple of walks ago.

"Perhaps," El said. "I suppose you've heard about the petition?"

"What petition?" Aggie stopped again, and El had to shoo her on.

"I found out last night. There's a move to force an election."

"An election? You mean, for mayor?"

"That's right."

"Isn't it too late?"

"They've got two weeks from when I was appointed. That still gives them plenty of time. They only need 130 signatures."

"They?"

"The people I've talked to don't know who's doing it." Just some of Aggie's good citizens of Jackson, El wanted to say, but didn't.

"Oh, El." Aggie had turned around and was jogging backwards.

"I must say, Ag, that all in all the last few days haven't been the best in my life."

Aggie laughed. "Boy, I guess."

"We should have just gone ahead and had an election in the first place."

"How could you know?"

"We just wanted to save a few dollars. And, of course, nobody likes to campaign. I certainly don't."

"But there was no way you could know."

They rounded the corner that brought them into full view in the display window of Keefer's Market. El looked at their reflections, Aggie bobbing along like a cork in a stream, while El resembled some waterlogged thing about to go to the bottom. Yet, for the moment at least, she didn't feel that way. Her fitful and oppressive night thoughts had gradually been reshaping themselves into something firmer and more determined.

"I'll tell you one thing, Aggie—I am going to run. Last night, after I found out, I was seriously thinking about not doing it. Better that I should concentrate on the job while I still have it. But not now, no way. If they think they can scare me, they're wrong."

"I could have told them that."

"I won't be elected. In the privacy of the voting booth, people will vote with their hearts."

"You don't know what they'll do." The decent-people-of-Jackson argument again.

"Well," El observed, nothing to be gained by arguing the matter, "we're going to find out."

Aggie said wistfully, "If only Bugsy Dolan had gotten the contract at the track."

"I'm sorry it didn't go to a local guy." But of all the might-have-beens in her life, this one, El decided, had been a pipe dream from the start. "As for Dolan, no matter how many times I kissed that particular frog, he was never going to turn into a prince."

Aggie snorted, "The story of my life," but that was another subject, for another time.

They picked up the pace and went on in silence. El's thoughts returned to the eerie vision of the truck pulsating at the foot of her driveway. In her years on committees and commissions and finally the council, she'd had trouble with people from time to time, but nothing like this. Yet she experienced a kind of recognition, too, a clarity. Perhaps it was just as well that she had no chance of being elected mayor.

"I've been thinking that maybe it's time to go back to the idea of recruiting black professionals to come live here," she told her friend. An old idea, much debated, often rejected. And, to be sure, not a great idea, but so far as El could tell, there were no great ideas.

"Won't that just make matters worse?"

"I don't know. We've talked about it enough. And after the *New York Times* story and what it's done to the reputation of the city…"

Aggie considered this and said, "If you do it, you'll want to do it quietly." El noted how solemn her friend had suddenly become.

"No," El told her, "we've got to shout it from the rooftops."

They were moving at a fair clip again, back down Grandview toward their starting point. Daylight struggled in beneath the solid cover of storm clouds. Yet another storm, but a small, quick-moving one, Walter had promised, nothing to worry about.

"It's not good enough, getting blacks and whites to live together," Aggie warned her, "not even cheek by jowl. They've got to work together, too. Solve problems together."

El, in her contrary state of mind, seized the pointed end of this idea rather than the handle. "I wish you'd tell that to the black community."

"Perhaps they know something you don't."

"And perhaps I know something they don't," El countered. How many of them had been the victims of the kind of hate mail El had been getting?

As they walked on, with these decisions made, El felt better, almost as if her depression had lifted. Which, of course, it hadn't. But Aggie was a sympathetic devil's advocate. That helped. Thank God for Aggie.

They chatted now, mulling over the hopelessness of the situation.

"Who's going to manage your campaign?" Aggie asked.

El hadn't given the matter a thought. "Anybody who wants to, I suppose." Seemed pointless to waste somebody's time on such a fruitless enterprise.

"What about me?" Aggie asked.

"You?"

"I know I haven't got any experience. You could get somebody better. But I'd be honored. And I'd work my fanny off."

"I'm sure you would, dear. And do a super job. The problem wouldn't be you, it'd be your candidate."

They continued on, haggling over the matter, El finding herself buoyed up, despite her better judgment, by Aggie's enthusiasm.

Animated now, their steps lighter, they picked up the pace a bit more, then a little more, until by the time they arrived back at El and Walter's old Vic they were chugging along as of old.

CHAPTER 24

~

When Deuce walked out of the water plant at 7 a.m., the yellow city pickup had already arrived, parked not in the plant lot but on the other side of the street, a symbolic gesture, he understood. He crossed over and got in. Bob One sat at the wheel, Bob Two slid over to make room.

"How you doin'?" Deuce asked as he climbed in.

"No complaints," Bob One said pleasantly. Deuce hadn't been part of the hostilities between water and wastewater, which was the reason, he assumed, Bob One had been willing to talk to him at all.

The two Bobs were on their daily round, checking the pump stations that lifted the sewage so that it could gravity flow down to the treatment facility.

"Not too cherry a day," Bob Two said. Pellets of snow, a thin scattering, peppered the windshield.

If the water plant people were meticulous about their work clothes, their carefully pressed shirts with the little water symbol above the pocket, the shit plant guys were a good deal less particular. Bob One's were worn to a dull purple color, with a ragged red-and-black hunting jacket and encrusted boots. He drove with his chin above the steering wheel, his arms wrapped around it. His beard had begun to go white, the long white hairs reminding Deuce of the guard hairs of a wild animal.

He parked at the Mechanic Street pumping station. Inside, much of the equipment was similar to stuff in the water plant: pumps, controllers, gauges.

Deuce followed as Bob Two clattered down the iron stairs to the intake. In the dimness below, he raked rags and other debris from the grating which screened the incoming sewage. Sewage had its own stench, not like shit, less repugnant, more sinister.

Deuce took stock as he waited. Peeling green paint on the concrete walls. I-beams. Flow meter box on the side of the effluent pipe. Red wheels used to open and close the valves. Heavy piping with elbows and bolted flanges. Thin electrical conduit hung from trapezes. Rusty metal catwalks and switchback stairs. Next to him rotated the shaft of a pump, the catwalk vibrating slightly, the sounds of spinning shaft, rushing water below, motor overhead. All very familiar…except the smell. He climbed back up the stairs.

"Heard you were gonna take over the negotiations for the big union," Bob One said.

"Might."

Bob One nodded, a gesture of mild curiosity. Didn't have anything to do with him. He tapped the gauge on the chlorine cylinder.

"Need chlorine!" he yelled down to Bob Two, who yelled something back, his voice like howling in the deep, narrow, concrete structure.

"To control odor?" Deuce asked. He knew a little about the operation down at wastewater.

"That's right, don't want to kill the bugs. Need them healthy."

Deuce watched as the two Bobs switched chlorine cylinders using a small overhead crane.

"If I do take over the negotiations," he told them, "we're not going to get much done unless we're all in it together."

"That right?" Bob One said.

Bob One and his friends didn't give a rat's ass about employee solidarity. The people down at the shit plant thought of themselves as the elite among the grunts working for the city. They collected the city's sewage and treated it mechanically, chemically, biologically, every which way. They filtered it, set armies of bugs loose to devour it, cooked it, chlorinated it, chlorinated it again. They had machinery up the wazoo, constantly being corroded and plugged up and overloaded because, of course, of all the crap people disposed of in the system, thinking, out of sight, out of mind. The wastewater boys stood at the asshole of the city, and dealt with all the shit, and as for recognition, well… So they hung out together and had an attitude, and Deuce could talk about employee solidarity all he wanted, but it didn't mean squat.

Deuce was sorely tempted to leave them be, but he knew that if he was going to put any kind of pressure on Paul Cutler and the city council, he needed Bob One and his friends back in the union.

In the truck once more, they headed on out.

"Tell me what your major problem is right now," Deuce asked. Bob One remained mute. This was Deuce's show. He'd have to do the talking, like it or not. "Okay, I'll tell you. JackPack's closed, so you're screwed." The Pack had sent a huge load of organics down to the treatment plant, and, of course, had paid to have it processed. Now the organics were gone and with it all that income.

"So we're screwed," Bob One said. "What's it to you?"

"How many layoffs you figure?"

"Dunno."

He probably had a good idea, but he wasn't about to volunteer any information.

"Anyway," Deuce told him, "what you want is no layoffs."

Bob One hunched up over his steering wheel. "You get us that, Houdini, you can write your own ticket."

Deuce thought about his father. In Deuce's shoes, the old man would've sought a no-layoff pledge from the city, then not budged an inch as he went down in flames...the self-righteous bastard.

"We could try," he told Bob One, "but no way will Cutler go for a pledge like that."

"Yeah," Bob One agreed, "I believe you're right."

"And I didn't come here to make all kinds of crazy promises I got no way of keeping."

"Why then, Houdini? If you got no rabbits in your hat, what good are ya?" Bob One spoke mildly, his questions perfectly reasonable.

"Notice how the fire department's started to flag the hydrants?" Bob Two said as they passed a street corner where a hydrant had been dug out of a huge embankment of snow. Bob Two kept his eye on the road and limited himself to incidental comments. He was a young guy and knew his place.

"Maybe there ain't no rabbits," Deuce told Bob One. "Maybe, maybe not. Let me ask you—suppose you was in charge, what would you do, lay people off?"

"Hell, no. Look," Bob One said, suddenly animated, "for twenty years we've gone from one catastrophe to another. Never done a lick of preventive maintenance. You put me in charge, I don't lay off nobody. I'd take the extra guys and make up a team to do nothing but preventive stuff. Double the lifetime of the plant that way."

"What are the chances of that happening?"

"The Cubbies'll win the World Series first."

They pulled into the Terminal Street lift station, which sat in the middle of the tank farm south of the Ice Harbor.

Inside, Bob Two turned off the pump, filled up load cells with distilled water, and then turned the pump back on.

"Listen," Bob One said.

From deep in the well came a faint squealing sound.

"Cavitating," Bob One said, "that's what it sounds like to me."

"Could be."

"Impeller gettin' eaten away, maybe. That's what I'm talkin' about, Houdini. Preventive maintenance. But nobody gives a shit."

Back in the truck, Deuce said, "So okay, what's the problem then? What's the real problem?"

Bob One shook his head.

"Management," Deuce told him. "Layoffs ain't the disease, they're just the damn symptom."

"Paul Cutler," Bob One said. "You know, we've never seen his ass down at the treatment plant, not once. The guy has no idea what goes on there."

"My point, exactly."

"Yeah, right, Houdini, but knowing the problem's one thing, doing something about it somethin' entirely different."

"True enough," Deuce admitted. He'd been looking for that something. He'd talked to union guys in other cities. He'd poked around in the Jackson library. He'd even been up to the U. and picked the brains of a couple of the professors in the poly sci department. Nothing he'd read or heard so far had much interested him. Maybe nothing would. Maybe this was all just a fool's errand.

"I know one thing, Bob. If we're going to be successful, whatever the hell we do, like I said, we've all got to be in the thing together."

"Roadkill," said Bob Two.

Bob One said, "Humph."

"I'm not asking for any commitment now," Deuce told him.

"So what are you doing?"

"Okay, this is the deal, you don't think much of the water plant guys, fair enough, I'm not in love with all of them myself.

But suppose, just suppose, the union's got a chance of getting something done—not now, but whenever—then I'm asking you to join again."

Bob One said nothing.

"An open mind, that's all I'm asking for. Check things out. See what's coming down."

"And what do we get out of it?"

"Get?" Deuce knew that Bob's people would be looking for some sort of payback. The old grievance with the water plant guys still stuck in their craws. Well, that was tough. But he was willing to put his cards on the table. "How the hell do I know? I don't even know what I'm going to do yet. Basically, it'll be all or nothing, we either win some concessions or we get our asses handed to us."

Bob One nodded.

The road curved down into the valley of Catfish Creek. Below, the wastewater plant hove into view, attractive in the distance with its towers and rectangles and domes. Bob One stopped the truck.

He looked across at Deuce. "You can get out here."

"What?" Deuce's car was up at the water plant, clear on the other end of town. Bob One's expression was set.

Deuce stared back at him. "You're kidding."

"You heard me."

What a contrary fuck, Deuce thought, but he knew Bob One wasn't kidding, so he opened the door and climbed out.

"Have a nice day," Bob Two said.

CHAPTER 25

~

Since his wife's death, Fritz Goetzinger didn't drive into the city to do what little shopping he had but out to Baney's Crossing, on the Kleinburg road. Coming back, he might stop at Poor Man's Cafe. He'd known the regulars since before his years in public life, since before the city had annexed his farm, which had started the whole business. So he might stop for a cup of coffee and a little human company at Poor Man's. This morning he stopped, but he didn't have the inclination for human company.

Harley Grant, who had gotten himself into financial trouble in the seventies and hit on the idea of converting his milking shed into the little cafe, was holding forth at the round table in the back. As soon as he saw Fritz, he hailed him over and started gabbing about all the nonsense going on down in the city.

"Nothing to do with me anymore, Harley. Tell me, you got a rifle I can borrow. Something happened to mine."

"Hmm, that right? Well, sure, come on over to the house."

It had been sleeting all day, off and on, salting the road and the old snow. There was no accumulation, no substance to it.

As they were walking across, Harley asked him what he had in mind. Another man, more taciturn, might have loaned the gun, no questions asked, but Harley's natural curiosity always got the better of him.

"Gonna slaughter one of my hogs."

Inside the farmhouse, Harley fetched the gun out of his hall closet and a box of shells from the shelf overhead. "How many?"

"One."

"Here, take a couple. Might miss."

Fritz hefted the weapon, opened and closed the breech, then put the shells into his pocket. "I ain't much of a shot, Harley, but expect I can hit a pig at two paces."

As they walked back, Harley asked him if he was selling animals to Modern Meat.

"No."

"Aim to?"

"Probably. Don't make much difference. Gonna lose the farm anyway."

"The hell you say."

"Yup."

"Damn. A man had as much adversity as you…"

"Way it is."

Harley leaned down to look into the window as Fritz started his pickup. "Anything I can do, you let me know, you hear?"

"Appreciate it," Fritz said through the glass.

He drove back to the farm, the rifle tilted against the passenger's seat.

From the foot of the driveway, where he'd stopped to pick up his mail, he spotted a car parked up above. Maroon. He wondered who it might be. El Plowman, most likely. She favored maroon cars.

His first impulse was to turn the pickup around. He'd never had much use for Plowman. Nothing but a tool of the city manager. Yet she wasn't a stupid woman, and he could only marvel at how fast she'd gotten herself into a peck of trouble as mayor.

He wondered what she wanted. Must want something, no other reason to be there. She had to be pretty damn desperate to come begging at Fritz's door. He contemplated the prospect of refusing her request, whatever it was, and so climbed back into his truck and drove up to the house.

She stood next to her car, her back to the wind, shoulders hunched, unhappy. Fritz got out with the rifle, and they stood silently for a few moments.

"See where my old job don't much agree with you," he observed.

"Tell me," she said, then peered carefully at him before asking, "And how are you doing, Fritz?" They hadn't seen each other since Plowman paid her respects at the funeral home. She glanced uneasily at the rifle he held.

"I'm okay," he said.

He walked toward the house, and Plowman followed and said to his back, "I understand your son is going to take over negotiations for the big union."

Fritz stopped. "What?"

"Haven't you heard? That's the rumor going around, at least."

He wondered if it could possibly be true. Edna would have been pleased. It was a few moments before he could speak again.

"In my experience, rumors ain't worth a damn," he told her.

"Well, maybe not, but that's the word… Anyway, it's not the reason I came. I wanted to discuss something else."

He waited.

"I've been talking to former mayors. They've all agreed to sign a public letter."

"Not interested."

"Don't you even want to hear what it's about?"

He propped the rifle inside the back door, then scooped two cans of birdseed from the container next to it.

"The words of these men still carry weight in Jackson," she told him. "Yours, too, Fritz. We need that now, before things get any worse than they already are."

He cocked an eye toward her. She stood on the doorstep, buffeted by the cold.

"Whose fault is that?"

He walked out toward Edna's feeder, kicking the snow aside as he went. Plowman followed. Now she was talking about some hate mail that she'd gotten.

"Something needs to be done," she said.

"Hell, I got mail. No big deal."

"Not about that. About the whole situation. The fact so few blacks live here. The paranoia people seem to feel. I've been thinking maybe we should go back to the idea of attracting black professionals."

"Wrong time, not with people from the Pack out of work like they are."

"Is there ever a good time? Anyway, we're talking about it again. As for the Pack workers, these new people won't affect them. If anything, they'll help. They'll create new jobs, not take them." She was talking quickly, nervous, or maybe just anxious to get out of the cold.

"They'll have wives and children," Fritz told her. "Everybody in the family works nowadays." One way or another, there'd be less jobs for the locals.

"This is only a hundred families all told, spread over five years."

"Don't make any difference. You talk about bringing one black family to Jackson, the people are gonna be up in arms."

As far as Fritz was concerned, what Plowman had to worry about at the moment wasn't the racial stuff. That came and went, like some kind of recurrent fever. But there were issues all right—discrete, hard, divisive. For instance, the city budget. Cuts would have to be made. And there wasn't anything left to cut, not without somebody got hurt.

The seed made a sound like sleet as he poured it onto the feeder.

"What you gonna do about the budget?" he asked her.

Plowman stood glumly by, snow collapsing into her low boots.

"We haven't decided yet," she said, clipping the words off, since this was not the conversation she had come there to have. But it was the one Fritz was suddenly interested in. He might as well try to do some good. Probably wouldn't get him anywhere, hadn't in the past, but he might as well try.

"You gonna cut back transit again?" he asked her.

"I hope we won't have to, I don't want to, but as you well know, we've got a big shortfall to make up."

He broadcast the remainder of the seed across the snow, then started toward the farrowing shed, Plowman trailing behind him, trying to get back to what she wanted to talk about. "Maybe we can come up with something innovative, some way to maintain the service. We need everyone involved. You, too."

"An innovative plan, huh, like people giving their weekends over to driving little old ladies to the supermarket? Like that?"

"You've never had much respect for volunteer work, have you?"

"Respect got nothing to do with it. It's emptying the ocean with a thimble. It's wishful thinking."

"If you ever wondered, Fritz, why people like myself have always had so much trouble with you, it's because of attitudes like that."

It was fascinating, Fritz had always noticed, how people assumed you just naturally wanted to avoid trouble.

In the farrowing shed, he looked around, making sure everything was in order, adjusting the heat lamp clipped to the slats of the last farrowing crate although it didn't need adjusting.

"You wanna know what to do about the bus system?" he asked her finally.

"Yes."

"Don't cut it."

"That might not be an option."

"The hell it isn't."

Still carrying the cans used for the birdseed, he walked over to the corn storage bin. Out of the corner of his eye, he saw birds at the feeder, a flash of red as a cardinal swept down, scattering the smaller birds. Plowman was chattering about other ways they might cut the budget.

He filled the cans, carried them out to the old oak beyond the machine shed, and dumped the corn on the ground. From the thick lower branch of the tree, he'd rigged a block and tackle.

"There is one other possibility," she told him, "one thing we haven't tried before. If we could do it, most of the rest would be unnecessary."

"What would that be?"

"We're asking the unions for a 10 percent wage concession."

He thought about his son once more.

"Paul came to the council—you missed the meeting, the last one before you resigned—and asked for permission to propose the giveback. It would eliminate the need to lay anyone off. Or cut transit, either."

"You're gonna do that, what about across-the-board cuts?" he asked.

"That's not going to happen, and you know it."

He did know it, knew all the arguments, too. Didn't make any difference.

"We've had our differences in the past, Fritz, but can't we, just for once, lay them aside? Too much has gone wrong already. Look at poor Edna, at your own tragedy. Look at all these other troubles, and more on the way. We need to speak as one now, Fritz, we really do."

This sounded phony to him, nothing but words. "The people I represent, they always got troubles, El. Maybe it's some worse now. Might be."

He had returned the cans to the back porch, and picked up the rifle. "Anyway, you ask me, that ain't why you came up here. Anyone got trouble right about now, it's you." He stared hard at her. "You got your tit in the wringer for sure." She winced. "What the hell were you thinking of, trying to get in bed with the likes of Marion Dolan?" Fritz had no use for Dolan.

"Damn you, Fritz, I was trying to keep jobs in the city."

Fritz shook his head. "Okay, but going to Dolan was stupid."

"Bugs approached me, but yes, it was stupid."

"Stick with what you know somethin' about. If you really wanna do a good deed, like I said, leave the bus system alone. Those people got no other way to get around."

They had arrived at the finishing shed, filled with market-weight animals. Fritz never pretended he could really understand people like El Plowman, whether they were cynical or just naive.

"Tell me, Fritz," she said as he chose an animal and separated it from the others, jockeying like a cowboy cutting a calf out of a herd of cattle, "are you going to organize the opposition, like you did last time?"

The question, blunt as it was, surprised him. "That an invitation?"

"Just a question." She had to speak up so as to be heard over the racket raised by the hogs.

"Don't worry," he told her, "I'm through with you people."

Fritz herded the animal with the barrel of the rifle. The banks of snow formed a chute leading toward the oak. He could hear El's footsteps behind him, a hesitant crumping across the hard-packed snow.

The hog kept looking back. Birds, apparently those displaced from the feeder, had found the corn on the ground, but at the approach of the small procession were scattered once more.

"I'm out of it," he repeated. "I'm sick of trying to get you people to do what you oughta." He thought about something else. "I'll tell you one thing, the employees ain't gonna sit still for wage cuts, and no way you'll make 'em stick. Don't think you and Paul Cutler are gonna eliminate weekend service or whatever just like that, either. Maybe you got such a low opinion of the people who ride the buses you think they can't mount a fight on their own. You got another think coming." And this reminded him of something else. "That holds for blacks coming to Jackson, too."

"It's talk like this, Fritz, which does nothing but make matters worse. All I'm trying to do at the moment is calm things down. Then we can sit down and deal with these matters. I'm open to suggestions. And, okay, I agree, everybody ought to be involved. All I'm asking you to do now is sign this letter with the other mayors. It's a token of goodwill, Fritz. It's a starting point."

"Not interested."

The hog went straight for the corn. Overhead the birds perched in the branches, complaining. The block and tackle swayed slightly in the wind.

"If you're not willing to do even this much, Fritz, then what chance is there that we'll ever settle our differences?"

"Ain't no chance, not without you change first. And I'll tell you what, it pisses me off no end that people like you go around pretending that all we need here is a little goodwill and everything'll be just hunky-dory." Fritz pulled the bolt back, took a shell out of his pocket and snapped it into the breech. "Life ain't like that." In a single quick movement, he lifted the gun to his shoulder, aimed behind the animal's ear, and fired.

CHAPTER 26

~

Aggie Klauer shut the door to her office and limbered up, as she always did before a session with the big union. Then, given the uniqueness of the occasion, she took an extra few moments to compose herself. People imagined she was always in charge, bouncy and upbeat, as if there was a bouncy-and-upbeat gene. Today, anticipating a new negotiator on the other side of the table, she'd fussed more than usual over her getup, but each adjustment seemed to make matters worse, so she'd finally decided to hell with it. She closed her eyes, exhaled, and reminded herself that whatever happened, life would go on.

Then she was off, moving briskly down the hall, thinking hard-nosed thoughts to get in the proper frame of mind. As usual, the others were already in the little room used for negotiations. At other times, she would smile and nod at the union people as soon as she came through the door, but today she refrained from looking at them. She sat down, resting her fingertips briefly on the wrist of the steno by way of a greeting and nodding to the city finance director on her other side. She placed the legal notepad she used on the table, folded her hands before her, and only at that point looked up, into the cool and distant gaze of Deuce Goetzinger.

Since she hadn't received any formal notification of the change, she said, "Well, what have we here?"

J.J. Dusterhoft, sitting next to Goetzinger, did the honors. "The starting pitcher got a little tired, so we've brought in our relief ace."

Aggie chewed the corner of her lower lip and looked back and forth between the two men. "Strange, nobody mentioned anything about an ace to me."

Aggie and Goetzinger sat back and regarded each other. In the son, Aggie saw Fritz Goetzinger, although Deuce lacked his father's patchy hair and glowering look. As a matter of fact, the younger

Goetzinger was rather good-looking, and Aggie could see why he'd had success with women. Back from his smooth, pale forehead, his hair flowed—curly, silky fine, a honey brown color. She resisted the urge to reach up and adjust her own hair yet one more time. Goetzinger's eyes were gray and vivid, his mouth ironic. He had the practiced passivity she imagined to be the hallmark of the good poker player.

"Well, Mr. relief ace, I believe it's your pitch."

Still without having said a word, Goetzinger opened his folder and passed out the union's counterproposal. The session began.

Even as they went from item to item, Goetzinger said very little, and Aggie found this off-putting after J.J.'s expansive devil-may-care style. She found herself moving not from statement to statement, but from silence to silence. She felt his eyes on her, appraising.

She must have encountered Goetzinger before, yet try as she might, she couldn't remember. She'd been the administrative assistant to the former personnel director when Goetzinger was hired. She'd done most of the orientations for new employees, but still, she just couldn't remember him. He'd gone to work up at the water plant, of course, so he didn't often turn up at the Hall. And the city employees at the outlying facilities tended to form their own little closed-off subcultures.

No, she didn't remember. Of course, she knew about Deuce. Everybody knew about him.

In the counteroffer, the union repeated its wage demand. No movement there. A new article about no-layoffs. She expected that. A couple of others, familiar stuff. Not much to work with.

"Looks like everybody got to put in his favorite demand."

"His or her."

Aggie smiled to herself at this jibe. Deuce Goetzinger, the great woman's libber.

As she idly leafed through the document again, back to front, she noticed something she'd missed the first time in her haste to get to the union counter on wages. Another new article, inserted just after the boilerplate at the beginning. Barely two lines long, easy to miss.

"Hmm," she said as she read it, then looked across at Goetzinger.

His eyes were such a startling gray. A slight smile settled on his lips, the upper rather thin, the lower plump and pale. Between his eyes and mouth a certain tension resided, as if the eyes took back what the mouth gave.

"What's this?" Aggie wondered aloud.

"Just a little something we tossed in." He made the motion of a poker player dealing a card.

"A committee?" The new article called for the formation of a committee, made up of members from each city department.

Deuce nodded.

Beyond the demand for the committee, however, and the requirement that it be broadly inclusive, the article remained mute. "And just what's this committee supposed to do?" Aggie asked.

"No instructions."

"None?"

She waited for him to elaborate. He didn't.

"It's beyond the scope, you understand," Aggie pointed out. In a matter such as this, the city wasn't required to negotiate.

"But it's permitted," Deuce quickly rejoined. That was true as well. The city could negotiate, should they choose. Aggie imagined what Paul Cutler would say.

She leaned back and clasped her hands together behind her head. "A committee, huh?"

He nodded slowly.

"Frankly, you don't seem like the committee type to me."

"I love committees."

"Oh?"

What was she missing here? Seeking a friendly face, she turned toward J.J. "Committee?"

Deuce didn't give J.J. a chance to answer. "I'm the negotiator for the union now, I believe."

Barbara Amos looked mighty pleased with herself. As for J.J., he raised one eyebrow and tilted his head slightly to the side, as if to say, "A new disposition, hon."

A new disposition, indeed. But what the hell was it? A committee with no instructions?

Aggie turned back toward Deuce, who sat with the same deadpan cardplayer's expression on his face. She gave him her best imitation of a sage nod and said, "I see. All right, but you understand, this isn't an item we're required to negotiate."

Deuce looked at her with his cool, penetrating, gray eyes. "But you can," he said.

∼

As she walked upstairs to report to Paul Cutler, she mulled over the union's proposal. It had always annoyed Aggie that she thought more clearly when alone than under the gaze of others, a miserable failing in a negotiator, one she tried to paper over as best she could with all her prep work. People often told her what a sharp little cookie she was, but Aggie knew the truth.

Anyway, the pressure gone, her mind began to roam freely over the possibilities.

And suddenly she understood; she knew exactly what Deuce Goetzinger was up to. "Of course." She snapped her fingers. "Ha!"

After Paul had wrapped up the meeting he was in and the two of them were alone, she quickly outlined the union's latest offer. The city manager was not pleased.

She left the odd new article for last.

"A committee?" he said, reacting with the same incredulity she had.

"That's what they call it."

Catching her tone, he asked, "What they call it?"

"Right. But in really it's a little different from your usual… oh, I don't know, strictly functional, let's-get-this-job-done set of bureaucratic drudges. In fact, it's sort of a legislative body, that's what I think the idea is."

His expression contracted. "A what?"

She smiled. Only in the telling was she really beginning to appreciate the ploy. "A kind of representative body. Think about it. It's made up of people from all the city departments, given no instructions."

"They can't be serious."

She thought about that. "I don't know."

Paul frowned and shook his head. "So, tell me, just how is this 'representative body' supposed to work?"

"No instructions."

"And what, precisely, does that mean?" Aggie noted his impatience. He could have figured it out for himself quickly enough, had he been the kind of man who appreciated surprises.

She considered how best to present it. "Well, I suppose a suitable analogy might be the Constitutional Convention. When was it—1787? A bunch of guys in powdered wigs, everybody with his own agenda, starting from scratch. That's what Deuce Goetzinger has in mind, I think...without the powdered wigs, of course."

"He wants to make city hall into a democracy?"

"Yes, precisely, I think that's exactly the idea."

"A democracy?" Paul said incredulously. "But I like being emperor."

"Well, of course," Aggie agreed, "who wouldn't?"

Paul suddenly laughed, his laugh as low and full as his voice. He gripped the arms of his chair and stared up at the ceiling. "Unbelievable." He looked back at Aggie. Like Deuce's, Paul's eyes were striking, in his case as pale as if they'd been blasted by radiation, that's what Aggie had always thought, like a blind man or perhaps an alien in a movie. "They've *got* to be kidding," he said.

"I don't know," she repeated.

He shook his head. "Okay, so tell me about this Deuce Goetzinger person, the mayor's son—excuse me, the ex-mayor's son...what else?"

Paul leaned on his elbow, one finger laid upon his lips. He had an exaggerated, almost aggressive way of listening when something really caught his attention.

"Worked for the city for seven years. Water plant operator. Good employee. One interesting item, up until a few days ago he wasn't even in the union. He went to the clerk last Friday and authorized checkoff..."

"I understand he has a reputation."

"Oh, my, does he." Aggie shook her head. She told Paul what she knew about his womanizing and gambling.

"They must think," he said meditatively, "that there's some sort of connection between poker and union negotiating." He sat up and made a halfhearted attempt to straighten his clothes, which always got more disheveled as the day wore on. "So, do you suppose this democracy ploy is Goetzinger's idea?"

"I don't know."

"Maybe he got it from his father."

"Maybe, but I understand the father and son don't get along."

Paul rubbed his hand down his tie, an ironing motion, and said, "Well, no matter. Obviously, given his background, it's not principled," the statement flat, the collegial atmosphere of a few moments before now replaced by the power of authority to define the situation.

"I don't know," Aggie said one more time, not willing to concede the point. As Paul was obviously dismissing the union proposal out of hand, she realized that the idea interested her, maybe a lot.

"Consider the source, Aggie," he told her brusquely. "Clearly, they mean to use the committee as a bargaining chip, to trade their MX missile for ours or whatever."

"We could call their bluff," she suggested.

"You know," he said, as if he hadn't heard, "what annoys me is that these people really think that they've got a legitimate proposal, as if they can just make up anything they want and, poof, it becomes a bona fide item of negotiation. Amateurs!"

"We could call their bluff."

"Come on, Aggie. And do what? Offer to exchange the giveback for the committee? As soon as you offer to trade the committee for anything, it's part of the negotiations. No, I don't think so."

Paul's mind was closed. All Aggie would accomplish by pursuing the matter was to call her own judgment into question.

"What did you tell them?" he wanted to know.

"That it wasn't mandatory."

"Good. Next time, you can tell them no dice."

As she left the office, Aggie was bothered. She trailed slowly along the hall. What bothered her wasn't her own instinctive sympathy with Goetzinger's proposal or Paul's utter dismissal of it, his characteristic sureness about things. No, these weren't the problem, but rather—as usual—herself, her own failure to realize how Paul would react and so be prepared to do something about it.

She walked on and soon had perked up again. Probably no big deal. Probably Paul had it right. The union couldn't be serious. When all was said and done, her own interest in some sort of workplace democracy had to be more genuine than theirs. After all, could a cardsharp and playboy like Deuce Goetzinger, practically a con man, surely someone with a low opinion of others, ever really take to heart such an idea?

No, she decided, no, he could not.

CHAPTER 27

~

"Another big storm," Walter reminded her. El had taken to eating in the kitchen now. Looking at Walter comforted her. His very oddness comforted her—the shades down, his weather chart on the fridge, his mind somewhere else. As many meals as she had cooked there, the kitchen was Walter's place, just as every other room in the house belonged to her…or neither of them. Old Vics, like spinster ladies, had a way of keeping to themselves.

Walter's enthusiasm for his work just never seemed to wane. He snooped after his snowstorms with a canine single-mindedness. People, who were always pretty incidental to his worldview anyway, became utterly superfluous. Whenever she came into the kitchen, he would either ignore her or seem as surprised as if some stranger had walked in on him. That was Walter.

"Another one?" she complained. "Are you sure?"

"As bad as the first is my guess."

"Could it miss us?"

He started to explain about the upper wind patterns and the storm track. Walter couldn't talk about the weather without sounding like a TV forecast, which annoyed El, so she cut him off.

Her flower catalogs, the reading of which had been a winter ritual in the past, now lay neglected on the sideboard. The terrible first storm had all but destroyed the makeshift and oft-used covers which were supposed to protect the roses, and so Walter's new announcement just burdened her the more. But what could she do? With so many other disasters to deal with, who had time to worry about mere roses?

"Pray to God," she said, "it misses us."

❧

They left together and stopped to look at the rose bushes and their shabby protection.

The house stood just below the brow of the bluff, partly protected, partly exposed, and snow storms sheared around it, scraping the lawn bare in one place and sculpting massive drifts in another.

Some of the bushes had been completely buried, others left just as completely exposed. Old canvas tarps, too heavy for the job, really, had been cut up and draped over the wooden frames, the frames now fissured and splaying so that the tarps sagged onto the plants, doing as much damage as the snow. One of the frames had completely collapsed, the tarp disappeared. The crown of one of the old roses had been caught and bowed into a drift, only its stem visible.

"Some rosarian I am," she sadly remarked as she surveyed the mess. She was letting her roses down, too, along with everyone else.

Walter came to stand beside her. He put an arm around her, and she rested her head on his shoulder.

She closed her eyes and felt the rough texture of his coat against the side of her head, and almost immediately sensed the beginning of a restlessness in him. Walter's kindness, as sincerely meant as it was, nevertheless had a certain awkwardness about it. He had to remember to be kind. So it wasn't the kindness that El cherished in him so much as the extra effort she knew it required.

"Well, what do you think?" he said. "I've got a couple hours. Maybe we can do something about this."

"Meetings."

"Oh."

Always meetings. She held him tight so he couldn't get away from her just yet. She burrowed her head into the harsh fabric and thought of hair shirts. He wiggled, on the point of trying to free himself.

Suddenly she let go. "Let's do it!"

She rushed inside to make a couple of calls, telling people to proceed without her, then she and Walter rooted around until they found the plans they had used to make the original frames. They drove with these to the lumber yard where they traded and soon had returned, followed by a pickup truck filled with wooden slats cut to size and new tarps, light ones this time.

El dug the snow out from around the plants, grimacing at the damage done to her poor dears, then went down into the cellar to help Walter hammer the frames together. Finally, Walter had to leave. El made more calls, cancelled one meeting, postponed another, then went back to work.

She would have banished all thoughts not containing roses, but no matter how hard she worked, her other troubles sat on her shoulder and simpered in her ear.

The image of the pig being shot returned again and again, as it had since the disturbing encounter with Fritz Goetzinger. She still heard the shot, and saw the animal go stiff-legged and drop, dead in an instant. The cold brutality of the act had shocked her, and it wasn't until much later, after she and Fritz had parted on worse terms than ever, that she realized how commonplace the whole business had really been. She simply never witnessed death, that was the problem. Acts like that occurred all the time. She was no vegetarian. What right did she have to feel shocked? She told herself this and attempted to forget the matter. But the image of the pig collapsing kept coming back, still intense and disturbing, and she would have to go through the whole business of rationalizing it away once more.

She stood up and stretched, then went back to arranging the new blue tarps so that they were stoutly supported above the rose bushes.

As she hammered in the nails for the tie-downs, the frozen ground chipped like rock and the nails refused to hold. She went down into the cellar where she found some spikes Walter used for who-knows-what and a small sledgehammer. She tried these. The frozen surface continued to shatter, but as she kept pounding, the point of the spike caught in a soft cyst or crevice and held. She liked the feeling of the small sledge in her hand, its head so heavy that the hammer almost swung itself and all she had to do was aim. She picked up the next spike.

All day she worked like this, begging out of meetings as she went. And finally, as the dusk settled around her, her mind grew calm. For a few minutes, the creature on her shoulder slumbered.

Finished at last, she stood back and inspected her work, satisfied. One thing, at least, done right. She lingered there and held that feeling for as long as she could.

What next? she wondered. But even in asking the question, she knew what the answer was.

She went inside. Her hands stung as she washed them. Cold sores lay in thick raw bands across her knuckles, spotted with dots of dried blood. The pain felt good.

In the kitchen, she sat on the Hitchcock chair next to the phone table and stared at her hands, large and raw, more those of a man than a woman. The seams on her fingers were thin red lacerations, like a myriad of paper cuts. She sniffed her fingertips, the bag balm she used for hand lotion, and beneath still a trace of the cold smell of soil.

She picked up the phone. Paul Cutler wasn't going to like this. No matter. She dialed the newspaper and asked for the city hall reporter and told him that transit system funds would not be cut, not if she had anything to say about it.

It sounded strange to hear Fritz's words coming out of her mouth, but that couldn't be helped. What they needed were more riders, not less service.

That call completed, she made a second, to Reiny down at the museum. She had told him before that he couldn't mount an exhibit laying out the history of racism in Jackson. Now she told him to go ahead and do it, that she'd changed her mind and would arrange a meeting of the historical society board to get formal approval. They needed to keep the bus system, but people simply had to confront their prejudice, too.

She hung up. Probably she'd live to regret these calls, but at the moment she felt liberated, righteous, happy…as if it really was a simple world…as if she really could do the right thing. There would be an election in a couple months and she wouldn't be mayor anymore. But in the meantime, she would live by her own lights. That promise she made to herself. A lesson her roses had taught her.

Part III

CHAPTER 28

～

El struggled into her coat and made the required good-byes and then hurried into the night, down the mansion steps and along the circular driveway past the cars of the other museum board members.

The wind had picked up, the moon fuzzy through a scrim of clouds, Walter's next storm almost on top of them already. She ducked her head into the folds of her scarf and walked faster. Her rose-protecting euphoria of a few days earlier had entirely disappeared. She felt like a woman who every day finds another chip in her best china.

Behind her the door opened and closed, steps coming after, sharp and quick, brittle like the midwinter cold. She sighed and turned to meet them. Reiny Kopp. He didn't bother with preliminaries, singing out while still several paces away, "I knew that was going to happen." He almost seemed pleased.

El waited for him to get close, so she wouldn't have to raise her voice.

"Certainly it fits your definition of the world." She should have known herself; that's what comes of being in a good mood. Yet, she had expected a little more openness on the museum board's part, a willingness to discuss the matter, at least, given recent events.

Catching up, Reiny lowered his own voice, the hint of pleasure gone. "You didn't even put up a fight."

Behind him, the Phillips mansion rose into the night, studded with salients and recesses and a long ridgeline with a dentition of dormers. In the faded moonlight, the large, elaborate structure cast shadows on itself. She looked at this as she decided what to say.

"It would have made a difference?"

"Might."

"As soon as Evy spoke, it was over." The others ever-mindful of the fact that Evy Phillips provided more than a quarter of the museum's budget. El ever-mindful, too. Only Reiny didn't care about such matters.

"Look, I'm sorry," she told him. "Sometimes you accept the inevitable. Now if you'll excuse me, it's been a long day…" She turned and continued toward her car.

There'd been another reason she put up only token resistance. As she'd listened to the arguments on the side of caution, she remembered the lack of enthusiasm in the black community. And she remembered something else that she already knew—her life seemed to consist of reminding herself of things already known— which was that the problem here lay deeper, far below the depth to which any museum exhibit might hope to excavate.

"Bunch of fucking cowards," Reiny sulked, walking beside her, his hands thrust deep into the pockets of his long topcoat, whipping its skirts impatiently around his legs, first one way, then the other. "Just like the others." He meant the black community.

"Put up the old exhibit as best you can," she told him.

"Why bother? It'll be shitty. It'll be worse than shitty, El—it'll be irrelevant."

"No, it won't."

Reiny's bony skull punched a hole out of the nightscape, a dark silhouette, like a rebuke. Thinking of her own gloomy state, El imagined that people like Reiny were never depressed. Their anger protected them.

"You're a genius at making do," she encouraged him. "You've done superb exhibits when you had nothing to work with. You can do it this time, too."

He jerked his thumb back toward the house. "They're just out to avoid trouble. Afraid to offend friggin' anybody. Shit, El, this town'll never change."

"What makes you think they want it to? Change is drugs in the schools and road rage. Change is what they see on the evening news. You can't blame them."

"There's already drugs in the school."

"All the more reason."

"All the more reason to do nothing? You've gotta be kidding."

El brought the conversation back to the matter at hand. "Good or bad, we have to put the exhibit back up."

"Bull," Reiny said.

He wasn't in control. El thought she should try to calm him down, if only it didn't take such an effort.

"Maybe we should try your approach, Reiny, I don't know, maybe. I was willing…but it's simply not going to happen."

"We'll see," he said.

"Like it or not," she repeated, curtly, "we remount the old."

Reiny said nothing. He was certainly capable of pulling some sort of Abbie Hoffman stunt if El didn't sit on him.

"Remember what I said," she warned as she climbed into her car. "No funny business."

She drove out the long, straight driveway, the straightness suggesting the power that families like Evy Phillips's once had in the city. Still had where the museum was concerned. The dark prairie uplands looped beneath the failing moonlight. Scarves of snow, still fresh from the last storm, blew in the rising night wind. Ahead of her, the lights of the city reflected from the thin overcast.

What had made her think she could twist the board around her little finger? Were all mayors touched by the mad belief they might force a scene?

Only with effort could she shunt her inadequacies aside for the moment and try to imagine what she might still do in the short time she had left as mayor. She'd lose the election, of course. The future was mostly opaque, but she knew that much. She'd lose the election. She didn't have a prayer.

So if she wanted to do something, she'd have to act fast. Most of her time had already been spoken for. The budget fight was under way. Plus the endless efforts to attract new business to the city, and to save the old. Around these monoliths would swarm the host of lesser problems that eroded each day away. She refused to consider the possibility of Walter's massive spring flood, too gruesome to contemplate. All this…all this…and now the museum vandalism and the *New York Times* story and the hopeless question of what they could possibly do about it all. What can you do after all the laws are in place but the evil remains, lodged in people's minds and hearts and souls?

Though she felt guilty worrying about herself, too, El did worry. She had finally become mayor. For forty years, in and out of the long, shallow troughs of depression, her life had been a preparation, even if, grappling with whatever matter was to hand, she had possessed little sense of that long trajectory. And now this, this brief and meager summation of it all.

Perhaps it was true that only the journey mattered. Perhaps destinations were always small deaths...or large ones. Perhaps the task she had been given at the moment was simply to accept whatever happened.

A few houses were scattered over the prairie, their lights like campfires. She would have turned off the road and stopped, just to be alone in the darkness, under the moon, but the snow banks crowded down to the edge of the road. So she drove on.

CHAPTER 29

~

Jack Kelley got up even earlier than usual—just after five. He sat for a moment on the edge of the bed, stunned, fighting the urge to lie back down. Janelle flopped over and mumbled unhappily and started to get up herself.

"It's early," he said. "Go back to sleep."

She ignored this. They'd been married thirty years, and she'd always gotten up when he did, whatever the hour. When he went to take a leak at two, she was sure to roll out of bed immediately afterwards and go take one of her own.

The mattress sagged, and he could sense her at his back, sitting on the other edge, shell-shocked, too.

"It's only five," she said, her voice husky. For any change in routine, she would seek an explanation. He wondered how much he could get away with not telling her.

What he had in mind, she'd never guess. He considered saying simply that he couldn't sleep, but she knew he slept like a dead man. A claim of insomnia would only make her more suspicious.

"Letters to write. I can think better when nobody else is in the office." This explanation had the benefit of being partially true.

He heard her rubbing her face vigorously. "Dictate them to whosits."

"Gayle."

"Her."

"I'm worried about the wording."

"What's so important?"

Once entered upon a conversation with his wife, Jack had no graceful exit. Janelle would get satisfaction, or they'd have a fight. One or the other. A finesse job was out of the question.

"I need to light a fire under the concessionaire."

"The concessionaire?"

"We should have plans from them by now."

"You don't have the plans?"

"That's right."

"So you're gonna get the plans?"

"That's right," he said warily.

"It figures."

"What do you mean, it figures?"

"Once again, Jack, yet one more time, you're gonna do somebody else's job. Anything with the concessionaire, the racing association's supposed to do it. Tell me they're not."

Janelle was always looking out for Jack's interests. She considered him unreliable in such matters.

He fended her off as best he could. "This is technical. The concessionaire will have hundreds of devices that need to be installed." He thought it might help so he added, "I want to set up a meeting out here to make sure we're all playing from the same sheet of music," but this turned out to be a mistake.

"The association's got nobody can set up a meeting? Can't set up a meeting, can't write a letter. An impressive bunch you got yourself hooked up with, Jack."

As they had been talking, they'd gotten up and started their morning ablutions.

"They can't write the letter I want to write," Jack called into the closet, where Janelle changed so he wouldn't see her naked. "These jokers are from out east. Jersey. I want to say some things, establish our bona fides." Jack sniffed under his armpits and decided not to take a shower. "Let 'em know we're not just some bunch of yokels right off the farm."

"Say what things?"

Okay, he thought, *this is good. Technical stuff, talk about technical stuff.*

"The standing seam roof for one. A sophisticated system. Eddie Blue chose it, don't ask me why. Nothing but problems. Typical architect's trick—to hell with how hard it is to install, just so it looks good." Jack was waking up. The pet peeve helped. "The concessionaire's gonna have stoves, big commercial jobs with hoods and ducts to vent through the roof. If we can penetrate between the seams, that's good. If we have to cut them, that's not good."

An indeterminate noise issued from the closet. His only tried-and-true method of turning Janelle off was to start loading her up with details.

He glanced in as he walked by. She was just slipping into her sports bra and turned sharply away.

"This is going to impress the concessionaire, this kind of talk?" she asked skeptically.

He went over to the chair she had given him a couple of Christmases ago. It had built-in hangers and a shoeshine drawer and other gadgets, an architectonic chair. Some furniture designer had tried to apply the Swiss Army knife approach to organizing a gentleman's daily outfit.

"I'm not trying to impress anybody. I just want 'em to get on the stick."

He looked at his clothes from yesterday, draped every which way over the device, and decided they had another day in them.

"Somebody else could have done this and given you a few more minutes of sleep," the closet said.

"You mean us a few more minutes."

When Jack left the house, Janelle was smoking and working away on her Nordic Track as she watched CNN.

The new storm had begun, and he drove downtown through that, looking at the snow, wondering how much they'd accomplish at the job site. Another day down the drain.

⁓

He didn't drive to the Jackson Building, where he had his office, but rather to the Cathedral. He'd decided to go to the daily Mass. That was the reason he'd gotten up, not because of the letter to the concessionaire, although he had to do that, too. Back at the house, he'd taken his rosary beads out of the drawer in his bedside table and put them in his pocket.

It was interesting what you lied to your wife about. Lied by omission this time, but a lie nonetheless. He supposed he was trying to avoid her approval. Or no, not that, not quite. In fact, he wasn't sure what her reaction would have been to this pious twitch on his part. Janelle had a limited interest in innovation.

Or perhaps it was simply that he didn't want to have to explain why he was going. Because he didn't actually know, couldn't have put into words, at least. That was, as a matter of fact, one of the nice things about going to Mass. It was a good thing to do, something you might do without knowing exactly why. He couldn't remember the last time he'd gone in the middle of the week. Probably somebody's funeral.

Mark O'Banion's. Yes, that was it.

He parked and walked gingerly up the worn marble steps and through the small door inset within the massive gothic gates with their iron strap hinges, then along the dim aisle through the nave, the chancel dark except for the backlit Christ above the altar. An old woman was praying the stations. He stood briefly and watched her, until he became conscious of watching. Then he genuflected and turned to the side, into the chapel where daily Mass was celebrated. He genuflected a second time and settled into a pew, last row, kneeling and saying the short prayer he used at Sunday Mass and then settling back and waiting, thinking about why he hadn't gone to the early Mass in his own parish, St. Columbkille's.

He could have. Father Mike Daugherty offered one. Part of it was that Jack didn't want to give Father Mike the satisfaction. Not very noble on Jack's part, but there you were. Part of it was that Jack had been so long involved with the secular end of things at St. C's that he'd lost track of the religious somehow, some sort of disconnect. Not a loss of faith, Jack would never lose that. The problem was actually more of a secular nature. Something else hard to put into words. Mike was part of it, of course. The difference in their ages didn't help, Jack a generation older, but Mike the priest, creating an uncomfortable crosscurrent of lines of force. Mike chafed under the constant irritation of Jack's seniority and long experience in the parish. Jack, for his part, found Mike's perennial bonhomie annoying, that and the pre-Vatican II impulses lying behind the Vatican II façade.

No, Jack would not go to Mass at St. Columbkille's. Instead he drove down here to the Cathedral Parish on the flats, the six o'clock Mass, an hour earlier than at St. C's, an accommodation for anyone who had to go to work early, cops and firemen and packinghouse workers, when there had been packinghouse workers.

The service began.

Father Rauch appeared abruptly, no procession or hymn, he and the Mass server coming briskly in from the side. Jack and the others rose. The priest recited the antiphon, kissed the altar.

The Greeting followed, then the Penitential Rite. Father wasted no time.

Quite a few present, more than Jack would have expected. A couple, middle-aged. Several men and women by themselves, one or two quite young. A trio of the expected elderly, perhaps retired religious from the teaching order's home down the street.

Jack was conscious of the dark nave at his back, of the somewhat histrionic solemnity of the Mass server, of the altar itself and the plainish crucifix, of the earlier exchange with Janelle and the day in store for him, of the fact that he hadn't gone to St. C's.

He adjusted his thinking and paid attention to Father Rauch as the priest clicked through the Liturgy of the Word, a workman-like job. So different from the variety shows Mike emceed up at St. C's on Sunday morning. Barely any homily, two or three sentences max, a lick and a promise of a homily. Nothing to prove here. The whole business almost callous, if you didn't understand. Jack had nearly forgotten that about these daily Masses.

The Liturgy of the Eucharist followed, and in less than a half hour, Father Rauch, with upraised hands, sent them away to live the Mass in their daily lives.

Jack and the others separated through the rising storm. He watched them go, people for whom the day had properly begun, people confident that death was the better half of life. Jack felt a touch of envy at their matter-of-factness, their belief beyond belief. He believed, too, threadbare as that had become over the years. He was like a marginal contractor, who did the work but had no gift for it.

⁓

He arrived at the office before anyone else. Unless the kid he had standing watch down at the job site cried an alarm, he wouldn't have to go down until the ten o'clock contractors' meeting. That gave him three hours. He could write a draft of the letter to the concessionaire. He could do other outrider kinds of things.

From one machine in the caf he got a cup of coffee, from another a sweet bun wrapped in cellophane. Then he sat at his desk, thinking about the Mass he'd just attended, still under its spell, which fact he hadn't really noticed until just then. A man with his makeshift breakfast, at the very rim of another workday, another day on a project he didn't really believe in, although it consumed his life.

CHAPTER 30

⁓

The flimsy pink paperboard containers slid back and forth, zig-zagging down the table. El Plowman laid out a Kleenex and when one got to her, chose a plain and placed it untouched on the impromptu napkin. The economic development committee meeting had begun, the beginning as informal as the committee itself, no chair, a floating membership, only the time and place set—every Friday morning, eight-thirty, the second floor meeting room in city hall.

Feeling somewhat disconnected, El squeezed the tea bag, then folded it over the rim of her paper cup, the little flag on the end of the string dragging on the table. While she listened, she dismantled the donut.

After a time, the conversation came around to Ultima Thule, the specialized catalog retailer they had been attempting to lure to the city.

"Brad asked about the bypass right-of-way again," Steve Ostertag, executive director of Jackson Development Corp., said, looking across at Chuck Fellows.

"Still negotiating," Fellows told him.

"What about going to condemnation?"

"Might have to. Take even longer then."

Steve shook his head, asked a couple more questions, then went on to other Ultima Thule matters, more niggling technical questions, last minute jitters the company was having, El guessed.

Her attention wandered. The walls of the room were bare. She really needed to do something about the starkness of the place. She missed the way it used to be, the ridiculously high Victorian ceiling, the poltergeists in the radiators, the echoey conversations, even the microclimates of drafts and heat pockets. What they had in exchange was this sensible box, economical to heat, no drafts, no poltergeists, not a shred of character, either. Well, she decided, she'd pick out a few pictures to put up, maybe that would help. Anyway, it was something she could do, a little civic beautification. Something that wouldn't get her into any more trouble.

She became conscious of a pause in the conversation and imagined that Steve had arrived at the end of matters related to Ultima. But when she looked toward him, she saw it was otherwise, that the pause was merely a small space left to fence off what had preceded from what was to follow.

"Brad mentioned something else." He took a drink and grimaced as if the coffee had become bitter between the last sip and this. "The *New York Times* story."

"He mentioned it?" Paul Cutler asked. Characteristically, the city manager had pushed his chair back from the table.

"Brought it up. Very briefly. Right at the end."

"What does that mean, brought it up? Is it a problem?"

"A concern. He said some of his people were concerned."

"The story was a distortion. Did you tell him that?"

"Yes. Brad knows. His people know. But they're hypersensitive to bad publicity. If they moved now, it might look like they were coming here because, you know…"

"He said that?"

"In so many words. I got the feeling that the only reason he'd mentioned it at all was as a courtesy to me. Over the last few months, we've gotten to know each other pretty well. He's a neat guy, and I think he'd really like to see this deal work out."

"Just how serious is this, Steve?" Paul said, clearly disgusted.

"I don't know. He didn't say, not directly. A problem, an issue, something they're concerned about."

At this repeated opaque statement, the room fell briefly silent. El thought, *Of course, it all makes perfectly good sense*. She kept this thought to herself.

The doughnut boxes, their cargoes dispersed, sat at haphazard angles, sagging and forlorn.

Ostertag continued. "They've got African-Americans on their payroll. I got the feeling that was maybe where the objections were coming from."

"What about black customers?"

"That's right," Ostertag agreed, "that, too. In fact, Brad said they've got a lot of black customers. Their stuff might be designed for the arctic, but it's also popular in, you know, inner city neighborhoods. Got a lot of cachet in the black community. That's what he said. Cachet."

"So it's a practical matter."

A couple of the men nodded at this. Now they were getting somewhere. Input started to come from different points around the table. Provisionally, El held her tongue.

"But we might not have to do anything," Paul said.

"Don't know," Ostertag responded.

"Wherever they go, they'll have the same problem, did you tell him that?"

"Could. Anyway, he knows it."

"And it's not really the problem itself. It's the way it looks."

"Perception. That's right."

At this, Floyd Hays, the executive director of The Main Street Project, looked into his lap and slowly shook his large, gray head. Perception. What a world.

Steve said the obvious. "We might not have to do anything. But this is four hundred and fifty jobs." And if everything went well, a lot more. "And it's not so late they can't back out."

"It's never too late," Paul said. "What about Deke McKeown? What do we know about his attitude toward all this?"

A discussion of the Ultima Thule CEO followed, McKeown with his fabulous buddies and serial Hollywood girlfriends, a cynosure of *People* magazine, stories of elaborate junkets to out-of-the-way places, where the junketeers wore Ultima Thule high-tech clothing, slept in Ultima Thule high-tech tents, ate Ultima Thule high-tech food. Certainly, the people McKeown hung out with were liberal types, Steve said. McKeown himself? Who knows? He made money, he spent money.

El listened with misgivings. Highfliers like McKeown made her uncomfortable. But she had the stirrings of an idea. He might be approachable. An innovation might catch his fancy.

Paul Cutler had the floor, cautioning everyone that most diseases cure themselves.

"You think so?" El asked, speaking for the first time.

"Yes, I do." He spoke more firmly. Perhaps he had picked up the hint of mockery in her tone. "In a few months, all this will be forgotten."

"And in a few months," she told him, "Ultima Thule might be on their way somewhere else."

"Possibly," Paul admitted. "But we've matched—we've more than matched the other offers. Any more and we'll all be walking around here wearing barrels."

El turned to Steve Ostertag. "What do you think? Is that what they're after, more freebies?"

"Could be, I suppose," he said.

"But that's not what you think. You think your friend Brad was drawing the curtain back a little, giving you a peek at the gears and cogs."

He nodded.

"That suggests, to me at least," El pushed on, "that this is more than angling for a further tax abatement. Tell me, Steve, do you think doing nothing is really an option here?"

Ostertag, unhappy with the position he found himself in, exhaled and grimaced, as if he'd just taken another sip of bitter coffee, although he hadn't touched his cup since this phase of the conversation began. Paul, for his part, having introduced a cautionary note, had settled back, as he typically did, to see how things played out.

Steve said, "You're probably right, El, this isn't just economic. Whatever it is. They're talking in-house. Most likely there are constituencies. You know. And all things being equal… Would it help if we did something? Can't say. Maybe. I suppose it depends on what you got in mind…"

"Did you tell him that we were remounting the vandalized exhibit?" Paul wanted to know.

"Yes, I did."

"Good. That's something we should be emphasizing."

"Would it be enough?" El asked doubtfully.

Steve shrugged.

"What," El asked, "if Deke McKeown saw we were trying to do something, something a little different, a little innovative? Ultima Thule's all about innovation, aren't they?"

Steve didn't react to this. Nobody in the room did.

"Suppose," El continued, "it was even something Ultima Thule could be part of?"

"Maybe," Steve said without much conviction. Normally he was a tub-thumper, so El found this reserve ominous.

"If perception's the problem, that's what we need to change, right?"

"Hard to do."

"But not necessarily impossible." El paused to remind herself of her recent disasters. "There is something we've been discussing on the integration committee. We all feel something ought to be done. Ultima Thule or not. Something substantial, beyond the usual professions of good faith. The proposal we've come up with is to actively recruit black professionals to come live in Jackson."

She looked at Ostertag.

"Really?" he said, his tone somewhere between curiosity and incredulity.

"Would that make a difference with Brad and his pals?"

"I don't know. I suppose it might."

"If we decided to do it, Ultima Thule would be exactly the kind of firm we'd want moving here. They've got black executives, the very people we'd be trying to attract. Deke McKeown could use that in his ads, in his PR, turn the negative into the positive."

"I suppose," Steve conceded, not exactly warming to the idea, but acknowledging that what El said wasn't inconceivable.

"Even target their black customers, if they wanted."

Steve nodded, acknowledging that, as well. Paul sat alert and passive, his gaze having slipped off El and come to rest on a part of the room where there was nothing to see. The walls without pictures.

But now he roused himself again. "And Jacksonians, El, what about them? What are they going to think of this scheme of yours?"

Now was the moment for truth in advertising, and El leaned back and smiled ruefully. "To be honest, every time I talk to somebody outside the committee, they think it's a perfectly dreadful idea."

"Because of local reaction."

"Yes. Strong reaction. It would have to be done very carefully. And certainly it's chancy. But I don't know how you accomplish anything if you don't take a chance." Something Reiny Kopp might have said. "Anyway, we'll be after professionals, not people who could be seen as competitors of the locals, taking blue collar jobs from them, or for that matter bringing crime or drugs or anything like that to the city."

Now it was Steve's turn to lay back in his chair, appearing to relax a little. "So your idea, El, is to import people who'll take *my* job?"

El smiled back him. "Yes, that's exactly the idea."

The others laughed, but not Floyd Hays of The Main Street Project. His hair hung in loose gray crosscurrents as he stared into his lap, shaking his head slowly back and forth. O tempora! O mores!

CHAPTER 31

~

At ten o'clock, Jack Kelley drove down to the dog track for the contractors' meeting and spent the next two hours fencing over scheduling snafus and change orders and the rest. The black contractor wouldn't be on the job for several weeks, but Jack couldn't wait before taking steps, and so at the end of the meeting, after he'd asked the others if they had any comments they wanted to make, he said, "Well, I've got one. Dexter Walcott isn't here yet, but he soon enough will be. If you've got any troublemakers on your crews, I want them off the job site."

As the construction trailer shivered in the wind, the men ranged along the sides of the low, narrow room adjusted their poses and said nothing, perhaps uncertain for the moment in exactly what quarter their self-interest lay. Jack, looking to the far end where Chuck Fellows stood in front of the plan rack, wondered if it might be worthwhile to call on his support here.

Finally, someone spoke. "I got a question." Jack turned toward the speaker—Lonny Vasconcellos, the son of Tony Vasconcellos, the electrical contractor. Father and son sat side by side, both men bulky, the father darker, balding but with a knot of black hair still hanging over his forehead, the remnant of the Italian cut he'd worn as a young man. Jack had known Tony many years. They were in the same parish, St. Columbkille's, and therein lay a tale. The son, Lonny, of lighter complexion than his father, wore his hair in a crew cut, short and bristly. He was running the job for his father, and Jack liked him even less than he liked Tony, which was saying something. "Tell me, Jack," he asked, "you expect all of us to be ever-so-nice, but suppose Dexter Walcott's people start something, what then?" Lonny was the very definition of why they shouldn't be bringing a black contractor onto the job site.

Jack stared at him, uncertain what he could say that might possibly make an impression. Probably because he'd gone to Mass that morning, an outlandish idea occurred to him, certainly an outlandish idea given this group. But the Vasconcelloses were Catholics and members of Jack's parish and, in fact, wouldn't have even had the electrical contract except for the machinations of Father Mike Daugherty.

So he said, "You turn the other cheek, Lonny."

The kid half-grinned. "You can't be serious."

"I'm dead serious."

Young Vasconcellos hooked his thumb back toward the outside, toward the electricians and ironworkers and other tradesmen on the site. "You think those guys will turn the other cheek?"

"At the moment, I'm not worried about them, I'm worried about you."

Jack stared at Lonny and then around at his father—sitting stoically, betraying no hint of what he might think himself—and decided to ignore the Vasconcelloses for the moment. He turned back to the others. "We got all kinds of potential for trouble here, folks. The best way to deal with it is to deal with it before it begins. As for Dexter Walcott, well, I'm going to tell him the same thing. He's got troublemakers, he should keep them off the job site... And if anything does happen, I expect you to come to me. Don't try to take care of it yourself. I'll do it."

Nobody, except Lonny, felt inclined to comment. The others were older and kept their own council, and their silence meant that they'd make up their own minds about the thing and act accordingly. Maybe they'd come to Jack, maybe they wouldn't. Perhaps, if Jack got lucky, Tony Vasconcellos would even do something about his loudmouth son.

But not at the moment. At the moment, Lonny said, "These are men out here, Jack, not friggin' pansies. Somebody gets in their face, they take care of the problem themselves."

Why Lonny Vasconcellos had appointed himself defender of the construction workers' honor, Jack didn't know. Maybe it had something to do with the fact that his father ran a union shop. Maybe he just hated blacks. Made no difference either way. The Vasconcelloses were the last people in that room who should have been giving Jack a hard time.

He supposed he'd have no choice but to take Lonny on at some point. His impulse was to ignore him. Contractors and their minions had been bullshit artists from the time of the pyramids. One way or another, jobs got done. Best to turn your back.

At the end of the meeting, he sent Gayle back uptown to type out the notes for distribution, telling her to leave out any mention of Dexter Walcott. Then he toured the job site with Sean Greene, the student he'd hired out of Plattesville when his original field man went AWOL on him.

They walked gingerly over the deck of the grandstand, swept by the storm and cluttered with gang boxes and spools of wire and scissors lifts and stacks of siding and ductwork and slanting guy wires. Down the ladder into the crawl space below, they found a couple of the plumbing contractor's people installing runs of pipe on trapezes. No sign of Tony Vasconcellos's electricians, who should have been there, too, doing the electrical rough-ins, hanging pipe and pulling wire and so forth. The air clung to Jack, cold and still and moist, almost clammy. Curtains of snow sifted from above, through the spaces between the ledger beams on the sloping north side, where a topping slab would eventually be poured and grandstand seating installed.

At each end of the football-field-sized space stood industrial fans, still crated, to vent any methane that seeped through the vapor barrier from the old dump lying beneath the site. The fans reminded Jack of the earlier controversy over the methane system, ancient history now, a fight that could have easily been avoided, had anybody cared.

Back outside, he checked progress on the paddock building, then walked toward the kennels.

Sean asked him what he was going to do if there was trouble when the black contractor arrived.

"You got a plan?" The kid seemed pretty enthusiastic at the prospect of general mayhem. The video game mentality of the young, Jack supposed.

"Something happens, you call me. That's all you need to worry about."

As they went on, Jack thought, a plan? Who could plan for such a fucked up situation? His plan was to wait and see what happened. His plan was to hope to hell that at the end of the day these guys would think about their wallets and forget everything else.

Nick Burns, the local homebuilder putting up the kennels, had his small crew still going in the snow, nailing together stud walls. Burns worked right alongside his men.

"If you're looking for Vasconcellos, he's over there," he said without prompting, pointing with his hammer toward one of the kennels which had already been enclosed. Having spoken, he immediately returned to his work.

Burns's assumption irritated Jack. Wasn't a worker on the site didn't know about the situation between him and Vasconcellos. Jack could imagine what people were saying behind his back.

He told Sean to go back to the construction trailer and then took himself off in the direction Burns had indicated, listening as he went to the ragged echoing rhythm of the hammering behind him.

The makeshift, temporary door on the far end of the kennel resisted opening and then yanked free as the wind caught it. Jack regained his balance and grabbed the door, with effort closing it behind him as he stepped over the wooden skirt and into the rich aroma of Doug fir, sweet with a touch of warmth. Tony and Lonny were there along with an electrician. Tony looked toward Jack without expression. The electrician was using a Sawzall to notch out a section from the bottom of a truss, obviously to give himself room to drill through the upper plate of the stud wall so he could feed conduit down to a junction box already installed below. Nearby, a portable generator banged away.

"Word, Tony," Jack said.

"Sure."

Vasconcellos sauntered aside to where they could speak in private.

Jack had no clue what might be the proper approach. He regretted the exchange already, even before it had begun.

"Tony, what the hell's going on?"

"Going on? Wha'd'ya mean?"

"All this damn trash talk from Lonny at the meeting. Walcott this and Walcott that."

Vasconcellos shrugged. "You know."

"No, I don't know. And now I go over to the grandstand. Nobody's there. Where the hell are all your people?"

Tony didn't reply at once. First came a short pause for marshalling.

"Weather's shitty, Jack, in case you hadn't noticed."

"Not that bad. Too shitty to go up on the steel, maybe. But not to pull wire."

"I don't know, Jack, deck's pretty damn slippery. Snow doesn't help. Gotta look out for the welfare of my men."

This was a crock. Tony was taking advantage of the situation to send his people to other jobs, that's what was really going on. Jack pointed out that there was plenty to be done in the crawl space.

Tony simply ignored this. He said, "What are you worrying about, Jack? The work'll get done. I got a penalty clause, remember? You got complaints, save 'em for the guy from Waterloo. He's the one could be diddling around a year from now, holding everybody else up."

These statements were a further crock, so far off the mark that Jack didn't know quite where to begin. Tony didn't give him a chance.

"You got a situation here, Jack. You want to keep the lid on, you better be prepared to cooperate. We'll get your job done for you. But these threats, and telling people what to do, they don't go over big."

An invitation to let the contractors run the job themselves, more vintage Vasconcellos. Sure as shit, thought Jack, he'd been right, this was a conversation best avoided. He should turn his back and walk away.

But still he could not quite abandon the effort. "Tony, Tony," he pleaded, "Walcott's gonna finish and head back to Waterloo as fast as his legs will carry him. I know that, and you know that."

"I do?"

"And that's what you should be doing, you and everybody else. Let's get this job done and over with."

Out of the corner of his eye, Jack had been watching Lonny closing in, itching to pile on.

Jack had no intention of staying long enough to let him.

"Just do the fucking job, okay, Tony?"

Outside again, the exchange with Vasconcellos over almost as soon as it had begun, Jack stopped to watch the work on the other kennel and calm down. What did he think he was trying to accomplish talking to Tony? A fruitless exercise, a waste of time. He should have walked away sooner. He should never have gone.

The carpenters were about to raise one of the stud walls they had been nailing together. The wind felt good against the side of

Jack's face, the pinpricks of melting snow. Burns and his men, blurred in the heavy slanting storm, spaced themselves along the foundation and on the count of three lifted, the long rectangular frame swinging upward, its vertical studs, on their sixteen-inch centers, so fragile appearing, mostly empty space. Something in the curve of the men's backs and the immemorial act of lifting the framing, the echo of millions of earlier house raisings and barn raisings, something in it reminded Jack of the gestures of Father Rauch at Mass that morning.

He really should try again with Tony Vasconcellos. It wouldn't do any good, but that didn't mean he shouldn't try. And keep on trying.

As the storm swirled around him, he stood watching the carpenters and tried to visualize himself being a better person than he was.

CHAPTER 32

～

From the contractors' meeting, Chuck Fellows drove out to check on the dredge. On the way, he stopped briefly at the end of the pipeline from which the sand and water slurry spilled, foaming down the slope to where Albert Furlong jockeyed his dozer, the machine bucking and surging, water climbing its metal tracks as he worked the sand away from the runoff.

The first few times Chuck had witnessed this scene, the dredge at long last delivering sand the quarter mile along the linked sections of piping to the job site, he'd felt a deep personal satisfaction, almost as if the task he'd set himself three months earlier, when he'd seized the dilapidated equipment from the dock board, had been simply to get it up and running, and that done, he could forget about the rest. But this wasn't some old radio or clock that a teenager might tinker with until he got bored. Chuck's work had just begun. He had tens of thousands of yards of sand to place before the first race on June 15.

Furlong idled the dozer, climbed down into the soupy froth, and came up to where Chuck stood. Unlike his brother, Albert didn't have much to say. He spoke, when he chose to speak at all, in shorthand. And so the two of them silently observed the slurry, flowing from the pipe without great force, this being about as far as the little dredge was capable of pumping.

"Doesn't look like there's much sand in it, Al." Chuck could barely see the brown in the water, the color of old snow, or hear the rub of grains on the bottom of the pipe, only the occasionally larger pieces, stone or shell, which came banging erratically along the line and reminded him of desperation.

"Better ask Bud," Albert said.

"I will. Why don't you get on the horn and call on down? I'll need a lift."

"Already have."

They continued for a short time staring at the discharge. The flow made shallow transverse waves rippling down the slope, creating the illusion that it was moving backwards. At the foot, around the idling dozer, the water eroded the sand from beneath its tracks as if intent upon burying the machine.

Ten minutes later, Albert's fraternal twin Sidney, the noisy one, was giving Chuck a ride out to the dredge in the workboat, the dredge cozied into the northeast corner of the open water, where they'd found an area free of debris from the nineteenth-century cooperage. Chuck had met the local historian Walter Plowman knew, and learned more about tierces and bell scrapers and other tools of the ancient trades than he cared to know, but at least the bottom of the river wasn't about to be declared an historical landmark.

Old Orv Massey's harbor tug, which they'd been using to keep the water open, was docked at the south side, away from the dredging. A couple of unfamiliar cars were pulled up next to the river, which probably meant that some subset of Massey's endless stream of euchre-playing buddies were on board.

Chuck and Sidney followed the curve of the floating line out, approaching the dredge's stern, where the two spuds alternately rose and fell as the craft pivoted from port to starboard and back again, vacuuming the river bottom.

Chuck noticed the end of a cast poking from the sleeve of Sidney's coveralls.

"What the hell's that, Sid?"

"Broke her. Nothin' serious."

"What happened?"

"Stupid. Wasn't watching where I was goin' is all, slipped on the ice. I knew it was gonna happen sooner or later. Probably break a lot more before I'm through."

Chuck felt a twinge of sympathetic pain in his own reconstructed elbow. He'd been wounded so many times in 'Nam that he'd become an expert on human anatomy. "Which bone?" he asked.

"Radius."

They tied off next to the fuel barge. Chuck continued to question him as they went inside. Hairline fracture near the proximal end, about as simple as such things get.

"What about insurance?" Chuck said, yelling now, for they had entered the machine shed, into the maw of the noise. Chuck had warned Sidney and the others. They were independent contractors. They wouldn't get city coverage.

Sidney grinned. "Don't you worry, boss. Now that I've come up in the world, decided to get me a real package this time, yes, sir. Not like what they gave us at the Pack. A real good one this time, Cadillac coverage, all the bells and whistles—dental, drugs, catastrophic, you name it, I got it. Nothing can happen to me that I ain't covered for." He held up his arm as if he'd broken it on purpose. "Gonna take full advantage, too, you bet. Have it paid for in no time."

Up in the control room, Bud Pregler was engaged in the endless repetition of steps involved in sweeping back and forth across the cut.

Every time Chuck saw him, Pregler seemed smaller and his beard bigger. Without the beard, like Samson shorn of his hair, he'd shrink to insignificance, perhaps disappear entirely.

"Well?" he said as soon as he spotted Chuck.

"Saw Sid's arm."

"To be expected. Tub's an ice cube… Well?"

"And I was out at the end of the pipe. Looks like you're pumping nothing but water."

"That's a damn lie. Although, I'll grant you, I'm not pumping as much as I'd like to. I've got to make it last." By which he meant that when he finished in this corner, that was it. "Well?!"

"A week from tomorrow," Chuck told him. A week from tomorrow, the biologist from the U. would do some bottom sampling for Chuck in the area around the present permit area, looking for signs of endangered species of mussels. If he didn't find any, the Corps of Engineers would probably let Chuck expand his dredging operation.

Satisfied for the moment, Pregler concentrated on his work, pointing with his chin whiskers toward the bow. "You wanna know why the soup's a little watery?"

Chuck looked where the whiskers indicated and saw that the ladder with the cutting blade and suction was tilted at a sharp angle down into the river. Pregler couldn't dredge any deeper if he wanted to. He was gathering every grain of sand he could reach.

"Think you've got a week's worth left?"

"A week? Don'cha mean two? Three? How long's it gonna take you to light a fire under the Corps?"

"Don't know. Depends on what happens a week from tomorrow. As soon as it looks like we'll get the permit, we start on the new area."

Pregler had his back to Chuck and was disengaging the friction clutch and setting the brake for the port hauling winch as the dredge slowed, edging to the outside of the cut.

"Other problems?" Chuck asked.

"Sucker's overheating. Had to shut her down a couple times."

"The intake?"

"Yup." One of the ironies of cold weather work like this was that the water intakes wanted to freeze up, which starved the engines of the river water they required as coolant. Too cold outside, too hot in.

They talked about it, no big deal. They knew keeping the intake open would be a chore.

"Anything else?" Chuck asked.

"Nothing you can do anything about." Pregler engaged the other clutch to start hauling on the starboard winch, pulling the bow across the cut in the opposite direction, leaving just enough tension on the port brake so the cable didn't go lax. Slowly, slowly, they began to inch to starboard. "Being as how I'm not sluggin' the line much anymore, this job has gotten mighty tedious. Back and forth, back and forth. Can't say I'm unhappy when we have to shut her down for a bit."

"Yeah, I know. A bitch." If he'd had the time, Chuck would have taken over for a few minutes, given Bud a break. Before he'd managed to hire the guys from the Pack, he'd spent time mastering the concept of dredge work, even sat where Pregler was sitting and, as a mental exercise, gone repeatedly through the sequence of steps. He'd never done it live, though. Might be interesting, if he had the time, which he didn't.

But as he was about to leave, Pregler said, "Tell me, Chuck, that black guy from Waterloo, he on the job site yet?" He asked the question with a kind of feigned indifference, as a man will who had been thinking about the matter, waiting for just the right moment to bring it up, and the right moment never came.

"Not yet," Chuck told him, a little curtly, for he was getting tired of all this chatter about Walcott, people working themselves up into a state. He didn't know how many times over the last few weeks he'd stood at the edge of a discussion about race. Wherever he went. These people wasted one helluva lot of time on this crap. Made no damn sense to Chuck, who believed in disliking people one at a time.

Pregler was paying attention to what he was doing, lowering one spud and raising the other as the dredge swung across the middle of the cut.

"It's a bad business," he volunteered when Chuck didn't seem disposed to continue the conversation.

Chuck didn't react to this, either, not right away, and Pregler cast a calculating look in his direction, then turned back to what he was doing, setting and releasing the swing wires as the dredge swept to a stop and slowly started back in the other direction. Even with all the noise, Chuck could hear the metal warping as the torque on the old craft reversed. Like a nail bent one way, then another, then back, over and over until it split.

"Beyond me," Pregler said, "why a man would come where he wasn't wanted."

Chuck had one thing he could say, and one thing only. With some of the yahoos around there he wouldn't waste his breath, but he respected Pregler enough to say it.

"Bud, the guy I wanted covering my back in Vietnam when I got into really deep shit, he was black. A first-rate troop. And the worst goddamn day I had in 'Nam, and I had a lot of 'em, was the day he got killed."

Pregler nodded, and now it was his turn to say nothing, seeing where things stood, not quite where he'd figured. When he did go on, he'd become a little more thoughtful.

"Me, I never knew any blacks, not like what you say. Got no feeling one way or another about your individual blacks, I suppose. All I know is the situation."

Chuck had said everything he was going to say. "I've gotta get going."

Pregler kept on talking.

CHAPTER 33

~

The room wasn't normally used at this time of day. The dreary beer hall décor—paneling black with age, lights casting weak globes of color from stained glass sconces—required more human presence than the two of them to create any note of lederhosen conviviality. El Plowman wanted no eavesdroppers. Johnny Pond's tape recorder sat idly at his elbow. During the meal, they'd chatted about recent calls to *Sound Off*, his midday call-in show; at the moment, local people were apparently less interested in complaining about blacks than about the city's inept handling of the snow. The discontents ebbed and flowed.

El asked if he'd talked to Chuck Fellows about the snow problem. "Basically," she said, "I think there's no place left to put it."

Finally, the meal completed, a carafe of coffee come for Johnny and hot water for her tea, El told him about the economic development meeting that morning. She recounted the event precisely, word for word where she could, not to influence what he might choose to say so much as to give weight to her own thinking on the matter. He took one sip of the coffee, pushed the cup away—not up to the Austrian he drank at the Three Annes Café, no doubt—and leaned back, folding his large hands over his stomach and listening impassively.

When she had finished, she added, "Of course, I'm not telling you this because you're a reporter."

She wasn't talking to him because she entirely trusted him, either. And their recent conversations over similar matters had certainly been unhelpful enough. But despite all this, she would talk to him.

He thought a while and said, "And you think this changes things some. The company might not come here." These sentences could have been questions or not. They were like discards thrown down that either of them might pick up.

"It might not."

"And it might. Perhaps it's just, like Ostertag said, a concern, a guy expressing a concern. It's a moment." With one of his big hands, Pond brushed the moment away.

"We're going to try to find out. Steve's going to call his guy. I'm thinking of trying to reach Deke McKeown."

He nodded.

El leaned toward him. "For all the good it'll do us."

He nodded again, adjusting his expression to indicate…she wasn't sure what. Perhaps it was simply his big man's round features, the sense that what might have been legible in a thinner countenance had become submerged, beyond the possibility of discovery no matter how careful the observer. Getting to know him better, his habitual easygoing calculation, hadn't helped.

"Two things impressed the people at the meeting. First, Ultima Thule sells to the black community."

"Money."

"Money."

"You always know a man's serious when he starts talking money," Johnny said.

"Right."

"What's the second? You said two."

"The fact that the people at the firm are concerned with the way it would look. Moving here after the museum."

"The perception." The very word that had popped up at the morning meeting.

"Public relations, if you want," El suggested as an alternative.

"Perception's everything. That's the age." He meditated on this and said, "We're a nation of strangers, El, got nothing but perceptions to go on, you think about it."

"The point is that the people this morning understood the seriousness of the matter. And they're prepared to do something about it… Well, maybe they're prepared."

"To do something. To put another perception out there. A counter-perception."

"I suggested bringing more black families to Jackson."

"Ah. That." They had talked of this in the ad hoc integration committee meetings, but never just the two of them, never in anything more than a hypothetical way.

"Yes," she told him, "that."

"A city council resolution, then?"

"Perhaps. If we do it."

"But you're seriously considering it *now*."

"Yes, I am. I think we need to do something, and I think it needs to be...I don't want to say dramatic...but people need to notice."

"Ultima Thule needs to notice," Johnny said.

"That's correct. But only part of it."

"You want to show them the city has noble intentions."

"I wouldn't put it quite that way."

"And so you and I,"—he held a hand up and waggled his fingers back and forth to indicate the two of them—"we're here to talk about the rightness of the thing, is that it? Or maybe you just want to know if I think it'll work?"

"Either. Both. *Will* it work?" She wanted him to argue.

"Will you get black folks to move here?"

"Yes. Ultima Thule has black employees. If the company comes here, they'd come, too, which would be a start."

"But that's after the fact. That's not what you're interested in."

"No, it isn't," she conceded.

"We've talked about this before." His tone suggesting that the matter had been already settled and in the negative. But it wasn't true. On the integration committee, if he'd been cool to the idea, he'd never dismissed it out of hand. And El thought it had much to recommend it, lacking only the necessary spark. "The people you're after, El, these upstanding professionals, they've got lots of options. Why move to a place like Jackson?"

"Because we'd invite them. Because, I don't know, Jackson's a good place to raise kids."

"White kids, maybe." He looked at her, the look full of cold calculation now, his mood altered startlingly. "So...you want to do this now. You got a need. Want to lure this company. 'How can we do that? I got an idea. Why don't we import some black folks? Spruce up our image.'"

"I do want Ultima Thule to come here. But that's not all."

He ignored the second half of her statement. "You want to go to them and say, 'Look at us. Look at what good little boys and girls we are, scouring the countryside for African-Americans to come live here.' Going the extra mile and all that...shit." His gaze briefly seemed to turn inward, but in a moment had sprung back on her again, implacable and confident. "And suppose no black professionals come here after all. So what? Long as you get Ultima Thule. Hell, you'd get Ultima Thule and no niggers, the best of all possible worlds."

She knew that Johnny could be counted on to put the thing in the worst possible light. That's why she laid it out for his benefit. Let him trample on it, then see what was left.

"That's a lie. Ultima Thule has black employees. You don't think I want black families to move here?"

He merely said, "I'm not talking about you," and then, "I've got to get back to the station."

"Maybe you're right," she told him, "maybe this seems self-serving, but it also gives us an opportunity. Sometimes you can't do something *just* because it's right."

He heaved himself up out of his chair, grimacing slightly and flexing his legs, and started out, and El thought that was that. But he had second thoughts of some sort and stopped at the door.

"Look, El. You got a few minutes?"

"Sure."

"Something I want to show you."

In silence, she followed him out into the storm.

They didn't go far. After half a block, they stood across from Washington Park. He skirted the park and mounted the broad post office steps on the south side. Up on the plaza, in the lee of the building, stood a person with a sign. One of the Breitbachs, no doubt. El couldn't read the sign in the storm, whatever they were protesting against at the moment. Something in the way the figure stood suggested it was Emma, not Pete, although without going closer, it was hard to tell for sure. No matter how bad the weather, one or the other of the Breitbachs was sure to be there.

Johnny ignored the distant figure. At the top of the steps, he turned to face the park and waited for El to come up beside him. His anger had passed, leaving in its place not his usual studied pleasantness but a severity, almost a haughtiness.

"Yes?" she said.

"Look." He gestured toward the park. From their vantage, they could scan over the embankments of snow. "What do you see?"

The bandstand stood at the intersection of two walkways shoveled through the deep snow, diagonals connecting the four corners of the square. City crews kept the walks clear, but after all the storms, the paths had been whittled down to hardly more than slits. A couple of the park benches had been dug out, too, although anybody sitting on them would have had no view, only white walls almost close enough to touch.

El had expected Johnny to show her something special, not a vista seen unnumbered times.

"I don't understand. What am I supposed to be looking at?"

"That's right," he said, "nothing to see. You're right. But was a time this marked the center of Jackson. Bandstand there. Every Fourth of July, you'd have a band concert, Sousa tunes, people down here with their picnic hampers, bunting draped all over everything. Long before my time, but I've seen the pictures. Notice how the walks radiate from the middle. Back then people were conscious of the symbolic intent of things… Not today. You've got to be mighty nostalgic to think that way anymore."

He was, of course, right. The park had been abandoned to the retirees from the nearby retirement homes who came to sit and chat in good weather. The July Fourth concerts had been moved out to the fairgrounds where there was room for fireworks. And except for the post office, the buildings around the square paid little attention, fronting this way and that, as slovenly in their attendance on the square as bored teenagers. It was sad when you thought about it.

As she said nothing, Johnny continued. "Trouble is, Jackson's got no center anymore. Not here, not anywhere else, either. Or it's got a hundred, which pretty much amounts to the same thing. People aren't citizens, El, just residents. So, okay, you're mayor of the place, fair enough, but the word is old-fashioned, out-of-date, probably should be changed to something more fitting to your real authority. Middle manager, something like that. I don't mean it as a slam, I'm just describing the reality, you understand. You deal with individual problems zoning variances, noisy taverns, like that. You got no warrant to do anything else. Nobody brought you in to save Jackson from itself.

"This has happened, El. The museum. The *New York Times* story. The violation of these lives, Hiram and Pearl Johnson's. It's a true thing. Any business Jackson loses because of it is honestly lost. And as a practical matter, you can't do a damn thing about it. That's what I'm saying."

El listened to all this and in her heart acknowledged the degree of truth. More true than false, perhaps. But not everything.

"If the world is nothing but facts, Johnny, why does anything matter?"

He did not respond at first, and they stared out at the park, which had, like so many parks, been named after George Washington. In the northwest corner, the trees were smaller. Vietnam protesters had once managed to defoliate several of the original maples, a stunt that had been laid at the doorstep of Reiny Kopp, although nothing had ever been proved. A number of trees had to be destroyed, and the city gardener had hit on the idea of planting one each of several native species, along with plaques so that children visiting the park might learn to identify them. Something good had come out of the bad.

As they stood there, the snow continued to fall, blue, and seeming white only because she remembered the color it was supposed to be.

CHAPTER 34

~

A t the track consultants' weekly meeting—the architect, engineers, and so forth—the matter of Dexter Walcott came up, as it would, and since of those present, only Chuck Fellows had attended the contractors' meeting down at the job site earlier in the day, he described Jack Kelley's move to keep troublemakers off the site.

Eddie Blue, the lead architect on the project, slouched at the head of the table.

"If we get rid of the troublemakers, who'll be left?" he wondered.

Chuck rather liked Blue. He ran the meeting in a mock casual way, his pale, perfectly bald dome wreathed by a fringe of wiry brown hair, his mouth wreathed as well, by mustache and goatee, the whole effect suggesting a clown's makeup and reinforcing his trick of using humor to hide his determination to have things his way. He pretended an interest only in matters of design and a profound indifference to all things mechanical, electrical, and so forth, baiting the engineers at every opportunity and enjoying no end his architect-from-hell shtick. Blue was a talker. In fact, a lot of the men at the table were, even the engineers.

"We'll have you down there building the thing, Eddie," one of the engineers present twitted him, trying to exact a little revenge.

"I'm sure we'd all like to see me setting a toilet," Eddie admitted lazily. "What about security?" he asked Chuck.

"Walcott will be looking for someplace to store material, maybe even before he's got any men on site. So yeah, we're gonna need someone twenty-four/seven."

"Little Rock, 1957," Eddie said, shaking his head. "This in the budget, perchance?"

"Contingency." Chuck oversaw the dispersal of funds for the project. "I'll take care of it."

A discussion followed as to which of the local suppliers of private cops might be preferable, a conversation Chuck stayed out of. No telling who at the table had a brother-in-law in the security business.

When strictly practical issues gave way to less apparent considerations, Chuck would sit on the sidelines. He had a sense of the various styles and limitations and obsessions of those present. Mostly, however, they remained opaque, men who led calculated lives, their minds filled with many rooms and much furniture. Chuck thought it was all bullshit, of course.

After they had decided on the security firm that he should contact, he said, "And one more thing. Another matter. Next Tuesday, I'm going down to Davenport for the Corps of Engineers' first flood forecast meeting."

"This has an ominous ring about it," said Eddie Blue.

"You will have noticed," Chuck went on, "that we've got some snow on the ground. More up north, a shitload, as a matter of fact, and that's the stuff we've really got to worry about."

This pronouncement led to some chatter at the table, people's favorite snow stories.

When they'd gotten that out of their systems, Chuck told them that the snow wasn't the only problem and then described his discussions with Walter Plowman over the last several months, the sequence of stages that might lead to a massive flood and the uncanny match so far between what could happen and what had happened.

"A flood," Eddie said. "I love it."

Chuck continued. He hadn't talked to anyone about these matters before, but judged the time had come. He told them that he'd taken over the operation of the dredge not just because of the time bind for placing the sand, but also because of the prospect of high water in the spring, which could make it impossible to do any dredging for months.

Eddie Blue sat back and propped his loafers on the table. "I seem to remember, way back when, thinking, well, if we're gonna build this thing in the middle of the damn winter, we don't have the sense we were born with. Tell me, Chuckie lad, at this Corps meeting of yours, got any idea what they're gonna say?"

"Probably won't make a prediction, if that's what you mean. Too early."

"Okay, to hell with the Corps, then. What about Walter Plowman, what does Walter think? He's never been shy about getting out front on a thing. Is water going over the wall? I mean, if the whole city's gonna get washed down the river, then that takes care of all our problems, right? We can all move to Vegas and become high-stakes gamblers or prize fighters or something sensible like that."

"Can't give you a definite answer," Chuck told him. "Mostly I've been focusing on the dredge. That's what we've been talking about."

"And you figure, at a minimum, you're gonna have to stop dredging at some point."

"Yeah. And I've just about run out of room in our current permit area. I've scheduled some sampling." He told them briefly about the biologist from the University of Jackson who was going to sample south and east of the permit area, looking for signs of endangered species of mussels.

"Higgins Eye," Eddie said.

"If he doesn't find any, then we'll probably be able to get a permit from the Corps to expand the dredging area."

Eddie, not much interested, went back to the flood prospect. "Have you told the CM about this?"

"Kelley? Still a bit premature." Although, it was true, he was going to enjoy telling Kelley. "Plenty of time to place the riprap."

Blue put his feet down and leaned forward, elbows on the table, head ducked between his shoulders, something of the vulture added to the clown effect.

"Premature? So all you're trying to do here is scare the bejeebers out of us."

"Why not? That's your prerogative, isn't it?"

"To have the bejeebers scared out of us? I suppose. Well, let us know when it's time to start building arks in the backyard. If you need me, I'll be down at the track setting toilets."

❧

Chuck's day wore on, meeting following meeting, his life reduced. After the track consultants, he went back to city hall and defended his revised public works budget before the city manager. Finally, he assembled his own people for their weekly gabfest, one get-together he couldn't blame on somebody else.

They talked about the usual stuff—the status of projects, problems that refused to go away, whiney city council members, whiney civilians—basically the fallout from living in a universe ruled by the second law of thermodynamics. When it was Chuck's turn, he broached the subject of the dog track, the phases of the work they were responsible for—access road and lift station for sewerage.

Finally, he mentioned the Corps of Engineers' flood meeting down in Davenport.

"Who knows where the flood plan is?"

Wayne Nevers, chief of the survey crew, said, "I can probably put my finger on it." Nevers was the kind of guy who talked behind people's backs, and Chuck didn't think much of him.

"Has anything been done with it since the wall was built?"

"I don't think it's much more than a schedule for closing gates during the spring rise," Nevers told him.

Chuck slung one leg over the other and wondered why, aside from the necessity to act, the prospect of a flood didn't much interest him.

"Find it. See what's there." He would have preferred putting somebody else on it, but with so much snow on the ground, Nevers was the one at the table underemployed at the moment.

Chuck turned to Seth Brunel, the assistant city engineer, also no prize, but the only other P.E. on staff.

"You're the lead on this, Seth, but we're gonna function as a committee of the whole. We need a plan to deal with the worst case scenario."

"Water over the wall?"

"It's my understanding that the system is designed for a two-hundred-year event. Check that." Not that anybody actually knew what a two-hundred-year event was. He turned back to Nevers. "Have your people figure out exactly what gets flooded if the system is overtopped. While they're at it, they might as well figure who will get their socks wet if we add, say, five feet to the wall and levees and water goes over *that*."

Nevers looked at Chuck as if he didn't quite believe what he was hearing. "You think?"

Chuck addressed them all. "I don't think anything. But we're damn well gonna be prepared. Each of you needs to look at your area of responsibility." Once again back to Seth. "Give some thought as to the best way to add to the wall." Chuck resisted the temptation to give him guidance. Let's see what he came up with on his own.

And, one last time, back to the others. "My intention is to keep water out of the damn city, whatever happens. In the meantime, it would help if you didn't go nosing this around. Maybe the exercise is for the hell of it. All right? There's no reason for people to go bugfuck just yet."

Not that Chuck had any hope that Wayne Nevers would keep his yap shut.

~

After the meeting, Chuck took Glenn Owens, the supervisor in the drafting room, aside and asked about Sam Turner.

"What about him?"

"How's he doing?"

Chuck listened as Glenn described the work Sam had been given recently, the drawings for the foundation of a controller.

"So you can still find stuff for him?"

Glenn, more loyal to the organization than Chuck, looked as if what he wanted to say didn't match what he figured he'd better say.

"We've split the work up a little different. That way, we can funnel some things his way."

"And his drawings, they're still okay? The quality?"

Glenn nodded. "He's pretty slow, but yeah, they're still okay."

"Are you getting more work done?"

"More than we would if he wasn't there?"

"Yeah."

Glenn shrugged. "To be truthful, no."

"What about less? Are you getting less done?"

"About the same, I suppose. A little less."

Chuck was conscious that he could cut the conversation short. Some time ago he'd told El Plowman he only went upstairs to deal with situations. He'd been forced to move Sam into the drafting room. So be it. Now Sam was on his own. In Chuck's mind, once a matter had been settled, whether it came out his way or not, he stopped worrying about it. Useless to worry.

Nevertheless, he continued to question Glenn. Perhaps, he thought without enthusiasm, he should have a talk with Sam.

~

An hour later, Chuck sat alone in his office. Johnny Pond had just left, having come to discuss the snow removal problem. Chuck leaned back, arms folded, and contemplated the seven-and-a-half-minute U.S.G.S. maps on the far wall, slightly separated but arranged so that the Mississippi flowed out of one and into the next, something about the maps suggesting the dissection of a brain. He thought about the snow. He thought about Sam Turner. Pond, at the end of their interview, had asked about Sam.

Now Chuck gazed morosely at the map. He wondered, as he had earlier, why the flood promised no adrenaline rush. More work, that's all.

He remembered his favorite mantra when he started feeling sorry for himself—Was it the central highlands? Was it the monsoon? Was anybody shooting at him? Then he was having a pretty good day.

His old boss Mark O'Banion used to stop in at the end of the day and give him a hard time, and they'd walk out together, talking about whatever. Chuck missed that. He missed Mark. Mark made the horseshit endurable. Immediately after his death, he had still lingered in Chuck's life, a shade haunting the places and situations that they'd shared, but the sense of his presence had gradually faded. Now Chuck could remember, but he could no longer talk to Mark and feel that someone was listening.

He remembered Rod Williams, too, his black point man in 'Nam, the one he'd mentioned to Bud Pregler. He remembered Rod, and then he remembered all the other men he had known in Vietnam, the legions of the dead.

And here Chuck was, still alive, still going through the motions.

He stopped thinking and let his consciousness sink into his body. He felt the pressure of the floor against the soles of his feet, of the chair on his ass and back, his folded forearms against the edge of his rib cage. The tug of gravity.

Beneath the calm lay an insinuation of restlessness, and beneath that, another stratum of calm, more profound, like the coral reefs where he used to scuba dive, where he would listen to his breathing, regular and slow, the conserving of oxygen like the slowing down of life itself.

When he roused himself, he called upstairs and countermanded his order. He wouldn't have that little talk with Sam Turner after all.

CHAPTER 35

~

El got back to the house at four thirty and went in past her rose bushes, their new covers still secure. Inside, before taking off her coat, for fear the impulse would be lost, she put in a call to Ultima Thule, to Deke McKeown, the company's flashy CEO. She didn't get through and didn't expect to. She left her home number and said she'd be in the rest of the evening and would appreciate a callback.

She dropped her coat across a chair, wondering if she might conceivably hear from the man. Company presidents felt it unwise to ignore certain public officials—congressmen, heads of permitting agencies. Small city mayors, on the other hand…

She wandered from room to room, trying to decide what to do. No meeting to go to, nothing else, either, a rare unscheduled night. An opportunity. She should be out knocking on doors, but her campaign handouts weren't ready yet. Much else beckoned, every nook and cranny in the house suggested something left undone. But having more to do than humanly possible gave her permission to do nothing.

She sat at the kitchen table and stared at the double reflections in the double pane windows that she and Walter had installed when they restored the house. A modern touch, those windows, blithely decided upon despite the fact that the two of them had so slavishly adhered to authenticity in other matters. But then again, they had a modern furnace, didn't they? And electric lights? And telephones and computers and all manner of other modern conveniences, right down to refrigerator magnets. The house was already a chimera. What did one more thing matter? But those windows…she didn't know. They were like a truth that could have been told but wasn't. Just to save a few dollars on the heating bill.

That was her depression talking. *Good grief,* she thought.

Food. She had to eat. She hunted around in the fridge, looking for something that appealed. Each possibility came with a packet of inertia attached, until she hit upon the idea of eating something she shouldn't. Eggs. Cholesterol. Perfect. Bacon, too. That's it, she'd have a Walter breakfast. If she timed it right, she could watch him giving his weathercast while she ate it. Just the thought of Walter comforted her.

That was Walter, a comfort without even knowing it.

She set about preparing the meal with a will. Under way, however, it was hard for her to stick with a purely authentic Walter breakfast. Three eggs, not two, with pepper, not salt. The bacon cooked until rigor mortis set in. Toast, white toast, ugh, but white toast it would be. He ate it dry, his one concession to good health. Coffee. Coffee? No, no, she couldn't do it, that was asking too much.

As she worked, she was not exactly happy, but for the moment she had a program. At six, she turned on the TV and listened to Walter giving his preview of the weather at the top of the newscast. Turned out he was the star of the show, the lead story. This storm had put the city over the top, a record annual snowfall, 63 inches, with two months left in the season. As she hurried to put her meal on the table, this fact diverted her thoughts for the moment from her other, more strictly human travails. She remembered the callers to *Sound Off* complaining about the crummy job city crews were doing getting rid of the snow. Time for the city council to have another chat with Chuck Fellows, she decided. No doubt they'd need to wring a few more drops out of the old budget to add to snow removal, more than a few drops. Feh.

She ate slowly, rather enjoying the unaccustomed combination of tastes, the peppery eggs and crumbly sweet bacon and ascetic toast. When Walter came on again, giving the regular weathercast, she paid less attention to his words and more to him. Watching on TV, she seemed to see him a little more clearly, less of a given than he was in person, and she studied him somewhat critically, her slightly uncombed, slightly lumpy Walter. He belonged to an era when perceptions didn't matter so much. Speaking of perceptions.

Moving his hands in age-old gestures, back and forth across the weather map, he unveiled his forecast, practically a Delphic oracle in the eyes of his many longtime viewers. She knew that he was actually standing in front of a blank blue wall, waving at nothing, the program engineer using the chroma key process to insert the weather map into the picture sent out to the viewers, and it seemed to El that, despite Walter's expertise, she could detect a certain trace of graceful awkwardness, like a blind man who has learned to get around in his apartment so skillfully that only the initiated knew the truth.

Halfway through the cast, he mentioned Hazel, the name he had given his computer. Whenever he mentioned Hazel by name on the air, that was a code, telling the engineer that some sort of technical glitch had cropped up. El peered even more closely, trying to figure out what had gone wrong, but everything seemed okay. Walter had been doing this so long that—

The phone rang.

She got up, balling her napkin and tossing it aside, and turned down the set, but continued to watch Walter as she went to the counter and answered, thinking—although it made no sense—that the call must have something to do with his problem.

The voice on the other end of the line was cheerfully aggressive, filled with competencies, and it took her a few moments, even after he had told her his name, to realize that the unexpected had happened— Deke McKeown, the Ultima Thule CEO, had returned her call!

She had been sure he wouldn't, hadn't even bothered to prepare an opener, and so, to say something, she told him what she had just been doing, watching her husband on the tube. It turned out McKeown was a secret weather channel addict, which got the conversation off to an undeserved good start. Of course, given the merchandise that he pitched, El realized, it made perfect sense that he loved the weather. No doubt he and Walter would get along like a house afire. He even said he thought he'd seen Walter once or twice, when the national station had done feeds from Jackson for one reason or another.

Thus begun, El and McKeown talked for fifteen minutes like old buddies. He had some sort of banquet he had to attend and put her on a speakerphone as he dressed, adding another odd bit of intimacy to the conversation.

For fifteen minutes, they talked, chummily, frankly, and then McKeown, being on a tight schedule, rang off rather more abruptly than he perhaps intended, his last words fading away like a shifting of attention. El, left by herself, hung up.

The newscast long over, she went and switched off the set. After watching Walter, and then the energetic conversation with McKeown, she found the total silence unpleasant, and the euphoria of the last few minutes began to wear off. She realized that the exchange hadn't been as frank as all that, nor McKeown's friendliness anything more than the friendliness of professional courtesy, McKeown being very good at what he did.

She had, of course, brought up the city's recent racial problems, that had been the whole point, and he'd been the soul of sympathy and she could—she now realized—interpret that sympathy any way she chose.

She glanced at the unfinished Walter meal, her appetite gone, but sat down in front of it again anyway, since she didn't know what else to do.

She stayed there for a long time, watching the eggs congeal. After a while, her mind began to seek out the positive bits which might be gleaned from what had just happened. It had been a foregone conclusion that the call wouldn't lead anywhere. It was simply a possibility that had to be exhausted. She knew that some intensity of unhappiness festered at the company over the city's recent unfortunate publicity, and that was all she was likely to know, no matter how many conversations she had with how many people at Ultima Thule.

She remembered her head-butting with Johnny Pond, who believed that she would fail and who might be right, probably was right.

This thought set her mind off in another direction. How curious it was, really, this being driven by the practical, by the possible. But what was it except discounting the future, playing life on the safe side, taking no chances, and so not seeking what might be possible at all but some lesser thing? Reiny Kopp was different, of course. He positively courted failure. But he wasn't the mayor of the place. If he ran for office on his flat-out do-the-right-thing ticket, how much of the vote would he get? Five percent? Ten? Anybody who was utterly honest could only represent himself.

And thus El's untethered mind drifted, as it always drifted, day or night, seeking that one point, that fulcrum, from which she might truly understand, might at long last launch the single correct act that would serve as the legacy of her many years in public service.

~

Chuck Fellows finally got home. The dogs were already inside and came clicking across the kitchen tile to greet him. He roughhoused with them and checked the length of their nails as he listened for signs of human occupation.

In the cellar, he found Diane wrestling the heavy old Army surplus tent off the storage rack he had built for it. The tent had caught on something. She stepped back and turned her head, just enough to note his presence, then without waiting for help seized the tent again and gave a yank. With a pop, the thing came loose, folding itself over the lip of the rack, then sliding off and performing an ill-tempered jackknife dive to the cement floor, dust shooting to the sides. Diane skipped out of the way.

The floor space had been whittled down by its littoral of packing cases and mothballed toys and Chuck's half dismantled motorcycle. They dragged the tent into the small open area and folded it out section by section to inspect for tears and mildew. Then Chuck hauled it upstairs and deposited it with the rest of the camping gear in the living room, which Diane had converted into a staging area.

The kids came downstairs to see what was up, Todd's disappointment at the reappearance of the old army tent at once made manifest. He wanted a tepee. Only pilgrims went to a rendezvous with an old army tent, and only pork eaters were a more degraded form of humanity than pilgrims. He went tramping back upstairs, exaggerating each step, lost in some fantasy of being bigger than he was. Grace raced up to the tent and stopped dead, as if surprised. She squatted down and touched it gingerly. Almost four now, she was taking more of an interest in her surroundings, as if she had noticed the gap between herself and the world and begun testing ways of bridging it. She decided the tent might be serviceable as a seat and sat down, rather demurely, bounced a couple of times on her little rump, then without comment got up and went to do something else. The dogs sniffed at the linseed oil-impregnated canvas and wandered away. Everybody having commented, the tent was abandoned.

After dinner, he trimmed the dogs' nails. Later, he read Grace a bedtime story. She was surrounded by her stuffed animals, her favorites at the moment Wally the Manatee and Flash the Turtle, this apparently being the natural history phase of her childhood. In Todd's room, Chuck watched his son playing a computer game and followed as best he could Todd's disjointed explanation of the object of the game. Something about saving the universe, a proposition which Chuck couldn't work up much enthusiasm for at the moment.

Down in the cellar, he tinkered with his motorcycle, which he hadn't touched in months. Fetching the tent upstairs had reminded him of it. On the workbench were piled back copies of *Engineering News-Record*, a foot-high stack, each issue with some story he had meant to read. He leafed through a couple of copies and came upon an article on failure analysis, which seemed appropriate, and so, standing up, he read that and sipped his beer, and listened to Diane moving about overhead, doing something in the living room.

～

Jack Kelley got home at 7:15. Janelle was cooking a new dish, which meant that she was even more testy than usual. "Talk to me," she said.

He gave her an edited version of his day, not mentioning that he'd gone to Mass. Not mentioning that he'd written the letter to the concessionaire, either, since he could do without one of her comments. Instead he told her about the inevitability of racial problems at the job site and that Tony Vasconcellos, who should be helping out, was doing anything but.

Fish fillets lay on paper towels next to the sink. Various foodstuffs and mechanical weaponry were scattered about the culinary battlefield.

"Maybe," she said, as she diced a bundle of chives, "what you need down there is a, whajamacallit, a chaplain. How about your friend Mike Daugherty?"

This suggestion fell under the heading of provocation.

"I hadn't thought of that."

"That's his job, isn't it?"

"What? Doing chaplaincy kinds of things?" He didn't know if *chaplaincy* was actually a word, but it sounded close enough.

"Keeping the lid on."

"Smoothing troubled waters? I suppose. What about the Protestants?"

"There are Protestants?" Janelle thought all construction workers were shanty Irish.

"I expect. Haven't asked."

"Anyway, doesn't one size fit all in these sorts of situations?"

"You mean, like in wartime?"

"Like Father whozits on *M.A.S.H.*"

Since getting a chaplain wasn't a serious suggestion on Janelle's part, the conversation was pointless, but she'd push it as far as she could. It was her way of needling him about the Vasconcellos situation, which she considered another bonehead Jack move, Jack saddling himself with more trouble. This time, she was right. She didn't, in fact, know Vasconcellos from Adam, the Vasconcellos family belonging to the Saturday congregation at St. Columbkille's, but she knew Mike Daugherty—oh, yes, indeed—and she knew the circumstances surrounding Vasconcellos getting the bid for the electrical. Not that Jack had had any intention of ever telling her. For that he had Father Mike to thank, Mike blabbing to Janelle, thinking he was doing a favor by telling Janelle what a good boy was Jack.

At the moment, the best Jack could hope for was to nudge the subject in a somewhat more neutral direction.

"Mulcahy," he said, "but that's just a TV show."

"It's based on real life."

"It is? I don't think so."

"I heard somewhere."

"Quote your source."

"Don't be ridiculous. Shit!" She was hovering over the recipe. She'd made some sort of mistake. That was what the "Shit!" was about.

"Okay," he said, "but no way I'm going to use Father Mike down on the job site, even assuming he was willing, which he wouldn't be." Mike had enough lives to interfere with already.

"Suit yourself." Janelle still hovered over the recipe, and he could tell she was trying to figure a way of repairing the damage. But she continued to talk. "Anyway, isn't this the city's problem? Chuck whatzisface should be doing something about it."

"Chuck Fellows? Let me tell you about Chuck Fellows." He already had, of course, more than once. With other people who gave Jack a hard time, there was always a bill of particulars, something he could list on the indictment. With Fellows, such niceties weren't necessary.

"The man doesn't care, simple as that. I'm through trying. I'll deal with him when I absolutely have to, but that's it. I need something done, I'll figure another way to do it."

Janelle was reaching up to the top shelf to get a little-used bowl. "That's my Jack. Somebody doesn't do his job, Jack does it for him."

This was, of course, her old sweet song, which Jack mostly let slide. But not at that moment.

"You know Fellows, Janelle? Do you?"

"No, of course not, what are you talking about?"

"Then give it a rest."

"I'm just saying."

"I know what you're saying."

"You let people take advantage, Jack, you know you do. Don't get all huffy with me." Janelle had this interesting tactic when fighting, a matter-of-factness, as if she had one hand tied behind her back just to give him a chance. But casual or not, once sure of her ground, she could not be moved. When she got to the pearly gates, St. Peter would let her through just to avoid the hassle.

Jack decided to keep his thoughts to himself for the moment. He watched her going about her business, tracing a cat's cradle between counters and sink and pantry and fridge, stopping time and again to stare suspiciously down at the recipe.

Neither of them was speaking, but Jack knew he could expect another zinger at any moment. He thought about Janelle's whimsical proposal for a chaplain at the job site. Totally impossible, of course. Second best would be to go to Father Mike and see if something couldn't be done about Vasconcellos. That was worth thinking about.

The back door opened, and their daughter Kitty came in, pulling her cap off, shaking out her hair and scattering snowflakes.

She looked at Jack, then her mother, and started poking around the kitchen, inspecting preparations.

"When's din-din?"

"Eight," her mother said. "Is your friend going to join us?"

"Suppose. You know him better than me."

Kitty's current fiancé was soon to be an ex-fiancé, although he apparently didn't know it yet.

Below her parka, she had on her nurse's whites. "It's awfully quiet in here."

"Your mother and I are taking a breather."

Kitty sniffed suspiciously at the fish lying translucent and defenseless next to the sink; then, having satisfied herself as to the current state of the household, told them that if Kenneth showed, she was upstairs getting changed. She left.

The two of them alone again, Janelle stopped what she was doing long enough to turn and say, "You're the construction manager, Jack. Something will happen and they'll blame you."

"That's right."

"Everybody will blame you, and you'll let them."

Unlike Jack, Janelle did not feel compelled to accept the world as it was.

When the doorbell rang, either the first of the guests arriving or Kitty's almost-ex-fiancé, Jack was thinking that, yes, for once he wouldn't mind Father Mike sticking his nose in.

CHAPTER 36

~

In the storm, the board planking leading down to Reiny Kopp's houseboat, though it had been salted, still looked too treacherous for any but the suicidal, or so it seemed to Sam Turner. Yet as he hesitated, a woman carrying a platter of food went by him and down like a dancer, holding the plate high over head and laughing, caught at the bottom by others before her momentum carried her over the dock and out onto the ice-covered harbor.

Sam had been born with no sense of balance. He couldn't even walk along the top of a roadside curb without falling off. But at the moment, shamed by the woman's giddy descent and seeing no alternative to some sort of attempt of his own, he began to go timidly down, sidestepping, slipping, and tottering. Halfway down, his legs went out from under him, and the rest of the way, he slid on his ass and rolled and scrambled backwards on hands and knees.

At the bottom, the others clapped and helped him up and dusted off the snow and gave him style points. Sam knew that he should join in the merriment at his pratfall, but felt too ashamed, and the others, seeing his discomfort, hesitated and then left him alone. More people descended in his wake, using different techniques, carrying stuff and aahing and oohing as they came.

Inside the houseboat, in the steamy heat given off by a woodstove in the middle of the large, low-ceilinged room, all the old activists of Reiny's generation were gathering. Sam had been the only black in so many groups of white people that he hardly noticed anymore. But he noticed the other differences, and wondered just what Reiny had in mind inviting him, him being younger than all the rest and not any kind of activist, past or present, just a dude trying to make do and get along. He and Reiny weren't friends or anything. Reiny only knew him at all because Sam had been helping out on the museum exhibit.

Kate Sullivan, Reiny's wife, took him over to the drinks table and listed the possibilities—soda, beer, wine, and also a bottle of rum to make Cuba libres, which Kate said that Reiny had decided to call Jackson libres for the evening. "You know Reiny." The comment seemed less a matter of fact than her way of making Sam feel welcome. He asked where Reiny was.

"Went to Chicago. Surprised he isn't back by now."

"Not much of a day for a ride."

"You know Reiny."

She left Sam to make his choice among the drinks. He took a beer although he wanted a Jackson libre. But the rum hadn't been opened, and he wasn't about to do it himself.

All around him, conversations were rocketing along. These people shared a past and had much to talk about, and Sam figured that any group he butted in on would right away get awkward, so he went over and looked in a big fish tank along one of the walls, filled with murky water and ugly looking fish. Most likely right out of the Mississippi, he decided. The fish twitched slightly as they eyed him out of one side of their heads.

Next he walked along the tables where the food for the potluck had been set out, peeking under lids.

He felt a light touch on his arm and, startled, turned his head and found himself staring into the encouraging smile and blue eyes and white hair of an old woman.

She said, "We saw you standing here and decided we just had to come over. The others are shy, you know."

For a moment, he didn't know who "we" were, but then saw an old man behind her, coming forward with his hand already outstretched.

"I'm Pete." He took Sam's hand and shook it with very small up and down motions.

"And I'm Emma," said the woman.

Sam shook her hand, too, and introduced himself.

"You're the Breitbachs," he said.

Emma nodded, matter-of-factly. "Everybody knows us... although not everybody approves."

The Breitbachs must have been in their eighties. Many times he'd seen them standing vigil outside the post office, occasionally both of them, but mostly one at a time, taking turns, protesting U.S. involvement in Central America or the Middle East or somewheres else. He'd never stopped to talk with them, although he'd been tempted. Somebody told him they were communists back in the thirties, maybe still were.

He wondered how they'd managed to get down the embankment outside.

"I've seen you at the post office."

"We've been doing that for twenty-seven years," Emma told him.

"It was Emma's idea," Pete added.

Emma was fairly heavyset and twinkly, Pete thin and grave, so they didn't look at all alike, despite what was said about people who had been married forever.

"And, of course, we've heard about you, too," Emma replied slyly, as if they were three famous people, long known to the general public, meeting face-to-face for the first time.

The Breitbachs introduced Sam around, and in this way he started to get a little more comfortable, although he still didn't know why Reiny had invited him.

As for Reiny, he finally arrived. Wasting no time, he opened his arms wide. "Let us deal with the eats first, my friends. Then to the serious business at hand."

He went over and lifted the first lid he came to. The food, it turned out, was supposed to reflect the revolutionary spirit of the group. "Let's see what we've got here. A tureen of borscht." He sniffed at it suspiciously. "Hmmm...I have to say, folks, the Russkies have been a major disappointment."

"We brought that," admitted Pete Breitbach.

"Let the minutes show that Pete and Emma confessed."

"It's for what might have been."

"What might have been." Reiny meditated on this thought. "I tell you one thing, the Soviets could've learned a thing or two from Pete and Emma."

Someone clapped, others joined in, and soon everybody in the place had risen and was toasting the Breitbachs.

Reiny lifted the next lid. "Stew."

"Diggers' stew," the contributor informed him.

"Ah, yes, the Diggers. Haven't thought about them for years." He shook his head. "Ahead of their time. Ahead of our time. I trust all the makings were stolen."

"Liberated," someone corrected.

Sam didn't have any idea who the Diggers might have been.

Reiny continued down the table, picking the covers off the Crock-Pots and chafing dishes, inspecting the food for adequate left-wing ardor. He came to a pot of greens.

"Soul food," the man who had brought it said, a white guy.

"It just looks like spinach to me," Reiny said. "Where's the collards? Where's the—help me out here, Sam, what do you need for an official mess of greens?"

Sam didn't know. His momma sometimes cooked something she called soul food, but he never paid much attention to what was in it. After a moment of panic, he tried to fake it. "Kale." He seemed to remember something about kale. Anyway, it sounded right. "I think maybe okra, too. And...red...—red something.

"I thought okra was for gumbo," Reiny said.

"Turnip greens," someone suggested, one of the women.

"Turnip greens and mustard greens," another woman put in.

"Yeah, that's right," Sam said.

Reiny had already continued down the table. Sam's tentative good mood took a tumble. Okra? What a damn fool thing to say.

Arriving at the desserts, Reiny inspected a pan of brownies. "Are these things store-bought?"

"Not hardly," the man who had baked them assured him. "Couldn't get the right ingredients in any store I know of."

"Most excellent. I knew I could count on you, Jerry. We'll save these beauties for afterwards." The Breitbachs had introduced Sam to Jerry, who had gray hair pulled back into a ponytail and showed bad teeth when he smiled and was smoking, his fingers stained with nicotine. He was the only one present who looked like a genuine ex-hippie to Sam.

Reiny had arrived at the end of the last table. He looked quizzically at a bowl of fruit.

"And what have we here?"

"Fruit," the donor said cryptically.

"Fruit is nice."

"No grapes."

"No grapes! Right, yes, a most excellent compote, then! No grapes. That's what every meal should end with. No grapes!" And this call was taken up by the others, until the room echoed with the cries of "No grapes!"

"My friends," Reiny said when the chanting ended, "dig in!"

Sam went over to get himself another beer, and finding that the rum had been cracked, poured himself a Jackson libre. Then he filled his plate and walked around until a group made a space for him to sit down, his plate on his lap.

Close up, these people seemed even older. Maybe they used to raise some hell, but now they looked pretty much like everybody else. Except for the one called Jerry.

As he ate, Sam listened to the stories. He kept his drink between his feet, took a pull on it from time to time, and when it got low went to refresh it. After a time, he started to feel all right again. He preferred listening. When someone spoke to him, asked what it was like growing up in the projects, he told them a little—about his momma trying to raise three kids by herself and his father who sometimes came around for a few days, always bringing something for Sam and the others. He even mentioned the fresh air camp he'd got to attend a couple of years, which made him determined to get out of the city for good one day. There had been a lot of bad shit, too, but mostly he didn't talk about that, although he knew it was what these white people really wanted to hear about. Sometimes, if he got drunk enough, he'd talk about it, but he wasn't drunk enough yet.

By the time Reiny rapped on his glass for attention, the people around Sam had pretty much lost interest in him. Whatever the image of the proper black man they had in their heads, he wasn't it.

Reiny wandered around the room. It didn't take him long to get up a head of steam. "I invited Hiram and Pearl Johnson here tonight, but they didn't want to come. They've washed their hands of the exhibit. Figure Jackson is pretty much beyond redemption is my guess."

Reiny walked behind Sam and Sam felt his hands on his shoulders, and it soon became clear why he had been invited.

"Some people believe it was the museum started everything. Not true. Others say the closing of the packinghouse and Sam here getting a job some people thought ought to go to a white boy, that's when it started, they say."

Sam felt the hands lift off his shoulders, and Reiny wandered back into view, still talking.

"But that's not true, either. It didn't start last year or the year before or the year before that... I'll tell you when—1619. When the first slave ship landed in Virginia, that's when this shit started. It started then and it's still going on. Isn't that right, Sam?"

Reiny didn't wait for an answer. He asked another question.

"Tell me, Sam, what do you think? You think we're beyond redemption?"

Sam hesitated.

Reiny put the hesitation to good use. "If you know Sam, my friends, you know he never has a bad word to say about anyone. One of the real ironies of the situation. Here's a man just trying to catch a break. Make a life for himself. Get along with people. Never a bad word for anyone... Of course, a black man who lives in Jackson would be a fool to say what he really thinks. Isn't that right, Emma?" Emma Breitbach nodded, but Reiny didn't see the nod. He had already turned his back and continued pacing.

Halfway across the room, he stopped and said, "Vietnam," just the single word, and then continued his transit, circling a table laden with the ruins of the meal, then stopping again, once again only briefly and looking at one of the people Sam hadn't met. "You remember Vietnam, Sid, right?" And on he continued, the others held in a kind of thrall like the characters in one of the fantasy novels Sam liked to read.

Finally, Reiny arrived back at his starting point and turned to face the room.

"In 1968, we refused to live in a country that would go to war against a people that had never done us any harm. And we did something about it. And we didn't worry about whether we could stop the war, either. Did we, Mac? Hell, no! We knew we couldn't change anything, not by ourselves. But that didn't matter!" He was picking out people at different points in the room, now a woman even more middle-aged and housewifely looking than the rest. "You remember, Sally, don't you? Taking a stand, that was all that mattered." He cranked his head around on that stalk of a neck of his and picked out someone else. "Remember, Jerry, remember?"

"I hear you, brother," Jerry called out.

"Why is it, then, that we're willing to live in a city that every day goes to war against its black citizens? Who in this room—except Pete and Emma, Pete and Emma are always the exceptions—who in this room has ever put himself on the line for the black people of this city? Tell me, Margaret, why is that? Is it that racism is lodged so deep in the soul of this town that nobody could root it out, is that what you think?" He continued to move, swinging his head this way and that, letting no one off the hook. "Isn't that what you say, Mel? Isn't that what we all say?" Nobody, in fact, was saying much of anything except Reiny. The whole evening had suddenly got very heavy duty. "Racism in the bone. Nothing to be done, nothing to be done." He moved several paces without speaking. "We didn't worry about this sort of thing in '68. We did what we had to do, period. Why is it any different now? Tell me. I want to know." He scanned the room and let this idea hang in the air briefly, then dropped it.

"Okay, so this is the thing…what we have here is an opportunity. You can forget about anybody else doing anything. The question is, what are *we* gonna do?" He continued to look around, to take everyone in.

Sam could sense the uneasiness of the others, white folks who had long ago made peace with whatever they had to make peace with.

"Where's the old perversity, people?" Reiny asked. "We used to be good at flipping these assholes the bird. We're older now. We oughta be smarter. We oughta be better at it."

Sam studied the faces around him, trying to read in the settled countenances the traces of the troublemakers they had once been. Not being himself a troublemaker—except by accident—he felt a little envy at their rambunctious pasts and, it was true, a little glad at their present reluctance, being as how he was so habitually reluctant himself. Most of all, he was glad to be out of it, to let white folks worry about other white folks for once. Or relieved, maybe that was a better word.

In the silence, Reiny stood, bony and unrelenting.

Chapter 37

~

Deuce Goetzinger returned to the union's proposal and picked another article to haggle over: safety eyeglass policy. He sat on his side of the table flanked by the union people, while Aggie Klauer lounged across from him, the finance director and steno as her seconds.

Deuce had gotten precisely nowhere. He and Aggie jockeyed back and forth, new arguments to him, but obviously heirlooms as far as Klauer was concerned. She spent part of her time gazing at him speculatively and the rest shooting the wobbly edifices he erected in the union cause full of holes. Deuce had sat opposite enough marks in his life to see, reflected in those blue gun-sight eyes of hers, the same fatal signs in himself.

Yet he liked the tension. He remembered it from his earlier days of playing poker. The edge that came from the withholding of information. The edge of fear, too. He might lose, and losing mattered, which was strange, since nothing much was at stake. He hadn't changed his mind about that.

Next to him, Barbara Amos shifted uncomfortably as he took his lumps. He'd told her to keep her drawers on, no matter what happened.

J.J. was out somewhere driving around on his truck, so Deuce could forget about any comic relief.

The session wore on. From funeral leave, they went on to casual days, then longevity, then shift premium pay.

Aggie smiled often, versions of disbelief and irony and the invitation to capitulate. The arguments she made held no evident interest for her, but her eyes remained alert, making small adjustments as she concentrated on his face, like a photographer touching up a portrait.

"Okay then, what about Article VI?" she asked with a kind of mock exasperation, rifling through the union proposal as if in search of one thing, just one thing they might agree on. "Nondis-crimination. Of course, we're all against discrimination, but the article serves no purpose. Such matters are covered by other legal instruments. What say we take it out?"

Deuce hadn't given Article VI a thought. He'd read it once and then forgotten about it. Now, surreptitiously, he tried to read it again. But he had to talk, he had to say something. "Can't hurt, Aggie, leaving it in. The more remedies the better, right?"

"The grievance procedure is simpler than going to court," Barb Amos put in, eagerly leaping to the attack. "Anyway, suppose cases are backed up or something. It could take forever. This way, people can settle the thing faster."

Aggie responded to Barb's argument, but she didn't look at Barb. Instead, elbow propped on table, chin propped on her fist, she gazed at Deuce. "Grievances just add another layer to the process. These are the kind of issues that go to arbitration, but arbiters don't have a background in discrimination procedures. So you end up in court anyway. Time lost, not saved." The cool gaze aimed at him seemed to say, "You don't know anything, do you?"

Deuce had mostly been ignoring the minor provisions in the contract. Stupid. No matter how trivial, each one of the fuckers had a history. It pissed him off. He'd always had the answers—in school, to his father—he'd always known what to say.

"What about Article VII, then?" Aggie asked, her tone sug-gesting she had no expectations here either. "Military leave. This is already in the state code. It's redundant in the agreement."

Another article that Deuce had ignored, another opportunity, no doubt, to make an ass out of himself.

When Barb started to pipe up again, he reached out and put a hand on her shoulder.

"Might be it's in the code," he said to Klauer, "but the code could be changed. In which case, we want language in the contract." This instantly concocted rationale seemed to have some merit. He congratulated himself.

Aggie, however, didn't appear to be exactly devastated by the outburst of logic. She was leaning far over the table, sagging on her elbow, either slightly amused or bored out of her gourd.

"Section 6 says the Iowa code prevails in all instances. If the law changes, so does the contract."

"That doesn't apply to the earlier sections." Barb said fervently.

"'In every case, military leave shall be granted in accordance with the Code of Iowa, Section 29A.28,'" Aggie quoted from memory.

"We don't agree," Barb insisted.

Aggie waved her hand lazily to show it wasn't a matter worth fighting over. Her eyes weighed Deuce. He had done nothing to redeem himself.

They continued. Arriving at last at the pay provisions proposed by the union and city, where they were farthest apart, Aggie talked about keeping layoffs to a minimum and Deuce about pay raises in comparable Iowa cities. And finally, nothing having been accomplished, a silence descended upon the table.

The session had ended.

Almost. Deuce had no intention of leaving it at that. Klauer thought he was an idiot, that he'd been sitting around with his thumb up his ass all this time, but she was wrong. He'd taken his lumps. Now it was his turn.

"Not doing too well, are we?" he began, leaning back, arms crossed, smiling.

Aggie, being smart and thus instantly aware that something was afoot, adjusted herself in her chair and paid attention. "No, we're not."

"Trouble is," he said, "all we do is talk about this...trivial stuff. Waste of time, don'cha think?" She gave no indication one way or the other. "And, I know," he told her, pausing for effect, "there are all these issues the city would like to—how shall I put it?—explore." Before he continued, he reached out and, without looking, touched Barb Amos's sleeve with his fingertips. She wasn't going to like what came next. "Making work rules more flexible, for instance, how about that? There's something we might talk about. Or increasing efficiency? Paul Cutler just loves talking about increasing efficiency, doesn't he? More bang for the buck and all that. And what about... aaah, I don't know, I'm sure you'd be better at making suggestions then me." He smiled pleasantly at Aggie. "How about a two-tier pay system, how about that? There's something to hash over."

This was too much for Barb Amos. "Deuce!" He turned toward her for a moment and mouthed the words, "Take it easy." Barb was, indeed, very unhappy.

Aggie had sat up straight. A union man broaching the possibility of a two-tier system? Efficiency? Flexible work rules? Here was something not covered in the city manager's charge to her. She leaned forward, blinking, too startled to hide the fact that she was startled.

"Or flexible benefit plans or...," he continued.

But as he continued to retail this list, management's wet dream, her eyes suddenly narrowed. "Oh, I get it," she said. "It's the thing."

"The thing?"

"That committee of yours, the one with no instructions. What we're not going to talk about."

"Did I mention any committee?"

"No, you didn't. How cute."

"The point is, here are all these things you're interested in. Right? But not the union. Not us. We hate every one of 'em."

"So this committee of yours is going to be my secret garden of delights, is that the idea?"

He shrugged and smiled his best poker player's smile. "Never can tell. No instructions."

"That's right, you never can tell." She grinned back. "And you never will, either, because this is the last time the matter is going to come up. The city isn't required to discuss this, and we're not going to. I've told you before, I'm telling you again."

"Teamwork," Deuce said. Aggie looked at him suspiciously, alert now that she realized he might be a rank amateur but wasn't altogether incapable of launching sneak attacks. "Next time you talk to Paul Cutler, Aggie, you might ask him just how serious he is about this teamwork business. He talks about it enough. Is he serious? Or isn't he? A lot of people got their doubts. But he can prove they're wrong. Easy."

She closed her eyes and exhaled. "I'm not going to talk about the committee."

"We're not talking about it."

"Oh?"

"No. We're talking about whether we should talk about it."

"I'm not going to talk about that either."

"Why not?"

She folded her arms and snorted, a little ladylike snort.

All this was amusing enough, but he saw that it wasn't going to get him very far. So he changed his tone. "Ask Cutler if he's interested in teamwork, Aggie. You can do that much. If he is, then the committee's just the ticket. If he isn't, then tell him to do us all a big favor and stop wasting our time with all this rah-rah bull. Let us do our damn jobs and go home."

Deuce didn't have any threats that weren't empty, but what the hell. Aggie immediately adjusted herself to this new serious tone. She ignored the content, however. Her amusement at his little ploy had been replaced by consideration. And a decision, apparently, that the fun and games were over. She ran her hand back over the top of her hair.

"We're not going to talk about the committee, Deuce. We don't have to and we're not going to. If you bring it up again, I'll end the session. Okay?"

"You're missing an opportunity."

"And if you try to slip it in all unawares again, I'll end the session, then, too. Do you understand?"

He leaned back and they regarded each other in this new grave manner. Perhaps, he thought, he should have kept things whimsical. Small arms fire, since Aggie, after all, was the one with the howitzers.

"Well," he said, "I guess that's it, then."

Now, having gotten her way, something of speculation came back into her gaze for a few moments. She held a clenched fist in front of her mouth and tapped her lips thoughtfully and then took the fist away. "I guess it is," she said.

CHAPTER 38

~

Mostly, Aggie didn't bother Paul Cutler with the details of her negotiating sessions. A comment or two at Monday morning staff meetings sufficed. She'd only gone up the time before last because of the sudden appearance of Deuce Goetzinger. And she only went up this time because...because she went up. She had a plan. Well, *plan* was rather too swell a word for her half-a-loaf of an idea.

Paul wasn't in. Aggie worked out with his secretary when she might have a decent shot at cornering him later, and then trooped back to her office, feeling restless and uninterested in other matters.

On top of her desk lay a phone message from Lucille: "Crisis. Call home at once."

Aggie sat down. With one finger, she pushed the message to the left. To the right, equally unwelcome, squatted a folder stuffed with paperwork, sheaf after sheaf like geological strata, her friend Joyce Pins's unending attempt to get herself reclassified. No, she'd told Joyce, no and no again. But even with practice, she didn't like the chore. Getting reclassified had become for Joyce a moral crusade, as if she were striking a blow for downtrodden clerk-typists everywhere. Doing for others by doing for herself. Now Joyce had a new champion: Chuck Fellows. Made no difference.

Aggie stared at the folder, then back at the message from Lucille. Scylla and Charybdis.

This being a good day to seek third ways, she wondered what else she might undertake. But then again, there was always the chance, however remote, that something was actually wrong with her mother. Suppose, just suppose. Aggie would never forgive herself.

So she made the call, to be on the safe side, and as she predicted, it was unnecessary. Lucille had taken care of the problem herself, whatever it was, and even seemed a little surprised to hear from Aggie, even a little miffed. Vintage Lucille. Her mother's annoyance, despite the absurdity of it, made Aggie feel guilty and, as if to make amends, she promised to stop down for a visit before bowling.

The phone call disposed of, Aggie stared at the fat folder. Might as well deal with that, too. She wrote another cease and desist memo to Joyce, thinking what a pain mothers and friends could be. At least, she consoled herself, she didn't have a lover, too. Which reminded her of Deuce Goetzinger, the cardsharp and lothario turned workplace reformer.

She took a break from her labors and leaned back for a few minutes and thought about the union's impossible proposal. Which she loved.

~

When they did the makeover of the second floor of city hall, the manager's office had been left alone, its august Victorian dimensions intact, as befitted the dignity of the city manager. Entering the room from the low-ceilinged antechamber, Aggie always felt a little bit like she did when she went outdoors, as if she might look up to see the clouds drifting overhead and gauge the weather.

Although, of course, looking up to gauge the weather in that room wouldn't help. It was necessary to turn your attention to the man sitting at the desk.

Paul glanced toward her, nothing friendly in the look. "Yes?"

"I met with the big union again," she told him, trying to strike a tone somewhere between the businesslike and casual, but realizing too late that she wasn't as well prepared for this as she imagined.

"I see." Paul paused only for an instant, puzzled no doubt why this wasn't something that could wait. "Any progress?"

"No. We pounded our chests and hooted is all."

He continued to look at her as if he didn't understand why in the world she was there, which, of course, he didn't, not until she got up the nerve to present her idea for a compromise.

The room was filled with the odor of buttered popcorn. A half-empty bag sat on his desk, which reminded her that it was her bowling night. And wouldn't it have been nice if she'd been bowling at just that moment?

"Perhaps," he said, "you ought to have a word with your friend Dusterhoft on the side. Show him the instruments of torture."

"J.J. wasn't there today."

"Off the committee, do you suppose?"

"Out plowing."

"Ah, of course."

"Anyway, makes no difference. He's in disgrace now, or at least nobody's listening to him for the moment."

"I see."

"I didn't expect any movement, and we didn't get any," Aggie said, speaking rather too quickly. "The 10 percent giveback freaked the union. They're just waiting for the impasse procedures is my guess."

Paul, having apparently accommodated himself to Aggie's intrusion, got up and walked over to the window and looked down on the street traffic. It being the end of the day, his clothes were disheveled, his shirt askew from many casual retuckings, his suit trousers riding low on his hips. His attitudes, Aggie had always thought, were the attitudes of a taller and thinner and neater man.

"They've got to understand that now's the time for concession bargaining," he told her.

She looked at his back and thought, *Easy for you to say*. She imagined his view of the streetscape below. "To make it work, you need trust. You need respect," she told him. "J.J. and I had it, but Mr. Goetzinger—forget about it. And, what's more, he doesn't know much. Not about negotiating, at least. Probably not about the union, either."

"What could they have been thinking?" the manager said from the window, where he continued to look down, his tone hinting at a sadness, as if he had already passed beyond the acceptance of her interruption and onto some other matter entirely.

"I don't know," Aggie said. "But..."

He waited.

"We've never gone to arbitration before unless we thought we could win." Mediation, first, and when that failed, arbitration. The city would lose. No arbitrator in the world would grant them a pay cut that large.

"Then let's not go to arbitration," Paul told her. "Up to you, Aggie. You've got to convince them."

He spoke now of the union's responsibility to save union jobs, the employees' responsibility to protect city services. Aggie looked at the mottling on the side of the popcorn sack where the butter had soaked through, and comforted herself with thoughts of bowling.

When she judged the time was right, as good as it would ever be, she said, "Deuce Goetzinger *did* bring up the workplace democracy idea again, by the way."

"What did you tell him?"

"No dice."

"Good."

"I told him I'd end the session if he brought it up again."

"Very good. If he wants to act like a child, we'll treat him like one."

"But despite all that...," she continued timidly and then stopped, cutting herself off, not even waiting for Paul to do it.

He craned to inspect the sky toward the west, like a man looking for signs of clearing. Aggie imagined the clouds, a solid gray stretching west and disappearing over the bluffs.

"I just hate it when we get back-to-back storms like this," he said. He had legal obligations to keep city hall open, no matter what.

Aggie screwed up her courage. "I've been thinking. Why not revive the idea of employee involvement teams? You remember: 'Here's the problem; here are the parameters; we accept what you do if it's done within these.'" Whatever Paul had thought of this scheme of hers the first time around, it ought to look a good deal better now (although, as a matter of fact, it looked a good deal worse to Aggie herself).

Paul glanced at her over his shoulder, then turned around and thoughtfully returned to his desk and sat down. "Yes, I suppose that's something we might consider."

Aggie perked up a bit. "Anyway, it would be something I could bring to the table."

"No, no, no, no," Paul said quickly. "It'd be a response to the union proposal. Can't have that. No, no. Afterwards. When the dust has settled. Then maybe we can talk about it. We'll see."

She wanted to argue, but her little boomlet of enthusiasm had already collapsed. "I suppose."

"Good."

And that was it. Moments later, she was out the door and on the way back down to her office.

What a wuss, she scolded herself, but in fact she felt worse than wussy. She'd blown it. It wasn't a matter of getting him to agree or not. He had the power, and nothing she could do about that. But she'd been afraid to stand up to him. She brought her little idea up, he'd said no, or almost no, and she'd been out the door as fast as if she'd stepped into an elevator shaft. She was afraid of him. She'd always been afraid of him. Afraid of his certainty. How could a man be that certain? She'd been afraid of his scorn, too. If she turned around now and went back up to his office, as soon as she got through the door, she'd wilt again, she knew it.

And he could have let her make the offer to the union. He wasn't trading it for anything. If he wasn't such a dinosaur, he would've seen that he wasn't trading it for anything, not a damn thing.

All the joy had gone out of the day. She'd even lost her appetite for bowling.

CHAPTER 39

~

J.J. Dusterhoft wasn't quite asleep yet. Or perhaps he was. Hard to tell. It being after five, Jimmy, the street department clerk, had gone home for the day, and J.J. had requisitioned his chair and now lay as prone as humanly possible, his eyes closed, the only noise the static coming from the intercom between the office and the gas pumps outside.

Someone had come in and was standing nearby. J.J. didn't hear the door open or footsteps. Not necessary. He could feel the adjustments in atmospheric pressure as the person moved around, the subtle torquing of the air in the room, and then its cease. He opened one eye. Deuce Goetzinger, hatless and ruddy from the cold, standing a couple of paces away, contemplating the corpse. J.J. closed his eye, Goetzinger's image swelling to fill the screen inside his head.

Deuce said, "Your pal Aggie Klauer had me for lunch."

"Of course she did." J.J. considered this and found something attractive in Goetzinger's forthrightness. "You're too light in the ass, my friend, to meet her on the open field. Now kindly go away. I need my beauty sleep."

J.J. waited, eyes still closed, for the atmospheric change that would announce Deuce's departure. He waited in vain.

"You're a hard man to find," Deuce said.

"Obviously not hard enough."

J.J. gave up on the idea of sleep. "Three weeks of twelve-hour shifts. Not as young as I once was." He climbed stiffly out of the chair and reached around to knead the sore muscles of his lower back, conscious of the middle-aged thickness of his body.

A cop car had pulled up at the pumps and the cop gotten out. "Anybody home?" he said into the intercom.

J.J. went over to the control panel, got the vehicle number and odometer reading from the cop, then pushed the button that activated the system. As he waited, he said to Deuce, "I suppose you might as well tell me what happened."

After the cop had finished filling his tank, J.J. wrote down the number of gallons dispensed on the fuel sheet and then pressed the bar which cleared the meter. Trailed by Goetzinger, he headed out back to see how they were coming with his truck, all the time Deuce telling him what had happened. "Klauer doesn't appear very taken with our proposal for the committee."

"Even if she loves it," J.J. said, "not much she can do, not unless Cutler decides he loves it, too."

"So Cutler hides in his office, tells Klauer what to do, and waits for us to cave. That's supposed to be negotiating in good faith?"

"Hobson's choice. But you've gotta understand we're not talking about poker here. Or a shoot-out at the O.K. Corral. Anyone with real authority would be a damn fool to sit down at the table himself." J.J. and Aggie, of course, had always known this to be so and never gotten too exercised over the fact, life being short and all that.

Out in the shop, he walked around his truck, looking for Brian, the mechanic who took care of most of the breakdowns. Found him rummaging around for something on his workbench, chewing on gum or tobacco or his tongue.

"Well?"

"Transmission. Two weeks."

"Knew it," J.J. said.

This was not necessarily bad news. All the other trucks were either out on the road or out of service. For one blissful moment, J.J. had a vision of himself asleep at home. Two weeks ought to be just about enough time.

"You can use forty-two," Brian told him.

"It's running?"

"Had her out for a spin just last month." Brian loved forty-two.

Rubbing his hands on an old oil-and-grease-soaked rag, a time-honored gesture among the mechanical brethren, Brian turned his attention toward Deuce.

"J.J. here was tellin' us about this committee thing of yours. I got a question for ya." Brian asked his question, his tone not the sort which would give a person encouragement. "What if Cutler calls your bluff?"

Deuce remained expressionless.

"Because," Brian told him, "you can forget about a giveback. No way I vote for that. Cutler can suck my dick for all I care. He don't get one friggin' cent."

"You can see," J.J. explained to Deuce, as if the words required interpretation, "Brian has some reservations."

J.J. and Deuce walked back toward the storage barn, and Deuce asked him about forty-two. "I didn't even know there were any vehicles left with two-letter designations."

"Waste not, want not."

They circled around the trash haulers, drawn up for the night in two rows, nose to nose like square dancers beginning a figure, and moved deeper into the dim, echoey building, past the tow truck, through the vacated spot where the graders were normally parked, gone now because they had every available piece of equipment out on the street, except for forty-two. They sidled past the SnoGo trucks which would be pressed into service when the snow stopped and it was possible to start hauling the accumulation, past the end loaders, past the small dump trucks, past the sewer cleaner, the TV van, the oil tanker parked for the winter, the walking mowers, the street sweepers, and the flusher, until, in the very ass end of the cavernous space, they arrived at forty-two, old and humpy and modest.

J.J. thumped it on the fender. "A 1949 REO Speed Wagon, first truck I ever drove when I started with the city. Still got her original paint job." In the gloomy recesses, however, it might have been any color. The truck's plow blade rested on the concrete. J.J. did a quick circuit. The salt spreading equipment had been installed but no salt.

"Let's see if we can get her outside for a look-see." J.J. had his doubts. Yet, it was true, Brian did love that machine.

They moved stuff to clear a path and then climbed into the old, rounded cab of the REO. The reedy steering wheel and gear shift didn't inspire confidence, as fragile looking as flower stalks. But she turned over a couple times and started right up.

On the short ride out of the barn, Deuce said, "Tell me about Klauer."

"Ah." J.J., who liked to talk as much as the next chap, nevertheless remained a mite chary here.

"Her father was a boozer and she married another one, is that right?" Deuce asked.

"Well…never met her father. I'm told he had a gift for making friends, but, alas, not much else. A tragic figure, by all accounts. Many attempts made to rehabilitate him. Aggie, I believe, was much taken up with the effort herself, although one wonders what impact a daughter can have in such a situation."

They had arrived at the gas pumps.

"What about the husband?" Deuce asked. "You know him?"

As J.J. climbed out, he said, "No, not him, either." Deuce got out, too, and they walked around the REO again as J.J. inspected her in the light. "But it is true, she did have a husband once, a hard-drinking, unemployable sort of husband, and after her dad, you'd think she would've known better. Then again, we human beings being generally bonkers, who knows. Maybe she blamed herself, failing with her dad and all, and tried to get it right the second time."

"She got a boyfriend?"

J.J. perked up at this question and stopped long enough to eye Deuce suspiciously, Deuce maintaining his usual facade of false pleasantness, the falseness as apparent as the pleasantness. *Go ahead, guess what I'm thinking*—that's what the look seemed to say.

"Why, are you contemplating becoming an alcoholic?" J.J. asked.

"Is she desperate?" Deuce wondered.

"Not so you'd notice. How is this relevant?" J.J. immediately regretted the question, which betrayed his divided loyalties here.

"You said it yourself," Deuce replied, "we can forget about conventional warfare."

"Yes, I did," J.J. acknowledged, although he wished he hadn't. He had to be more careful what he said around Goetzinger. Trying to salvage the moment, he suggested, "But what we oughta be looking for here is some kind of win-win situation, something just too damn attractive to pass up."

"Think Cutler's interested in win-win?"

"Or you."

Deuce nodded, pleased perhaps to think he and Paul Cutler were men who agreed on the need for one of them to lose.

J.J. went back to what he had been doing, completing his walk-around—the tires looked okay—and then climbing into forty-two long enough to get the mileage before heading inside to activate the pump. Deuce followed.

"So, okay, tell me, J.J., if we're gonna do this thing, where do the negotiations have to take place? I mean, the real negotiations?"

"Where?"

"Not in that little pissant room down at the Hall."

"I suppose not." J.J. considered and proposed the obvious. "Between Aggie and Paul Cutler."

"Maybe."

"Where else then?" J.J. wondered.

"For this game, we need a wider playing field."

The system activated, J.J. returned to the REO and started to gas up.

"Ah...yes. A wider playing field." J.J. found something rather ominous in this sentiment. "A little premature, don't you think, to start firing grapeshot?"

"The rules are out the window. We use what we got."

J.J. remembered all his reservations where Deuce was concerned. The man might do more than fail. He might make matters worse.

His hand was about to freeze to the handle of the pump, so he stopped long enough to put his gloves on. "Tell you what," he suggested, "why don't I go see Aggie, feel her out? Maybe she's a secret admirer of our idea for a committee. Maybe we can get her to go to bat for us."

"Turn her? Sure, why not?"

J.J. laughed. "You mean, make her into a double agent? Send her into meetings with Cutler wearing a bug? I'll ask."

Deuce said, "Not you, me. I'll go."

Oh, dear, J.J. thought. He craned his head back so that he could cast a skeptical eye on Deuce. "She might be a mite more up front with me."

"Wouldn't expect her to show me what she's holding. Don't care. I'll go."

J.J. still had the impulse to protect Aggie. A sharp-looking fellow like Goetzinger, famous deflowerer of the local maidens. Suppose Aggie fell for him, what then? Suddenly J.J. became aware of his own emotional stake here. No way he and Aggie would ever step out together, but did he want his fantasies trampled on by this joker? "Might be better if I talked to her," he repeated, trying for the right note of gravity, the man of superior experience admonishing his younger and inexperienced associate. Deuce wasn't buying. In fact, his mind had gone off in another direction.

"If she won't fight with me," he said, "what are the chances she'll ever fight with Cutler?"

"I suppose. Then again, if she fights with you, what reason she got to fight with Cutler?"

Deuce smiled and didn't reply. Once again, J.J. had to remind himself of the new disposition. He went back inside to fill out the fuel sheet.

That was it, then. Deuce would go see Aggie. They'd fight like cats and dogs or hop into the sack together, no middle ground. The negotiations were either pitched battles or foreplay. Or both. Could be both. Probably both. J.J. was still too much taken up by the sudden appearance of jealousy in himself to see any other alternative. The seduction of Aggie. Seduced and abandoned.

"I'd better talk to her," he tried again, even firmer this time, one last try.

"Nope. No way. This is my show."

Back outside, J.J. stopped for a moment to admire the REO Speed Wagon, sitting next to the pumps, grumpy at being pressed into service, its original paint job chipped and discolored and rubbed away, its rounded fenders suggesting a middle-aged spread, not entirely unlike J.J. himself, J.J. with his foolish young man's dreams of love.

He got in and rolled down the window. "I'll be honest with you," he said to Deuce, and then proceeded to lie, "I'm afraid you're gonna screw it up. You're new at all this. You've already learned you can't go head-to-head with Aggie. Now you're just going to alienate her totally and then where will we be?"

Deuce looked at J.J. in the cool way he had, as if he saw effortlessly through J.J.'s logical camouflage, like a man whose polarized vision screened out the better impulses in people, but never missed the unworthy.

"I'm going to talk to her," he told J.J.

J.J. reminded himself yet one more time that, like it or not, Deuce was now the negotiator. "You do have some of your old man in you, you know."

For once, Deuce didn't bother to deny it.

CHAPTER 40

~

Aggie wondered if she dared bring up Deuce Goetzinger's idea. She and El were walking Indian file along a slit trench cut through the snow. For two weeks, storms had kept them from their morning jaunts, so they had much to catch up on, and Aggie for the last several minutes had been waxing enthusiastic over El's campaign for mayor—as any campaign manager must—while El talked about it desultorily, as if some other person entirely was running.

Finally, Aggie abandoned, for the moment, the effort to pump up her candidate and considered what else she might talk about and realized that although it was entirely inappropriate, a violation of one of the cardinal points of bureaucratic etiquette, and Paul Cutler would have her head if he knew about it, she dearly wanted to discuss the union's unorthodox proposal.

At the end of the trench, they climbed over an embankment and kicked through snow uncleared from the last storm and squeezed between parked cars and drifts, dodging the traffic. Since it was Saturday morning, they'd started a little later than usual. In the east, the early February sky blazed with light, and a battery of blue clouds retreated over the horizon, the remnants of the last storm. Finally, it had stopped snowing for a minute. The sky overhead had a laundered appearance, like faded jeans.

At a corner, they waited for a bus to pass and El craned to look inside. Aggie knew what she was doing: counting the house.

"It's early yet," she said, trying to be helpful.

"Um-hmm."

They moved on.

The road swung gradually around toward the southeast. In front of them, the Blufftop Boulevard water tower rose, a great blue mushroom, its eastern edge wrapped in a crescent of sunlight.

As they crossed the next street and were able to walk abreast, Aggie volunteered, "My talks with the unions are going nowhere fast," still uncertain how far she dared go. "They're looking for a no-layoff pledge."

"Transit?" El asked, her interest stirring slightly, since the bus system was obviously much on her mind.

"Wouldn't they just love no layoffs," Aggie said.

They had arrived at an unshoveled section of the sidewalk— unshoveled for several storms, it appeared—and paused to reconnoiter. "We need to get the sidewalk inspector out here," El said. "I don't care how much snow we've had, there's no excuse for this."

The best course seemed to be back over the embankment to a space that someone had shoveled out for their car, the car gone and the space saved with a kitchen chair.

As they scrambled over, Aggie said, "We could maybe link no-layoffs to a wage concession." Even talking about this with the mayor was verboten, hierarchically speaking, but more in the nature of a venial sin compared to the other matter.

"It would tie our hands," El pointed out.

"But if we did it, even just with transit at first, I bet we could get them to settle. And that'd give us something to club the other unions with." Being small and vulnerable and paranoid, transit might very well be manipulated. And as far as Aggie was concerned, swapping a no-layoff guarantee for a cut in wages made sense, something for the city, something for the union.

They passed the chair—Aggie had an urge to sit on it—and continued out into the street, skirting past cars that were still plowed in.

Engine noise approached from behind, and they hustled for the safety of a driveway and stopped to reconnoiter again.

"What about negotiations with the big union?" El asked. "Fritz Goetzinger's son. How's he doing, by the way? Competent?"

"No."

"Too bad."

Aggie described Deuce's sketchy grasp of the issues. "But actually, it makes no difference, El. He'll just stonewall, and we'll end up going to arbitration and losing."

Aggie told herself that in a strictly by-the-rules sort of way it was true, she shouldn't mention Deuce's idea, but on the other hand, wasn't this something new under the sun and didn't that count? Paul was the one being unreasonable, afraid he was going to lose some of his precious prerogatives or something.

"Well," El said at last, "the council told Paul. He could try for givebacks if he wanted, but it was a waste of time."

They were wending their way along another narrow defile, El in the lead, in no rush today, not like the last couple of times they had walked.

From the ragged ridge of snow next to the sidewalk, coal-sized pieces had been dislodged and rolled into their path, good for kicking. Aggie kicked one, which disintegrated, a fine cold mist flying back and stinging her calf.

"There was one thing," she said to El's back and then, taking a deep breath, feeling the cold air searing her lungs, she threw herself into a description of the committee with no instructions. She gave the history. She narrated the trap Deuce had laid for her on Thursday. She recounted her later run-in with Paul, what at least she thought of as a run-in although she knew that Paul would have described it somewhat differently, as a setting-straight maybe.

El listened, but didn't react one way or the other, failing to ask the questions she might have asked if the idea had caught her fancy or, alternatively, seemed a threat. Aggie addressed both possibilities, telling her that the manager and council would always enjoy a veto power, but otherwise Deuce's committee would be totally independent, nobody's tool but its own.

"And Paul doesn't like the idea," El said after she finished.

"Of course."

"And obviously you do. What about the union? Just how serious are they?"

"I don't know."

"You don't?"

"How could I?"

"You must have some idea."

"No. Maybe the rank and file are enthusiastic, but I haven't heard anything to suggest that." Without a dedicated cadre, Deuce's proposal was, alas, nothing more than vapor floating in the void. "Anyway, I told him if he brought it up again, I'd end the session."

"Paul told you to do that?" El asked, the question mostly rhetorical.

"Yes. It's beyond the scope."

"Of course it is," El said. "And so, that's it."

"Except…as you already said…I obviously like the idea, sort of at least."

"But *not* Paul."

"Not Paul." Aggie didn't know where to go from here. Rather timidly, she said, "We might trade it for a small giveback."

"Paul," El said.

"Paul," Aggie agreed.

"I hope you don't want me to…," El laughed.

"No, no," Aggie told her friend at once. Perhaps if El had shown more enthusiasm…

"Because Paul's mad enough at me already," El pointed out.

"The buses."

"That. And now I'm a politician running for office and so by definition anxious to give his money away. And of course there's the business of attracting blacks to the city. He doesn't think I'm sound on that, either."

Aggie, finding herself rather relieved to get off the Deuce business, said, "I don't think you're sound on that."

"Nobody does. Well, the members on the committee. We've come up with some language. Sort of splitting the difference."

"Really?"

"Everyone will be unhappy, of course."

"I guess."

"We've given up on making people happy," El informed her. "The goal now is that nobody should be too unhappy."

"A nice blend of unhappiness."

"Precisely. Nobody so unhappy they'll do something about it."

"Ah."

They had arrived at the end of another block. A wall of snow of alpine dimensions rose before them, and they could find no way over it that didn't involve peril and a complete loss of dignity. As they turned back, El said, "Anyway, sometimes you've just got to do what's right."

"Yes," Aggie agreed. El still seemed gloomy enough, but she had finally, once and for all, made up her mind what to do. And wasn't it a nice thing, Aggie thought, to make up your mind.

～

Walter was futzing around in the kitchen when they got back. He had one of El's campaign buttons pinned to the lapel of his bathrobe. Aggie lingered there a bit longer than she would have on a workday. Walter was campaign treasurer, so the occasion had the feel of a strategy session even though no one was strategizing at the moment.

Stacks of El's campaign literature stood on one of the counters. "Ah, they finally came," Aggie exclaimed.

El said, "Mm."

"What's Lucille up to these days?" Walter asked, for he never failed to ask after Aggie's mother, confident no doubt that Aggie would have something new and amusing to report. It was sad but true that Aggie usually did have something to pass along.

"She's on a new diet. She can eat anything she wants as long as it's orange."

"You mean, *an* orange?"

"No, orange, the color. Of course, oranges are okay, being orange. Nectarines, apricots, quite a few fruits are actually orange. For some reason. After fruit, the choices get a little thin. Carrots. Sweet potatoes. Salmon."

"Pumpkin pie?"

"For dessert."

"Why?"

"You'll have to ask Lucille. It has something to do with antioxidants, or maybe that was the last diet. Anyway, I figure it won't kill her." Which was the criterion Aggie used when deciding whether to intervene.

While she talked, she'd unfolded one of the campaign brochures and glanced down the list of El's accomplishments, a row of bulleted, pithy sentence fragments. As El's campaign manager, Aggie had been involved in the design of the handout. Sort of. El insisted she wasn't going to waste a lot of money on a lost cause and so they had resuscitated, mutatis mutandis, the one she'd used when she ran unopposed for the ward seat on the council.

"I should think presentation would be something of a problem," Walter mused.

"That's right. It's hard to even look at a plate with nothing but orange food on it."

She turned the flaps over, running her eye down the panels, gauging the visual impression the brochure made—better than Lucille's dinners, at least—then back at the bulleted list, which was nothing more than a valediction by someone who had already accepted her fate. That's what she and El had fought over.

"I still say we ought to have some kind of slogan," Aggie complained. "Gosh, El, everybody's got a slogan."

"You mean, 'Let's bring more African-Americans to Jackson,' like that?" El was going around the kitchen opening and closing cabinets and the fridge, looking for something.

Aggie snorted. "Don't be silly. Not one that actually *says* something. Who ever heard of that? No, no, what you need is more like 'Going forward together' or 'A bright tomorrow.' Isn't that right, Walter?"

"Doesn't do much for me," he said. "How about 'Partly cloudy followed by clearing'?"

Rather than comment on this meteorological suggestion, El said to Walter, "Tell Aggie what you'd do about the buses."

"The buses? Sure. Paint 'em psychedelic colors and put in video games, that's what. You want people to ride, you got to give them a reason." El gave him one of her what-planet-did-you-come-from looks.

Aggie enjoyed the Plowmans. Their marriage had been made, if not in heaven, exactly, at least in some interesting place.

When she was ready to leave, Aggie said, "Two o'clock then." She was to return for a meeting with the volunteers who would be going door-to-door when they kicked off the campaign in earnest.

"I won't be here," El told her blithely. "People to see. But you know what to do, you don't need me."

"Yes, but...but..."

"I know, I know, Aggie. Sorry. I've got other things I just must do. I'm seeing the superintendent of schools this morning, the archbishop after lunch. There are many, many people to see." She was obviously talking about this crazy scheme of hers to import blacks from Chicago, St. Louis, Manitoba.

"What about the volunteers?" Aggie complained. Whined, really. "How do you expect them to go all out if you don't buck them up?"

El stopped what she was doing and stared at Aggie impatiently. But then she smiled. "I forgot. You still think I can win."

Just at that moment, Aggie was feeling balked and frustrated, and so she said, "No, I don't, but gee whiz, El, you've gotta try. What good is it if you don't even try?"

El came over and hugged Aggie and kissed her on the forehead. "I'll try, dear. I promise. I'll try."

CHAPTER 41

~

Chuck Fellows watched as his son Todd's gaze swung in a slow arc, taking in everything while they tramped by the buckskinners' tepees.

With their olive drab wall tent, the Fellows were once again consigned to the lowly ranks of the pilgrims, except that there were no other pilgrims gung ho enough to drag their camping gear out into the middle of the worst winter on record. So the Fellows family had the lower camping area to themselves. Todd was mortified. As for Chuck, well, his son's persistent complaints were getting on his nerves.

He picked a site partially scoured by the wind and shucked off the harness he used to pull the Army surplus Ahkio sled on which their gear was stowed. Diane immediately started loosening the straps. They had a lot of work to do to set up.

Using his shovel like a post-hole digger, Chuck chopped through the crusty snow, marking out the campsite, and then began to clear the area. The children scooped out the soft snow beneath and tried to make snowballs, but it was too dry and just crumbled away in their disappointed hands. Diane searched through the pack until she found her list. She never went anywhere without her lists.

Almost immediately Grace was over and whispering something in her ear.

"We've got to go for a walk," Diane told Chuck. "Go learn how to not piss in our boots," she stage-whispered.

Diane had outfitted herself and the kids so that at least when they got away from all this modern camping equipment, they'd resemble the genuine article. Grace, a miniature French voyageur in midwinter, was completely enveloped in woolens. She looked like a mitten. Pissing was not to be taken for granted.

Chuck continued clearing the area. Again and again, Todd stared toward the primitive camp, where the spires of the buckskinners' tepees, like a village of churches, stood out proudly against the sky. Chuck didn't like buckskinning any more this time around than he had during the summer rendezvous Diane had dragged him to on the mistaken belief that since he liked camping, he'd like this ersatz version of voyageur days. It took all his energy to remain more or less civil and, for his son's benefit, put on this show of participating, but Todd couldn't understand such adult cop-outs. He wanted nothing less than true belief. And Chuck, if he didn't think much of buckskinning, didn't think much of himself just then, either. His anger mounted.

By the time the girls returned, he had the Gore-Tex ground cloth laid and had hauled the tent off the sled and begun to unfold it.

Diane looked at the blue sky. Chuck stopped what he was doing and looked up as well, the blueness partially bleached out to the south, in the quarter of the morning sun, but more intense in the north, a clear icy color, so perfectly cloudless that it seemed false in some way.

Conversational voices from the upper camp slipped easily between the layers of cold air. With them came reports of hammer blows as pegs were driven into the frozen earth, another tepee having risen among the spires.

Diane rested a hand briefly on his arm, then turned back to the unfinished tasks.

Todd walked the perimeter of the cleared area like a horse circling the fence of a paddock. "C'mon, sport," Chuck said to him, "let's set this thing up."

Wherever Chuck was, he had to be somewhere else. As soon as camp was pitched, he needed to go back into town. But for the moment, he checked his impatience. He had a few minutes. Teach the kid a thing or two, he told himself. Be a damn parent. To his son, he said, "Remember when we pitched this last fall? I want you to tell me what to do."

But Todd just mumbled underneath his breath. He looked angrily at the tent, the emblem of his shame, and halfheartedly kicked at it.

Suddenly, Chuck's anger flared. "Look, Elsie, you can help or we can go home. Which is it?"

"Help your father, dear," Diane called softly.

Even if his son didn't, his wife understood the effort it took. Chuck heard the bitterness in his own voice. The line between hard-ass and asshole was narrow, and somewhere along the way he'd passed over. "This won't take long, sport." He held his son by his shoulders. "Give me a hand, okay?"

As an act of amends, Chuck took his time, showing Todd each step, not proceeding until he had elicited at least a spark of understanding.

"I'll try to get back in time so we can go on the shoot," he told him after the last metal pin had been driven and nylon guy rope cinched, the camp stove set up with boughs spread under it to prevent any snowmelt, and stovepipe run up through the fiberglass thimble to the outside.

"If you're not here, I'll go," Diane said matter-of-factly.

"You don't know how to handle the flinter."

"I'll get one of the men to show me."

Chuck grumbled. Diane was taking this "perfect wife" business too far. Teaching the kid how to shoot was his job.

Brooding, he drove back into town, then down to the dredge. Of the two of them, his son was the more honest. It might be a child's honesty, but what difference did that make? Todd wanted to go buckskinning; he didn't want Chuck's half-baked substitute. Yet Chuck remained powerless to enter his son's make-believe world in any genuine way, either that or refuse to have anything to do with it at all.

And then there was the matter of his job. When he'd agreed to take over as public works director, he'd promised himself he would be stone honest, that much at least. But he hadn't. He couldn't map out the ways he'd violated that oath. Made no difference, signified nothing but the deviousness of the adult mind. Taking over public works had been like agreeing to go buckskinning and then not doing it all the way up, dishonesty built right into the thing.

When he arrived down at the river, the others were already out on the ice, below the square of open water where the dredge and harbor tug sat idle. Young Massey, the great grandson of the tug skipper, had been drafted to core holes, although at the moment he just leaned idly on his auger. Jeff Hawthorn, the biologist from the U., was there, of course. And Bud Pregler from the dredging crew. And old man Massey himself and Walter Plowman. Nobody doing much of anything at the moment. Chuck didn't like the look of it.

The sun glared from the river ice where wind had stripped off the snow cover, and Chuck watched his step as he picked a way out to the others.

"Guys," he said, arriving at the motionless little group, "tell me you've got some good news."

A bucket and Hawthorn's bottom sampler lay on the ice beside him. The biologist nodded at Chuck and reached out to shake his hand.

"The only good news is good news for Jeff," Walt Plowman volunteered.

"'Fraid so," the biologist agreed.

"Let's see," Chuck said.

Hawthorn had a face mild but blasted by too many years in the sun and cold and wind. From a pocket he extracted a cloth bag and poked around in it until he found what he was looking for. A mussel valve.

He took off his gloves so he could handle it more readily. His hands were large and soft, as splotchy as his face.

He held the mussel shell up, stepping so close to Chuck that the two men were touching.

"Lampsilis higginsi."

"Higgins Eye? You sure? You absolutely sure?"

The others had crowded around to eavesdrop.

"Amateur might mistake it for a Hickory nut," Hawthorn told Chuck. "They often got a thick shell like this." He held it edgewise. "But the beak on a Hickory nut's more pointed." He ran one finger over the raised area on the back of the shell. "Or maybe they'd mark it as a Pocketbook or a Fat Mucket. But they'd be wrong. This is a Higgins Eye all right. Seen enough of 'em in my lifetime. Mostly dead like this. A young male by the look of it."

Chuck sought a loophole. "Maybe there aren't any live ones down there."

The biologist shook his head. "This critter was alive a little bit ago. Shell's intact, surface layer hasn't been abraded. I can keep on lookin', but it doesn't make any difference. Find 'em or not, they're down there."

"Shit."

"Sorry."

Chuck felt frustrated as hell. Now what the fuck was he going to do? "So tell me, Jeff, how many potential Higgins Eye sites haven't you looked at?"

"A lot," the biologist conceded.

"So it's like streetlights, a light here, a light there, everywhere else, who the hell knows. Higgins Eye might be all over the goddamn place."

"Don't know. Could be."

That the mussel might be plentiful, its endangered species designation unnecessary, just pissed Chuck off all the more.

"Better safe than sorry," Jeff said.

"Yeah, sure…the Higgins Eye, God's gift to man." Chuck stared off into space. "Damn it!"

"Chuck's been having a bad year," Walt explained in mitigation when the biologist gave Chuck an unsympathetic look. Hawthorn was another of Walt's many pals. Walt had recommended him to Chuck for this emergency work.

Chuck contemplated his situation. "Wha'd'ya think, Bud?" he asked Pregler. "Farther down the river?"

"Could, I suppose." Pregler wore a vivid orange hunter's cap above the great black shovel of his beard. "Dredge is already pumping pretty near as far as she can. Have to pump the sand partway, truck it the rest."

"Use a scraper maybe. Or rig up some sort of booster pump." Either way a real pain in the ass. And Chuck just didn't have the time.

There was one more possibility.

"Okay," he said, "let's go out there." He pointed to the area beyond the open water, out toward midstream. "How deep is that sampler of yours good for?"

"I can go down ten feet."

"That'll do."

As they were lugging their gear out farther onto the ice, they heard yelling and turned to see a tall figure rapidly nearing, stumbling but coming on, rushing across the ice, ignoring the ragged surface.

"I'll be damned," Chuck said.

Of all Chuck's old Army buddies, Diane once said she hated Jake Podolak the least.

Podolak came straight for Chuck, a shit-eating grin on his face. Suddenly he spotted Walt.

"Hey, Walter, son of a bitch, should've known you'd be here, too." He detoured over to shake Plowman's hand. Podolak was gimpy. Like Chuck, he'd gotten fucked up in 'Nam. That's how they'd met.

"You know Plowman, Snake?" Chuck asked, surprised.

"Shit, everybody knows Walter. He's a fucking legend."

"Aw," said Walt modestly.

"Sure enough is," Podolak averred, standing still long enough to admire the fucking legend. "Full of all sorts of crackpot theories, ain't that right, Walter?"

"Well, since you put it that way," Plowman said.

Podolak laughed, a sudden laugh, as if a grenade had exploded among them. "Totally crackpot theories. Makes no difference. Knows absolutely everybody, does Walter. River rats, goddamn U.S. senators, you name it. Likes everybody, too, near as I can tell. Hell, he associates with you, Fellows. That proves it."

"Walt's a helluva lot more help than you've ever been, Podolak."

Jake nodded. "There you are. What'd I say?" He gave Chuck a bear hug. "Good to see you, compadre." Into Chuck's ear, he whispered, "What say you and me go out and get hammered a little later?"

He gave Chuck a tiny space into which to assert a word or two, an opportunity lost. Chuck was remembering his family with the buckskinners.

"It's not snowin', Walter!" Jake bellowed. "What's the matter with you?"

"Another storm starting to form up in the Gulf of Alaska. Won't be here for a bit, though."

"That right? Shit, what a winter. Just here for the day, had to come up and see this dredging operation of yours," Podolak boomed on, talking to Chuck again. Jake worked for the Corps of Engineers down in Rock Island. That's where he would've found out about the dredge. "Talk about crackpot schemes. In the middle of the friggin' winter." He laughed, delighted. Jake was a man with a true appreciation for the hopeless. "Do you have any idea what the fuck you're doing?"

"Not a clue," Chuck told him. "Making it up as we go along."

"Figures!"

Podolak didn't wait for introductions. He went around to each of the others and stuck out his hand.

He gripped young Massey and looked at the auger he was lugging and said, "I can see who's doing the work."

"Now that you're here, Podolak, we can give him a rest."

"I'll cut two holes for every goddamn one you've done, Fellows."

"Fair enough. I've done fifteen."

"Like hell you have."

"Okay, don't believe me. You always were a goddamn gold-brick, Podolak."

In this way, Chuck and Jake continued baiting each other as they all resumed the march out to the area to the east of the dredge and a new round of coring and sampling.

Jake was interested in everything. Unannoyed by the racket of the auger, he watched intently as the kid drilled hole after hole and Jeff Hawthorn lowered the sampler, pushing it firmly into the bottom sediments before releasing the messenger that slid down and tripped the catch holding the jaws open.

"Not too deep to dredge out here?" he asked Chuck.

"We'll manage," Pregler told him.

The dredge was working on the inside of a bend, the center of the channel toward the far shore, the bottom sloping only gradually toward it. Not ideal, but they could make do.

Each time the sampler came back to the surface, water draining from it, the material grabbed from the river bottom cascaded with a slithery pebble sound into the biologist's bucket. He picked through it, but didn't have much to say. The stuff all looked more or less the same to Chuck. He thought, Higgins Eye mussels, for Christ's sake. As bad as the goddamn Snail Darter. Still, despite the circumstances, he respected the kind of expertise that Jeff Hawthorn possessed, Hawthorn seeing something where others saw nothing. And studying the biologist's ruined face and hands, Chuck admired the life he would have led, outdoors, year after year, committed, unconcerned for himself, caring only for the work.

"Shitload of ice to cut off the river if you plan to dredge out here, my friend," Podolak observed.

They went on to the next hole and the next. From each, the biologist saved a little, tossed the rest, leaving dark, glistening crescents strewn on the ice. Then, he stopped saving anything. And finally he told the kid not to bother cutting any more holes.

He brought the cloth bag over and showed Chuck his stash, bits and pieces of shells, not a whole one in the lot.

"Hard to tell. There might have been an active bed here at one time, but not now."

"No Higgins Eye?"

"No Higgins Eye."

"Hallelujah."

Jake, who had stuck his head into the middle of these proceedings, nodded sagely.

"Now all I need," Chuck said, "is the go-ahead from the Corps."

"See what I can to," Podolak volunteered, putting a hand on Chuck's shoulder. He wasn't in the permitting section, but he knew people. "Expect we can speed things up a bit."

They gathered up their stuff and headed back, Chuck and Jake and Walt Plowman walking a little off to the side.

"As for getting hammered," Chuck told his friend reluctantly, "no can do."

"How come? What's up?" Podolak demanded. What could possibly preempt getting hammered?

"Camping with Diane and the kids."

"Winter camping, eh? Neat."

"Chuck's a buckskinner," Walt put in, and Chuck winced.

The Snake howled. "Dan'l Boone! I don't believe it! That's funnier than shit."

"Up yours," Chuck said.

Back at the dredge, Chuck showed his friend around while Walt and the others went onto the tug to have a drink and play a little euchre.

"And how is Diane?" Jake asked.

"More like me every day."

"A hard-ass, then. And the kids?"

"Them, too."

Jake chuckled.

The guided tour over, Jake said, "A handsome craft," and then they stood silently.

"Well," Chuck told him finally, "gotta get back." He envisioned Diane and Todd walking toward the shoot, Todd with his flintlock.

"Buckskinner," his friend winked.

"Did I say, up yours? Anyway, it's Diane's idea…for the kids."

"Ah."

"You were too goddamn chickenshit ever to get married, Podolak."

"I was married once," Jake said with umbrage.

"Oh, yeah, right, I keep forgetting. I've known cuppa coffees lasted longer. Good ol' what's-her-name. Pookie."

"Bubbles, please. Her name was Bubbles. Pookie was just a nickname."

They laughed, an old joke, and then fell silent again. It was part of the tradition between them that Chuck never remembered Jake having been married.

The time had come to part. No reason to put it off any longer.

Jake nodded toward the harbor tug. "Guess I'll wander on over, see if I can cadge a drink, maybe work up a little poker game."

Jake grabbed Chuck in a brief bear hug.

"Next time."

"Yeah," Chuck said, "next time."

"Don't let 'em get you down."

Chuck watched as Jake strode with his familiar limp toward the tug, yelling, "Permission to come aboard, Cap'n!"

Standing out next to the 4x4, Chuck paused and looked back. Inside himself, he heard not his own voice but Diane's. Her sarcastic remarks about his war buddies. Of course, that was the old Diane. Maybe the new would accept even his scruffy pals from 'Nam days. And, it was true, she had become more like him in some ways. But his sense that one of them would win, the other lose, remained as strong as ever. He was still the heathen, she the missionary.

The dredge lay low in the water, shabby, encrusted with ice, the cutter head and booms and spuds sticking out this way and that, like some daffy erector set project. Chuck remembered Jake's enthusiasm, dredging in winter an act sufficiently insane to meet with his approval...just the kind of overreaching, in fact, he'd measure a man's life by. Chuck shook his head. Jake.

And yet, as he climbed wearily into his truck, he realized that he didn't really want to stay. He didn't want to go back to the buckskinners' encampment, either. He couldn't remember the last time that he'd driven to a place where he really wanted to go. Probably when he'd gone out on his motorcycle two summers before, a long weekend by himself, one of his rides to nowhere. But at the moment not even that interested him. Nothing interested him.

He was a little frightened, too.

CHAPTER 42

~

At the end of the news conference, El watched Johnny Pond stuff his tape recorder into the capacious pocket of his flowing winter coat and leave the city council chamber, not exactly stalking out, but close enough. They'd barely acknowledged each other. He'd asked no questions. *Just as well*, she told herself.

The other reporters stayed behind for follow-up. El wasn't the only member of the integration committee present, thank God.

Finally, in ones and twos, the rest drifted out, until only she remained, although the WPA mural on the back wall always made the room appear populated. The mural had faded over the decades—the council talked occasionally about restoring it—and to El the disappearing images seemed less like people than the opinions they held.

She walked down the long corridor to Paul Cutler's office and described the news conference for his benefit.

"Don't start on me," she said, to forestall one of his cracks.

Probably she needn't say anything. Paul usually accepted faits accomplis, if rather sourly. Now he contented himself with, "You're trying to do the right thing."

This comment patronized, the word *trying* stretched out and taut, like a rope she was using to hang herself.

"Assuming the council doesn't change its mind," he added.

"Why should they?" she asked sharply. Did he know something she didn't?

"You talked to Roger Filer recently?"

"No. Have you?"

Paul shook his head.

"As far as I know, he's still undecided." Paul hadn't picked Filer's name out of a hat, Filer being the one council member who had been making noises about running against her in the mayoral race, although he was taking his sweet time deciding.

"Be nice if it was unanimous," Paul said.

He had gotten up from his desk when she came in, and the two of them sat across from each other at the small conference table. They no longer saw eye to eye. Their friendship, which had once seemed so solid, was turning out to be only professional after all. El regretted it. Perhaps Paul did, too.

They discussed Roger Filer briefly, not a topic El had any intention of wasting much time on. A week remained for candidates to collect signatures and should he at long last make up his mind to run, that was his business. If she wasn't paying any attention to her own campaign, she certainly wasn't going to pay attention to anybody else's.

Paul reached back and fetched the popcorn off his desk and offered her some. She declined, then changed her mind, and the two of them took turns with the bag. Paul seemed to be putting on weight again. He always had had the look of a man burdened by his physical existence.

They talked about Ultima Thule and Deke McKeown and how they were going to make sure that the mail order retailer found out about the city's initiative.

"Since Ultima Thule is the whole point of the exercise," Paul felt compelled to point out, a statement by which he both salvaged some value for the effort and distanced himself from it.

"The occasion, perhaps," El replied.

The manager leaned back with his hands cupped behind his head.

Although he would not like the sound of it, she said, "I've been thinking what else we might do."

"What else? To entice more blacks? Why, nothing. Do nothing, and, if you're lucky, nothing will happen. McKeown will move his operation here, and"—he waved his hand lazily—"that's that."

"No," El countered. "that is *not* that. Anyway, it's about something else. The opposite, really. How do we help the people already here, the longtime Jacksonians? For one thing, we need to keep layoffs to a minimum. An absolute minimum."

He paused and then said, "Of course," peering more intently at her.

"I'm serious, Paul. No layoffs."

"You're not talking about a pledge to the unions, I hope."

"Actually...," she started and then hesitated. "Don't look at me that way. You know the problem as well as I do. People think the number of jobs is fixed. A job lost is a job lost forever."

"You'll tie my hands."

"Bringing more entry-level positions into the city is important. Like Ultima Thule. Fine. The more the merrier. But we absolutely do need to keep the jobs we've already got. Good grief, look at the Pack, look at the domino effect from that. And what can we do about it? Nothing. But now we're talking about city employees. Here, surely... And yes, why not a pledge?"

She knew why not. The shortfall. How in God's name were they going to balance the budget?

Paul remained perfectly still, leaning back, hands still cupped behind his head. She tried to read the pose. He seemed too relaxed. He wasn't hastening to trot out the usual arguments. Must think he didn't have to. Must think that with this proposal to bring blacks to Jackson, El had hopelessly compromised herself—Don Quixote in a blouse and skirt. She could be safely ignored.

He asked, "And so, tell me, just how many votes do you think a no-layoff pledge would be worth?"

El folded her hands in her lap and stared at the abandoned popcorn bag and thought, *So that's it*. She paused long enough to get a grip on herself. The question deserved no answer, but she answered anyway, in honor of their long relationship.

"None. I'm going to lose the election."

Paul didn't, as he might have at another time, acknowledge her forthrightness, but merely said, "Because, El, if this proposal of yours were some sort of...campaign gimmick, then I guess I could understand it. But if you're really serious..."

"I'm dead serious. And since you dismiss the idea with such scorn..."

At this, he leaned forward and folded his arms on the edge of the table. "Not scorn. It's just not possible. You know that. And if you pursue the matter, it's nothing more than a cheap politician's trick. And frankly, El, I thought you were above that."

"I guess not," she said with a false smile. She got up to leave. At the door, however, she looked back and said, "I'm sorry," in a tone not of apology but regret at the bitterness of the exchange.

At once, Paul said, "So am I."

There seemed nothing else to do, but when she turned away, he began to speak quickly. "Look, if you want a pledge, if you're bound and determined, the unions have to agree to the givebacks. Then I'd be willing to do something. Give assurances in private, maybe that."

Surprised, El looked back.

"But nothing public."

"No."

Yet if the city agreed, it would become public, no way to keep it private. Paul had to realize that.

"Can Aggie take the union reps aside?" she asked.

"Uh-uh. The unions have to make the first move."

"They never will. Not unless there's some kind of signal from us."

"I won't have Aggie going to them."

"Something more indirect, then."

"Very indirect."

After a few moments of hope, El decided that there was less here than met the eye. She sought for some way forward and remembered something she and Aggie had talked about on their last walk.

"What about this proposal the big union has made? A committee."

His demeanor changed at once. "How did you find out about that?"

"Why shouldn't I find out? Aggie told me. It sounds like something worth exploring."

"It isn't." His sudden bluntness betrayed his anger. He was seldom angry, annoyance being a more congenial emotion. But he could get mad.

"Why not?" she challenged him. "Aggie seems to think it might be a good idea."

"I'm sure she does."

"And maybe that would be a way of getting the unions to make the first move on the givebacks. Or we could package the committee with a no-layoff pledge in exchange for the givebacks, how about that?"

Paul rubbed his face, a quick motion, then dropped his hands into his lap, the gesture like an idea entertained for an instant and immediately abandoned.

"A committee of second-guessers? No, thank you," he told her. "No city manager would be willing to work under such conditions."

Hyperbole, the preemptive strike. "I'm sure," El said, "managers would *prefer* not to." The softening that had occurred moments earlier when they both said they were sorry had been nothing more than the eye of the storm. "Are you telling me you'd quit?"

The frankness of this obviously startled him, but he responded at once, "I hope it doesn't come to that."

"So do I," she said.

They left it at that.

Chapter 43

~

Quarter to five. Too late to start something new. Plenty of old stuff left over, but nothing that Aggie absolutely, positively had to do at that very instant. A catnap perhaps. Experimentally, she closed her eyes and wiggled around in her chair to get comfy. No good. Her eyelids slid back open, like blinds that wouldn't stay down.

She had never been any good with odd moments. Other people put them to good use, scraps of things saved for scraps of time. Aggie's mind would go slack, an indolence pleasing only so long as she didn't think about it.

Someone knocked, and she roused herself. Ah, good, rescued. But when the door opened and she saw who her rescuer was, her hopes for a pleasant distraction until it was time to go home quickly disappeared.

Not waiting for an invitation, Deuce Goetzinger closed the door and slipped into the chair opposite her.

"Hi," he said.

"Hi," she said back.

They stared at each other. He wore the smile that didn't quite agree with his eyes.

"Well?" she said.

"Well."

"You were just passing by?"

"Came to see you."

"That's nice."

They sat looking at each other some more, and Aggie found herself thinking roguish thoughts. He *was* cute, no doubt about it…but, she decided—summoning her usual distrust for men who were better looking than she was—cute in a rather conventional way, don'cha think? A little androgynous, even. Yes, that was it. They'd make cute androgynous babies together. She banished this idea at once.

"I suppose you've come to talk about the thing."

He shrugged, as if that wasn't the reason, but since she'd brought it up. "A good idea."

"It is, huh?" She smiled, feeling the tug at the corner of her lips as she lifted her chin and scratched under it, warning herself, *Don't do it, Ag, don't take the bait, leave it alone.*

But she was divided against herself. One of the contrary beings that lived inside her skull dearly wanting to take him on. *Do it*, the inner imp inveigled, *you can take this joker down a peg or two!* If she could actually succeed, excavate beneath the surface of his bland, really quite annoying self-assurance… How much easier she'd rest once she had exposed his ploy as nothing but a shameless negotiating tactic.

But instead she told him, with an internal sigh, "No matter, we're not going to talk about it, not now, not here, not anyplace."

He slung one leg over the other and smiled his sleepy cat smile.

"Okay," he said. "What about something else? How about democracy? Let's talk about that. Oughta be a safe subject. Nobody's against democracy, right?"

"It's the same thing."

"It is?" He seemed genuinely shocked, and Aggie had to laugh. "I've never mentioned democracy before. Have I? I've talked about the committee, sure." Deuce settled back and began to wave his arm around in a loose-limbed way, as if this was just something he was saying. "So, okay, you don't like that, even mentioning it. But I'm just doing it, you know, right now, mentioning the committee again, because I want to point out that that's what I've talked about: the committee. But not democracy. I've never said diddly about democracy, not until now, and now only so we don't have to talk about… well, you know, the other thing."

"Participatory democracy," Aggie said, but she was thinking, *The weasel's rehearsed this, it's all a setup.*

He nodded, a faraway look, as if hearing the expression for the first time.

"Participation is good," he said.

Aggie warned herself again, *Cut this off, Ag, you can't win, you'll say something you'll regret.* The very light in the room, the glow swaddling them from the late afternoon gloom outside, conspired to create unwise confidences. And there was always the chance, however remote, that he was actually serious. What if he was actually serious? How tempting! How fascinating to explore the idea with this man if he really, truly meant what he was saying.

And except for the accident of what happened next, their relationship might in an instant have been caught in this spider's web of possibilities. But no, it did not happen, for at that moment, a third person appeared, Aggie becoming aware of this new presence in a quick decrescendo, first as movement at the periphery of her vision, then the bulk and attire of a man pushing his way into the room and finally the person himself—shortish and stout and rumpled—the one person in the world that she could have done without at that particular moment in her life.

"I'd like a word with you," the city manager told her without preamble.

Goetzinger turned with interest toward this new arrival, but the manager barely noticed him, and Aggie realized with a start that Paul must not know who he was. She wondered what chance she had of making Deuce disappear before the manager ID'd him. Not much, apparently, for Paul had already turned and begun peering at him suspiciously. Deuce resembled his father too closely to remain incognito for long.

"You're young Goetzinger."

Deuce raised a hand, toasting Paul's success.

Paul, for his part, had the look of a farmer who has just discovered a corn borer in his crop.

"What are you doing here?" he demanded.

Deuce contemplated the manager placidly, not the least bit unsettled apparently by his sudden appearance. No doubt he'd played poker with local mucky-mucks, no doubt he beaten them, too, and was not to be cowed by the powerful. Now he took his time, perhaps sorting through possible responses. He settled on simple confrontation.

"You won't let Aggie talk about the committee on the record, so I came here."

"Whatever you've got to say, say it at the table," Paul told him.

Deuce elected to misinterpret Paul's meaning. "Great. So we *can* talk about it, then."

Paul cast a withering look upon him. "You cannot. And a word of advice. You want to accomplish anything at all, forget the funny stuff.

"Why don't we discuss the matter, you and me, man to man," Deuce suggested pleasantly.

Aggie cringed, but all Paul said was, "Aggie's the city's negotiator. Now if you'll excuse us."

After another somewhat insolent pause, Deuce heaved himself up from his chair. He seemed about to say something else, but changed his mind and, with brief glances first at Paul and then at Aggie—a small knowing smile for her benefit—he sauntered out of the room.

The manager closed the door behind him.

Aggie braced herself and couldn't help saying in self-defense, "He just showed up."

Brusquely, Paul told her, "I don't care about him," and then moved the chair Deuce had been sitting in, as if the act of moving it removed some taint, and sat down. "There's something else concerns me. Did you talk to El Plowman about the union proposal?"

Oh, shit, Aggie thought. For a desperate instant, her mind went blank and she had to struggle against the impulse to lie.

Finally, overcoming this baser instinct, she mustered a weak, "El and I talk all the time."

"Oh, you do. Is that right?"

"I mean, jeepers, I'm her campaign manager. And we walk. For exercise. You know that. Don't you know that? We've been doing it for years."

In her panic, Aggie couldn't imagine what had possessed her to discuss with El something she knew would absolutely tick Paul off. She'd always been a law-abiding creature, Aggie had. And she hated getting yelled at. Getting yelled at was the worst.

Paul leaned back in his chair, shamming ease, his right arm slung over the top of his head, hand hanging limply on the other side, forming a kind of picture frame for his face.

"You think it's okay then," he asked, "torpedoing me behind my back?"

"No, of course not. I wasn't… That wasn't what I was doing… trying to do."

"It wasn't?"

He waited for an explanation.

"El and I talk, Paul. Whatever comes up, we talk about it."

"I see." It was after five o'clock now. The faint sounds of people leaving, not voices but the constant opening and closing of doors, left her with a sense of being abandoned. "I don't know about you, Aggie, but I don't tell *anybody* everything."

Good grief, Aggie thought, and reminded herself that she didn't have a leg to stand on here, no point trying to pretend otherwise.

So, hoping she didn't sound too defensive, she said simply, "I like Deuce Goetzinger's idea."

"Well, yes, we already know that, don't we? But at the moment that's not the point."

She ignored the point. "You don't like the idea. Neither does the union, that's what I think. So I'm left holding the bag. Because it *is* a good idea." So there!

Paul said nothing. He had slid down farther in his chair, arm still draped over his head, flicking the top of his ear with his middle finger. If he was going to yell at her, she wished he'd do it and get it over with.

"I am truly sorry that I talked to El about it," she told him, something which needed to be said, although what she was truly sorry about was the dressing down she was now getting. She even found a little bit of her courage returning and amended her earlier panic with, So, okay, talking to El was a no no, technically speaking, bureaucratically, whatever, and she knew Paul would climb all over her if he found out, but she'd done it anyway.

At the moment, Paul's eyes seemed to be weighing her apology against the seriousness of the crime.

"You think you're in the middle, do you?" he asked. "In the no-man's-land between me and the union?"

That was exactly what she felt like, but she said what she had to say. "I negotiate for the city."

"You don't seem very convinced."

"I know what my responsibility is."

He took his time, flicking his ear until he was ready to speak.

"And it's not going to happen again, this going behind my back?"

"No, of course not."

He roused himself out of his chair. "Make sure it doesn't."

"I just wish…," she started, unable to quite leave it alone. But what could she say? She'd already done enough damage.

"Yes?" Paul paused. An invitation to dig the hole she was in deeper.

"Nothing."

"That's right, nothing. Make sure it stays nothing."

Finally alone again, Aggie listened in the stillness to his retreating footsteps, the hard leather of his dress shoes ticking off the yards along the hallway, past the deserted counters and up the stairs and along the second-floor corridor, still audible in her inner ear long after the building had become perfectly silent.

CHAPTER 44

⁓

At the city council work session on snow removal that night, as others talked, El slowly swiveled in her chair and contemplated her various wrecked relationships with the men in the room, not all the men, to be sure, but an impressive number. She was leaving quite a swath in her wake.

Chuck Fellows stood, one hand clamped on either side of the podium, as if about to rip it out by the roots. Of course, she'd never gotten along with Fellows, even before the Sam Turner business, so strictly speaking there had never been anything to wreck. Just to go from bad to worse.

Johnny Pond. Johnny was back in his usual seat at the reporters' table with his tape recorder, doing his job, not quite so somber as he'd been earlier in the day, but hardly his old self. She and Johnny had had a decent relationship once, although his friendliness had always had something calculated in it. An improvement on Fellows, at least. She wondered just how mad Johnny really was because she hadn't followed his advice to stay out of the bringing-blacks-to-Jackson business. The anger seemed misplaced, but she didn't pretend to understand him.

Slowly she rotated back in the other direction. Her headache had started to intensify, small stabs of pain. She drew her palm across her forehead, extracting the last vestige of coolness.

On the other side of Chuck Fellows, Paul Cutler slouched in his accustomed place, at the far end of the staff table, the city clerk and city attorney serving as a kind of buffer, a first line of defense between him and the council. Paul had lousy posture, which El had once tried to do something about. At the moment, he doodled with his pen, listening with an air of faint distaste. El contemplated him only briefly, the flare-up between them that afternoon still raw in her mind.

At the corner of her eye, among the council members to her left, she caught Roger Filer, her opponent presumptive for mayor and undoubtedly the next of her relationships scheduled for demolition. She almost liked Roger, his seriousness a little too put on, perhaps, but nothing done to camouflage his unhandsomeness, sporting a nose once broken and never straightened, his thinning hair combed to emphasize rather than hide his bald spot. Truth in advertising, as befitted the Chevy dealer he had been all these years. At the moment, he was concentrating on what was being said.

El turned back toward the podium, where Hank Kraft, the street commissioner, was leaning across Fellows to speak into the mike, answering a technical question, supplying the council with more information than requested, as was his habit.

"The total was forty-three, the operating cost per inch of snowfall, $8,174. The year before the figures were…"

Fellows seemed barely conscious of his starring role in this little drama about the perilous state of the snow budget. Unlike Hank Kraft, he supplied what was requested, not a jot more. To give Hank more room, he had backed a pace away, in what she would have called in another man a state of dreamy distractedness.

Hank ran on.

"There's a twenty-four-hour operation on a snow fight. We're really reaching deep to run twenty-four hours. In storms like we've just had, we call in every part-timer we got, put every piece of equipment we can lay our hands on out on the street, graders, end loaders, the whole shebang…" He continued, repeating himself, while Fellows stood indifferently by, looking past El toward the street maps which laid out the snow plowing routes and had been hung on the wall behind the council members. A man like Fellows, she supposed, must have a special affinity for maps.

"What about private haulers?" Roger Filer asked.

Fellows stepped forward to answer.

El listened, taking the opportunity to turn once again and contemplate Filer. The man was taking his sweet time gathering signatures. And giving such coy answers to questions about his intentions you'd think he was a potential presidential candidate fending off reporters years before the next election. El didn't know what to make of it. He could beat El, of course. He and everybody else.

As the work session wore on, El became aware she wasn't the only person doing the watching. Paul was watching her. She stared boldly back.

"The fact is that we're using the streets for storage," Chuck was saying.

Paul's attention left El immediately. He interrupted Fellows. "*Storage* isn't quite the right word here. We've been hit by back-to-back storms. Twice. It takes longer to clean up."

Fellows ignored this correction, continuing to speak to the council. "We can't plow curb-to-curb. We'd lose the sidewalks."

"I'm concerned," Paul persisted, also talking to the council, "that we not give the wrong impression."

Fellows hadn't lost his trademark bluntness, nor his disdain. Paul didn't bother to hide his annoyance, either.

Observing the tension between the two men, El thought how much more pleasant it was when other people were having the disagreement. She wondered why Paul and Chuck didn't get into it more often.

To a further question from Roger Filer, Fellows adjusted his expression and said, "According to long-range forecasts, we're looking at above average precip at least 'til March." El knew where he'd gotten *that* from. "I'm projecting 25 percent above normal. Costing it out, we'll be $240,000 over budget."

There was a stir in the room. One of the men on the council whistled.

Paul was nodding. Whatever his irritation with Chuck Fellows at the moment, he enjoyed problems like this. Acts of God. It took the heat off him in other areas. Acts of men. And it gave him something else to hold over her head. When their eyes met this time, there could be no doubt about the message. Enough of this foolishness about no layoffs. There would have to be layoffs.

She shook her head.

The pricks of her headache became sharper. She rubbed her forehead once more, but the heat of her palm only seemed to intensify the pain.

She took her hand away. The aspirin bottle in her purse was empty.

CHAPTER 45

~

Paul Cutler got home before ten, a lot earlier than if it had been a regular council meeting. Brenda's car was missing from the garage. As he walked through the house, the sound of a clarinet, the familiar, slightly wheezy cascade of notes, hesitated, then died away altogether. Resentment had formed a thin scab over his anger. He knocked softly on the music room door and, without waiting, entered.

"Where's your mother?" he asked Zoe, his seventeen-year-old.

"Out at Grey Poupon." When he gave her a puzzled look—even for Brenda, it was awfully late to be at the fellowship—Zoe added, "Planning her big whatchamacallit. Second wind."

"Ah, yes." Despite his foul mood, he smiled. "Second blessing, you mean."

"Whatever."

He'd been so taken up with his own problems that he'd forgotten for the moment Brenda's preparations for her week of revival. At the Fellowship of the Mustard Seed, aka Grey Poupon, Paul's jokey and hostile nickname, more hostile than he'd intended, the creation of a moment of irritation and immediately adopted by Zoe as a taunt of her own, another cold war weapon to use against her mother. He felt badly about the name. Things were tough enough without making them worse.

Zoe played a few more notes and stopped.

"What?" she asked.

"Nothing. Go on, don't mind me."

As she played, a romantic piece, the instrument rose and fell, light playing hide-and-seek along its complex surface. Paul preferred Bach.

Like earthshine, reflections from the music stand light touched the furniture in the room. Zoe—too intense for her years, too much the child of her parents—reminded him now, as she often did, of a lost soul.

She stopped after a few more bars and lowered her instrument. "You look so sad, Daddy."

Sad? Irritation came so quickly to hand, other emotions never got the chance to announce their presence. But, yes, he supposed she was right. How strange.

If Zoe had been an adult, he might have confided and been comforted.

"All city managers look like this, pet, after a few years. Nothing to be done, I'm afraid. Probably time to move on."

"Sad Daddy," she said, her sympathy tinctured with irony, for she was a bright girl and knew when he was being condescending.

She took up the clarinet again, the same piece, her lips tense around the mouthpiece. She looked more like Brenda when playing, Paul imagined, more like him when at rest.

"Don't let your mother catch you," he suggested as he started to leave. She stopped playing again, but only long enough to make a face. After all, the whole point in practicing late into the night was to irritate her mother. Probably if Brenda didn't get home until two a.m., Zoe would still be practicing away. Paul couldn't remember when she'd hit on that strategy—pursuing the virtuous to excess. She'd probably become a world-class clarinetist, all because she was trying to get her mother's goat.

Closing the door softly behind him, he thought, "Husband, wife, daughter, all the same." They were rockets arcing in separate directions, growing farther and farther apart.

Except that, at the moment, his own rocket was none too steady on course. This reminded him of the fight with Aggie, even Aggie of all people getting mouthy with him, going behind his back. As he walked down to the basement, his irritation settled back in.

Evidence of the Cutler family's separate trajectories littered the family room: in one corner, a guitar and piano, Zoe's false musical starts; in the opposite, the pottery gear Brenda had purchased when she thought she might be saved by art. His office, a room within the room, enclosed a third corner.

There he took a tumbler and bottle of whiskey out of his desk, and tossed off a shot while still standing. He poured a second drink, fetched a cigar from the humidor, and settled himself in the swivel chair, his feet propped on the desk. Since Brenda had given up drinking herself, she didn't approve of his drinking anymore, either. She didn't say anything, but in that house, words weren't necessary.

Anyway, city managers drank. That was their occupational disease. He waited for the booze to kick in.

The best way to stop thinking of one irritant, he had found, was to concentrate on another, so he put Brenda aside and took up El and Aggie again.

A place like Jackson was riddled with covert linkages. You never knew when somebody was somebody's cousin or people belonged to the same fraternal organization or had gone to high school together. Nothing to be done. And it was true, the situation with Aggie and El was a little different. He'd known about the relationship between them. Nevertheless, it possessed in his mind the same covert quality as all the ones he didn't know about.

He regretted El. They'd done good work together in the past. Now, for some reason, she'd lost it. She'd become like some poor schlub living on disability in a transient hotel somewhere and concocting fantastic schemes for saving the world.

As for Aggie, he didn't regret a thing. She'd asked for it. He'd be damned if he'd have a subordinate going behind his back. And that committee idea she'd fallen in love with… If Aggie had her way, Jackson would end up like a Third World country, where people talked to each other all the time and nothing ever got done. Of course, she was a woman, a fact he'd been willing to overlook in the past. The problem with women in Paul's view was simple: they were nurturers; they got trapped between the general and the particular. Choices became impossible.

Brenda, he thought. Yes, well, Brenda was the exception that proved the rule.

After a time, he held his tumbler up and turned it so the liquor coated the inside of the glass, shining amber in the light. Cigar smoke hung in strata. He was still stone-cold sober.

Even from his cubicle in the basement, he could hear Zoe's instrument, the sound finding its way through walls and closed doors and ceilings, like water through fissures in a dam.

Some city managers had city managers for friends, people they'd met at professional meetings, shoulders to cry on. But no real spark had ever been struck between Paul and any of the other managers of his acquaintance.

He'd have to tough it out on his own. The way it had always been.

Probably, he thought, what he'd said to Zoe was right; his time in Jackson was coming to an end. Managers were hired because people couldn't be trusted to govern themselves. You came to town and were reasonable, and people hated you for it, your fate sealed the day you arrived. A city manager was a man with a good deal of power and very little influence.

Such thoughts rose in the fumes of his whiskey. He had, he reminded himself, no right to be surprised and no right to self-pity, either. He would have to settle for paranoia, and so he thought about all the different things all the different people of Jackson were doing at that very moment, the conversations, the private thoughts, the slow drift of convictions beneath those private thoughts.

At the edge of his desk lay a copy of the current issue of *Public Management*. He opened the magazine at random—an article on motivation—and with disgust flipped it back onto the desk.

The periodical lay open before him, filled with its earnest practicality. He nursed his drink and his sense of grievance. Overhead, he could hear the clarinet, muted, barely reaching into his monastic quiet.

A cardinal rule of his profession was keep your distance, don't start forming alliances, don't conspire, don't try to pit one group against another. A rule he kept in spirit, even as he broke it in fact.

He pulled on the cigar, sipped his pick-me-up, and let this idea mellow.

Later, he lit another cigar, poured himself another drink.

And still later, he heard the front door slam shut. The music hesitated, but only for an instant.

CHAPTER 46

~

Chuck Fellows didn't have much time—city council meeting. Every time he turned around, another council meeting—work sessions, budget hearings, you name it. He'd bust his ass getting there on time just so he could sit around listening to a bunch of politicians run their mouths. The city council reminded him of what he had hated about the Army.

Diane hadn't bothered to change out of her clothes before preparing dinner, just put an apron on over what she'd worn to work, so that some of her daytime efficiency still clung about her.

Of the children, only Gracey present at the moment, Todd nowhere to be seen.

Chuck just had time enough to feed the dogs before Diane said, "I'm about to serve." He noticed her curtness.

As they were sitting down at the table, Todd still hadn't shown his face. Diane called out sharply for him to come, and from her tone, Chuck could tell the curtness of a minute earlier had come from more than the hassle of getting him off to his meeting.

"What is it?" he asked.

"I'm going to let Todd tell you."

Finally Todd came moping into the kitchen.

"Sit down, sport," Chuck told him. "You've got something to say to me?"

Todd wiggled onto his chair, then slumped down. Usually, when he had done something wrong and the piper must be paid, he was more animated, even garrulous in his own defense, but now he merely looked at the edge of the table in a hangdog fashion.

Chuck checked his watch and started to eat. "Well?"

Diane said, "I got a call at work today. I had to go get him. Apparently it's not the first time they've had a problem, although up to now they've tried to handle it themselves."

What the problem was, however, she still would not say. That was up to Todd.

Chuck stopped eating and turned his full attention on his son. "Well? Out with it."

Todd mumbled something.

"Speak up." Chuck didn't have time for this.

"I got into a fight."

"A fight? Is that all?"

"No," Diane said, "that's not all. He's been making a habit of it. Bullying. Picking on smaller children."

"Is that right?" Chuck asked his son.

"He started it," Todd complained, hunkered down, unrepentant. Chuck told himself that he ought to be patient here. He didn't want to make this into a kangaroo court.

"Who's 'he'?"

Todd said, "Jamie," and then mumbled the last name. The name being irrelevant, Chuck decided to let it ride.

"How did he start it?"

Chuck watched as his son struggled to come up with a plausible explanation.

"He's a dumb jerko asshole…"

"Todd!" Diane snapped.

"Watch your mouth," Chuck told him.

Todd dragged the tines of his fork across the tablecloth.

"I'm waiting," Chuck told him.

"Nobody likes him." His voice rose with sudden inspiration. "The teachers, they don't even like him!"

"That's why you hit him? Because nobody likes him?"

Todd nodded, a hopeful nod, the nod of someone who thinks that maybe he can get away with one.

Chuck looked at his watch and went back to his dinner. "You know what it means to rationalize?" he asked.

"No."

"Of course he doesn't," Diane said.

Chuck gave his wife a look. She wanted him to deal with this. He would.

"It means," he said to Todd, "you don't want to tell the real reason why you did something, so you make something up, something that sounds good, but isn't true. It's a lie."

Todd remained mute.

"It's not just this time," Diane said. "It's other times, too."

"You're making a habit of this, sport?" Chuck asked his son.

"He's bigger than almost all the others in his class," Diane continued. "Apparently, he's turned himself into quite the little tyrant."

"Why don't I know about this?" he asked her.

"I didn't want to bother you. You've got enough to worry about. But it's more serious than I was led to believe."

Confronted so suddenly with a full-blown situation, Chuck found himself uncertain how to proceed. He looked down at his son, but instead saw himself, himself at eight. He had gotten into fights at that age. Had he picked on kids? He didn't think so, but he didn't really remember.

Diane had found her voice now. "He's got to learn not to fight."

"He does?"

"That's right."

"You mean, I can never beat up a kid littler than me?" Todd asked, following his own line of reasoning, and in a tone suggesting that such an idea seemed preposterous. What were little kids for if not the occasional pummeling when they forgot their proper station in the third-grade hierarchy?

"No, dear," Diane said, "you can never beat up a kid littler than you."

"I'm doing this," Chuck reminded her. "Kids aren't adults, and elementary school isn't the United Nations. Sometimes the only way a kid gets respect is by punching some jerk in the nose."

"I don't agree. Anyway, I don't appreciate getting pulled out of work to go fetch your son because he's been picking on children smaller than he is. Perhaps the next time, you'd like me to tell them to call you, and you can deal with it."

Diane hated disagreements in front of the children, but Chuck didn't mind. Part of life, and they might as well get used to it.

But he still wasn't sure what to do. Or what, in a larger sense, he wanted for his son. Did he want to turn Todd into the man he was now? Did he want Todd, in thirty-five years, to be sitting at the dinner table staring down at *his* son and feeling the way Chuck felt now, the way he had felt over the last couple of years, basically not giving a shit, basically going through the motions. Maybe Diane was right. Maybe they should try to make him into a regular little Mahatma Gandhi.

Chuck couldn't do it. No way he wanted to breed all the perversity out of the little bugger. Not cruelty, though, not this tormenting of the weak, which Chuck despised.

"Listen, Todd," he told his son, "I don't hear anything about you getting into fights with kids bigger than you. How come?"

Todd had no response to this.

Diane said, "Fighting with bigger children? Now there's an idea."

Chuck folded his arms across his chest and stared down at the boy. "If you're going to fight, you don't fight with people you know you can beat up. Only cowards do that."

Todd sat mutely.

"You hear me?" Chuck waited.

"Yes," Todd said under his breath, staring down, still dragging the tines of the fork slowly across the table cloth. His food remained untouched. Chuck took the fork away from him.

"Speak up!"

"Yes," Todd said a little louder.

"Good. But if you've gotta defend yourself, that's okay. You don't back down from anybody. You got that, sport?" He continued talking to his son, driving home the point. "You don't pick fights. But you don't take anybody's guff. Big, little, makes no difference." Todd hazarded a brief look at his father.

For a moment, Chuck felt satisfied, like a man who had been struggling up a slope covered with dislodged stones and suddenly found his footing. He pointed a finger at Todd. "But no more bullying. All right? All right. Enough said."

Diane looked disgusted, although whether more with Chuck or Todd it was impossible to say. Little Grace, sitting next to her brother during this interrogation, had remained silent, eyes wide open, staring at her father and, as she still did in moments of stress, sucking her thumb.

CHAPTER 47

~

Janelle Kelley had her interior decorator's paraphernalia all over the dining room table, the table attended by a rabble of Federal, Windsor, and mongrel side chairs. Janelle didn't apply her art to the Kelley house any more than Jack did his builder's expertise, the place cluttered and mismatched and, to the practiced eye, slightly out of plumb in an old house way. One of Janelle's legal-sized notepads sat next to the telephone, the city council meeting on the TV at the far end of the table, the dishwasher in the other room just clearing its throat, contemplating its prewash cycle, and Janelle already on a call to one of her clients, flicking her cigarette impatiently against the rim of an ashtray. Jack listened to a couple of sentences and realized it wasn't a client but one of the craftsmen who supplied her with reproductions. The poor fool had missed a deadline and was trying to fob off some excuse on her.

Jack watched the TV long enough to witness his boss Harry Steadman's biweekly performance before the council, Harry back in town and taking over that duty. Harry looked good on television. He scattered confidence and geniality like benedictions. He stood upright at the podium, relaxed, one hand in a pocket, the other shaping his reassuring words. True, he conceded to the council, track construction remained behind schedule, but only on the grandstand and this break in the weather had been a godsend. He'd been assured by his people that they'd make up most of the lost time. Maybe all of it. Going great guns now—exterior skin on tote board—site utilities—ahead of schedule on kennels—20 percent of the primary and secondary steel up on the grandstand, and if the good weather held, he'd been assured they'd be buttoned up in three, four weeks max. Then it'd be Katie bar the door.

Janelle put her hand over the phone's mouthpiece and looked skeptically at Jack. "Who's doing all this assuring? You?"

"I told him we'd need the weather with us the rest of the way."

The grandstand controlled, all the other stuff which Harry had dangled like silver trinkets before the eyes of the council members—tote board, kennels, utilities—just the usual bump and grind, barely worth mentioning.

"That's a lot more than four weeks," Janelle pointed out.

"Yeah. And no way the weather's gonna hold. He knows it. Council knows it, too."

"I don't like the sound of the word *assured*," Janelle said suspiciously before she removed her hand from the mouthpiece and resumed berating the poor doofus on the other end of the line.

Jack went up to his office and unrolled the preliminary drawings he'd finally managed to badger out of the concessionaire; he spent the next couple of hours trying to estimate the breakout for the work.

He stopped from time to time, his mind, which had a mind of its own, dragging back the issue of the construction schedule for further mulling. He remembered the day of the groundbreaking the previous September, when he'd promised the then city public works director Mark O'Banion the job would be done according to the specs and on budget, but, most of all, on time...*on time*...winter or no winter, the track ready to open on June 15. A promise made in their professional capacities, of course, construction manager to project owner, but yet...

He and Mark had known and respected each other for a very long time. Now Mark was three months dead. And the project? Well, after all, when you really thought about it, whatever the potential financial payback to the community—and Jack had his doubts on that score, too—the track could hardly be counted a worthy civic enterprise. A mere dog track. Even this far along, considered strictly on the merits, Jack would have gladly walked away.

He heard steps, light and quick, ascending the stairs, followed by a rap on his door.

"You'll never guess who I met today," his daughter Kitty said as she breezed into the room.

She came filled with a bright expectancy that was rare for her, but Jack could only look dully back, his mind taken up with these other matters.

"Diane Fellows," Kitty informed him.

"Who?" He'd never heard of her. "Fellows? Any relation to Chuck Fellows?"

"Wife."

"He has a wife?" Some woman would actually marry Chuck Fellows?

"So she claimed. Two kids, too."

Jack thought, *So Chuck Fellows has a wife.*

"If she's anything like her husband...," he said.

"She seemed quite nice, actually."

"Where did you run into her?"

"I took a patient over to Medical Associates. She's an administrator there."

Jack studied his daughter and wondered, mindful of her personality, what he thought of her having a little chat with the wife of the director of public works. "What did you talk about?"

"You and Chuck Fellows, of course, what else? I was nice," she assured him, reading the expression on his face. "Jeepers, Daddy, give me that much credit." Kitty had what Jack called her nurse's bluntness, and, being a loyal daughter, if in her own rather offhand way, she thought nothing of tossing brickbats that he had inadvertently handed to her. "Anyway, don't you suppose she already knows what you think of the man?"

"I have no idea." Jack, who still hadn't entirely accommodated himself to the idea that Fellows had a wife at all, couldn't imagine what he might talk to her about.

"You would've been proud of me," Kitty said. "Not only was I nice, but I plumped for you, told her what a great guy you are and how you're giving your all to build the dog track for the city, and blah blah blah. I put on a good show. Say thank you."

"Thank you."

"You're welcome."

"And what did she say?"

"That she was sure her husband appreciated what you were doing."

Jack smiled at this preposterous statement. "So basically you stood there trading lies."

"Well, of course, what do you expect? I'd just met the woman."

Kitty flounced out of the room, gone as quickly as she'd arrived.

Left alone, Jack attempted without luck to take up his estimating. So Chuck Fellows had a family. Jack imagined them—a mousy wife tiptoeing around, the children, probably mousy, too, tiptoeing around, too, the household tactics being to stay downwind of the old man. Jack closed his eyes and envisioned the house itself—colonial, garrison colonial, hunter green, three years old, very quiet, with a few scrappy shrubs and trees around about, pickup truck in the driveway, the kind of place where some ghastly crime is committed and the neighbors say they never imagined anything was the matter.

When Jack finally went back downstairs, Janelle had abandoned her work and poured herself a drink. In her lap, a woman's magazine lay open but ignored. The city council meeting droned on. Janelle waved her cigarette at the screen.

"This is quite interesting."

One of the councilmen was speaking.

Jack considered scotch and decided no and went into the kitchen to get a beer, followed by the councilman's indistinct words, unhurried and sincere, as if he'd been going on for some time.

"Who is it?" Jack asked from the kitchen.

"Filer."

"Is he going to run?" A rumor had been floating around for some time.

"Yes. Today was the last day to turn in signatures."

As Jack carried his beer back into the dining room, he was reminded of contractors who turned in their bids at the last moment. And this reminded him of Tony Vasconcellos, for he never thought about contractors in general without thinking about Tony Vasconcellos in particular.

In the dining room, he remained standing. "Interesting?"

"They're about to vote on the resolution to recruit black people to move to Jackson."

"For or against?"

"For, of course. Five to one probably."

"Filer the one?" Jack wasn't quite sure whether he was surprised or not. The Roger Filer that he knew from Rotary didn't seem like much of a boat rocker.

"He's saying if we're gonna invite anybody to the city, it oughta be the sons and daughters who left because they couldn't find jobs here. He's saying that and he's saying the city ought to be run like a business." Janelle flicked her cigarette against the edge of her ash-tray with characteristic impatience.

"Hmm," Jack remarked.

The camera had moved to a close-up of Filer, still talking. Jack wondered why on earth he would run, the racial business being pretty much a lose-lose situation as far as Jack was concerned. Although, it was true, there were a lot of people in the city, even people who weren't necessarily racists, who had no interest in rolling out the red carpet. So from a purely demographic point of view…

Jack thought of something suitably cynical that he might say in Janelle's presence. "I suppose he imagines he's gonna sell more Chevys."

"That's not it," she retorted at once.

"Oh?"

Janelle, the pundit in the Kelley household, made it a point of honor to have strong opinions. Knew everything. Knew stuff people had no right to know.

"It's his inferiority complex."

"Always seemed like a pretty confident sort to me," Jack opined.

The camera was slowly panning down the council table.

Janelle lit up another cigarette. "Feels he's never been accepted in Jackson. Been here how long? Since the sixties at least, involved in all kinds of civic stuff, but never invited to join the Masons, never invited to join the Shooting Club."

"He's a Protestant?"

"Methodist."

"You're not a true Jacksonian unless your mother was born here," Jack said, resurrecting the much-repeated local saying. By which criteria Jack himself didn't qualify, although Janelle did.

"There's something weird about the man," she said, "something not quite right, too friendly or something. We've never had him over."

"Why would we?"

The camera had come to rest on El Plowman. Jack wished it would pan back down to Filer so that he might get another look at the fellow. Maybe he actually believed what he was saying, sincerity being an option, too. But the camera remained steadfastly on the stoic and glum mayor.

Had Janelle once considered having Roger Filer over and abandoned the idea because Filer "wasn't quite right"? Interesting what went on inside your wife's head that you had no inkling of.

The camera remained determinedly on El Plowman, so Jack took his beer and went away and spent another hour working on the drawings from the concessionaire.

CHAPTER 48

~

The consent items, tacked onto the end of the city council agenda, always contained an item or two about which some council member might wish to question staff, so Chuck was forced to sit through the entire fiasco, five hours to accomplish a half hour's worth of work. He returned home after one a.m., still in his city council mood, and got a beer and went out to the sleeping porch he'd converted into an office. He tried to unwind by studying the next move in the chess game he was playing by mail.

A kid or dog had jostled the board again, and he restored the pieces as best he could, too impatient to replay the moves. Made no difference. He'd blundered early in the game and was playing for a draw. He studied his crumbling position, castling the obvious move, his king about to be set upon by a horde of white pieces. Or he could concede. Experimentally, he lay the black king on its side and stared at the fallen piece. Finally, he turned it back upright and went ahead and castled.

After a while, sick of his own company, he went upstairs.

The day, however, had not quite ended. As soon as he got into bed, he realized that something was missing: the medley of noises Diane made when asleep, her side of the bed at the moment as quiet as outer space. Chuck clasped his hands behind his head and waited.

After a time, she began, although not where he expected.

"I met Kitty Kelley today."

"Who?"

"Kitty Kelley. She's Jack Kelley's daughter."

Chuck was surprised for an instant and then not surprised. In places like Jackson, ingrown, practically incestuous, you were always among people who knew people you knew. "I was going to tell you at supper, except we got into that other thing. She's a nurse at St. Rafael's. She brought in one of her patients for therapy."

"How did you find out who she was?"

"She made the connection. Saw the name on my badge. She was amused."

"Amused?" An interesting way to put it. "Kelley thinks I'm a flaming asshole. No doubt he's been passing it around."

"She didn't say what was funny."

"And you, what did you say?"

Diane had propped herself up on an elbow and was looking down at him in the dark. "That you're a sweetheart. Then Kitty said her father was a sweetheart, too, and we went on like that." Chuck snickered, imagining the exchange.

"Of course," Diane added, flopping back down, "the conversation made no sense unless you understood the real relationship between you and Jack Kelley."

Chuck considered delivering a shot against Kelley, Diane having created a free-fire zone, but then decided it was late and what was the point. He waited in the silence for whatever else she had to say, the encounter with Kelley's daughter too slight a matter to have kept her awake.

"I thought you were going to start on me again about the business with Todd," he put in after a time, just to see how she'd respond.

The bedsprings creaked and then went silent. The longer the silence, the more uncertain he became of what was coming, although something. She had learned to rise to his provocations.

"Does it ever occur to you that you might do more harm than good?"

Yes, it did, but Chuck said, "Kid's got to defend himself."

"You know what you mean, but you don't know how Todd takes it. Whatever children hear, it's not what we think we're telling them."

Interested by this point, Chuck didn't launch a counterattack at once.

"Anyway, never mind," Diane continued, "we'll do it your way this time. That's not what I wanted to say. What I wanted to say is that I'm worried about you."

"I'm okay."

"You are, huh? Have you looked in the mirror recently?"

"Do it every day."

"I mean, *really* looked? I can see it in your face, dear. The strain, the unhappiness. You need to get off by yourself, like you used to do. Why don't you go for a ride on your motorcycle? Take a day, take two days."

"I'm okay."

"I know why, too," she said, skipping over his assertion. "It's because I made you stay in Jackson when you wanted to go to that awful place in Canada."

"Like hell. You gave me an ultimatum, and I made a choice."

Diane was quiet and then said, "All right, yes, that's a better way of putting it. You made a choice. And now you don't have a minute to yourself. And all the joy's gone out of your life. I can see it in your face."

"I'm okay."

"You need time to yourself, you really do. Why don't you take the weekend off, go somewhere on your bike, one of your—what do you call them?—rides to no place."

That wasn't what he called them, but it was close enough. "It's winter. The bike needs work." He envisioned the Suzuki, disassembled in the cellar.

"Take your truck, then." Diane was propped on her elbow again, warming to the chase.

"Too much to do." He listened to himself with disapproval as he went on. "I've got all these goddamn jobs, remember?"

"Pfft," Diane said, "don't give me that. You always have too much to do, and anyway, you think most of it's trivial."

"I finish what I start," Chuck said self-righteously.

"Of course you do. But we're not talking about that. We're talking about you. We're talking about all the sleep you're losing."

"I sleep fine."

"You do, huh? For a man who prides himself on telling the truth, you can sure be full of it sometimes."

Chuck didn't answer. Diane was right, he had been having trouble sleeping. He'd never had trouble before. In 'Nam, he'd trained himself to sleep anywhere, to sleep just below consciousness, like an alligator with nothing but its snout above water. He'd liked the challenge of it; he'd liked the idea of the NVA so close they could almost smell his sweat as he snoozed away. But now nothing was at stake and he couldn't sleep. That was his life.

Diane had lain back down.

"You can take a day or two off," she said. "The world won't come to an end."

Chuck understood his own unworthy petulance here, and the contrary satisfaction he took in working the hell out of a job he thought pretty much for shit.

"I've never seen a man more responsible than you are," Diane said. She insisted on inflating his worth. Part of the wife's job, he supposed, but he thought it was a crock.

"I do the work. But it's no big deal. Whatever else happens, it happens. The world goes to hell, that's just tough shit."

"Chuck, the world-class cynic. Baloney. It's all a big act. You know what I think? I think it's all because of Vietnam, this tough-guy, I-can-take-anything, I-don't-need-any-time-for-myself act. That's what I think. I think you've seen too much. You've lost your faith in people. You spend all this time with them, but you're basically afraid to trust anyone. Or you turn it all into an in-group and out-group thing, people you really, really like—for instance, Walter Plowman—and people like Jack Kelley, who's probably a perfectly decent man but you've decided to make into the enemy."

Statements like these really ticked Chuck off. Who the hell was she to tell him what he felt?

"'Nam's got nothing to do with it."

"I think it does. But I don't want to fight about it. All I'm saying is the budget or the dog track or whatever it is you think you've got to do this weekend can wait. You need to take some time for yourself."

Chuck said nothing. Diane wasn't such a great fucking wife, after all, he decided. She still thought she knew so damn much.

The conversation had ended. He lay staring at the ceiling. He thought about what had been said. He thought about 'Nam. He thought about the surprise visit the week before from his old Army buddy Jake Podolak. He thought about the Suzuki lying in pieces down in the cellar. He thought about Yellowknife in the Canadian Northwest Territories, where he'd almost gone. And thinking about that, his mind trailed off to the north, across the tundra, across the white wastes where no man lived.

CHAPTER 49

～

Jack Kelley had disliked men before. When a contractor gave him a tough time, Jack would typically turn his back, deal with situations when they came up, try, if necessary, to work things out so the other fellow saved face, even do his best to keep him afloat long enough to finish the job. It was true, all right, that sometimes Jack scanted a bit on Christian love. He'd always been a better Catholic in his deeds than in his heart; he knew it and regretted it, but there you were. Yet, he did try. Even with Tony Vasconcellos, he'd tried.

In the construction trailer, he glanced over Sean's attendance sheet for the day. Good weather, a run of good weather and all hands on deck, for it was make hay while the sun shined. They didn't have that long, another storm coming onshore in the Pacific Northwest. His eye ticked quickly down the list, stopping only when he reached the electrical contractor's manpower. Jack seemed to see the number even before he looked at it: four. And no mention of a superintendent.

Four? Four electricians? Four lousy electricians? Should have been a dozen guys on site, minimum.

Jack pointed at the offending number.

"Is this right? You sure?"

Sean nodded.

"And no foreman? Where's Lonny?"

"One of them said he went to Manchester with his dad to look at dogs."

"Say again."

Sean repeated himself.

"Greyhounds?" Jack asked.

"That's what he said."

As Jack headed out the door, Sean told him that he'd organized the payment requests and didn't Jack want to go over them? Jack ignored him. Up on the deck of the grandstand, he talked to the senior electrician on hand and confirmed what Sean had said.

"Greyhounds?"

"Tony heard somewhere there was money in them. You know Tony."

"We all know Tony."

As he stalked back to the construction trailer, Jack kept on repeating, "He's gone to look at dogs, the son of a bitch has gone to look at dogs." That was just too goddamn much.

He called Vasconcellos's office and told the secretary he needed to talk to him at once, then slammed the receiver down and sat pounding a fist into his thigh, Sean hovering nearby.

～

Vasconcellos didn't call back. At four-thirty, Jack drove down to the contractor's office. No one there but the secretary. She assured him that she'd passed along his message.

Jack left. He would talk to Vasconcellos, one way or another; whether the shit wanted it or not, Jack would talk to him. He got back into his car.

The early February days were slowly growing longer, and a remnant of daylight survived as Jack pulled into the dead-end street where the Vasconcellos family lived.

The ranch house, brightly lit, sprawled across a double lot at the end of the cul-de-sac. Jack parked on the curve, next to the heaped up ridge of plowed snow. From where he sat, he couldn't see the house, only the glow above it. The electrician had turned his place into a carnival of lights.

If there had been pleasure in Jack's onrush of anger that morning, he took no such pleasure in the loathing he now felt for Tony Vasconcellos. Only once before had he been consumed by such an intense hatred, beyond reason, beyond control, and that had been long ago, for a boy who had started out as a childhood friend. Jack barely remembered what had led to the change. Even at the time, his hatred had seemed entangled with something deeper than mere events. What he did remember, only too well, was the satisfaction he'd felt when the boy was killed in an auto wreck, the satisfaction and the fervent hope that his former friend would burn in hell. Jack had gone to

confession and been absolved, but the absolution failed to dis-
lodge either the satisfaction or the guilt, which he still carried
all these years later. And as with that boy, so with Tony Vasconcellos. Might he rot in hell.

And yet, and yet...what were Tony's sins? Not mortal certainly, hardly even venial, merely the schemings of a typical low-life
contractor. Jack understood this. Made no difference; made not a
fucking bit of difference. He absolutely loathed the man.

The temperature had begun to drop sharply as the daytime
warmth disappeared into the cloudless sky. Jack skirted the tall
ridge of snow. In the floodlit driveway, a number of vehicles—
pickups and SUVs and luxury sedans—were parked at angles to
one another before the three-car garage. Next to the building, a
massive RV hunkered in the snowpack. He did a quick estimate,
pricing out this gross excess of vehicles, another item for his bill of
particulars against Vasconcellos.

Angela Vasconcellos came to the back door, smiling as if nothing was wrong and saying what a pleasant surprise, but not opening
the storm door all the way.

"I need to see Tony."

"Oh, dear," she said, still smiling, so sorry, "it's not really a
good time, Jack."

Jack stared at the wife, in her late forties, still attractive, very
attractive, carefully dressed, as if off to some function or other.
Why such a woman would settle on the likes of Tony Vasconcellos,
he had no idea.

"Angela, I want to see Tony. You go get him."

The smile disappeared.

"I don't know, Jack. He really can't."

Jack leaned closer.

"Believe me, Angela, you don't want me to go away without
seeing Tony."

She hesitated, then withdrew, closing the storm door, but leaving the other ajar, the warm air from inside leaking out and misting
along the edge of the glass. Jack had a powerful sense of people
inside living lives at acute angles to his own. He waited, practicing
what he would say.

After a while, Tony appeared, showing no sign that he had
been occupied in anything other than avoiding Jack, and at once,
the best defense being a good offense, said to Jack, "I've got a bone

to pick with you. You went to the priest again. You keep on going to the priest, Jack. It makes me look like shit, and I don't like it."

"Come out here and close the door," Jack told him.

"Let me go get my coat."

"You don't need your damn coat. This won't take that long. Believe me."

"Stop going to Father Mike," Tony said, closing the door gingerly behind him.

"Why didn't you return my call?" Jack asked.

"What call?"

"This morning. Your girl said she passed the message along."

Tony shrugged, unconcerned. "Never got it."

Jack started to say something else, then stopped himself. This is not a surprise, he told himself, don't waste your breath.

"You and your son were out to Manchester today looking at dogs?"

"That's right."

"There was no foreman on the job."

Vasconcellos shrugged again, massively unconcerned. "My people know what to do."

"There were only four of 'your people' on the job site."

"That right? You sure?"

"There were only four, Tony."

"I'll have to look into it."

"You do that."

"What about your young gofer there?" Vasconcellos asked.

"Sean? What about him?"

"You sure he didn't miscount? Frankly, Jack, he hasn't impressed me, no experience, not much on the ball. If you wanted a youngster with some potential, you shoulda considered my Lonny, not that I have any intention of letting him go, heh, heh."

"I asked your man Gene. He confirmed it."

"He did, huh? Up on the deck, was he? You shoulda gone out to the kennels. Probably more of my guys out there."

Although it was a pointless exercise, Jack said, "Let's be frank, Tony. I know the game you play. You bring a full crew out there for a day or two, go like hell, then start pulling guys off and sending them to other jobs." Vasconcellos had the track contract in his pocket. A done deal. When other work came up, maybe something he could run off the books, he snatched at it. The shit.

As if Jack had just proved his point for him, Vasconcellos said, "That's right, the track's not the only thing I gotta do." He changed the subject. "You know, Jack, you really oughta think about going out to Manchester for a look-see yourself. Invest in a couple of puppies. Bruce Huizinga's got a real interesting operation out there." Placidly, Vasconcellos began a disquisition on the art of dog breeding, the tone of his voice making Jack homicidal.

"Stop it, Tony! I don't give a shit about the dogs, to hell with 'em. And let me tell you, you haven't got time to fuck around 'em, either."

Vasconcellos paused and then countered with a bland, "I still say that your man musta counted wrong. I'll look into it, just to make sure."

Get a grip, Jack told himself. Forget about trying to reason with the man.

"Okay, Tony, fine, you do that," he said. Knowing that Vasconcellos would stonewall, Jack had not come unprepared. "I'm just here to make a record, anyway. That's what I'm doing, Tony, making a record. Just so you'll know." Jack took one step away, and then delivered his parting shot. "Oh, and by the way, you can forget about the electrical work for the concessionaire. There's twenty or twenty-five thou you could've had. But not now, no way. And I'll tell you one more thing—you keep on like this and I'll take the rest away from you, too. You watch me."

As he walked away, he said, "Nobody fucks with me, Tony."

CHAPTER 50

~

They left the flood until last.

"Before we begin," Chuck Fellows cautioned his engineering staff, repeating the warning he'd issued two weeks earlier, "this is all preliminary, okay? We don't nose it around. Probably nothing's gonna happen. There's no damn reason for anybody to get his balls in an uproar yet." He turned to Seth Brunel, the assistant city engineer. "And before we talk about water over the wall, I want to make sure the protection system functions as designed. That's what I'm really worried about."

"All right, so here we go," Seth said as he taped a map of the riverfront on top of the blackboard and began describing the preset sequence of events as the river rose. "Zero river stage, the Coast and Geodetic Survey Base Datum, is 585 feet above sea level. Pool is seven feet above that, so that's basically when nothing particular is going on…"

Seth was gaga over the prospect of a big flood. But he was young and had grown up in the middle of Nevada, where water was more a rumor than a reality. Chuck made an allowance for him. The interest of the old-timers was less excusable. They should have known better, but they'd been telling stories about the era before the flood protection system had been built and remembering with ill-concealed pride the long days and nights of sleeplessness, of adding to the levees until nothing more could be added, ringing sand boils and reinforcing seeps, waiting desperately for the crest. For big-river floods were massive and drawn out, water pressure slowly mounting against emergency dikes, week after week. There was nothing in the least amusing about them. Chuck, for his part, thought about people building in the floodplain where they had no business building, and the river coming to take back what was hers.

Although he didn't expect it, not this time. Even after a bunch of Walt Plowman's preconditions had been met, others remained—more winter storms, a sharp break in the weather come March, torrential spring rains—the odds still long. Chuck was fatalistic, but unlike the fatalism of others, who expected cataclysms—even, if these jokers were any example, looked forward to them—his resembled the heat death, the death by whimpers. Probably nothing would happen, but that didn't mean the world wasn't going to hell.

Seth continued, indicating the relevant points on the map and describing the intensifying response as the river rose—what happened at fourteen feet when sixteen was the predicted crest; at sixteen feet, more than eighteen predicted; and so forth. Flood stage was seventeen, at which point the river began to climb out of her natural banks, but the floodwall and levee system were designed to hold back as much as a thirty-foot crest, four feet above the flood of record. Chuck's main job as the river rose was closing gates to prevent water from backing up through the storm drains. After that, he had to pump any rainwater that ponded behind the system over the wall and into the river.

Seth, with his newfound enthusiasm for high water but also his long-standing nutso love of caves and lead mines and under-ground passages of all kinds, mentioned the possibility that there were old abandoned storm drains that nobody knew about. Chuck told him to forget about ghosts.

"I wanna talk about the wall and the levees. You've walked them?"

"The wall. Sections of it. There's too much snow to see much, particularly the levees. As the snow melts, I'll check the rest."

"Okay." Chuck decided he'd have a look for himself. He didn't trust Seth, who seemed competent enough, lanky and blond like an all-American kid, but possessing a secretive streak which Chuck assumed had something to do with his love of things below ground and left Chuck with the feeling that he never quite knew what Seth was up to.

Chuck asked him, "How do you propose adding to the system if the stage goes over thirty feet?"

Seth taped two drawings over the waterfront map, one the cross section of a temporary levee on top of the existing, the second his proposal for adding to the wall.

Chuck listened and studied the drawings, which could have been rough sketches at this point in the proceedings—Seth himself called them first approximations—but had been rendered in detail. For the floodwall, he'd add flashboards to the top, the only sensible solution, the question being how to attach them to the existing concrete.

"What about spalling?" Glenn Owens, the drafting supervisor, asked. "Your bolts seem pretty close to the edge."

"The top fastener you want as high on the wall as you can get it to minimize the moment on the vertical member."

"Not a problem if you work from the outside," Chuck pointed out.

"I assume we won't be able to," Seth said.

"Assume?"

As they continued talking about the wall, Chuck turned his attention to the drawing of the emergency levee. Seth had used flashboards there, too, secured by stakes driven into the existing levee and backed by earth fill. He must have thought since he was using boards for the wall, why not the levee, too. No doubt it would work, but it seemed to Chuck too elaborate, probably more expensive, too, not to mention the problem of finding all the lumber.

When Seth began to describe the emergency levee, Chuck cut him off at once. "Have you costed it out yet?"

"Haven't had time. Thought if I could come up with a design we liked, I could go from there."

Obviously, Seth liked this Mercedes Benz he'd come up with. Chuck told him what *he* thought, which deflated his subordinate, who lost some of his patent cheerfulness for a moment. "I wanna know how much it's gonna cost us," Chuck instructed him. "Make sure you can put your hands on enough plywood sheeting. We've got six miles to work with here, a shitload of wood if you're gonna use it all the way. And we need to know where we can find clay locally." He suggested a couple of places to start looking. "Good fatty clay. If we can get it for free, why not make the whole levee out of the stuff and use sandbags and poly on the front. The levee's not an engineering problem, it's a money problem." If it had been Chuck's baby from the beginning, he would have called around, sourcing different materials and obtaining current costs, maybe guaranteed costs, then tried to figure out how the situation would change during a flood, and all the time as he was doing this, designing and redesigning on the fly, in his head, not like Seth here, who treated the assignment as a paper-and-pencil exercise, as if he was still back in engineering school. But Chuck had known that would happen, part of Seth's underground personality, no doubt.

You had to delegate and let people get it right or screw up, that's what Chuck thought. Diane imagined that he didn't trust people, but she was wrong. He just didn't have confidence in them, that was all. Like his favorite drill sergeant from basic training used to say, trust begins where confidence ends. Sometimes you maybe had no choice but to trust a man, although not when his ass was on the line. In 'Nam, he'd made damn sure he only went out in the boonies with people he had confidence in. But here in Jackson, nothing was on the line. Why not trust Seth? Not to mention the fact that it just pissed Chuck off no end to have to tell somebody something he should've known already.

Wayne Nevers, the chief of the survey crew, replaced Seth's visuals with a map of the city on which several contour lines had been drawn, the areas that would be flooded at different river stages if water went over the protection system.

Everyone at the table was gabbing now. This was really interesting, this beyond-the-edge-of-the-known-world stuff. If water capped the wall, the downtown would fill up fast. People would have to be evacuated. Maybe evacuation should occur earlier, as a precaution. "Not our job," Chuck told them. "Just concentrate on what we've gotta worry about." The physical infrastructure.

The others applied themselves to this more-limited mandate. Electrical substations would be flooded. Maybe they should be talking with the people at Tri-State Power. The water plant would be flooded, too, and they'd have to start trucking in water for sixty thousand people. What about wastewater? Probably they'd end up dumping untreated sewage. Could they do that without the EPA jumping down their throats? Traffic signals? Should they pull the controllers to prevent water damage? Did they have enough temporary stop signs to do that?

As Chuck listened to the chatter, his impatience rose quickly, for he realized that he'd made a mistake. No need to talk about any of this extreme stuff yet. They were too far ahead of the curve. His fault. He'd been paying too much attention to Walt Plowman. The Corps of Engineers hadn't even made a preliminary prediction yet. Nobody knew what was going to happen. All they knew was that there was a shitload of snow up north.

"Enough," he said sharply, getting to his feet. "Enough. You can put all this away. Just worry about the wall and levee for now." The others looked at him, startled at the suddenness, still with plenty they wanted to say about Armageddon.

CHAPTER 51

~

"Sister had to go home—illness in the family—so I'm baching it," Father Mike Dougherty explained, leading the way. "Why don't we use the west parlor?"

In the foyer, Jack Kelley noticed that Mike had shifted around the two stands, one with the Bible on it and the other with Flower's treatise on the virtues of octagonal buildings. He'd added a third, on top of which lay open the recently published history of the diocese, which he tapped as they passed.

"Wonderful book. Read it yet?"

"No."

"Worth the effort. Interesting chapter on St. C's. You're in it."

Mike had been recommending books for years, although this was the first time he had this particular enticement to dangle in front of Jack. Jack had no interest in reading his name among the lists of past and present spear-carriers in the diocese.

They entered the parlor, where amber afternoon sunlight slanted sharply from the southwest through the leaded windows, cutting the legs off nearby furniture. A half-finished glass of what looked like sherry stood on a small table between two of Janelle's rococo reproduction chairs. Mike motioned to one of the chairs and took the other himself, which had a footstool on top of which papers were scattered.

"Homily," he said, gesturing toward the papers. "It's tough coming up with good ideas anymore, so I've started migrating around the place, hoping the change of venue will bring inspiration."

"Has it?"

"Why don't we wait 'til Sunday, then you can tell me."

Father Mike had on his black clergy shirt today, a little unusual since he usually wandered around the rectory in mufti. The shirt lay open at the throat, no white tab collar, as if he'd just come off duty.

Jack refused the offer of a drink, and Mike performed the ritual of asking after Janelle.

"I was sitting here, where, as I said, I don't usually, and it struck me again what a wonderful job she did." He made a motion with his hand as if blessing the scene. "Look at the way the pictures and rugs just naturally draw the eye to the wonderful old upright. All that's missing is someone playing."

Mike loved Janelle in the Christian sense, but he did not like her. Yet he had found a thousand ways to praise her remodeling job.

"I'm gonna get you two on a cursillo weekend one of these times." He smiled as he said this, having said it so often that it had become a kind of joke between them, as if Janelle would ever willingly subject herself to the charismatics in the parish.

Jack found himself more impatient with the niceties than usual.

"What can I do for you, Mike? Up to my ears."

"I bet," Mike clucked. His friendliness didn't waver, but Jack seemed to glimpse beneath the professional composure a suggestion of strain. He had noticed this before, and it softened his attitude toward his priest. Perhaps it had no more noble cause than the effort required to run a growing parish, nothing more lofty than ambition pursued, but Jack always suspected it also had something to do with the toll that celibacy must take on a man.

"And how *is* the track coming, my friend?" Mike now asked.

"Behind."

Mike shook his head sympathetically. "All this snow."

"That too," Jack said, for one way or another, the conversation now entered upon had to do with Tony Vasconcellos, not the vicissitudes of the weather. "Just for your information, Mike, Tony has instructed me not to talk to you anymore."

"Hmm, interesting. He didn't mention that." Before Jack could react, Father Mike went on. "But no, actually I wasn't thinking about Tony, I was thinking about the work, I really was, thinking about what it must be like out there. Terrible weather, a rush job, the complexity of it all. Wonderful challenge, really. And frankly, just to anticipate a bit, if Tony really isn't pulling his weight, I can't understand it. If it was me—"

"I wish it was."

"I almost left the seminary to go work on the Trans-Alaska Pipeline, did I ever tell you that?"

"You did." Mike had his store of tales and talked to many, many people, apparently forgetting what he'd said to whom.

He nodded, but finished the thought anyway. "A great help it would've been to my parents. They had a desperate need, and there I was, off with my begging bowl to become a holy man." As he continued, Mike made a fist and jabbed the air, short jiggery punches. "But the challenge of it, that would've been the thing. Not the money. Working at thirty below. Building across the permafrost. Every day a test of a man's fortitude."

"Frankly, Mike, I'd think seminary would be enough of a test of any man's fortitude. Anyway, we've had this conversation before."

"Ah! But still…"

Father Mike often spoke like this, half jocularly of his envy of Jack's life of bricks and mortar, just as he professed to envy the Trappists out at New Melleray their contemplative existences, as if the priest occupied some impossibly compromised place between two perfections.

"I remember hearing somewhere," Jack once twitted him, "that envy is one of the deadly sins."

"True…true…," Mike had said at once, "if fully consented to. And particularly—which just goes to prove your point—when the envy is of sanctity."

"The brothers."

Mike had nodded with pleasure.

Jack suspected, however, that Father Mike, like the rest of them, only spoke so lightly about sins that didn't tempt him.

Another device of the priest was to lead conversations into byways of his own choosing, like a cabby expert at taking the long way around. Jack didn't have the time.

"Vasconcellos came to see you, did he, Father?"

This had the desired effect. Mike adjusted his expression and blew out a puff of air and propped himself up on his thighs.

"Yes…yes, he did. Very upset."

"Is that right?" So Vasconcellos had gone whining to the priest. Unbelievable.

"I have to tell you, Jack, that Tony feels you're holding him up to a higher standard than the rest…you know, the other contractors. He thinks you're bending over backwards just because you two are both from St. C's."

"I can't tell you how amusing this is," Jack said. "Two days ago, he tells me not to come here, that this thing is between him and me. And so what does he do?"

Mike lifted his eyebrows and nodded in mild surprise. "I suppose he figures turn around's fair play."

Jack took only a moment to decide how he was going to deal with this. He was now very clear with regard to the matter of Anthony Vasconcellos.

"I don't know what he figures, Mike, but I'll tell you—he doesn't get treated any different from anybody else. And right now he's that far from getting canned." Jack held up thumb and forefinger a fraction of an inch apart.

"You've told this to him?"

"I have. He doesn't believe it. He thinks the fix is in." Jack stared meaningfully at Mike.

"He's telling me what he's doing is standard operating procedure, but you seem to want him to drop all his other commitments. He says the building isn't even enclosed yet, and he can't really go to town until it is. Is that right?"

"He has plenty to do." Jack had no intention of getting into a negotiation with Mike over the nature of Tony's service. "I'll tell you what the trouble is. Tony doesn't give a shit about the project. Tony cares about Tony. And he uses people. And he's very good at it. And don't think he won't use you because you're a priest. He will, and frankly my guess is you'll let him get away with it." Another time, Jack wouldn't have dreamed of leveling such an unmanning remark at Mike, but where Vasconcellos was concerned, all bets were off.

"Dear me," Mike said and briefly seemed stymied by Jack's outburst. Mike was never stymied for long. "He mentioned some work you've taken away from him."

"For the concessionaire."

"You have, then…taken it away…definitely?"

"He's not doing the work he's already got. No way I'm gonna give him more."

"Wouldn't it be better to, I don't know, the carrot-and-stick thing. Seems to me if you're trying to get him to work harder…"

"He's lost the work, Mike. I've told him he's lost it. That's it."

"Still… Has a decision been made who's to get it?"

"No."

"Well, then..."

Jack would be damned if he'd ever give it to Vasconcellos, but he let the matter drop.

Mike tried another tactic. "You should get to know the family better, Jack."

"No," Jack said.

"No? Just like that?"

"No. It's a bad idea for construction managers to start hob-nobbing with contractors...or their families."

"I see. Well, that's okay then."

They became quiet. The sun had gone behind the bluffs, the room quickly dimming. Mike reached over and turned on the light, another one of Janelle's reproductions, this a faux oil lamp. Then the priest picked up his drink, but didn't raise it to his lips. He tapped the side of the glass, his head turned, studying Jack. "Father Rauch tells me that you've started going to daily Mass down at the Cathedral."

This remark, out of the blue, stopped Jack cold. Shit. Father Rauch had ratted on him. Of course, Mike being plugged in, every-thing came back to him, sooner or later.

"The Cathedral Mass is at six. I need to get to work."

Mike paused to consider these words, continuing to look at Jack. "You didn't even tell me... But never mind, it's good that you should be doing this thing, wherever you're going." This show of equanimity didn't fool Jack for a second.

The priest wasn't through. "I also remember, Jack, the day last fall when you came up here and we sat in my study and I browbeat you into paying a visit to Tony, to encourage him to submit a bid...the first day, I suppose you might say, that Tony came between us. Remember?"

"What do you think?"

"You had something else on your mind that day, but we never got around to it. Not after the Tony business. You must remember that, too."

Jack said nothing.

"A question you wanted to ask, perhaps."

Jack shook his head.

"Well," Mike said, "that's okay. If you ever need to talk, I'm here."

Perhaps, Jack thought, he *would* talk to Mike one day, perhaps something would happen to make that possible. But if so, it would be to the careworn Mike that Jack bared his spiritual doubts, not this Mike so anxious to fulfill his priestly office.

And thus, when the interview ended and Jack went away, he had freely admitted his dislike and distrust of Tony Vasconcellos—who, indeed, had come between them—but he had not confessed his violent loathing for the man, the loathing to which, borrowing Mike's words from the conversation about envy, Jack had fully consented. On such a fulcrum, Father Mike could have balanced Heaven and Hell.

CHAPTER 52

~

It was after five when Chuck Fellows finished his meeting at the wastewater treatment plant, so he didn't bother to go back to city hall but headed straight on home. No meeting that night, just some letters to write. He stopped at an Okey-Dokey to pick up a six-pack, walking toward the cooler past the rack with the hot rod and muscle-builder magazines, the gallon-sized soft drinks, the shelves packed with comfort food. Hot dogs revolved inside a steamy glass cooker. In the fish-eye mirrors set overhead, figures came and went behind him.

With the beer, he stood at the end of the checkout line, the cans dangling from one finger, his attention flagging in this fallow time between life at work and life at home. At the register, a young woman cashed out purchases, her teased black hair piled on top of her head and falling in thick tangles. She bit her lower lip as she made change, pressing money into hands as if afraid to drop it. The line jostled forward and she repeated her ritual, glancing up for a fleeting moment, her pointed white face peering out from the mare's nest of hair.

The following transaction was handled more briskly, something odd and rushed and jittery about it, in the way she rang up the purchase and made change, this time laying the money on the counter rather than handing it back and turning immediately to the next person in line.

The bills and coins remained untouched, and she looked back toward the previous customer, who was speaking to her, but too low for Chuck to make out the words.

"No, you didn't," she said.

The customer said something else that Chuck couldn't make out. Leaning out from the line, he spotted Sam Turner.

"No, it wasn't. It was a ten," the girl said to Turner.

Turner said something else, and the girl didn't answer this time.

Another store employee, a man, working on the other side of the cashier's island, noticed the onset of a situation. He hesitated and then came forward. Chuck did, too.

"Sam," Chuck said, nodding. "Problem?"

After a momentary flicker of recognition, Turner showed no surprise at his boss's sudden appearance. He barely reacted at all.

The girl spoke. "He says he gave me a twenty dollar bill, but it ain't true. He gave me a ten."

"That right?" Chuck asked Turner. "You gave her a twenty."

"Yeah."

"It was a ten," the girl said.

The male employee, who wore a name tag which read, "Gary," and below that, "Shift Manager," showed no inclination to thrust himself into the middle of things. He had taken up a position behind the girl and slightly to the side, from where he could observe.

Chuck looked at the girl, then Sam, then Gary, then back at the girl.

"Didn't you put the bill on top of the cash register as you made change?" he asked her.

"I know what he gave me."

Chuck turned to the woman next in line. "See what happened?" She frowned and shook her head.

Gary the Manager adjusted his position uneasily under Chuck's gaze, but wouldn't speak. He looked to be in his early twenties, not much older than the girl.

"Why didn't you put the money where you could see it?" Chuck asked her again. Whatever Sam had given the cashier, it was up to her to make sure this sort of thing didn't happen.

"Hey, some of us got things to do," a guy waiting in the back of the line bitched.

"Hold your horses," Chuck told him, then said to the girl, "If you didn't put the bill on top of the register, who the hell knows what he gave you?"

"I know how much it was," the girl repeated, the sum total of the argument she was prepared to make on the subject. Her black crazed hair and a pair of turquoise loop earrings seemed meant to set off her pallid complexion to advantage, but it didn't work.

"Forget it," Sam said. "Ain't worth it." He was gathering up the bills and coins from the counter.

"But you gave her a twenty. You're sure about that?" Chuck believed that a certain amount of nastiness was required in situations like this.

"Hey, the man said 'forget it.'" This from the complainer at the back of the line.

Sam retrieved the last of the coins. "It's okay, man," he said to Chuck. "Forget about it."

Chuck was not of a mind to forget about it, but Sam obviously lacked the stomach for this sort of thing beyond a certain point. He was black, everybody else in the place white, so probably that had a lot to do with it. If it had been Chuck's twenty, no way he'd let it ride. No damn way. He'd give the girl and her mute boss something to remember him by.

"You sure?" he asked, one last chance.

"Yeah."

"Have it your way. Wait outside for me."

When it was Chuck's turn to pay, he gave the cashier a twenty and watched as she put the money on top of the cash register.

The shift manager, who had had a word with her after the aborted altercation, lingered a short distance away, keeping his eye on Chuck.

"When you cash out tonight," Chuck told him, "if you're ten dollars to the good, you'll know whose money it is."

The cashier glanced up briefly, biting her lip as she thrust his change toward him. She wore a shapeless blue smock over her own clothing. Perhaps she had been attractive as a teenager, but now, twenty or so, life had already begun to slip away, and in her hostile and hesitant expression, Chuck seemed to read self-knowledge, too. He took his change and left.

Outside Sam waited, shoulders hunched against the cold, wearing dark glasses, although the sun had already set, and a hunting cap with the flaps turned down. Chuck went over.

"I wouldn't abandon ten bucks without getting a piece of somebody's hide in exchange."

"Yeah," Turner said, the word not quite a question, not quite a statement.

"Yeah... Tell me, you got a few minutes?"

"Gotta be someplace."

"It won't take long."

"Okay, I guess." First he'd gotten stiffed out of a tenner, and now his boss wanted a word with him. Obviously, Sam's evening wasn't off to a good start.

"Where can we have a little privacy?" Chuck asked.

They might have walked over to a tavern just a couple of doors away, but Chuck decided against it and suggested instead a diner around the corner, which Sam told him was crowded at this time of the day. They settled on a nearby donut shop, and drove in separate cars, Chuck already having his doubts about this impulse to speak to Sam.

The deserted, too-bright franchise shop with its molded furniture bolted to the floor and pictures of donuts blown up to the size of automobile tires didn't improve matters.

They took their stale coffees to a back corner and wedged themselves into the emplaced seats. Sam turned up the flaps of the cap, then laid it next to his cup. In the manner of some blacks, he had shaved his head, but it was hard to see what sort of effect he was after. It certainly didn't make him appear more formidable.

"Gotta be down at the museum," he said, the words less a matter of information, it seemed, than a justification for getting the hell out of there as quickly as he could.

"You're involved in that, the repair of the exhibit?"

"Yeah. I helped the first time, too, when they were making it."

Chuck asked how it was coming along. Fewer people were working on it now, Sam told him, and mostly, they were just trying to patch it up as best they could. It wouldn't be nearly as nice as the original exhibit. To Chuck, this seemed a little strange. He didn't know Reiny Kopp well, but Kopp had the reputation of being pretty damn obsessive, a stickler for details, and it was hard to imagine him simply packing it in. Kopp had been protesting the Vietnam War at the same time Chuck was fighting in it, but Chuck didn't necessarily hold that against him.

The subject of the museum quickly exhausted, they fell into an awkward silence until Chuck asked, "You go in there often?"

"The Okey-Dokey? It's on my way home."

"Get shortchanged before?"

He shrugged. "Few times, other places, not there."

"You can forget about the ten bucks." Chuck related what he'd said to the manager after Sam left, but even if the guy found that Sam had been right, he'd no doubt pocket the money himself.

"Most likely," Sam agreed.

"Unless the girl beats him to it."

"Maybe. I dunno." Sam looked down and dropped his voice. "Sometimes people surprise you."

Chuck looked at Sam with interest. "Been known to happen."

"She's worked there maybe six months, something like that. Longer than most. It's a pretty crummy job."

Sam apparently gave people the benefit of the doubt. Chuck was not so charitable. "In six months, she should've learned to keep the money in sight until she made change. On day one, she should've learned that much."

"Expect she knows it now." In Sam's smile, a touch of sadness seemed to linger, sympathy for another fallen creature.

Chuck crossed his arms. This inclination to kindness raised Sam slightly in his estimate, but kindness at the moment was beside the point. The reason for this spur-of-the-moment get-together had nothing to do with the incident at the store, and it was pointless to belabor the matter. On the other hand, now that Chuck had Sam in front of him, he regretted the impulse to sit down at all. Any number of times he'd thought he might talk to Sam, and any number of times he'd put it off. Sam didn't impress. What could Chuck possibly say to him that would make any difference?

But it was too late now. They were there.

"Tell me, Sam, how you doing up in the drafting room?"

Turner pulled back slightly, his eyes darting down and to the side. He sat perfectly still for a few moments and then said, "All right, I guess."

"What's Glenn got you doing?"

"Just finished a couple drawings for Seth."

"The emergency levee and floodwall?"

"Yeah."

In his mind's eye, Chuck visualized the drawings, which he'd seen only a few hours earlier, not realizing they were Sam's work. Except for the excessive detail, they had seemed unremarkable. A good sign, perhaps, except that Chuck remembered Glenn telling him that the problem with Sam wasn't the quality of the work.

"Have you picked up your speed?"

Sam shrugged.

"You need to do that," Chuck told him. "What about more complex drawings? What are you doing to prepare yourself to handle them?"

"Got a drawing board and some stuff at home."

"So you're practicing on your own?"

Sam sent a glancing look in Chuck's direction, then leaned forward, elbows on the table and staring down. "Probably should be doing it some more."

Which meant he wasn't doing it at all. "Yeah," Chuck said, "probably you should be doing it some more."

Chuck might have asked how he was getting along with the other guys, but that was an invitation to rationalize his spotty performance.

Nothing much had been said, nothing much remained to be said.

"If you're serious about a drafting career, Sam, you need to get a lot better."

Sam nodded mutely, then for the first time since the exchange began, looked squarely at Chuck. "Might be, if I could get some time on the computer..."

"We've only got the one unit."

"That was what I worked on mostly in school. People got CAD nowadays."

"There's no money in the budget for more systems, not this year, not next, either. Like it or not, you'll have to master the traditional methods. Maybe a few years from now..."

Balked in this direction, Sam said, a little more glumly, "Or I could go back to hauling trash. Didn't mind that."

Chuck inhaled, annoyed. If Sam thought he could undo all that had been done... "You bid the job. Why, if you weren't prepared to do the work?"

"I try, man," Sam told his coffee cup.

"Don't try. Do it."

Sam was hunkering over the table and fingering the handle of the cup. He might have continued to speak. Chuck had the impression of a great press of words welling up just beneath the surface. But nothing came out. He pressed his elbows into the Formica and hunched so far forward that he seemed on the point of rising off his chair. The unnaturally bright lights in the place reflected in patches from his skinny, bald dome.

"Just because you don't like a job," Chuck told him, "is no reason not to bust your ass trying to do it."

Sam nodded vaguely and continued to play with the cup. "It's an okay job. Liked haulin' trash better."

"We're probably going to two-man crews."

Sam didn't react.

Chuck told him, "You couldn't have loved collecting garbage all that much. You bid off the job."

"It is sort of shitty, I guess," Sam agreed. He settled back into his chair. "But, you know, you gotta pick up the garbage. People gotta have their garbage picked up."

"And nobody has to do drafting work, is that it?"

"Gotta do that, too. I dunno, it's not the same." Sam seemed to be relaxing a little, in a tense sort of way.

"True, it's not the same," Chuck told him. "It's harder, for one thing."

If Chuck imagined Sam would become defensive at the derision implied by this comment, he was mistaken. Sam immediately agreed. "That's right, you hafta have a calling or something. It ain't just a job."

"Like hell. It's the time. You gotta put in the time. That's all."

Sam was shaking his head. "It's not just a job, man."

"But you bid on it. Why, if you weren't prepared to perform?" Chuck paused for emphasis. "If you weren't prepared to do whatever the fuck it took?"

Sam grabbed his hat and started slapping it against the table. "Yeah, you got that right. I bid on it."

"So now you've got it. It's your responsibility."

Sam nodded several times. "Yeah."

"That's life, Sam. You make your bed, you sleep in it."

Chuck could not say this without becoming aware of his own situation, his own unhappiness, the bed he had to sleep in. There was a conversation he and Sam might have here, no doubt, but it wasn't one that would do either one of them a bit of good.

Sam continued to slap his cap against the tabletop. Whatever else was said, the exchange had ended.

CHAPTER 53

~

Jack Kelley didn't drive the short way onto the job site, through the nonunion gate, but instead around by the southern shore of Apple Island. He had decided to check out Chuck Fellows's dredging operation.

In the distance, as he dipped down off the elevated highway, he spotted some sort of activity out by the river, or on it, a glimpse gone as he gained the flat of the island and made his circuit between the hedges of old snow. On the road, occasional patches of bare asphalt had been worn through the hardpacked gray and white leavings of the many storms.

The turnout where the dredge crew parked was jammed with vehicles, leaving no room to pull off, so Jack stopped in the middle of the road and got out for a better view.

He'd given up on the hope they'd have enough sand to finish the parking lots by opening day. Probably they'd have to bus people. Probably they'd have to bus people all summer. City was nuts thinking they could do the job with their little dredge. Fellows was nuts thinking he could do it in winter, too.

Beyond the dredge, in its rectangle of open water, a cluster of workmen stood on the river ice, along with a pickup truck and farm tractor. The truck was plowing the snow off the ice, forming a long windrow to the south, while the workmen gathered around a makeshift assortment of equipment: chain saws, crosscuts, various kinds of what looked like grappling tools. Jack peered toward the operation, parsing it. Fellows must have gotten his permit from the Corps. The largest apparatus, a circular saw resembling something salvaged from a lumber mill, had been rigged to run off the power takeoff of the tractor, probably to score the ice before the other tools were used to cut it free and hoist it out of the river. Quite a scene, Jack decided—the dredge, the plow, the tractor and saw, the

men dark and bundled up against the wintry white surroundings.
Fellows was a pit bull, Jack had to give him that much credit. A
man who had the defects of his virtues.

Mostly, however, Jack felt only relief. Thank God this particular headache wasn't his.

Hearing someone approaching along the road, he got back
into his car and drove through the union gate and onto the job site,
where the headaches *were* his.

~

People jammed the construction trailer, the place so smoky
that one of the nonsmokers joked about bringing a class-action
suit. Not enough seats for everyone. Some of the old-timers had
brought their own. As projects wore on, the number of trades pro-
liferated and construction trailers began to resemble subways at
rush hour.

Everyone at the moment was busy ignoring one of the new-
comers: Dexter Walcott, the black contractor from Waterloo, a
man guaranteed to wreak havoc on the site. Walcott stood in front
of the plan rack and drafting board, beside Chuck Fellows.

Tony Vasconcellos had made himself comfortable at his usual
station near the door, next to his foreman son Lonny. The elder
Vasconcellos bestowed on the world his usual what-me-worry
smile, the expression out of joint with his dark, meaty complexion
and the knot of tortured black hair hanging over his forehead. He
seemed mighty pleased with himself for some reason. Perhaps he
was still enjoying his gambit of having gone to Father Mike. Maybe
he imagined that the ploy had something to do with Jack leaving
him alone the last few days. It hadn't. Jack had simply given up. He
was turning his back. He'd keep a file, he'd make memos. The next
time he went after Vasconcellos, it'd be for keeps.

"The only submittals we don't have in to you are the specialty
items," Walcott said when the conversation about the status of shop
drawing came around to him. This piece of business should have been
matter-of-fact enough, but Jack could feel the charged undertow.
"Finish doors and hardware have been submitted but not returned."
While the black man had been standing silently and waiting, he
appeared insufficient, tall but too thin, thin even wearing a winter
coat, his straightened hair so different from Tony Vasconcellos's, as

orderly as a wig, the skinny mustache perched at the edge of his upper lip, his eyes cloudy. But his face came alive when he talked, like a machine with many moving parts, suggesting the elaborateness of speech. "The interior studs should begin to get here middle of next week. Need to know where I can store 'em."

Jack shifted his attention from the man to what he was saying. Storage? Leaving stuff just lying around. No, no, wouldn't do. Have to find someplace off-site. Otherwise they'd be creating an attractive nuisance, just asking for trouble.

In an instant, Jack was oppressed by the difficulties off-site storage presented. Walcott would want credit so the place would have to be bonded. That, plus who'd pay? Walcott? The city?

"Let's talk about it afterwards," he told Walcott, and the contractor nodded, and the meeting moved on.

Walcott wasn't the only newcomer. Two men who would operate the facility once the city had turned it over to the racing association had shown up to introduce themselves—the track's general manager and racing secretary, the latter overseer of all matters relating to the greyhounds.

Jack did the honors, and then they each said a few words.

The meeting wore on, the usual bump and grind—deletion and in-fill of two overhead doors in the grandstand; no color picked yet for the countertops in the kennels; trusses and beams now up in the paddock building; standing seam roof three to four weeks behind...

From time to time, Lonny Vasconcellos stared about himself, trying, it seemed, to catch people's attention. He resembled his father in general structure, being large and already showing signs of running to fat, but he possessed his mother's fair complexion and almost could have been called pretty, something nobody would ever say about Tony. Lonny also lacked his father's deviousness, replacing it with a bold assertive quality, as if he'd been converted to adulthood rather than growing into it. He specialized in the declarative sentence and spoke with the fervor of a true believer. At the moment, however, he contented himself with this craning around at the others, trying to share a knowing look. He wasn't having much luck.

When they got to the subject of work scheduled for the next two weeks, Walcott said he planned to begin a week from Monday. "Best start with the paddock building. Stud work and insulate the outside walls. Hold off on the grandstand until the steel's a little further along, if you don't mind. I got a lot of boys I can put to work soon as it looks right."

Jack noticed that this information, which another time would have been welcome, only filled him with more foreboding. One week left to enjoy the normal tensions of a job site. After that…

As Walcott spoke, Lonny stopped staring around and sullenly contemplated the linoleum at his feet.

~

Finally, when the meeting broke up and people left or formed small clusters to transact a bit of private business, Lonny sprang into action, first cornering the general manager of the track about something or other. Jack moved closer and listened, the subject turning out to be the hiring of people to run the place once it was finished. Naturally, Lonny had some suggestions: unemployed construction workers who happened to be friends of his and who he thought deserved first crack at the jobs.

The GM answered patiently. Jack considered intervening, but remembered his resolve where the Vasconcelloses were concerned. Besides, he had something to talk to Chuck Fellows about, and Fellows was already out the door.

A dozen paces from the trailer, Chuck had stopped to listen to the racing secretary, jawing at the contractor doing the site work. Jack joined them. The track official, down on his haunches, was weighing a fistful of sand, grains and fragments of mussel shells sloughing off the sides of his hand as he explained why such material wouldn't do for the track surface. Too coarse. The dogs would cut their feet on the shells. Also, too loose. They'd be sliding all over the place.

Jack had given the track consultant's specs for the racing surface only brief consideration, and he listened with interest to these unsuspected complications. He found such problems almost soothing after Lonny Vasconcellos.

"On the other hand," the racing secretary was saying, looking up at the group accreting around him, "it can't be too hard, either. Too hard, it gets rutted and an animal can break a hock." He gave off the impression of a man utterly dedicated to the dogs, in fact, a bit like a dog himself, although not one of the long-snouted sort, like greyhounds, rather a pug or boxer, with a dished face and the suggestion of something inbred and unstable.

The discussion continued, but was ruined for Jack when Tony Vasconcellos joined the group and at once began retailing all his newly acquired dog expertise.

Jack took the opportunity to draw Chuck aside for a private word, well away from the others.

"Walcott's request for a place to store his interior studs."

"What about it?" Fellows asked.

"If we leave the stuff lying around, who knows what'll happen."

"Have to wait and see." Fellows spoke bluntly, his sentences without any hooks that Jack might hang his own ideas on.

"Walcott could store off-site," Jack suggested.

"Could. Where you think you're gonna get the money, general conditions?"

"Walcott maybe. Or share the costs."

Fellows folded his arms. Jack had learned that when he did that, he was prepared to be particularly obnoxious.

"Walcott's got an interest here, too," Jack argued. "We all do."

Out of the corner of his eye, Jack watched Tony Vasconcellos and his son approaching. Or rather Lonny approached, his father lagging behind, appearing to abandon the conversation with the track secretary only reluctantly, figuring perhaps that he'd better keep an eye on Lonny, who was making a beeline for Chuck Fellows.

Fellows ignored them. "I've talked to the consultants about the situation," he was telling Jack. "We'll use private cops if we have to. Not right away. First, we give these yahoos a chance to behave themselves. Until something happens…"

"Until what happens?" Lonny Vasconcellos asked, smiling as he came up.

With a composure that suggested he had been well aware of the approach of the Vasconcelloses, Fellows turned to Lonny. "Until you or one of your friends starts to give Dexter Walcott a hard time, that's what. Then we're gonna bring private security onto the job site and charge it against your contract."

"Whoa," young Vasconcellos said, holding up his hands and leaning back, but still smiling. "I just came over to talk."

"Okay. Talk."

Lonny, not quite prepared for the abruptness, took a moment to reset himself. "My dad and I were just wondering who gets the jobs when the track's built?" Jack noticed that he spoke in a some-what conciliatory tone, even including his father by reference, although it was clearly Lonny who had a burr up his ass.

"Who gets the jobs is none of your business," Chuck told him.

Good grief, Jack thought. Fellows was in an even nastier mood than usual, which was saying something.

"Really?" Lonny shot back at him, his smile hardening. "I guess I'm a citizen like everybody else. And this is a city project, ain't it? And you represent the city."

Chuck observed young Vasconcellos narrowly. "All we're doing is building. You got a concern about staffing the facility, talk to the racing association."

"It's still a city project," Lonny persisted. "I mean, shit, city people oughta get the jobs."

"Tell them to apply," Chuck said.

"Yeah, apply, right. A lotta good that'll do." Lonny, seeing nothing was to be gained by diplomacy, had fallen back into his normal whining manner. He plunged on, giving free rein to his sense of violation. "I don't believe it. I mean, shit, this ain't right. A lot of my friends are outta work. They got wives, they got families. Tough shit, right? Probably what's gonna happen is they'll truck a bunch of blacks in to run the track, that's what I think. We gotta give the blacks everything." And then, maybe figuring this was a little strong, he added, "I mean, shit, I got nothin' against them. But damn, we're not trying to go where they live and fuck things up for them."

No one spoke, so young Vasconcellos continued to run his mouth. Chuck had continued to inspect the kid with some mix of speculation and hostility.

"My dad and I was out to Manchester the other day. Talked to a guy, and he said, 'You got a good thing going in Jackson. Don't know why you'd want a bunch of niggers moving there.' Guy was right, you ask me, we got a good thing going. Now it's all gonna get taken away."

"That's enough, Lonny," his father said, but Lonny wasn't through. He stabbed a finger at Fellows.

"Something's gonna happen, you better fuckin' believe it. And you can't take it outta our contract. It's not us. It's everybody. Nobody fuckin' wants Walcott here."

"That's enough, Lonny," Tony repeated.

"No," Chuck Fellows countered, "let him talk. In fact, why don't we get Walcott over here so we all can hear?"

"Let's not," Jack said.

Some distance away, Walcott, who had been looking around the site, was just arriving back at his truck. *How convenient*, Jack thought.

"I got nothin' to say to him," young Vasconcellos told Chuck, but Chuck ignored him and hailed Walcott over.

"This isn't gonna help," Jack said to Chuck, to no effect. Jack's protest had been halfhearted anyway. He felt removed from the scene, disconnected from these compulsive and self-indulgent people, this stampede toward confrontation.

Tony Vasconcellos stood mutely a couple of steps away, his placid smile back in place after the failed attempt to call his son off.

"I got nothin' to say to him," Lonny Vasconcellos repeated. The black contractor approached deliberately. Just as his words had suggested the elaborateness of speech, his articulated manner of walking suggested the intricacy of the human body. He nodded as he got near. "How ya doin'?"

"The kid here's got something to tell you, Dexter."

"Yup," Walcott said, as if he knew as much. He turned his attention toward Lonny, but Lonny obviously wasn't about to say anything.

"Okay," Chuck said, "I'll do it." And he repeated everything said earlier, word for word, beginning at the beginning.

Walcott listened without expression.

"That really the way you feel, son?" he asked the kid.

"Don't call me 'son.'" Lonny started to leave.

"Why don't you stay?" Chuck suggested.

Lonny countered with, "Why don't you fuck off? I don't work for you. I work for my father."

Chuck wagged his head this way and that, grinning. Then he stepped up to Lonny, inches away. "What was that, asshole?"

Lonny, startled, tried to back up, but caught his heel and went down on his butt.

Fellows immediately glanced toward Tony, but Tony was going nowhere, so Chuck turned his attention back to Lonny and with a little come-hither gesture said to the prostrate form, "C'mon, kid, let's see what you got."

For a moment, it looked like Lonny might take Chuck up on the offer. He was about Chuck's size, even a little bigger, and twenty or more years younger, but something in Chuck's manner suggested a fight with him would be a thoroughly unpleasant affair. Anyway, for whatever reason, Lonny decided to stay put.

"Dexter," Chuck said, still glowering down at Lonny, "you or your boys gonna start anything?"

Walcott stood composed but unhappy. "All my boys are good boys, not lookin' for trouble, no, sir. Come here to do a job. I trained 'em real good. They're professionals, every one of them."

"All I need to know." Fellows turned toward Tony Vasconcellos. "I expect you to control your men. If there's trouble, we'll deal with it and dock your contract. You got that?"

Fellows glanced at Jack. "Okay?"

Jack, dispirited, made the necessary effort to pull himself together, and thinking that Walcott hardly needed this kind of demonstration to tell him what he was up against, said, "It doesn't help, Chuck, it makes matters worse."

"Don't give a shit, Jack."

Fellows and Walcott walked away, Fellows talking as they went. Lonny was back on his feet. "That fucker's insane."

It only makes matters worse, Jack repeated, this time to himself. Matters were out of his hands. He'd play the cards Fellows had dealt him—what choice did he have?—but words seemed such a flimsy bulwark against the mounting of desire all around him.

"He might be insane," he told Lonny, "but Chuck Fellows signs the checks." He turned to Tony. "See, Tony, it's not just me. It's Fellows, too. You want trouble? He'll give you all you can handle." Vasconcellos wasn't smiling anymore.

"Fucker's bluffing," Lonny said, still looking after Fellows, now in the distance, standing next to Walcott's truck.

"I don't think you want to find out," Jack told him before turning back to his father. "Well, Tony, what's it to be? Your choice."

Tony just shook his head. "A bad business."

"I say he's bluffing," Lonny repeated. "And I'll tell you what, Jack, something happens down here and we defend ourselves, we'll be heroes."

"Heroes? Is that what you think?"

The father just shook his head and said again that it was a bad business. Jack wondered what influence, if any, Tony had on his son.

When Mike Daugherty talked about troubles in the Vasconcellos household, Lonny must have been part of what he had in mind.

He turned to Lonny. "You go to Mass?"

Surprised again, as surprised as he had been when Fellows challenged him, Lonny said, "None of your business." Jack also remembered Father Mike's desire that he should get to know the Vasconcellos family better. Who would want to know such people?

Jack stared at Lonny and said, "I hope not."

To Tony he merely repeated, "Your choice." The father was buttoning up his fancy black leather jacket, in preparation to depart.

Jack turned his back and walked away. He saw that several workmen had come to the lip of the grandstand deck and that overhead, the ironworkers hanging steel had stopped to watch, too. Someone had probably spotted Lonny's fall. They continued to look, even though there was nothing more to see.

CHAPTER 54

~

From the low ridge, probes of morning sun struck through the leafless canopy and mottled the pickup truck. The truck stood alone, surrounded only by the treads of other, now absent vehicles. Perhaps an expert tracker would have been able to trace the recent trail on top of the older tire marks and footprints fossilized in the white ice, these newer steps leading away from the truck and across a broad wooden bridge and, on the far side, over an embankment and down to the creek below, where anyone might now have picked the trail up and followed the boot prints in the deep and undisturbed snow.

Next to the stream, the hiker had stopped long enough to put on snowshoes and then continued on, first in the dim light beside the creek, the creek itself cloaked in ice and snow, except where the cover had been abraded away by the black water beneath.

Several hundred yards from the bridge, a steep hillside, thick with saplings, descended to the creek edge, blocking the way, and the snowshoe tracks turned into a shallow valley, through a gap toward the uplands and finally into the sunlight. Trails left by deer and other animals came and went, avoiding the deeper drifts. At one spot, the snow had been disturbed and a mound formed, a cache perhaps left by some fox or coyote or bobcat. The human steps went on, the snowshoes making faults in the old, crusty snow, following the contours of the land and probably, hidden beneath the deep cover, the trails broken and worn into the landscape by summer hikers. Now only a single line of steps marked this solitary winter passage.

Eventually the hiker, perhaps bored, perhaps with some goal in mind, abandoned the natural path and turned up into the woods, where the temperature remained more constant and the snow not so deep, but softer, the snowshoes sinking in and kicking wakes behind them. The land rose sharply, and the tracks became ragged and irregular, seeking the best way, avoiding stands of blackberry canes and fallen timber and rock outcrops. Finally, after several false crests had been climbed beyond, the air brightened once more, and the slope gentled.

On top, the woods opened into a small goat prairie, besieged by red cedars and staghorn sumacs. The snowshoes had packed down a space next to one of the sumacs, as if the hiker paused to observe the tracks made by birds and mammals beneath the small tree and the missing bark and twigs and seeds stripped away by the animals, nature's efficiency.

The hiker had paused again, this time at the center of the prairie remnant, the snow deep once more, the prairie grasses buried except for the turkey-footed spikes of the big bluestem, man-high in summer, but now barely sprouting above the snow. From here, the sweep of the western sky could be seen, the blue overhead and the approaching storm front with its long shoreline, as if the good weather had been a sea that the clouds had finally crossed.

Possibly the vision of the approaching storm had reminded the hiker of the passage of time, for now the tracks moved restlessly on, without pause, down from the hilltop and then almost at random, through a dense wood, past an ancient refuse pit, over a plowed dirt road, and into a wooded area as open as if it had been swept by a brushfire, past a stone foundation and briefly along an old farm or logging road. Where railroad tracks cut obliquely across the road, the hiker turned down along the tracks for no obvious reason. But not for long. In a short distance, the footprints cut away from the tracks, into the heart of a low, swampy tract where light faded and snow sagged in gray swales and no signs of human activity were to be found, no foundations or refuse pits or roads.

The snowshoes broke through the rotten ice as they crossed the stream that fed the swamp, leaving behind small, shallow pools of standing water.

At places, where the snow remained soft, the slurring of the trail suggested that the hiker had become leg weary but continued doggedly on, struggling over a rocky knoll, breaking through a stand of saplings that might easily have been skirted, until at last a slough of the Mississippi appeared and then railroad tracks again, a main line, and an abandoned quarry.

The quarry road looped around and struck out north. Scuff marks showed where the snowshoes had been removed. Boot prints continued on, still easy to follow at first, but mingling with more and more human tracks and becoming indistinct. And finally leading back to the parking area from which they'd begun, where Chuck Fellows tossed his snowshoes into the back of his pickup, got in, and drove away.

PART IV

CHAPTER 55

～

Only a few cars were out, their headlights burrowing into the storm. Snow dunes blocked the side streets. Harold Anglin pulled over to the stop at Church and Highway 40, although nobody was waiting to get on or off. He didn't want to get ahead of schedule.

He got up and stretched. Kirk and Janey, two of the regulars, had been arguing as usual, the only other rider a big fellow who'd gotten on at Locus and Fourth. Harold knew him from somewheres, but couldn't quite remember. Not from riding the buses, Harold didn't think. A real big man. He sat a few rows back, reading the flier Kirk had foisted on him.

Strings of meltwater leaked down the plastic runners laid along the walkway. Harold looked at his watch, then swabbed the inside of the windshield with a towel.

"Hope you're not in a big hurry," he said to the others. "Headway being what it is at this time of the day, I don't want to leave some poor soul stranded out here." He tried out a joke. "Somebody dies of exposure, it don't reflect well on the system."

"Going to visit to one of my LOLs," Janey said. "Expect she can wait." Kirk didn't say anything, but Harold figured he was probably going out to the mall to do some leafleting.

The big fellow came forward to hand the flier back.

"Keep it," Kirk said.

"That's all right, give it to somebody else."

"Wha'd'ya think?" Kirk asked.

"I don't know. Don't ride that often myself."

The fellow went back to his seat, by the look of him not particularly anxious to get dragged into the argument Janey and Kirk had been having.

345

"I'll tell you one thing," Harold said. "Except they figure a way to increase ridership, the service is gonna get cut again. Maybe not this year, maybe not next, but sometime."

"They don't want more riders," Kirk declared. "They did, it'd be easy enough. Just hike up the parking rates downtown."

As Harold checked his mirrors and pulled back into the travel lane, he said, raising his voice so he could be heard above the surge of the diesel engine, "The way I figure it, they ain't anti-bus, just pro-car."

"Amounts to the same thing."

"Pretty much," Harold had to concede.

"Or they could cut fares," Kirk continued. He wasn't the type to leave a matter alone just because he'd already made his point. "Planner down there at ECIA showed how a ten-cent cut would increase revenues by $74,000. They buried that quick enough."

Harold didn't know how Kirk found out what was going on inside the intergovernmental agency.

Janey said, probably trying to end the argument, "I just get tired of begging. If they're gonna cut it, they're gonna cut it."

"Ain't begging," Kirk declared. "People got rights."

"All my life, it seems," Janey went on with her thought, "I never got nothing except I begged for it."

Harold tacked onto Highway 40, a four-lane, and started the long climb toward the top of the bluff. Traffic unusually heavy for midmorning, cars and semis and everything in between, people driving too fast.

"The mayor says she's not gonna stand for cuts," Janey said. "It's up to her."

"What the mayor says and what's gonna happen ain't necessarily the same thing. She's only got one vote, even if she ain't blowing smoke." Kirk had a mouth on him. Stubborn, too. His stubbornness was what made him a good activist, that and the fact he had plenty of time on his hands.

"What about Roger Filer?" Harold asked, a little jittery now, dividing his attention between the too-fast traffic and the conversation. "How you think he's gonna vote?"

"You gotta be kidding. He sells cars."

"Maybe." Harold hoped that, being a candidate for mayor and all, Filer might leave transit be and vote to cut something else, something without a constituency.

"I'll tell you what Filer'll do," Kirk said. "He'll wait to make sure there are enough votes to eliminate weekend service, then he'll vote against cutting it. Have his cake and eat it, too."

At Highway 40 and Langworthy, they picked up three kids, off school for the day and probably, like Kirk, heading out to the mall to hang. They went way to the back.

"This time ain't any different from all the others," Kirk said. "Without we fight, they're gonna stick it to us."

Kirk was right, no doubt about it, but Harold sympathized with Janey. People shouldn't have to parade their neediness in front of the city council year in and year out. They weren't crippled beggars in India or something.

"What you gonna do, Janey," he asked, "they get rid of weekend service?"

"Haven't the faintest idea. I can't, like, mothball my little old ladies two days a week."

On the brief sharp rise just below the crest where the highway crossed Grandview, Harold had to slow for a car creeping along. Other vehicles moved steadily by in the passing lane. At the top, the light changed to yellow. The car in front of him timidly slowed, although it could easily have made it through, and that forced Harold to stop, too, the bus tilted back at a steep angle. Damn.

"Everybody got to come together on the thing." Kirk never gave up, but Harold could tell from his voice, he was getting tired of arguing, for the moment at least. "Everybody oughta be up at the city council screaming bloody murder, Janey. You, too."

The light changed, and the car in front of him crept ahead. Harold pressed the accelerator gingerly, listening to the rising pulse of the diesel, waiting for the bus to begin to move. He eased up and over the top, the tire chains beginning to sing as they crossed Grandview. This was the corner where Harold sometimes saw the mayor out walking with Aggie Klauer. Not at this time of the day, though.

Nobody waited in the shelter at the stop, a major transfer point. Harold pulled over anyway and checked his watch. He'd be glad when he was off the highway and back on city streets.

"You got that right, mister, you want a thing bad enough, you gotta fight for it," the large man suddenly said, agreeing with Kirk. Harold glanced in the rearview. The fellow was coming forward again, taking a seat near the activist. Must have changed his mind about putting in his two cents worth. "Used to be, I worked at the Pack. We had our chance. Could've bought the company. You know about that. Company would've been ours. But like you said, everybody got to be behind a thing."

JackPack, Harold thought. Yes, that was it, that was where he remembered him from.

Harold looked in his mirrors and pulled back into the traffic. "Say," he called back over his shoulder, "didn't the paper do a big story on you, couple months back?"

"That's right."

"Ha! Knew it! Tell me, what's your name?"

"Billy Noel."

"Billy Noel. Right. I remember. It was just before the big vote you had. I read the story. A real good one, too. I remember thinking at the time, 'Man, that's tough work, glad it isn't me'—on the kill floor there, where you was."

Noel moved even farther forward, sitting on the bench seat right behind Harold.

"You're right. It's not a job for everybody. I did it for twenty-seven years. Other stuff, too, I moved around some, but mostly it was on the kill floor."

"What I heard," Kirk said, "is no way the company was gonna survive anyhow."

"You're wrong there, mister," Billy Noel replied, taking exception. "We could've made a go of it. Been thinking about it a lot since I got laid off. Would've been tough, don't deny it, but that don't make it impossible. The trick is, like you say, everybody's got to get behind the thing. People start second-guessing…"

"Yeah," Kirk agreed, "but what I heard was the company planned to close all along. Just looking for an excuse to blame it on the employees."

Harold waited for the response. Billy Noel said, "All I know is, seven weeks now I been laid off… I'm used to working. All my life, I worked."

Harold thought about that, about whether he'd have a job himself when they cut transit back. His situation wasn't so different from Billy Noel's there, although no way the transit employees could ever even think about buying and running the system themselves.

Outside Henry Wallace Elementary School, two more kids, with large homemade disks, boarded, and jostled each other the way kids will as they plopped down near the door. They've got to be crazy, Harold thought, going sliding in the middle of a blizzard.

After he double-checked his mirrors, and while he swept the large, horizontal steering wheel around and the bus hove into the wind and snow once more, he said, speaking to the adults clustered at the front, "I'll tell you what I'd do if I was El Plowman. I'd cut everything the same. You talk about everybody being in on a thing there, Billy. That's what I'd do. Equal cuts. Everybody the same."

The others remained quiet.

He'd caught up to another car going slowly, barely moving.

"There's an idea to die for," Kirk said.

"Then nobody'd have to beg," Harold defended himself. "That's what you want, isn't it, Janey? Sharing the pain, like. Everybody hurtin' a little, but nobody, you know, gettin' absolutely hammered. All of us together on the thing, like Kirk and Billy there think it oughta be."

The others seemed to have nothing to say to this idea, which had just come to Harold out of the blue, and he started to think he maybe should have kept his mouth shut.

The car moping along irritated him, and he glanced impatiently into his mirrors. He had crept to within a few feet and looked almost straight down on its roof. Barely moving. He looked in his mirrors, the snow swirling thickly, hard to see, but no headlights bearing down on him, and so he pulled out to pass.

A deep muffled sound rushed from behind and clamped around his head. The bus jerked, his arms wrenched in their sockets. Another sound, low and hollow, rolled forward, then a third. The bus vibrated, shock and aftershock.

When he had managed to stop, Janey was the first to react, heading toward the back. A couple of the kids had been thrown to the floor but were already scrambling to their feet, apparently okay. "Open the door, Harold," Janey yelled up to him, "I gotta see if anybody's hurt." She paused for a moment on the top step and looked back. The two men quickly followed her.

A sensation, like the shocks that had passed through the bus, now cascaded down Harold's body. He felt very strange and fumbled with the radio receiver, shaking, as he called for help.

CHAPTER 56

～

J.J. Dusterhoft followed the usual routine, pulling the REO around behind the long gable-shaped storage shed and up to the salt pile. As the end loader dumped scoops into the box, he revved the auger and then, while he waited, picked up a pleasant reverie where he'd left off a bit earlier. Reveries with Aggie Klauer in them were always pleasant.

He looked at his watch. Just about time, in fact, for Deuce and her to start going at each other again.

"Are you going to be there this time?" she'd wanted to know when she'd phoned him the night before.

"Probably not. Another big storm."

In point of fact, J.J. wasn't in a position to tell her the truth, that storm or no storm, he wouldn't have been there, although he wouldn't have minded being a fly on the wall, just to check out the expression on Aggie's face when she walked into the room and saw what Deuce had cooked up this time.

"I was just hoping against hope," she said, "I can talk to you."

"We've had some good times, haven't we?"

"Yes, we have," she said brightly. "And we negotiated good contracts, too."

"Under the circumstances."

"There are always circumstances."

"How true."

"Deuce Goetzinger wants to walk away from the table with his pockets full. But we—you and I—we walked away from the table friends, too. People don't appreciate how important that is." Aggie had the gift of friendship. No doubt, she had a gift for love, too, J.J. thought wistfully.

"We were never appreciated," he said.

"Amen." She spoke in mock seriousness, then laughed, the laugh trailing off into, "Paul will impose a settlement, you know. Goetzinger's leading your people into the sea."

"Perhaps, dear. But alas, what can I say, I'm not the head lemming anymore."

Aggie laughed again. "I wish you were."

The truck shuddered and settled more firmly over the drive wheels just as the radio squawked to life, and the pleasing, mellifluous tones of Aggie's remembered words disappeared, replaced by a decidedly less pleasant voice: the street commissioner's.

"J.J., before you do anything else, punch out Alpine, will you?" Peppered with static, Hank Kraft's words became strained and anxious. *Shit*, thought J.J., *Alpine?* He had to be kidding.

"You're breaking up, Hank," he said into the radio. "I can't hear you."

"There's been a big pileup out on 40," Kraft continued, ignoring this standard ploy of J.J.'s. "St. Rafael's is calling in their emergency room people, and one of 'em lives on Alpine. A nurse."

"Where are the cops?" They were the ones supposed to give people a lift in situations like this.

"Out at the accident. The chief called me."

"How serious?"

"Don't know. A bus. A big rig. Several cars. It's a mess."

Probably the cops didn't want to drive down Alpine any more than J.J. did. Nobody in his right mind would. Call Kraft, the chief must've thought, get him to do the dirty work. Kraft was infamous for being a patsy…unless you happened to work for him.

"Where's Ralphie?" Ralphie drove a little pickup they used to plow in tight quarters like Alpine.

"In the shop."

Conscious that they were talking on the radio and anybody might be listening in, J.J. had to watch what he said. But shit, Alpine?

"What say I just give the nurse a ride to work myself?"

"I got no address." Kraft sounded real uptight. Might just be the radio, another piece of geriatric city equipment. "C'mon, J.J., for you it's cake."

That's right, J.J. thought, *appeal to my vanity*. The man had no shame.

Nothing to be done. "Yeah, sure, okay, Hank, anything for our friends in blue."

J.J. looked toward the river. When he could see the other side, a storm wasn't any big deal. At the moment, he couldn't even make out the floodwall on this side.

He put the truck in gear and headed over to the scales to weigh in.

Then, plowing the arteries as he went, he skirted around to the top of Alpine. In weather like this, when the snow was heavy, he liked to plow downhill whenever he could.

Of course, he thought, if he had any sense, he'd leave the truck right where it was and knock on doors until he found the nurse and then haul her over to the hospital himself and forget all this plowing-Alpine shit. Any sensible person would.

From where he sat, he could see only the very brow of the street, framed on either side by houses blurred by the storm. Nordic ski jumpers hurtling into empty space had better views.

He mumbled to himself, "You'd think emergency room people would have enough sense to live on the flat somewheres."

Shit.

"Do it." He shifted into low gear and hit the accelerator. The truck tipped forward and the street swung into view below him, a narrow file between two rows of cars, the cars nothing but white mounds.

He talked himself down, riding the crown, trying to keep some speed on her without losing control, glad it was the REO and not one of the bigger trucks. "Okay, baby, that's it. Not too fast, not too fast." His eyes moved rapidly back and forth between the two pieces of rebar sticking up as guides on either end of the blade.

Halfway down, some joker had parked his car angled way out from the curb, sticking into the single traffic lane. People who didn't know how to park ticked him off. He'd caught a little luck this time, though. Nobody was parked along the curb opposite, and so he moved to sidle around, steering down off the crown. It was tight. "Easy, easy." The rear bumper of the car neared, disappearing behind the right-hand edge of the blade, then slid by. He shifted his gaze, toward the car parked immediately down the hill on his side of the street, and began to steer back up onto the crown.

The truck didn't respond. He touched the accelerator. Nothing. He was being sucked slowly along the gutter. He pumped the brake, trying to ease to a stop. The truck slowed, holding its position, nose pointed slightly toward the center of the street. Just as it stopped, he heard a sound, so soft that a moment later he wondered if he might have imagined it.

He leaped from the cab, doing a brief jig before landing on his can. Beneath the snow lay a sheet of ice. Swearing, he scrambled up and around to the blade of the plow, where he wiped away enough of the snow to see the crumpled fender and shattered taillight of the car he'd hit.

"Goddamnit!"

He'd barely been moving, but with a load of salt the truck was a heavy sucker and generated all sorts of momentum. It didn't take but a tap to do the job.

"Shit...*shit!*" He would've been okay if he'd stayed up on the crown.

He swore again, and then, after calling the garage and chewing Hank out, began knocking on doors, looking for his victim.

CHAPTER 57

~

In her office, Aggie paused long enough to go look out the window. The weather had gone from bad to perfectly dreadful. Beneath the eaves of the building across the way, pigeons huddled piteously, the street below nearly deserted, no cars passing by, only a solitary pedestrian bent to the storm and, wearing no boots, struggling unsteadily forward in footprints left like stepping stones.

Aggie went back to her ritualistic, pre-negotiation limbering exercises. Arms akimbo, torquing first one way, then the other, she wondered what Deuce would have up his sleeve this time. The prospect of another sly proposal from him, something delicious and utterly impossible, set her a bit on edge.

She held her arms out to the side and twisted each way again, then doubled up, legs ramrod straight, and placed the palms of her hands on the floor. She should find an improv group somewhere and make her mind as flexible as her body. Then when Deuce put something witty on the table, she could skewer him with…well, she didn't know, that was the whole point.

But suppose he did nothing? Suppose he gave up and started negotiating like a normal person? She stood up straight and did a couple of deep-knee bends with her knees sticking out like a ballerina practicing plies. How boring! She could have the usual negotiations any time she wanted. Heck, she was having the usual negotiations at that very moment with police, fire, and transit, who'd all mentioned Deuce's revolutionary gambit—the committee with no instructions—sort of half included it in their own proposals, but then abandoned it with hardly a whimper after she'd said no dice. So much for union solidarity.

It was all so utterly depressing. She did a couple more angry flexes and then gathered up her stuff and headed on down the hall.

When she entered the little room where they did their negotiating, any fear that Deuce would simply throw in the towel
immediately evaporated. On the other side of the table, he sat, as
usual, but this time not among the same old faces. He'd assembled
a new team for the session. And not just any old new team, not just
some random sampling of the union faithful. As a matter of fact,
Deuce himself looked somewhat out of place in the midst of this
reconstituted group, for it was composed entirely of women.

Aggie snorted. Barb Amos remained from the old days, everyone else a first-timer at the table.

"Well, well," Aggie said.

"We thought it would help if some of our people got to experience what it was like negotiating with the city," Deuce said with a
pleasant smile, his eyes alert for her reaction.

"Is that what you thought?" The group resembled, Aggie imagined, a convocation of Deuce's ex-girlfriends, everybody turned out
for the occasion, a couple of the newly-pressed-into-service sup-
pressing giggles.

As Aggie took her seat, she said, "So every time I come through
the door, there'll be different people across the table, is that the idea?"

"Could be."

"And you don't think that makes a travesty of the negotiations?"

"Some of our people think the negotiations have been a travesty all along."

This was a typical union provocation. Changing the committee was a provocation, too, of course, but at least an amusing one.

Barb Amos—who seemed to alternate between great pleasure at having brought someone with Deuce's odd talents in as her
negotiator and what could only be described as abject terror at the
prospect of what her loose cannon might actually do— was mighty
pleased at the moment, positively full of herself, wearing a dress
suit in a woolen fabric with large patches of black and white which
made her look like a playing card.

Deuce was still the best-dressed person at the table in a royal
blue dress shirt open at the collar and a tan houndstooth sport coat,
the Brooks Brothers man squiring his gaggle of ladies.

"Nice outfit," Aggie said as she took her seat.

With a slow nod, he acknowledged both the compliment and
the little stiletto of irony she had inserted beneath it.

She looked left and right at each woman in turn, saying each name. Then back at Deuce. As usual, his eyes and mouth didn't agree, his eyes studying her rather coolly even as his mouth invited her to come out and play.

It occurred to Aggie that this new move on his part wasn't entirely unrelated to the committee-with-no-instructions proposal, although, of course, in much too indirect a way to call him on it. Anyway, something else interested her at the moment. Since the union had always been dominated by men, this newest tactic was a gender-bending exercise as well. Aggie decided she was pleased. Good, give the women a chance. But, of course, she couldn't just let Deuce off the hook.

"Well, I'm glad Barb is still here."

Deuce considered that and responded, "You mean, someone who knows what the hell she's doing."

"Why should I want to imply that?" Their eyes were locked on each other. "Someone who provides, shall we say, continuity."

"We don't think much of continuity."

"So I've noticed."

"In fact, today," he said, and let the word hang in the air between them, "...today, we thought we'd talk about the virtues of the four-day week."

And so, with this proposal, the session had been launched. Ten-hour workdays, however, were an old item from the union's hope chest and thus not something sprung completely new from Mr. Goetzinger's fertile brain for the express purpose of knocking Aggie for a loop. As for the all-girl orchestra, well, that *was* new, but considering the matter, Aggie decided that maybe she could put it to use.

In fact, she was sure she could.

CHAPTER 58

~

S hare the pain."
In the excitement after the bus accident, Janey Roche had forgotten all about Harold the bus driver's suggestion. But now, up in
Fionna Henefy's bright and steamy bathroom, Janey remembered.
Fionna was one of Janey's little old ladies.

Janey had been two hours late, but Fionna wasn't the type to
notice a little tardiness. And once she'd been assured nobody had
been killed, Fionna wasn't much interested in Janey's account of the
accident, either. "Accidents happen," she said.

Fionna used a walker and couldn't get up the stairs without
help, so she lived on the first floor of her tiny house, and once
a week, she and Janey—thin, humpbacked Fionna and heavy,
awkward Janey—would make the perilous ascent for Fionna's
weekly shower.

Fionna was sitting now on the commode, her feet on a towel,
Janey carefully drying between each toe. These were the only times
Janey could get her to sit still. She liked having her feet done.

Janey's visits were the last luxury Fionna could afford; luxuries,
after all, were often quite humble.

"Share the pain," Fionna said. "Umm."

"It was Harold's idea. Harold drives the bus I come out here on."

The corner of Fionna's large toenail turned down into the flesh,
and Janey carefully worked a piece of absorbent cotton under the
nail with an orangewood stick and then clipped and filed it.

"That way everybody has to give up a little, but nobody a lot."
This idea, Janey knew, had been suggested before. What appealed
to her was what Harold had said afterwards, that nobody need go
anymore to the city council hat in hand. Not that she would have,
anyway. But what with Kirk pestering her all the time, she felt
guilty. Damned if you do, damned if you don't.

She started on Fionna's other big toe. The room smelled of roses from the after-bath lotion. Drafts of chilly air had begun to slip through the cracks.

"Umm," said Fionna.

Back downstairs, Fionna inched along on her walker, restless, always restless. She turned on the television with the remote and channel surfed for a while.

The living room had been converted for sleeping, the only room in the house big enough for a hospital bed.

To ward off bad weather, Fionna had placed the Blessed Virgin in the picture window, facing the rising sun. The Blessed Virgin was having an off day. Not that Fionna would have admitted that. "Think how much worse it could've been," she'd say.

Candlemas just passed, Fionna had laid in a new stash of blessed candles. During electrical storms, she would light one of these, say the proper prayer, and hobble around the house sprinkling holy water for good measure. Father had stopped by and blessed her throat, it being the Feast of St. Blaise, as well. Early February was the time of many blessings.

Janey went into the kitchen to prepare their meal, listening to the storm as it whipped around the eaves of the house and thinking about Harold's idea as she worked. Harold wasn't the type to do anything about it.

After a while, Fionna shuffled into the kitchen. She never stayed in one place for long.

Her children were scattered, as restless, Janey imagined, as Fionna herself. Fionna never talked about them. She liked ideas. She liked plans.

Janey heard her nearing, the clumping of the walker at each step.

"Huey Long," Fionna said suddenly.

"What?"

"Share the Wealth, that was his idea. Huey Long. Ever heard of him? Before your time. He was governor of Louisiana, maybe senator, I forget, who can remember stuff like that? He wanted to share the wealth. Every man a king, that's what he said." She stopped speaking abruptly, the words submerging out of sight, but still present, Janey knew. Fionna seemed to make little distinction between the word spoken and the word thought.

"I've heard of Huey Long," Janey said, stopping and turning around. "People said he wanted to make himself into a dictator or something, like Hitler."

Fionna held her thin, blue-veined hand up and made little backward flips, the way she dismissed an idea beneath contempt.

"He wanted to share the wealth…that's what he said anyhow. Who knows?" Her eyes suddenly focused and came to rest on Janey. "You want to share the pain. Dear, dear."

Janey saw the point at once. What a silly idea. With relief, she decided to forget about it. For a few minutes, she felt lighter and went about her dinner preparations, humming, listening to the scraping sound behind her. Fionna on the move again.

CHAPTER 59

~

Deuce had been dressing for work when J.J. called. "How you getting to the water plant?"

"Cops. The mayor declared an emergency."

"Call 'em up and tell 'em to forget it," J.J. told him.

And so, ten minutes later, Deuce was standing out in the snow when the salt truck rumbled into view and J.J. threw open the door for him.

"Still driving the REO," Deuce noted as he climbed in.

"Therein lies a tale." J.J. reversed direction. "But all in due course. So tell me, how did it go? Was Aggie amused?"

"For a while. She even tried to turn the tables on me. Of course, the girls were just off the boat. She talked about what 'the guys' had always done, as if 'the guys' were, you know, morons by definition."

"I believe that's an attitude widely shared."

"Yeah. I'm sure it is." Deuce had to speak up to be heard above the whining of the engine in low gear and scraping of the snow-plow blade and blowing of the heater.

"But then you did what you said you were going to do."

"You bet." Deuce had broached the forbidden topic, the committee with no instructions.

J.J. turned onto Grandview Boulevard at its southern end and began plowing the loop road along the rim enclosing the flood plain. From all the jouncing, Deuce had begun to get a hard-on.

"Nice ride."

"Never said this was limo service. So she ended the session?"

"What choice did she have?" In Deuce's experience, nobody wanted to carry out a threat. Make the threat, the act becomes unnecessary, or at least that was the theory. Didn't work with him. A little something his father had found out when Deuce had been growing up. And now Aggie.

J.J. had become quiet. Being Aggie's buddy, he was no doubt unhappy because of the rough handling.

"At some point," J.J. said, "Cutler will impose a settlement."

"That's his problem." The union's position was so hopeless that it was pointless worrying about what the manager might do. Anyway, if you were gonna be chickenshit about the thing, you might as well just pack it in.

"Speaking of Aggie, I got a call from her last night." J.J. described the city's tentative offer of no layoffs, or almost no layoffs, if the union agreed to the giveback.

"So let me get this straight," Deuce said. "Cutler told Plowman who told Aggie who told you."

"I believe it's called back channel."

"We fall on our swords, and Cutler gives us private assurances."

"Since you put it that way, not terribly appetizing, I'll grant you, although some of the younger guys might go for it. Anyway, I was thinking. It looks like the mayor might be a sympathetic ear, so why not sidle over for a chat?"

"I told Aggie we were going public."

"What did she say?"

"Nothing. She was heading out the door."

"Maybe we could get El Plowman to do it for us."

"I suppose."

"Plowman and Aggie are great friends," J.J. said.

"I think maybe I'll go talk to Roger Filer," Deuce countered. If he was going to talk to anyone, why not Filer, who would probably be the next mayor? Assuming, of course, the union could hold out that long.

"I suppose," J.J. said over the whine of the motor. "Or why not talk to them both?"

"Yeah."

They drove without speaking for a couple of blocks, Deuce thinking about what he was going to do next. Go public. Had to go public sometime. Pretty much the obvious thing to do, although Deuce didn't give a fig about the obvious. He much preferred playing cat and mouse with Aggie, even though he was mostly cast in the role of the mouse. The expression on her face when she realized he was going to force her to end the session had been wonderful, going from shock to disgust to acceptance but with a certain

flair, a certain comic exaggeration after the initial surprise. At the
very end, she'd even smiled slightly, a smile mostly to herself, but
perhaps a little for him. It reminded him of the way a good poker
player will sometimes toss in a busted hand, a kind of acknowledg-
ment that the world wasn't necessarily made for his benefit.

Deuce and J.J. drove on. The plowed-up embankments on
either side were like high roadcuts. "Look at all this fucking snow,"
Deuce marveled.

"White is the color of mourning in India," J.J. said.

"You're a cheerful son of a bitch."

"It has not been a good day."

J.J. told him about an accident he'd had on Alpine.

"Just between you and me and the bedpost, if I'd been carrying a little less salt, I might've been okay. You got a full load, this
baby is heavy. You get sucked into the curb and that's all she wrote.
Hank had no business sending me down there."

"But you went."

"Yeah, I know. How bright am I?" Of course, Deuce understood that J.J. had to do it. If Kraft had ordered him to do something
rinky-dink, that would be one thing, but this had been tricky. This
was a matter of pride.

"Fortunately," J.J. was saying, "the gal I hit turned out to be a
sweetheart, in fact, the very nurse who needed to get to the hospital. I gave her a lift."

"You're running a regular taxi service."

They were approaching the Okey-Dokey at the corner of University. "Coffee?" J.J. asked.

Back in the truck with their drinks, J.J. inserted his big plastic
mug into its holder and rubbed his hands vigorously across his face.

"Twelve-hour shifts. I'm not as young as I used to be."

He put the truck in gear and headed back out.

"So, anyway, I gave the nurse a lift, and she tells me a little
story."

"Yeah?"

"Yeah, but first, I got a question for you." J.J. glanced over.
"And none of the close-to-the-vest shit you specialize in, please.
Tell me, just how serious are you about this here committee of
yours?"

This question brought Deuce up short. How serious was he? A
moment revealed the answer.

"I'm dead serious. On the other hand, I don't give a shit. It's a kick. It's more interesting than anything else we've got on the table."

"That's comforting."

"You wanted me to be honest."

"That I did."

At a brightly lit intersection, power lines dipped down, thick with snow, reminding Deuce of hog dust on cobwebs. In the street-lights, the snow sparkled.

"Well, okay," J.J. continued, in a ruminative mood, "so I asked myself, just suppose, just suppose we really are serious about this thing. Seems to me we've gotta start getting personal, naming names. Everybody's got a story, right? The boss from hell."

"Hank Kraft."

"Yeah, Hank Kraft. Although Hank has his points, but yes, people like Hank, people worse than Hank. I'm thinking this com-mittee of yours might be just the place for us poor peons to lodge our complaints."

"I thought you just wanted to go fishing?" Deuce challenged him, a little annoyed for some reason at this sudden taste for blood in a man famous for his willingness to accommodate himself to the realities.

"Well, yes, true enough. But, like I said, been thinking. And anyway, I enjoy chatting people up. Might even volunteer my ser-vice to the committee, who knows? Of course, I'm not sure how I go about doing that. Do I have to run for office? Or are people chosen by lot? Or maybe by reading the entrails of chickens?"

"Beats me."

J.J. laughed. "Exactly my point."

The blade of the truck, hitting something, tripped forward, then snapped back.

"So what's this story the nurse tells you?"

"Right. Well, it seems that there was a city crew out on Alpine some time back, fixing a water main, smack dab where I had my little mishap, as a matter of fact. Had a huge washout there accord-ing to the nurse."

"If they don't find a leak right off, it can wash away a ton of shit."

"I know. Anyway, they filled the hole. As they were leaving, the nurse goes out and tells them there's been a lot of water coming down

off the bluff. According to her, it'd been coming down for months."
At this point, Deuce's attention, casual before, became riveted.

"Months?"

"Since the summer sometime."

"How much?"

"She didn't say. Enough so she noticed, obviously."

"From where?"

"She didn't say that, either. When the cold weather came, it
stopped. Some of it froze, too. I got a bruise on my keister to prove
it… Anyway, that's the story, not exactly *War and Peace*, but it set
me to thinking about bosses from hell and whatnot. And not just
about Hank Kraft."

"Frank Lacy."

"Bingo."

The chief of the water distribution crew was a piece of work.

"You know Frank?" Deuce asked.

"Oh, yes. Had a little run-in with him last summer, I did."

"Yeah?"

"Doing some curb and gutter work up on Locust, and I busted
a water lateral. Lacy's crew happened to be working down the street,
so I trotted on over, thinking, how providential…"

"Let me guess. Lacy said, 'You broke it, you fix it.'"

"His very words."

"Frank likes to rub people's noses in it."

"He could've made the repair in no time at all."

"Goes without saying."

"Think of the goodwill."

Deuce laughed.

"I tell you, Deuce, if an easygoing, fun-loving fellow like
myself gets into it with the likes of Frank Lacy, imagine what happens with some of our touchier brethren."

Lacy had a few cronies, hard-core types, who'd worked for him
a long time. Otherwise, he was a revolving door, chewing up and
spitting out people as fast as they were sent to him.

"So," J.J. said, "I'm beginning to take a liking to this scheme of
yours. Give us peons a shoulder to cry on, like I said. Why not?"

Rather then welcoming this news, Deuce found himself
annoyed, although he didn't know why he should give a shit. It
wasn't as if he was all that much in love with workplace democracy.
On the other hand, just because you don't much care for the girl

you're dancing with, that doesn't mean you wanted some clown cutting in on you.

And, on the third hand, he *was* interested in the water.

"When the repair was made on Alpine, who did the nurse talk to? Lacy?"

"She didn't know his name. Anyway, he didn't seem very interested."

"Probably Lacy. Did she say anything more about the water? Anything at all?"

"No, why?"

"We're missing some."

"What? Water?"

"Yeah, we've got a break somewhere in the system. Losing maybe 30-35,000 gallons a day. Of course, Lacy doesn't believe it."

"No?"

"We're pumping more than the usage in the intermediate system, not a lot, maybe 10 percent. Lacy can't find the leak, so he tells us we're imagining things. I expect he hasn't looked too goddamn hard." Lacy had a low opinion of the operators at the water plant.

"Alpine," J.J. said.

"Maybe. Could just be groundwater from a seam in the bluffs. The leak might be somewhere else, down into one of the old mines. That's what we've been thinking." The city was honeycombed with abandoned lead mines. "But if Lacy's just dogging it, and every day the city's losing the cost of treating that water…"

"And therefore you could prove he has been somewhat remiss in his duties. A pleasant prospect," J.J. opined.

"You bet your ass."

They had arrived at the water plant, and Deuce got out.

"Even if you're not right," J.J. suggested, "Frank Lacy is still a great advertisement for this committee of yours."

The snow peppered Deuce, and he slammed the door shut and walked into the lee of the building, where the storm suddenly abated and he felt a flush of warmth. He lingered in the stillness and, as he watched J.J. plow out the water plant parking lot, fretted over his friend's newfound interest in the committee. Or rather his own lack of it. He felt like an outsider. Here he was the one who had introduced the scheme, and now J.J. was making it his own. J.J. and Aggie. Deuce was sure she must like the idea, too, even though she betrayed nothing as she acted out the script Cutler had handed her. Deuce didn't know why he was so sure. Maybe intuition. Maybe because she was a woman. Or maybe just the edge of whimsy in her manner, the slight smile that morning a moment before she had walked out the door. She must like the idea.

As the taillights of the truck disappeared into the storm, he thrust the union problem aside. At the moment, finding the missing water and screwing Frank Lacy interested him a helluva lot more than sitting on some piddly-assed committee and arguing over piddly-assed little bureaucratic nothings, which was, so far as he could see, what workplace democracy was finally all about.

He turned and went inside to work the graveyard shift.

CHAPTER 60

~

The piles of snow jamming the narrow, hilly streets cast long night shadows across Janey Roche's path.

A car turned downhill toward her, and Janey, hastening to get out of the way, stumbled and sat down abruptly in a snowbank. To get to her feet, she had to twist around and push with her hands, one plunging through the crust, snow sifting beneath her glove, the painful cold cutting her wrist.

Against the upwelling of city lights from below, the mayor's house loomed, an imposing pitch-black silhouette on its ledge near the top of the bluff. No one home. Figured. But she'd come this far, she wasn't going to go away without making sure. Muttering to herself, she advanced sideways up the edge of the steep driveway, planting her feet, first one, then the other.

She knocked, but nobody came. She knocked again and stood in the black entryway, listening to the silence inside.

She'd come on a fool's errand. The mayor had promised to meet her, but what are promises to a politician?

Out at the driveway again, she stared downward with trepidation, the air all about her sparkling with the night lights, but the foot of the driveway as dark as looking down a well. From the top, it seemed much steeper. She didn't see how she could get to the bottom without tumbling head over heels. She couldn't believe how stupid she was. This would teach her to be enthusiastic.

Turning sideways again, she began to inch her way downward. If she fell, it'd serve her right. She moved cautiously, sidestep by sidestep, keeping to the edge, and got halfway to the bottom before she began to slip, teetered, and only managed to throw herself down on her hands and knees to prevent a worse spill. She slid to a stop several feet farther down. Finally, knees stinging, she stood up and resumed her slow descent.

At the bottom, she paused only long enough to catch her breath.

She was almost back to the bus stop when a car pulled past her and halted, and a dark figure climbed out and looked back toward her.

"Jane Roche?"

~

"Here, let me take your coat."

Jane Roche shook her head. She sat with the coat wrapped tightly about herself.

El regarded her mournfully. Apologies seemed to make no impression on Mrs. Roche, a heavy middle-aged woman, about El's age, severe, her cheeks rouged by the cold. "Tea, then? Can I at least get you something to warm you up?"

"Don't have time. Just got time to say what I got to say. Last bus is at 6:30."

"Nonsense. I wouldn't dream of making you struggle back down that hill. I'll take you home."

"Used to be, buses ran 'til midnight," Jane Roche said. "Coffee, if you got any." As she spoke, she had been looking around, curiosity displacing part of her anger.

El filled a kettle with water, telling her a little of the history of the old Victorian. She had no idea why Jane Roche wanted to see her. Something to do with transit, perhaps. More likely, she'd come to complain about the plan to bring blacks to Jackson.

El turned back toward her guest.

"What happened to your stocking?" Mrs. Roche's coat had parted at the knees, exposing the ripped white stocking, hanging down below the hem of the uniform visible beneath. She looked down at the damage, then hiked up the hem far enough to expose her knees, one scraped, the other trickling blood. "I fell on your driveway."

"Dear, dear, let me get something for that."

"Got a kit in my purse. You're a nurse like me, you gotta be prepared."

El fetched a basin and filled it with warm, soapy water. Mrs. Roche insisted on attending to the wounds herself. El looked on, itching to help.

"After all you've been through just getting here," she said as the repairs were completed, "I hope I can be of some service."

"Doubt it." Mrs. Roche dropped her dress gently back over her knees. "You know how much these cost me?" she asked, brandishing her ruined stockings. "I'll tell you. $8.95." She repeated the figure.

"I'd be glad to pay for them. You wouldn't have fallen if I'd gotten home when I was supposed to."

"I don't want your money, Mrs. Plowman. Your honor."

"Please, call me El. Everybody else does."

Jane Roche merely frowned.

The kettle began to whistle, and El poured her coffee. "At the rate I'm going," El said as she carried it over, "I'll probably spill this on you." Mrs. Roche had wrapped her coat back around her, still clutching the stockings.

El pulled out a chair and turned it around so she could sit facing her visitor.

"Now, tell me a little about yourself. You're a nurse. That's all I know."

"An LPN."

El nodded. "And?"

Reluctantly at first, but then more readily, Jane Roche began to tell her story. Native Jacksonian. Catholic upbringing. Marriage. Two children. Working for the Jackson VNA.

Though Mrs. Roche spoke readily enough, the sullenness remained. She was, El judged, the sort who observed the proprieties, but, given a dollop of encouragement, would become confessional. "You've had a storybook life, then?"

"Not hardly." So the rest came out. Her abusive mother. A chronic weight problem. Marriage to the first man who'd come along, a weak, self-absorbed, cancer-plagued man. Children, into whose lives she poured her own with little return. Now all gone, husband, children, home. And she cking out her existence, taking whatever part-time, ill-paying jobs she could find.

As El listened, she realized that Jane Roche was depressive, like herself. A kindred spirit. And, judging from her story, with a lot more reasons than El had, not that reasons had all that much to do with depression.

But Jane Roche's tale clearly was twice-told, repeated too many times to serve as much of a bond between them. She spoke with dour determination, more as an argument is built in court than friendship formed with a fellow sufferer.

"I'm a survivor, Mrs. Plowman. You're a woman like me, no one cares. It's something you wouldn't understand."

"Don't be too sure."

Mrs. Roche ignored this. "I look out for others, no one looks out for me. But no matter what happens, Mrs. Plowman, I'm a survivor." A brag, of course, but El knew why Jane Roche said it. We accord moral authority to survival.

"I see, yes…" El found herself beginning to tire and decided that she wasn't up to whatever it would take to make vital contact with this woman. "So, tell me, please. What can I do for you?"

Mrs. Roche looked away and picked at the edges of her coat.

"I got something to say."

"Yes?"

"I'm not asking anything for myself, you understand. I don't want anything for myself."

"I understand."

"You're not going to like it."

Bringing blacks to Jackson, El thought wearily. "Try me."

"The other day, during the storm, I was riding on the bus, you know, the one that crashed."

"You were?!"

"Going out to see Fionna Hennefy. She's one of my little old ladies that I take care of."

"Then it was you helped all those people."

"Helped some. I was there. Others came along pretty quick. There were a lot of people to attend to."

"I know. But you're to be commended. Please, tell me about it." El's energy revived, and she questioned Mrs. Roche closely, letting her add firsthand details to what El already knew.

"The driver wasn't at fault, you're sure of that?" she said finally, repeating an earlier question. Thank God most of the injuries had been minor, but there would be suits regardless, personal injury lawyers mounting raids on the public purse.

"Like I said," Jane Roche confirmed, "I saw him check the mirror two, three times. I ride with Harold a lot. He's careful, Mrs. Plowman. Harold's not the type to do nothing reckless, believe me."

"Do please call me El."

"Okay. But like I started to say before, that ain't why I came here, although it's got to do with Harold."

"Tell me." El felt better. Halfway through her recollections, Mrs. Roche had wriggled out of her coat and draped it casually back over her chair.

"It's Harold's idea. Of course, he's pretty shy and some of his schemes are a little…strange. But this one I heard before, once in a while, and seems to me it's a good one, although it's true you never hear that much about it."

"Believe me, Jane—is that what people call you?—believe me, I'm always in the market for a good idea."

"Janey. Most people call me Janey."

"Janey, then. Well, proceed."

"It's got to do with the budget. You know how you spend all your time arguing about whether you should cut this or that or the other thing, you know, the bus system or the recreation department or, I don't know, the fire or something?"

El nodded.

"Seems to me, that just pits everybody against everybody, if you know what I mean."

"Everybody against everybody?"

"Yes. I mean, well, maybe it's okay if you're a higher up or somebody. But if you're a little guy, like Harold or me, it means you end up going to the city council hat in hand. I mean, Mrs. Plowman, you end up begging people. Begging. Ain't no other way to put it."

"Nobody who comes to the council," El said, "is a beggar."

"Well, that's what it seems like to me. I spoke to the council once. You wouldn't remember. It was the first bus fight. I stood up there and asked you not to cut the system, you know, but you cut it anyway."

"It won't happen this time, not if I have anything to say about it."

"That ain't why I came. I know cuts have to be made. It's making people fight over them, like dogs fighting over a bone or something, that's what I hate."

"I see. And you've got another idea."

"Yes, I do. Cut everything equal."

"Oh," El said.

"Across the board." Jane Roche made an abrupt, diagonal slashing motion. "Everybody the same."

"I assume you mean proportionally."

Janey Roche nodded sharply. "Fair's fair."

El felt disappointed. Even on occasions as unpromising as this one, she still hoped for some sort of insight, some creative suggestion, some magical something.

Naive. The reality was that people came to her, all charged up—with anger, with some hopeless scheme, it made no difference—and what she did, if she was any good at her job, was to gently dissipate the energy.

She wondered what she could possibly say to this woman.

"You ride the buses."

"You know I do."

"If we cut everything, then you understand the transit system will be cut, too."

"Fair's fair," Jane Roche repeated.

"But you need your rides. Other people, too. I don't want to cut the system."

"Frankly, Mrs. Plowman, and meaning no disrespect, nobody believes you."

"Nobody?"

"Everybody I talk to, they think it's nothin' but politics."

"I see. And politicians aren't to be trusted."

"No disrespect."

Annoyed, El turned away. Janey was skeptical, people were skeptical, but skepticism was cheap. The council did the best it could.

"Then we'd have to cut police and fire, too, programs that benefit everybody." El thought of a medical analogy. "You're a nurse, you know that when the body's under attack, it protects the vital organs. How can the city do any less?"

Undeterred, Janey responded immediately, "Broad programs oughta be cut first, you ask me. We oughta share the pain, not try to fob it all off on the little guy all the time. We got no sense of community, Mrs. Mayor. You think otherwise, you ain't seen all the abandoned old people in this town. I see them every day."

"I'm sure you do."

El remembered standing on the post office steps with Johnny Pond and looking out over Washington Square and Johnny telling her basically the same thing, another aspect of the same thing. Jackson was a city with no center, like a body from which the heart had been removed. Speaking of medical analogies.

Yet, Janey had struggled through the storm to talk to her. She hadn't come to complain about the plan to encourage blacks to move to the city. Or to ask anything for herself. And if her proposal was totally unrealistic, being realistic was not always such a virtue. It was a kind of giving up, too. And anyway, El was hardly the one to start going around and telling people to be realistic.

"I have a thought," she said. "Why don't you present your idea to the council?"

"Me?" Janey said, startled. "I came to see you. I came to tell you."

"I know, but this'll give you a chance to see what others think. I'm just one person."

"You're the mayor."

"I am the mayor," El agreed, "for the moment, at least. I'm afraid it means less than you might imagine. But look, you talk about the lack of community, and then you want me to be your stalking horse, you want to hide behind me." Janey sat rigidly, staring at El. "Frankly, even if I was willing, I don't see how I could do it in good conscience. I don't believe your idea is practical."

"Then forget it," Janey mumbled. The prospect of having to appear before the council had cooled her ardor quickly enough. She was struggling back into her coat and looking around for her purse.

El felt awful. Maybe this woman wasn't ready to face the council, but she *had* taken the trouble to come make her case, even had her battle scars to prove it.

"Wait a second. A couple of minutes ago, you were all but yelling at me. Now you say forget it, just like that?"

"If it ain't practical… If you ain't willing to do anything about it…"

"But you believe in it."

Janey stuffed her stockings into her purse. "Do you want me to make a fool of myself?"

"No, of course not." El started to tell Janey she wouldn't make a fool of herself, but stopped. She had a vision of Paul Cutler, sitting slouched in his chair, listening to the proposal. Cut everything the same.

Janey stood up. "I'm ready to go home, if you'll take me."

"Yes, all right." As El fetched her own coat, still searching around for some way to save the situation, all she could summon was a bit of frankness. "You're right. Some people would think very little of your scheme." El knew something about losing face.

"Still, one wonders," she mused aloud as they went out to her car, "whether you have to be at least a little foolish to have a good idea in the first place."

Janey Roche didn't react to this. El didn't expect her to.

CHAPTER 61

~

"New outfit?" El asked.

"I needed something to pick me up." Aggie inspected her Gore-Tex parka with its splashes of bright primary colors. "Also," she added, "to keep from getting run over."

Although, at the moment, getting run over wasn't an option. She and El had finally abandoned the snow-heaped streets and joined the early morning walkers indoors at the Kennedy Mall.

"I should get one, too," El said, and not, Aggie noticed at once, with the dour determination which in past months would have greeted any such proposal. Something had happened. El was positively cheerful!

"Do," Aggie encouraged her. "I got a new outfit for work, too. With a nifty vest and velvet slacks."

"Slacks?"

"Velvet. Gonna wear it to negotiations with the big union. I'm tired of looking like a sow's ear next to Deuce Goetzinger."

"What will Paul say?" Paul had made it known, more than once, how happy he was that dresses were coming back.

Aggie made a rude noise. She hoped Paul didn't like it.

El's laugh was her old one, full-bodied, uninhibited. Aggie was almost afraid to ask.

"El, El," she whispered, "what's happened?"

El boomed out another laugh. "I know. Even Walter noticed."

"But what happened? I can't believe it. It's wonderful!"

"Well, let me tell you."

Chin up, arms flailing—in the wide-open spaces of the mall, they could really make time—El threw one phrase after another back over her shoulder as she told the story of a visit the night before from a licensed practical nurse named Janey Roche.

"So that was her scheme. I said, why not speak to the council. That cooled her jets, I can tell you. Probably just as well. She didn't possess what you'd call a winning personality. Sullen, a little abrasive, sort of reminded me of me. And her idea...woo-eee.

"I took her home, thinking, that was that. Nothing to be done. Of course, you know me, I can't sleep. I was lying awake later, reviewing my life, as usual, and Janey Roche's scheme kept coming back, wouldn't go away. Didn't make any difference all the arguments against it. Just kept coming back, like one of those pop-up targets at a carnival. And suddenly—I have no idea what happened—suddenly I felt better. I felt like my old self again."

"Oh, El, I'm so glad!"

"Just like that, poof. And all thanks to Janey Roche."

"Hooray for Janey Roche." And hooray for Aggie, Aggie, the campaign manager, added to herself. Maybe now they could run a real campaign for mayor.

"Of course," El added quickly, "making cuts like she suggested is just plain nuts."

"Absolutely."

"And I wouldn't dream of doing anything about it, except here I am, feeling good again and thinking I owe Janey."

"You're actually going to do it, then, propose cuts across the board?" Aggie asked incredulously. "I suppose we could make it a plank in your campaign platform or something."

"Hardly. I'm not a complete moron."

Aggie listened with glee to El's laugh. "Think of what Paul would say," she said.

This slant on the matter just naturally put Aggie in mind of Deuce Goetzinger's proposal for a committee, participatory democracy, a coffee klatch, whatever you wanted to call it. Something else Paul hated.

The mall walkers were out in full force along the dim promenades, the kiosks and stores still shuttered. For a time, Aggie and El moved briskly and without speaking, the pleasant silence between friends bathed in a moment of perfect understanding. And for a time, Aggie didn't think at all, just strutted along, her elbows flapping jauntily, even pleased for once with her spruce little image, not just a glimpse in Keefer's display window hedged all around by snow and frost and icicles, but coming and going from the windows of the mall shops, a kaleidoscope of Aggies.

When she was ready to talk again, she caught her friend up on the status of the negotiations, particularly with the big union—Deuce's all-girl negotiating team, and, less amusing, his forcing Aggie to walk out of a session. He was also threatening to go public.

"It sounds like he *is* pretty serious about this committee of his," El said with interest. The lifting of her spirits seemed to put everything in an entirely new light.

"I don't know. Hard to think so."

"Did you talk to your pal J.J. Dusterhoft?"

"Yeah. He didn't hold out much hope. Maybe, with a no-lay-off pledge from Paul, the union might forgo a wage increase. That much. But a giveback, no way. Transit, maybe. But not the big union. And police and fire, fugedaboutit."

"Worth a try. Anyway, why are you so certain young Goetzinger isn't serious?" El said, returning to the earlier matter. "He's Fritz's son, after all."

Aggie never really thought of Deuce as the old mayor's son, aside from the family resemblance, so El's characterization threw her for a second.

"It does seem like the sort of thing his father might have come up with, doesn't it?" she mused.

"And if he had?" El asked rhetorically. Fritz would have shown no quarter.

"The son," Aggie said, "is different. He's...I don't know, more an observer."

"Yet, as you said, the proposal's the most interesting thing on the table," El persisted, all her old curiosity back.

"It isn't on the table," Aggie corrected her.

El snorted. "Okay, it's the most interesting thing not on the table."

"We could make it a campaign issue."

"O my gawd."

"Budget cuts across the board. Workplace democracy. El Plowman, the people's candidate."

"O my gawd."

"But we like these ideas. Sort of. Don't we?"

"I like lobsters, too, dear, but that doesn't mean I'm willing to make myself deathly ill." El was allergic to shellfish.

"Seems to me like you're already deathly ill. This is just...I don't know...a hair of the dog." Liquor analogies came naturally to Aggie.

El laughed. "Why continue rolling down the hill when I could jump off a cliff?"

In the food court, a couple of the fast food outlets had opened to cash in on the early clientele. Aggie and El approached a table where a bunch of old gents were taking their ease and making observations on the state of the world, and Aggie waited while a couple of the more vocal traded barbs with El, El giving as good as she got, but still not exactly the kind of performance a campaign manager liked to see out of her candidate.

At last, the two of them were under way again, heading in a new direction, and Aggie's froglike mind, hopping first one way, then another, came back to the subject of the union negotiations, and as she and El steamed along, Aggie told herself again what an irritating fellow was Mr. Deuce Goetzinger.

～

Aggie followed El back to her house to pick up some campaign literature for distribution. Walter was dumping his breakfast dishes into the sink and about to head off to KJTV, but he took the time to ask after Lucille. His hair was slicked down, he had on what appeared to be new clothes—everybody was getting new clothes—and he looked as sleek as a slightly overfed otter. Bad weather agreed with him.

Silently, El handed Aggie an envelope with a New York postmark. When Aggie wrinkled her brow, El just nodded at the envelope.

As she opened it and inspected the contents—a hundred-dollar check and accompanying letter—Aggie said, "Lucille found this weird radio station. I forgot to tell you, El."

"What do you mean 'weird'?" Walter asked.

"I didn't hear it. FM, I think. Really strange programming. Lucille was a little vague, you know Lucille. What is this, El, a campaign contribution from New York?"

"Read the letter."

"How did she find it?" Walter wanted to know.

Aggie perused the letter. "The station? My mother has entirely too much time on her hands, that's how."

"Strange programming?"

"You'll have to ask her. A lot of talk against bringing African Americans here, she said. Country and western music. No ads. Lucille always notices stuff like that."

"We're not *bringing* them here," El corrected, a little testily.

The letter dealt with the same matter, the city "bringing in blacks," which the writer favored.

"We're not 'voting whether to let blacks come here,' either," El fumed, something else suggested in the letter, which had obviously annoyed her enough so that she could quote it verbatim. The writer seemed to think they were running a referendum on closing the city to blacks entirely.

Aggie looked at the valediction. "How did he find out about the election, do you suppose?" The national press had done their stories on the museum vandalism, got bored, and gone away.

"Might be a pirate," Walter suggested.

"A what?" El asked him.

"Pirate radio station."

"Really?" Aggie said.

With extra emphasis, El plunked the saucepan in which she heated water for her tea down on one of the stove's burners, then looked sharply back and forth between Aggie and Walter. She pointed at the letter.

"I'm sending the money back. What do you mean, Walter, a pirate radio station?"

"I don't know. Could be. Somebody doesn't want blacks coming here and has started a little one-watt operation to advertise the fact."

"Why don't we keep the money?" Aggie suggested. Visions of an honest-to-God campaign danced in her head.

El was looking thoughtful.

"I want to know," she said to Walter. "Maybe somebody's just changed their programming. That would be bad enough. If it's a pirate, I'm going to the FCC."

"Why don't we keep the money?" Aggie said.

"I'll find out what I can," Walter said.

El glared at Aggie. "Because this election isn't about some new version of Jim Crow laws, that's why."

"Of course it isn't," Aggie agreed timidly. She'd forgotten how strong-minded her friend could be when she wasn't depressed. Nevertheless, Aggie couldn't simply abandon her effort, like that.

"But just think, El, real campaign money." If they'd gotten a contribution from New York, maybe they'd get more from other places. With a pile of contributions, they could hire a campaign consultant, run TV and radio ads, the works.

El was having none of it.

"This is a local election," she said. "I'm going to keep it that way."

CHAPTER 62

~

Deuce found the water distribution crew on the other end of town, repairing a leak in a quiet residential area, a subdivision that had once been farmland.

He parked the RX-7 and walked slowly toward them, preparing his mind for an encounter with Frank Lacy. The sun lay to the south, a perfect winter day, the next storm not yet making up on the western horizon. Living and working downtown on the floodplain, surrounded by bluffs, he felt the opening up of the landscape, the prairie sky, the houses receding toward the west, neat and silent and evenly-spaced, like infinitely repeating mirror images. Snow blew in ribbons from their roofs, atop which dunes had been sculpted.

He continued up the gentle slope to where Frank Lacy's men had opened up the street with a backhoe. Muddy water skirted the excavation and along one edge, dirt and asphalt slabs piled haphazardly.

Kevin Jungblut was down in the hole, standing on the bottom rung of a ladder, ineffectively shoveling mud away from the water main. Jungblut was low man on Lacy's totem pole. Foamy brown water pooled in the hole beneath his boots.

Frank Lacy himself stood next to the hole, glaring at a small pump.

"Goetzinger!" he yelled, without looking up, "come over here!" Deuce further girded himself and approached.

"Hello, Frank."

"Look at this bastard, plugged up again," Lacy said. He was talking about the pump. "You wanna unplug it for me?"

"I don't think so."

Lacy loved to pull people's chains. He peeked at Deuce, his lower lip twitching as he smiled, then laughed and knelt down, pulling the hose off the pump and with his bare hand scooping out the mud that had clogged the strainer and flinging it down a few inches from Deuce's shoes.

"What's a matter, Frank," Deuce asked, "couldn't shut the valves?"

"Pretty goddamn obvious, wouldn't you say?" Lacy yanked the starting cord and the little pump sputtered to life. The work had to proceed, even if they couldn't completely valve off an area. If it'd been anybody besides Lacy, Deuce might have sympathized.

Snow in a nearby yard, saturated with water, formed a sagging gray bowl.

Lacy gave Deuce a shall-I-clean-my-hands-on-you look, then laughed again and went over to his truck for a rag. As he returned, he surveyed the scene and then yelled at one of his men.

"Butch, get down there and do it right!" He motioned toward Kevin Jungblut, who was still trying to shovel the mud while standing on the ladder. Butch, one of Lacy's longtimers, routed Kevin, then jumped down into the hole and, standing in the clay-brown water up to his knees, started working energetically, cleaning the mud and water from around the main. Jungblut stood unhappily nearby.

"Can't get good help no more, Goetzinger." Lacy smiled, his lower lip twitching, his fair Irish face shamming benevolence.

He used to fight every year in the Tough Man Contests at the civic center, until they were discontinued. Lacy was pint-sized, a lightweight, maybe welter, not that anybody paid much attention to such niceties in the Tough Man Contests. Meanness counted for more than size, anyway. Lacy had always done very well.

They stood side by side and watched Butch digging around the base of the pipe and moving the pump's suction hose around in the hole, trying to draw the water down so he could make the repair.

"What's this goddamn thing you're trying to do with the union, Goetzinger?" Lacy demanded.

"What goddamn thing, Frank?"

"Democracy for the masses, whatever the hell you call it."

Deuce's natural inclination when challenged was to defend himself with silence. He eyed Lacy, whose jaw was working, chewing on his disdain.

"You think these clowns give a shit about that," Lacy said, a sweep of his hand taking in his crew.

"Why don't you speak a little louder, Frank?" Deuce suggested. "I don't think Kevin over there can hear you." Jungblut stood farthest away, staring disconsolately down into the trench, the site of his recent humiliation.

Lacy, taking up the challenge, yelled at him. "Come over here, Kevin. Don't stand there moping in your goddamn beer." He put an arm around his reluctant subordinate and positioned him directly in front of Deuce. "We're talking about this here, wha'd'ya call it, Goetzinger, this here participatory democracy shit? You heard about it, right, Kevin?"

Jungblut shrugged.

"Kevin here," Lacy said, "ain't even heard of it, Goetzinger. You're in the union, ain't that right, Kevin?"

Jungblut knew when he was being baited, but he made the mistake of staring at the ground hangdog, which just encouraged Lacy.

"You do know what you gotta do to get in the union, ain't that right, Kevin?"

"Yeah." Jungblut's irritation just peeped through, but he didn't raise his head.

"Good boy," Lacy said and patted him on the shoulder. "You'd be surprised, Deuce, what these guys don't know. Some of 'em don't even know Iowa is a right-to-work state. Hell, don't even know what it means to be a right-to-work state. Kevin knows, though, ain't that right, Kevin?"

"Yeah."

Lacy leaned toward Deuce. "Kevin here's one of the brighter ones. But this participatory shit, I don't know, Goetzinger. Sounds a lot like rocket science to me. Not something you can do sitting in front of the tube guzzling beer."

In the lull that followed, Lacy smiled at him, lower lip twitching, and Deuce tried to think how he might encourage him to act even more like an asshole, not that much encouragement was needed.

"Ah, but Frank, we've being thinking, wouldn't it be nice if the membership had a say-so every once in a while? I mean, some of our people work for real jerkoffs." Now it was Deuce's turn to lean, smiling, toward Lacy.

Lacy laughed and patted Jungblut. "I believe, Kevin, Mr. Goetzinger here is implying I'm a shit. Could that be true?"

Jungblut, of course, wanted nothing to do with this conversation.

"Tell him," Lacy demanded, "am I a shit?"

"No," Jungblut mumbled.

"No?"

"You're the salt of the earth, Frank," Jungblut managed.

"Damn right, I am!" Lacy boomed and pounded his subordinate on the shoulder, "The salt of the fucking earth, and don't you forget it." Lacy laughed, and then released Jungblut. "Okay, run along and try and make yourself useful. See if Butch needs anything. Butch, what's it look like?" Lacy yelled down into the hole.

"Circular," Butch yelled back up. He had finally managed to pump the water down and was feeling under the bottom of the pipe.

"Good. Kevin, go get him a 226."

Jungblut, obviously relieved to be doing anything other then taking part in the needling between Lacy and Deuce, hustled over to the truck and returned with a metal sleeve, which he handed down to Butch.

"You're something else, Lacy," Deuce said as they watched the sleeve being fitted around the pipe.

"A shit, right?"

Deuce didn't answer. Instead, after a pause, he said, "J.J. Dusterhoft was plowing Alpine the other day. He had a little accident."

"I heard." Lacy wasn't the type of guy to miss much.

"Got sucked into the curb."

"I know. A fucking shame."

"Said there was a ton of ice under the snow."

"Ice? What a surprise, and in balmy weather like this."

"Nurse whose car he dinged told him you'd been over there fixing a leak some time back."

"She did, uh? Well, let me see...believe we were. Hard to remember. Breaks all over the goddamn place. What a fucking winter. Ain't even March yet." In March, the frost came out of the ground, and things really got dicey for Lacy and his crew. "But, yes, believe we were over there. Couple months ago. A simple job, like this one. In and out."

"Woman up on Alpine said she'd told you there was all kind of water sloughing off the hillside."

"That right?"

"Naturally, Lacy, I thought about my missing water."

"Ah, yes, I see, it's your missing water, is it? Your so-called missing water."

"We got the numbers, Frank."

"So you say. Tell me, Goetzinger, is this like the towboats going by?" Lacy had never believed the operators in the water plant could tell when towboats passed on the river by subtle changes in the static pressure in the wells.

"This is exactly like that, Frank. We know when towboats are around, and we know when some of our water's gone missing."

Lacy looked at Deuce with a twinkle in his eye, his lip quivering.

"So what is it, Frank? Did you check it out or what?"

"Here's the thing," Lacy said, the quivering stopping, his eyes going cold. "We did a job on Alpine, yes, I do remember. Look it up, if you've a mind to. Wrote the thing up, like we always do. It's a matter, as they say, of public record. As for the rest, you people at the water plant can fantasize all you want. Ain't got nothing to do with me."

"I just wanted to check it on out, Frank."

Lacy nodded slowly, his expression gone blank. "I'm sure you did. Tell you what, Goetzinger, if I find your water, I'll be sure to let you know."

"Thanks, Frank, you're a prince."

❧

Deuce worked the second shift that night, on the pumping side. He got two interesting phone calls, the first from Kevin Jungblut.

"It was me the woman on Alpine talked to," Kevin informed him.

"Oh, yeah? You told Lacy?"

"Yeah, but Frank don't wanna hear that kind of shit."

"What did he do, anything?"

"Naw, took a ride around the block. Mostly, just blew it off. Said it was probably groundwater from all the rain we had last fall. Typical Frank."

Lacy had the perfect job for somebody who liked to hide things under the rug. The city was his rug. Who knows what they'd find if they dug up the whole water system?

"Frank's a piece of work," Deuce said to Jungblut.

"He's a fucking mick asshole, but I need this goddamn job, Deuce."

It occurred to Deuce that here was a perfect opportunity to push the democracy idea. J.J. was right, it was precisely jerks like

Lacy that the proposal was meant to neutralize. And what Deuce, the general with no army, obviously needed to do was recruit people like Jungblut. Yet he just couldn't summon the missionary energy at the moment.

"Thanks for the info, Kevin. I take it you don't want to be quoted."

"Shit, no. You never heard this from me. Lacy'd have my ass."

The second call came from Deuce's boss, Wayne Gourley, the water plant manager.

"Frank Lacy just called me, Deuce. Mad as hell."

The jolt Deuce felt passed quickly. Of course Lacy was mad as hell. Of course he called Gourley. Should have expected it.

"He says you were way outta line," Wayne went on, "trying to blame him for an accident a friend of yours got in up on Alpine."

"You're kidding."

"He said that one of the salt trucks—"

Deuce cut him off. "Yeah, yeah, Wayne, I know what happened." That bastard Lacy.

"You got a problem, you should've come to me, Deuce."

"Right, Wayne," Deuce said. Go to Wayne, nothing happens. Wayne was five months from retirement, but truth be known, he'd retired years ago. "You wanna hear my side of the story?" Deuce asked.

"Of course," Wayne assured him weakly.

Deuce gave him the rundown.

"It seems like to me," Wayne said, ignoring everything Deuce told him, "the distribution system's his operation. He says there's no problem, that's good enough for me."

"We're still missing the water, Wayne. It's out there somewhere."

"Yeah, I know, but just leave it go, will you? Ain't no big deal. Probably gone down one of the old lead mines or something." Wayne was a real go-getter.

"It's costing the city money, Wayne," Deuce said, reducing the problem to a form his boss could appreciate.

"Yeah, yeah, but we've left it go this long. A little longer don't make no difference."

"About five months longer?"

"What?"

"Nothin', Wayne, forget it. I won't harass poor Frank Lacy anymore."

"Do me a favor, okay, make sure you don't."

Disgusted, Deuce hung up. He sat staring at the wall of gauges and nursing his anger. For a time, he even regretted that he hadn't tried to arouse some enthusiasm for the democracy thing in Kevin Jungblut. It wasn't such a bad idea, he decided. Nobody gave a shit, but, what the fuck, come to think about it, it really wasn't such a goddamn bad idea after all.

Chapter 63

~

He should be looking for another city to manage. Paul Cutler slumped in his chair and listened glumly to El Plowman's campaign speech. Nothing else to call it—a campaign speech. Had no earthly place at a budget hearing. Of course, El wasn't the only offender. They all did it.

At the moment, however, Paul didn't much care. He was thinking about himself. As marriages sometimes straggle on, the life force drained out of them, so too the union between a city manager and the council at whose pleasure he served. Like husks, such spent relationships could crack and be dispersed to the four winds in an instant. At a bus accident, for instance, barely a year after he'd convinced the council to self-insure. He thought this and decided he should *already* be working in another city, enjoying another honeymoon with another city council.

El rattled on. She'd started by saying she understood the need to make budget cuts judiciously, then sounded for all the world as if she wanted equal cuts across the board, which wisdom she apparently received from some licensed practical nurse. Next she'd be going up to the psycho ward at St. Rafael's and asking the nutcases what they thought. She must have shaken her depression. She spoke with great energy and bluff good humor, cheerfully confessing the unsoundness of her proposals and making them anyway, as if any old idea was a good enough place to start from.

Paul wondered how he should handle this new evidence of apostasy. Or whether he needed to do anything. Perhaps, when the time came, he'd say a word or two, leave it at that.

In the back of the room, transit supporters were marshalling for the next item on the budget agenda. Out of the corner of his eye, Paul was aware of Kirk Moore, one of the organizers of the protest against cuts in the service, moving back and forth in a half stoop, an afterimage of Moore's ancient suit, of a kind of iridescent turquoise color, lingering at the corner of Paul's vision after Moore himself had moved out of range.

Paul went back to thinking about himself.

～

When El at last had finished, he realized with a slight start that nobody seemed in a rush to fill the void she had left, not even Roger Filer. Reminded of his intention to say a word or two, Paul roused himself out of his somnolence, putting aside the desire to treat her proposal with the scorn it deserved. Instead he agreed with her. That was really the only thing to do.

"Yes…," he began slowly, "It's true… The ideal is always to distribute the cuts equitably. We all want to do that, Madam Mayor. And certainly, in making cuts, when we have to, when it's unavoidable… We're concerned with quality of life issues. Surely, we don't want to cut everybody else and leave police and fire and streets alone. That would be a kind of fortress mentality. Even in closing the city garden a year ago, unavoidable, no alternative really, but done with only the greatest reluctance. What gives a city its identity and brings people back is what's unique or individualistic about it, like the flowerbeds along Grandview. Fortunately in that case, we were lucky enough to find volunteers, some little Dutch boys to plug that particular hole in our dike. We won't always be so lucky. But whether we are or not, we must never forget the ideal you've sketched so admirably."

Drily, El said, "Yes, of course." What else could *she* say? She was half smiling, understanding perfectly well his true feelings. "However," she continued, obviously not prepared to let him off so easily, "it seems to me, when we only have 16 percent of the registered voters participating in an election—that was the figure at the last local election, if you remember—then that suggests we have a problem, wouldn't you agree? It's not about equal cuts. Think about that idea any way you want. Impractical or not, it has been made in the right spirit, that's the important point. And beyond that, the critical issue is, how do we get the Janey Roches of this world more involved? Until we do, we've failed in our stewardship."

Roger Filer had been mighty quiet. He hardly seemed like a candidate at all, letting El hog all the airtime. But finally he felt moved to speak. "People don't trust us. That's what I think." His bass voice—which always reminded Paul of barbershop quartets—and his crooked nose and his bald pate all lent Roger an air of sincerity. "I was talking to a fellow came into my showroom the other day, fellow like me, you know, ran his own shop, well, not really, ran a one-man operation, but..." That was Filer's problem. He got off the point. Finally you stopped listening.

Paul returned to his private ruminations, happy to leave the posturing to El and Filer. It wasn't really his place to talk about such political matters; he was just the council's hired gun, after all. He mused over what he might have said, had the occasion allowed for total honesty. He sometimes had an impulse to tell the truth, to be as frank as Chuck Fellows, for instance, although frankness didn't seem to have made Fellows a happy man. People do distrust government, Filer was right, but mostly it was a way of covering their ignorance and indifference. They knew nothing about the issues and only voted when there was something on the ballot that touched a nerve. This time there was something that touched a nerve. This time there'd be more than a 16 percent turnout, El needn't worry on that score.

Paul also recognized the familial resemblance between this idea of getting more people involved and young Goetzinger's committee with no instructions. El, tainted by that as well, wanted more voices heard. They'd end up with a hubbub. And if truth telling had been an option, he would have pointed out that elections mostly served the purpose of giving corrupt politicians second thoughts. The city was run by the handful of people capable of running it. All societies were managed by small elites, Jackson no different from Lagos or Riyadh or Beijing. In Jackson, they were just a bit less honest about it was all.

Sometime later, after Roger Filer had made his point in the least interesting way possible and the exchange been exhausted to no particular conclusion, they went on to transit.

~

During the break, Paul returned to his office and discovered El with Johnny Pond in the reception area. El had dug the radio out of Paul's secretary's desk, and she and Pond were bent over it like a couple of conspirators, El slowly rotating the tuner through the welter of nighttime stations.

She waved him over, and the three of them listened as she turned past the weak, static-filled voices and songs and paused at the stronger ones only long enough to satisfy herself on some score before moving on.

"What is it?" Paul asked her.

"Aggie's mother stumbled onto a strange station last night."

"Strange?"

"A pirate," Johnny said. "FM. Low power. Whoever it is must have just set up shop. We heard a rumor about it this morning."

"A pirate radio station? Broadcasting what sort of stuff?"

"Against blacks coming here," El said.

Pond added, "Basically your good ol' boys' wet dream—country and western, Fourth of July music, racist vitriol—that's the skinny anyway. We tried to find it, but couldn't. Might be it's only on at night. Or could've already shut down, who knows."

"We should be so lucky," El said.

She landed on a station playing a C and W song, and paused, waiting for the tune to end.

"Speaking of rumors," Paul said to Pond, "I heard you're leaving."

"What?" El snapped her head around toward Pond.

"Who told you that?" Pond asked Paul.

"Is it true?"

"Oh, my gawd," El said, "just what we need. Tell me you're not."

In the way he had of distancing himself in conversations, Pond said, "Always found rumors interesting. Always wonder who stands to gain by them."

El looked at Pond narrowly. "Tell me you're not leaving."

"Got no plans to. Not at the moment."

"Good," she said, but kept on eyeing Pond. People denied true rumors all the time, and if Johnny left the city, it would be a slap in her face.

Paul was annoyed enough at El not to care.

The song had ended, and the announcer gave the station's call letters, a commercial outfit down in the Quad Cities. El exhaled, her head still canted up toward Pond, as if looking for some telltale sign in that expertly composed countenance, but when she spoke, it was to change the subject. "Tell Paul what you just told me." She returned to the radio and continued her progress across the FM band.

"Got a call on *Sound Off* today," Johnny said to Paul.

"Oh?" Paul had no use for the call-in program that Pond hosted, a megaphone for the local bellyachers.

"From David Duke," Pond said.

"David Duke? The Klan guy? You're kidding."

"Nope. It was him all right."

David Duke. Great. Wonderful. "Calling from where, Louisiana? How did he know about the show?"

"Got me."

"I suppose he didn't want to talk about the overage in the snow removal budget."

"Nope. Just El's plan to import people of color."

"We're not importing anybody," El corrected testily. "We'd like more African-Americans to move here. We want to create an atmosphere where they'll feel welcome. But we're not *bringing* anybody here, we're not *importing* people, we're not doing anything like that."

Such distinctions seemed mere hairsplitting to Paul. Anyway, whatever El thought she was doing, her scheme, if this latest development was any indication, was bearing strange and poisonous fruit. Paul could have predicted it.

The call to *Sound Off* would have been more than eight hours ago. He wondered why it had taken this long for him to find out.

"Tell me he's not thinking about coming here."

"Don't know," Pond replied. "I suggested it might not be such a good idea, being as how he's trying to reinvent himself as a Republican."

This statement, if you thought about it in a certain way, was truly depressing.

"Let's hope the hell he stays away," Paul said.

El continued her search for the pirate station. As she fiddled with the dial, trying to tune in another station more clearly, she said, "Whether he comes or not, we need to repudiate Duke in no uncertain terms. Duke and all his ilk."

On the station she'd just found, someone was making a speech. A calm, reasonable voice. She started to turn past the station, but something stopped her, and she jiggled the knob again, sharpening the signal. The three of them listened. As is often the case with reasoned discourse, it was difficult at first to understand exactly what point the speaker was trying to make.

"Speak of the devil," Pond said.

~

Making his way back to his seat for the second half of the budget hearing, a curious idea occurred to Paul. If things got bad enough, if Duke actually did come to Jackson and there were riots and who the hell knows what else happened, perhaps El Plowman would be elected mayor after all.

CHAPTER 64

~

See where you went and talked to the mayor," Fionna Hennefy said, startling Janey.

They were sitting at the kitchen table as Janey took Fionna's pulse.

"How did you find out?" Janey had told several people of her unhappy visit with El Plowman, but not Fionna, who'd been so scornful of the idea in the first place.

"On the TV there."

"What?" Janey was shocked, and she lost count and had to start over.

"Cut everything the same, wasn't that what you said? Had the city council meeting on for a little bit last night. The mayor was yakking about that. Figured she had to get it from you."

Janey shook her head. "That's right, I did go and talk to her, but she told me wasn't nothing to it, it was naive. Just like you did. I don't understand." Recalling the interview with the mayor caused sympathetic pains in her knees.

"Hmm," said Fionna.

"What did she say?"

"Don't know."

"You just said you were watching."

"Tried to," Fionna said. "Couldn't. Pish, who can sit still for stuff like that?"

Janey felt disappointed…and a little betrayed, although she knew perfectly well the old lady channel-surfed all the time. As she recorded the readings in her notebook, she wondered whether she should be mad. Had sharing the pain been a good idea all along? Had El Plowman stole it? If the idea was so stupid, as the mayor said, what business had she got bringing it up? Nobody made a fool of herself on purpose.

"I just don't understand," Janey said again.

After she finished in the kitchen, she went out to the bedside table and counted the number of pills in each of Fionna's vials of medication. The Blessed Virgin, no longer on storm duty, was back in her usual niche in the small shrine.

Before she changed the sheets, Janey paused and stared out of the picture window, thinking. For a moment, no traffic passed, and behind the silence she could hear a faint sound like water, like a river current heard far away. Perhaps, she mused, the mayor had changed her mind. Janey could almost believe that. Most of the time, when she recalled their talk, she just felt dumb. But a couple of times… It was like when she caught herself unawares in a mirror and for the briefest of instants looked pretty again.

On the tiny surviving strip of front lawn, only the very top leaves of a rhododendron struggled to hold themselves above the tide of white, the leaves still green, bowed down about the end of the upper branch, reminding her of prayer.

If only…

A big semi truck passed, and the storm door rattled in its wake. She heard Fionna behind her, and the momentary spell was broken. The curtain scraped as it closed.

Fionna liked to make little gestures of helping as Janey changed the sheets on the hospital bed. When, two months ago, the massive thing had arrived and Janey had been trying to contrive a way to avoid setting it up in the living room, all Fionna said was, "No matter. Make do." She dismissed social conventions with little backward flips of her hand. "All my friends are dead anyway. Nobody left to disapprove. Traipse around naked if I want to."

Fionna liked the bed. "Got all the bells and whistles," she had said.

The clean bottom sheet fluttered down.

"I don't know what I could have been thinking about," Janey mused. "I wonder if I should go see her again."

"Hmm."

Janey knew what that meant.

"Maybe Plowman's got something up her sleeve," Fionna said, talking mostly to herself. "Like to think so. Better rascals than incompetents, that's what I say."

Fionna approved of rascals. She considered Nixon the greatest modern president. "Went to China," she had once explained to

Janey. "Woulda given everybody a minimum income, if they'da let him. Look it up. He was a crook, too, of course." Little dismissive waves as she turned away, her mind already on something else.

The second sheet fluttered down.

"Don't know what I was thinking," Janey repeated.

She felt the pain in her knees.

CHAPTER 65

~

Lacy'd go bugfuck if he knew I was here."
Kevin Jungblut had agreed to meet Deuce only long enough to give him the sonophone and show him exactly where the break had been on Alpine. Jungblut was hardly an imposing figure. His eyes were watery and uncertain. He wore long sideburns, popular in the 1960s, and a mustache shaped like a dog bone.

"After you talked to Frank, he drove over here and looked around."

This surprised Deuce. He always assumed Lacy had the courage of his intolerances. "Find anything?"

"Nah. Not with all this fucking snow. He did what you're gonna do." Jungblut nodded toward the sonophone.

"Too bad he didn't do it two months ago."

Jungblut shrugged.

"Show me where the leak was."

Gingerly, the three men, Deuce and Jungblut and Seth Brunel, the assistant city engineer, made their way down the slope, Deuce hauling his paraphernalia: hydrant book, tape measure, and snow shovel.

"Here." They'd stopped along a stretch where no cars had been parked. Deuce looked for traces of J.J.'s accident. Long gone, of course.

"We opened her up down there first." Kevin pointed toward the foot of the street. "Worked our way back uphill until we found the break." Jungblut lined himself up on a nearby house, moving a few feet back up the hill, and then pointed down. "Right about here." Below the ice and hardpacked snow, the pavement remained invisible.

"So you had half the goddamn street dug up."

"Yeah."

"And Lacy tells me it was a routine job."

"Don't necessarily mean nothing. Breaks on hills are a bitch. Water can come to the surface way the hell and gone away from where it broke."

"That's right," Seth Brunel said, standing a short distance away, conducting his own inspection of the area. "On top of everything else, the carbonate rocks are porous. Water migrates through them, might come to the surface anywhere."

Deuce was well aware of all this, but it didn't make any difference, Lacy had been stonewalling all the way.

"Any sign of runoff while you were making the repair?"

"It was like the other day." Kevin told him, referring to Deuce's visit to Lacy and his crew. "We couldn't valve it off completely. But I don't know, didn't seem like there was a shitload of water or nothing, just enough to make the fucking job miserable as usual."

"When was this?" Seth asked.

"December 3."

"Good memory."

"Frank looked it up," Jungblut said to Deuce.

"Busy covering his ass, isn't he?" Deuce observed with some satisfaction. What a jerkoff.

"I'll tell you," Brunel, who had ignored this exchange, said, following his own line of reasoning, "it was mighty cold back then. The frost already pretty deep. Water follows the path of least resistance, so it could have been diverted. Fact you didn't find much doesn't mean it wasn't there."

"You need me for anything else?" Jungblut asked.

"No," Deuce told him.

"Just make sure you get that back to me, okay?" He indicated the sonophone.

Deuce nodded.

"Before tomorrow night. I need it for Monday, or my ass is grass."

"Don't worry. And thanks, Kevin, I mean it."

"Yeah, sure." As Jungblut backed away, he added, "Nobody'll go against Frank, you know."

"About what?"

"The democracy thing. Frank would figure a way to get one of his guys on your committee. I don't know how, but he'd do it."

Deuce held up the sonophone. "You gave me this."

"Yeah, well, the son of a bitch just went too far the other day, that's all."

"And usually he's so reasonable."

To this Jungblut merely shook his head.

"What was that all about?" Seth asked as they watched the receding figure.

Deuce told him the story while they moved slowly back up the hill themselves.

The leak, if there was one, had to be somewhere above. Deuce stopped to listen with the sonophone at a hydrant that had been shoveled out, then handed the instrument to Seth so he could listen, too.

"So you're the one proposed the committee with no instructions," Seth said as they continued upward. "I heard about that. Are you guys really serious?"

"Sure, why not?" Deuce didn't know much about Brunel aside from the fact that he had a fondness for caves and tunnels and such. Anyway, he was management, not to be trusted.

"Why not?" Brunel responded. "Well, for one thing, most of what we do in engineering is technical, not the sort of stuff you could, I don't know, take a vote on. If that's what this committee of yours is supposed to be doing."

"It's given no instructions."

"So it could do anything."

"That's right. Could decide to have a big blowout pig roast every year. Or to disband. Whatever."

At the top, they paused and turned their attention back to the matter at hand. Seth talked about the carbonate rocks of the Galena Formation.

"The carbonates are susceptible to solution by the groundwater, so you got sinkholes and caves all over the place up here."

"I figured the missing water could've ended up in one of the old mines."

"Could be." Brunel smiled and nodded. This was an idea that obviously appealed to him.

At the corner of Grandview Boulevard, they used the hydrant book and tape measure to locate the next fireplug.

"You'd think what with all the announcements, people'd dig out their hydrants."

After he'd shoveled the top free of snow, Deuce pressed the tip of the sonophone's metal stud against the operating nut and bent over to listen through the device, which was shaped like an old-fashioned telephone handset.

"Here," he said and handed it to the engineer, who took his turn. "Wha'd'ya hear?"

"Nothing," Seth said.

"Right. That either means no leak or a huge one. The bigger the leak, the harder to hear."

"I know," Seth said. "Silence is ominous."

"Or not."

"One might wonder, then, what we think we're doing."

"A question," Deuce admitted, "a lotta people been asking me of late."

Seth thought about that and said, "I've got an idea. Follow me."

At the Y-intersection a block farther along stood Keefer's Market, and it was here that Brunel led.

Unceremoniously, he asked the old man behind the counter, "Can we go downstairs, Andy?"

"Sure." Andy, the counterman, seemed utterly unsurprised at the visit. "Better take a light, Seth." He fetched a flashlight from the shelf below the counter. As Deuce and Seth began to move away, the old man added, "You'll need this, too," and handed the city engineer a claw hammer.

In the basement, they moved a bunch of boxes piled against one of the walls.

"You've been here before," Deuce suggested.

"Was a time, a bit ago, I practically lived down here."

"What is it?"

"You'll see."

A large sheet of plywood had been nailed to the studs and pink insulation stuffed behind it. Seth pried the nails out and peeled away the plywood and insulation to reveal a void large enough to crawl through.

"Okay, Alice," he said, grinning, "into the rabbit hole."

With the flashlight, he swept away the cobwebs, stooped over and inched his way through. Deuce followed.

"Welcome to the Gobaith Mine." They squatted on their haunches. "Gobaith is Welsh for hope," Seth explained. "Most of the old lead miners were Welsh."

Deuce thought about that. "Hope's okay, I suppose." But he didn't believe in it. To hope meant to be disappointed. "Patience is better," he said. Patience without expectations, the way he played poker.

"This used to be the biggest mine in Jackson." Brunel swept the beam of the flashlight along the tunnel to the right. "The main adit runs three quarters of a mile west, clear to the city golf course, with all sorts of offshoots." He swept the beam to the left, pointing with it. "That's what we're interested in. Only goes a couple hundred feet this way. Used to come out down on the side of the bluff. That's where the original entrance was. Got a couple of shafts go straight down, too. So better watch your step."

The adit was high enough to walk, hunched over as if they carried great weights on their backs.

Seth said, "They almost opened the Gobaith again during the Second World War. That's how bad the metal shortages got back then."

Deuce barely listened. He was thinking of his mother and father, of the night he and the old man spent in Whistler Number Two, while his mother was lost...slowly freezing to death in the snow. "Okay, here we are," the engineer said, "I told you it wasn't very far. I think there's enough room for you to squeeze up here beside me, but be careful."

Shoulder to shoulder, they peered down a narrow shaft; the beam of the flashlight illuminated masses of old cobwebs.

"Boy, you find cobwebs in the darnedest places," Seth said. Straight down, the beam reached only blackness.

"Ore deposits formed along the vertical joints in the dolomite, and the miners went down after it." He picked up a stone and dropped it. They waited for the sound as it hit bottom. Nothing. "If your water got into one of these shafts, it's long gone."

Around them, all was bone dry. A dusty, sterile odor. Deuce pressed the sonophone against the side of the shaft, and could hear a low rumbling noise, like the ruminations of the earth itself. He handed the instrument to Brunel, who listened for a few moments and said, "Traffic on Grandview."

"Yeah. Shit." Deuce felt like he was on a fool's errand. "Hardly seems worth it."

"Eh, who knows? Might get lucky."

They stepped gingerly over the hole and stooped farther along, to a second shaft, where they dropped another stone into the void.

Seth went on at once, obviously into the hunt now. A mystery to be solved. They turned back and started snooping along side passages, going down passage after passage, each one pretty much like the last, utterly dry, no sign of Deuce's water.

"I trust you know the way back out," he said.

"No prob. Been down here a million times."

Judging strictly by Brunel's avidness, however, the intricate way he traced along an overhead seam with the beam of his flashlight or stopped to peer at some little nothing, he might have been canvassing the place for the first time. As for Deuce, well, he decided they'd find no water no matter how many passages they searched. The whole thing was a waste of time.

"You really like this stuff, huh, old mines?" he asked Brunel as they snooped along yet another offshoot of the system.

"Yup."

"Why? What's the attraction?" For Deuce, who was interested in so little, the interests of others remained mysterious, like willful delusions.

But Seth only paused long enough to look back and say, "Do I have to have a reason?"

"Suppose not."

Maybe, Deuce decided as they resumed the search, that was why he didn't mind wasting his time, letting Brunel have his fun. There was always something suspect about reasons.

Finally, back up on top, they dug out more hydrants and listened with the sonophone. They talked to people they met along the way. They found no trace of Deuce's water. A day of busted hands.

But he didn't mind. That was the whole point about patience.

~

PART V

~

CHAPTER 66

~

Johnny Pond woke up. He listened. Beside him, his wife Chloe breathed softly. He lifted his head slightly from the pillow. The kids' rooms first. Front hallway. Living room.

Outside.

He threw off the covers and banged his bad knee against a chair as he lurched toward the window in the darkness and swept the curtain aside.

It took him one, two, three stabs with his leg before his trousers became unsnarled and he could jerk them up and buckle his belt, no time to zip up, no time for socks. Shoes? Shit, shit, no time!

"What is it?" Chloe asked sleepily.

"Call the cops. Keep the girls inside." He stopped for a beat and hissed, "Don't let them go out!" and then took the stairs three at a time, jamming the balls of his feet against the wooden treads, pain exploding in his bad knee. He limped past the coat rack, grabbing at his jacket, which caught and fell from his hand and was abandoned.

Outside, he couldn't see the burning cross, visible from the second floor window, but only sparks and a glow rising from behind the snowbank near the mailbox. The pickup truck, far down the street, had almost disappeared. He hardly felt the cold on his feet and bare chest as he limped around the front of the Toyota, scrabbling in his pocket for the keys.

The car started immediately. "Good," he said aloud and floored it, in reverse, bouncing hard across the apron of the driveway and into the street, swinging the nose sharply around as he jammed the accelerator down. The tires spun on the pavement, then caught, and the little car surged from gear to gear, gaining speed.

"Motherfucker!" he yelled after the truck.

Its taillights disappeared around a corner far ahead. "Couler Ave, Couler Ave. That's okay, I got 'em, that's okay." He kept the accelerator pressed to the floor, the car climbing the street, picking up speed as he massaged his ruined knee, his eye on the point where the taillights had vanished. He started his turn before he reached the corner, the car sliding as it yawed to the left and slammed sideways into a snowbank. The taillights reappeared, still far ahead. "Good, good, that's okay."

The wheel spun beneath Johnny—"C'mon, c'mon, c'mon!"— then caught, the car lunging forward. His sudden calmness surprised him. He drove without headlights. The truck disappeared again, and again Johnny kept his eye on the spot and then rammed around the corner, the taillights coming back into view.

But the situation had suddenly changed. The lights were closer, much closer.

Motherfucker had eased up. Must think he was in the clear, must not know Johnny was coming on, gaining, gaining. "Good, this is good, man," he said quietly to himself and then yelled, "I got your ass now, you motherfucking bastard!"

Suddenly the truck took off again. "Shit! Knows I'm here. That's okay, that's okay." No way he'll get away now. Had him dead to rights. Johnny rubbed his knee, and let his calmness settle back in.

The truck took another corner, starting the turn too late and for an instant rising up on two tires, almost flipping over. Johnny eased up slightly as he followed, in no rush now. It was like the old days, playing linebacker, as he'd drift along behind the line, almost amused, waiting for some running back to roll the dice. No pads today. And he was beginning to feel the cold, on his feet, on his chest, seeping through his fly and chilling his cock. His anger had withdrawn a short distance, lay coiled within him.

The car handled well. He regretted letting Chloe talk him into the cheaper model, not the V-6 with the overhead cam engine. "See!" he argued with her now. You never knew what was gonna come up.

The pickup seemed to hesitate, then swerved onto the access road separating one of the city's western developments from the countryside. They were heading out into the county where the roads were long and straight, and if they had anything under the hood, they could lose him. Johnny took the curve neatly, the taillights back in view. He was driving on rutty snow now, the car shimmying, the wheels spinning and catching, spinning and catching.

"Come on, come on, come on!" he yelled, jamming the pedal down with all of his 250 pounds.

The truck swerved again, right, left, fishtailing, then righting itself and darting down one of the streets in the development.

"Ya dumb motherfuck!" Johnny yelled. "Gotcha!" He slowed and swung wide, then cut the corner so tight he heard the snow-bank rubbing along the side door.

He was close enough to see in the cab now. Three of 'em. Gun rack in the back window. "Motherfuck," he said again, but quietly this time.

The truck kicked up a rooster tail of snow as it tried to acceler-ate between the rows of dark houses. At the last moment, it turned wildly again, sideswiping a parked car. Couldn't make up their minds. The dumb fucks were driving by committee.

They were heading back toward the county. Too late now, Johnny right on their ass.

They careened out of the development and onto the access road again, Johnny next to them for a moment but unable to cut them off, so falling back, thinking, *best not ruin Chloe's car*. At the county road, the truck again turned too quickly, drifting sideways. Johnny, anticipating, had already slowed and swung wide, into the oncoming lane.

The whole scene lay before him, the truck motionless, its back wheels spinning as he passed on the inside, cutting off the escape route just as the drive wheels caught, but now, with nowhere to go, the truck merely lurched forward, turning away from Johnny and into the snow bank at the side of the road, its nose riding up and over the snow, its taillights flipping abruptly up and disappearing.

Johnny was out of his car and over the ridge of snow, limp-ing, his bare feet plunging through the crust, but still coming on. Below, the truck sat, upright, buried up to its frame, its headlights flung far across the snow. He glanced at the gun rack in the back window. Fishing rods.

The three men were already outside, the biggest of them coming up the embankment toward Johnny. Cursing, the fellow crouched, beginning to circle, his fists held low. Johnny's anger had kicked back in, and he went straight at the man, ignored his feints and swung and caught him flush and put him down, motionless in the snow. He turned his attention to the other two.

His anger was really up now. One of the others stood passively near the truck. The third one, nearer to hand, a small, mean-looking fellow, held a tire iron in one hand.

"You got one shot, motherfucker. Make it good," Johnny told him.

The fellow stood his ground, waving the metal rod, waiting. Johnny advanced, limping, sinking into the snow, no longer feeling his feet. He swept his forearm up, blocking the iron, feeling a sharp pain, first on his forearm, then a stinging blow glancing off the side of his head. The fellow tried to launch a second blow, but Johnny seized the weapon and with a howl hurled it into the night.

The first attacker had begun to stir and the one over by the truck was scrambling on his hands and knees for the crest of the embankment, but Johnny ignored them. He wasn't through with the mean-looking one.

Stripped of his weapon, the little bastard was attempting to get away, but Johnny plunged through the snow and grabbed him and wrenched him around and up off the ground to get a better look before he destroyed the motherfucker. The light from the truck, reflected from the snow, illuminating the fellow's face from below, and Johnny saw with satisfaction the fear that had come into his eyes. How easy to smash this worm into nothing. Johnny felt the satisfaction of it. How often he'd wanted to bash some white face.

Rising in the distance, a siren. The fellow flopped around, trying to get loose, and Johnny shook him violently back and forth, and when he stopped, the white guy continued to cringe and try to twist himself free, making strange little noises. The siren came closer.

"Please," the other said, "please," and no longer struggled but merely whimpered, trying to fold himself up into the fetal position, to protect his nuts. Johnny hit him once and then, with disgust, flung the vile, insignificant creature into the snow.

Johnny's anger, unrelieved, grew, filling him, engulfing him, bursting from him, and he turned away and screamed into the blackness.

CHAPTER 67

❧

Chuck Fellows pushed the coffee cup away. Diane had turned off the radio, creating a local silence, against which beat the whoops of Todd and his new friend, playing in the living room.

"One of Johnny Pond's daughters is Gracey's age," Diane said.

"What, Mommy?" Gracey asked, looking up from the floor, where she was kneeling on the comic page of the morning paper, making up stories to go with the pictures, since she couldn't read yet.

"Nothing, dear," Diane told her.

The Des Moines Register had been divvied out, and Diane laid her section open on the counter and read standing up. Nothing in it about the incident, which had occurred too late to make the paper. The report on the radio had been sketchy, Chuck's attention drawn not so much to the ages of Johnny Pond's daughters as to the cross burners themselves, unemployed construction workers. At least the two who had been identified were construction workers, the third a minor and not named.

Chuck looked out the kitchen window, where the overcast and old snow drained the air of color.

"Think about having to explain something like that to your kids," Diane said. "We're very lucky."

Chuck patted his thigh and Gracey bounced up and came skipping over and sat in his lap. He asked her what she was going to do that day and she refused to tell him, grinning and shaking her head in the coy, stubborn way she had, a little game the two of them played.

Chuck joshed with her, making mock threats about what he was going to do if she didn't tell him and feeling her restlessness beneath his hands. Diane was right, he supposed, they were lucky. Chuck didn't feel it for himself, but for Gracey and Todd, who could grow up without the burden of prejudice. He looked for signs of the person his daughter would become, still invisible beneath the pug nose and the enormous dark pupils of her eyes, those pupils all but hiding the whites, as if she took in the world in great visual gulps. Sometimes—not this morning—they would stare at each other for a brief interlude, each baffled by the other, like strangers meeting on a journey.

Soon she had wiggled off his lap and gone back to be near her mother. She had been sticking even closer to Diane of late, since Todd had mutated, become disturbingly different, an object of awe. Suddenly, he had friends. The year before he'd been a loner and Chuck had worried that he was accomplishing nothing with the kid except instructing him in the art of chronic dissatisfactions. Now something had happened, some new flowering in Todd's neural system, and he had best friends and subsidiary friends and enemies of various sorts—even the recent troubles at school part of this new gregariousness—and Chuck realized his fears had been absurd. They'd had nothing to do with Todd, just his own egotistical imaginings. His son had a fate of his own.

As if these thoughts had conjured the boy himself, the sounds from the other room grew louder, on the move, and Todd came storming through the kitchen with his friend, in the middle of their game. On an impulse, Chuck asked him if he wanted to go down to the river, see the dredge again—his friend could come, too—but Todd dropped an indifferent "No" in his wake.

"Suit yourself," Chuck said, but his son had already disappeared, leaving the words stranded.

"You'll have better luck if you catch him alone," Diane suggested, coming over to switch sections of the paper.

"Up to him." Chuck pushed the coffee cup farther away. Despite this show of unconcern on his part, he felt the power of his son's indifference. "Anyway, I'm off."

～

In his truck, he turned on the radio and listened to the news, mostly a repeat from earlier: the cross burning the night before, the coming of David Duke on Monday. Driving through the quiet Saturday morning streets, he seemed to feel the rising tension of the place. The fermentation of hatreds.

He imagined Johnny Pond chasing the cross burners. He imagined again what he would have done if somebody pulled that kind of stunt on his family. His hands closed around the steering wheel, his foot tensed on the accelerator, but the 4x4 continued its measured pace from block to block.

Down on Apple Island, he stopped at the discharge pipe and told Albert Furlong, the endman, to get on the horn, he needed a lift out to the dredge. The call made, Chuck didn't leave at once, but lingered for the simple pleasure of watching the slurry of water and sand spilling onto the edge of the track site.

"When did you say you wanted this job done?" Furlong asked. Over his parka, he wore a stained orange work vest.

"Didn't say. How's your production?"

"Fifteen maybe. Better ask Bud."

"Just as long as we've got enough for the road." The site would be a swamp come the spring thaw, not long now. "Might need some for berming, too. When the water comes up." Sand was far from the ideal barrier material against floodwater, but it was usable in a pinch.

"Do the best we can," Furlong told him.

"All I ask."

Chuck looked past the idling dozer, along the winding artificial channel draining the dredged water back toward the Mississippi, where in the distance, partly obscured by the bare, black webbing of cottonwood branches, the runoff had melted the snow, forming a shallow lake atop the ice. The lake glinted, a sheen of silver in the gray morning light.

～

On the dredge, Albert's brother Sidney fetched a set of ear-plugs for Chuck, and they walked around, conversing in yells and pantomime. The port swing wire had frayed and would need to be replaced. Gunshot-like cracks rang out as the wire wound back onto the drum of the winch, fusillades of river water firing off it.

Chuck climbed the accommodation ladder into the lever room.

"Bastard's okay for the moment," Bud Pregler told him, as he set and released brakes and clutches in the leverman's intricate rhythm, all the time keeping an eye on his gauges. "Figured out there's a current, even way in here. Gotta step the bastard harder to port." Chuck could hear the triumph in Pregler's voice.

The dredge vibrated continuously. Around the base of his coffee mug, a spill shivered, like wind-scuffed water. Outside, up at the bow, ice fenders clung. Years in the future, when he had forgotten everything else, Chuck would remember the ice. Even on a dull day, the decks gleamed with it. Rinds of white, like crystals in the heart of a geode, coated the framing of the cutter head. They might have been an icebreaker in the Arctic Ocean.

Slowly the dredge swung through the black water, the snow-bound riverscape beyond. "Shift's mighty long when you're getting good production," Pregler said, a fixed complaint, made whenever Chuck came on board.

"Al Furlong said you're only pumping 15 percent sand."

Pregler glanced at his pressure gauge. "Hard to tell. Might be. Ain't like this is a science or anything. Anyway, the sand's good. Could pump more, I suppose, at least in theory. Problem is, we're pumping pretty near as far as we can, using up a lot of our capacity just pushing water. Got to keep it moving or the sand starts to drop out inside the pipe and we slug the bastard."

"What if we shorten the line?" They'd discussed this before—pump to a spoil area nearby and haul the sand from there up onto the track site.

"Your call, boss."

They talked about it, Pregler all the while engaged in his endless repetitions as the dredge moved back and forth across the cut, and Chuck said he'd do some calculations to estimate how much they could increase the dredge's output by pumping the sand only as far as the nearest point on the island that could be used for temporary storage.

"One more thing," he told Pregler. "At some point this spring, we're gonna be out of business. I went to the second Corps of Engineers flood meeting yesterday."

"They make a prediction this time?"

"Twenty-five feet."

Pregler looked back over his shoulder, making a small O of his mouth, a whistling gesture, his red lips surrounding coffee- and cigarette-stained teeth, the whole enveloped by his massive black beard. "That'd be pretty much a record, wouldn't it?"

"Except for '65. And not much below that."

Pregler went back to his gauges, shaking his head.

"Assuming they're right," Chuck told him. "But even if they aren't, we're gonna have to stop pumping at some point."

Pregler nodded.

"I figure," Chuck continued, "when stage gets to fourteen or fifteen." They'd known all along that the work would be interrupted by the spring rise, but the Corps announcement had the effect of a starter's gun. "Not much time," Chuck told Pregler, "and we'll need as much sand as we can get between now and then." They had maybe a month.

"Shorten the line," Pregler said.

"Tell you Monday morning."

"Maybe run around the clock."

"You think you're up for that?"

"What about the guy who used to run the dredge? Turcotte?"

"I'll never use him," Chuck said at once. "No fucking way."

Pregler looked forward toward the river and the large, ancient circular saw they had used to score the ice before they cut blocks of it free and hauled them out of the way. "Sometimes a man's got to swallow his pride," he said.

~

Chuck didn't go home directly, but drove around the city, looking at infrastructure, what little he could see, like a fence rider on a ranch. A new storm was tracking to the north, mostly sparing them this time, at least until the snow melted and ran off into the Mississippi and its tributaries and headed south. He hadn't talked to Walt Plowman recently, not since they'd been out sampling for Higgins Eye mussels. About time to start checking in with Walt on a more regular basis.

He turned on the news. Turned it off. Thought about John Turcotte. No way, no fucking way he'd ever go hat in hand to Turcotte. He thought about that and realized the strength and weakness in it, and that finally it made no difference whether he went to Turcotte or not, that he failed either way. If he did go, he might be able to pump more sand was all.

The garage door opener didn't work, and he'd forgotten to get a new battery for it. He parked outside the house and sat in the 4x4, staring at nothing in particular, reluctant to go inside. As the light snow landed on the windshield, gusts of wind blew some of it away, an intricate pattern of adding and subtracting.

Inside, he found Diane and Gracey in the dining room, Gracey learning how to do beadwork. But as soon as Chuck appeared, Diane decided it was time for Gracey's nap, which meant she had some matter to discuss.

"Where's Todd?"

"Over at his friend's house. They've been back and forth all day. I'll be right down. Don't go away."

She herded Gracey upstairs, and Chuck went out to the kitchen and got a beer and waited, remembering Todd's total absorption in his game that morning and his indifference to his father.

"What is it?" he asked Diane as soon as she returned. She noticed his beer and went to the cupboard for a wine glass, got the Chablis out of the fridge and poured herself a half glass, which she brought over to the table. It had been some time since they'd had one of their companionable chats at the kitchen table, him with his beer and her with her wine.

She didn't waste time. No nonsense, just like Chuck. One of the things she'd picked up during their marriage.

"It's Todd's new friend," she said. "I don't know, maybe it wasn't him, maybe it was his father. Anyway… It's about the cross burning. Or at least that started it." Diane paused, and Chuck waited. "And what they told him isn't…I don't know…prejudiced exactly. Basically, that Jackson's a white man's town, that blacks have their places and whites theirs, and people like to live among their own kind. You know the argument."

"Yes."

"If you're Todd's age, there's a certain logic."

"No matter what age, you happen to live in a place like Jackson."

"Yes, well… And he likes the little boy. Apparently the father, too. They might be likable, who knows? That counts for a lot with an eight-year-old. Likableness. As much as the logic."

In this simple way, Chuck found an action he could undertake unalloyed with baser impulses.

Chapter 68

~

El Plowman drove slowly up to the house, looking for signs of the cross burning. Nothing visible except an area directly in front where the snow had been disturbed and someone had placed a bouquet of flowers. As she pulled into the empty driveway, she wondered at the absence of cars. The place appeared to have been abandoned.

She turned off the motor and set the emergency brake and for a minute sat in the mournful silence.

The house seemed such an ordinary dwelling, neat and modest and traditional with its white clapboard siding and green shutters. The last place where this sort of thing should happen. She still couldn't quite believe it. Why Johnny Pond? Simply incomprehensible. Johnny, the football hero at the university, the popular newsman and call-in host, who time after time had gone to bat for his disgruntled listeners. It made no sense at all, not a shred, and some sliver of her mind still expected that in the end it would turn out to have been nothing more than a tragic mistake. As if that wasn't bad enough.

El got out and approached the front door.

She rang the bell once and waited, then a second time and continued to wait, and finally from some precinct deep in the house, steps approached, the heavy tread of a man. The door opened. For a moment, they looked at each other through the storm door. Johnny wore trousers in some sort of heavy material and a plaid shirt, which gave him the look of a lumberman, a black Paul Bunyan. His left arm was in a sling, the left side of his head bandaged. He pushed the outer door partway open.

"What happened?" El asked. The news story had said only that Johnny had been taken to the hospital and then released. "Are you all right?"

He ignored the question. "Glad you came," he said, but he didn't make way for her to enter. "Been thinking about you."

Behind him the house remained silent. Perhaps he had sent his wife and children away. He leaned on the doorjamb and started to talk.

"You know what your problem is, Eleanor? You think you're entitled. We warned you. The day you came to Pearl and Hiram Johnson's house, after the museum was trashed. Do you remember, Eleanor? They told you they didn't want nothing to do with the museum exhibit anymore. That was a warning. I spelled it out for you later that day. Expect you can recall that, too, if you try real hard. We went to the Three Annes Café. I told you nothing you could do but make matters worse. And then down at Washington Park—couldn't have been more than two, three weeks ago—I said it again. Nobody ever elected you to save Jackson from itself. I told you, we all told you, but you went ahead anyway. You imagined the good you were gonna do, and ignored the harm. Ain't that right, Eleanor?"

El didn't know what she had expected, but not this. She attempted to say something, but he just raised his voice and continued.

"The difference between you and me, Eleanor, is I don't forget what color I am. But whites like you, you act like you ain't got no color. Your whiteness is like the air you breathe. You don't understand your own color. What chance you got to understand anybody else's?

"None. You got no chance. And I'll tell you something else. Those boys I caught last night, they understood. They understood more than you do. They're mostly ignorant, those boys, the kind of lowlifes I wouldn't wipe my shoes on. But they know what color they are, Eleanor. They know color makes a difference.

"I blame them. But I blame you, too. I blame you more. They're rattlesnakes, but rattlesnakes don't strike unless they're provoked. Somebody's got to come along and start poking around in their nests. Somebody like you. That's when they strike.

"And you know who they hit? Who they sink their fangs into? Who gets filled up with their poison? Not you. Uh-uh. Not me, neither. Hell, I know all about this shit. Can't grow up in the projects without learning there are a lot of white motherfuckers out there. Not even my wife, not her, she knows. But my little girls, my dear, innocent little girls. What, for God's sake, have you done to them?!"

The words poured out of him. El could not say that he was wrong. She tried to speak, to apologize, to defend herself, but his words just continued to roll over hers, and finally he dismissed her, slammed the door in her face, and she went away angry and distraught.

As she backed out of the driveway, another car was stopping, out at the curb, and a little white girl got out and placed a second bouquet beside the first one.

CHAPTER 69

～

Perhaps it was just the blindfold she wore, but they seemed to have driven for a long time. Rachel Brandeis, the special assignment reporter for the *Jackson Tribune*, guessed the driver must be doubling back, trying to confuse her. Absurd. He must have seen too many spy movies. She balanced the camera on her knees and noticed that she'd closed her eyes.

"Wait," was all the man riding on the passenger side of the front seat said when she had asked a question. The driver said nothing.

Despite her nervous energy, she found herself beginning to lull off, swaying to the movement of the car. She remembered as a young child returning at the end of summer from their cabin in South Fallsburg, eyes closed and drowsy in the backseat, listening to the disembodied voices of her parents and brothers.

This pleasant memory vanished as she sensed something moving close to her, the sensation not visual, rather a minute shift in the air around her head, a prickling in her nostrils. She reached up to swat it away, but felt nothing. Her edginess returned.

She tried once more to engage the two men in the front seat in conversation, again without luck. But talking herself helped a little, creating the illusion that she partly controlled the situation.

She felt the object passing in front of her face again, again reached up to shove it aside, and as before felt nothing.

"Okay, kill the lights," the man in the passenger's seat said to the driver.

The car slowed, then turned, and the smooth humming of the tires broke up into a rough, gravelly sound.

They led her, still blindfolded, inside a building, going up several steps (she counted them, four) across a short porch (two paces) and through a door. She didn't know what possible use this information might be. More spy movie stuff. She stumbled on the sill.

"Oops, there," the voice said, and a strong hand gripped her elbow. She was guided through a room, perhaps two rooms, and then felt fingers working at the knot of the blindfold a moment before it was swept away to a flash of brightness.

"Welcome to Radio Free Jackson," the voice said as it came around from behind her. She blinked away the glare and looked up into a face covered with a ski mask, only the eyes visible.

"I'm Harlen," the mask said, the words partly muffled. "You can call me Harlen." He had stopped, like a man peering around a corner, his chin cocked at an angle beneath the rough fabric of the mask. The blindfold dangled from his fingers. "That's Ray over there, on the air." Ray also wore a mask. He sat in front of a microphone, surrounded by a semicircle of card tables on which several pieces of primitive-looking equipment had been arrayed. He acknowledged the introduction with a briefly lifted finger. Along with the mask, he wore surgical gloves.

"And this," said Harlen, indicating the last man in the room, "is Sparks, our technical wizard."

Sparks? Rachel thought. He had to be kidding.

The triumvirate of radio pirates all wore masks. Surgical gloves, too. Rachel found something more ominous about the gloves.

"Sparks is our main man," Harlen was saying. "We treat him real good. Had his radio engineer license when he was ten years old or something."

"Sixteen," Sparks corrected. His head was so distinctive, tall and narrow, his eyes at the very bottom of the eye holes, that the mask seemed barely to disguise him.

Now he left the room and she heard his footfalls on stairs and in the room directly overhead.

"Sparks is also our lookout," Harlen explained.

"You're expecting someone?" she asked. The windows were covered with blackout curtains, a World War II touch.

"Never can tell," Harlen answered. Unlike Sparks, his personality didn't burst out of his mask, his head of no unusual shape, his eyes an unremarkable brown, with crow's-feet at the corners the only distinguishing marks.

Rachel began to unpack her camera.

"Remember," Harlen cautioned her.

"Don't worry."

She knew the rules, frontal shots verboten, masks or no masks. These minions of David Duke were taking no chances. She hoped to snap a profile or two, for any help that might provide in figuring out exactly who these no-goodniks were. Although with only pictures to go on, even without masks, people were often surprisingly hard to identify.

Harlen held a finger up for silence, mouthing a "Shhhh," and then pointed at Ray the deejay, hunched over, talking into the mike, introducing a new song. Afterward, he promised his listeners, he had a story they would find quite interesting. A small mouth-hole had been cut out of his mask to allow clear enunciation and ear-holes, too, over which headphones were clamped.

Harlen whispered into Rachel's ear, describing the setup. "You know anything about radio stations? Don't need much equipment. See that there, it's the mixer. Ray uses it to switch from the mike to the tape deck. See." The song, some female country and western singer, died away. Rachel watched Ray's hands, wearing the surgical gloves, manipulate the slides on the machine. The gloves reminded her of medical experiments.

"Okay," Harlen said, raising his voice once more, "the mike's off while the tape's playing." He discussed the function of the transmitter and amplifier, but Rachel was less interested in the equipment than in Ray, who performed his manipulations of it with a certain delicacy of manner. The cutouts exposed a fraction more of his face. A telltale etching around the eyes. Like Harlen then, no kid. Ironic mouth. No, she decided, more sardonic than ironic, the sort of man who could ridicule his own beliefs but act on them anyway. She was sure she had never encountered him before. She wouldn't have forgotten that mouth.

On the floor nearby were car batteries being used to power the transmitter. A cable from the amplifier wound across the floor and up through a window, "the antenna," Harlen explained. His manner was graceful and ardent, as if he might cast a spell over this crude setup.

Rachel took her pictures, sidling this way and that, including as much of the forbidden as she could.

Except for the electronic gear and folding chairs and a pair of floor lamps, the room remained bare, an old place with faded, flowery wallpaper and wall sconces topped by elaborate glass chimneys. Cords from the floor lamps and a pair of space heaters were plugged into a power strip, the cable from the strip disappearing through a door left open a crack and from which came a continuous grumbling sound. She opened it wider and in the dimness made out another room, empty except for a generator.

"So," she said, "I guess you fellas don't live here. Where are you from?" Neither Harlen nor Ray possessed any discernible accent. As for Sparks, she didn't know. He had barely spoken.

"Why do we have to be from somewhere?" Harlen asked, his tone mischievous.

"Some people think you've come here to stir up trouble."

"Trouble? Hardly. We aim to stir up truth, that's all. And you know, it's interesting how people just naturally assume your average Jacksonian is an ignoramus, not smart enough to set up and run a little operation like this. In fact, we've all got deep roots in Jackson."

"In that case, I suppose you could name the current city council members?"

He went down the list quickly, then gave her the names of the city manager and several other city officials for good measure. "And what about you, Miss Brandeis, since you want to play this sort of game, can you tell me who the architect was that designed the Blair House on Hornbeam Avenue? Or where the old high bridge used to cross the Mississippi before they tore it down?" He threw out a couple of more questions even more obscure.

She couldn't answer them and didn't try. "If you really are locals, I'd think you'd want the credibility you'll get from identifying yourselves."

"Well, yes, that's right. But frankly we speak for the people. They know us by our words. And, of course, beyond that there's the little matter of the Federal Communications Commission."

The sound of the country tune had filled the room again, but only briefly as it ended. "Shhh," Harlen cautioned her. "You'll like this."

Ray reached for the mixer, turned the tape deck off and his microphone on. "Emmylou Harris, folks, 'Making Believe.'"

"Now, like I promised, I've got a news flash for all you good people of Jackson." He slipped a clipping out from beneath the mixer. "I have before me a story appeared in this afternoon's *Jackson Tribune* under the byline of a lady named Rachel Brandeis." As he said this, he didn't so much as glance toward Rachel, just proceeded to read the story verbatim—her account of the arrest of the cross burners. When he'd finished, he said, "Mr. Pond and his family are respected citizens of Jackson. We want to join the other good folks of the community in condemning this senseless act. We understand that the young men who performed the deed were frustrated and felt that nothing else would bring attention to the pain they felt because of recent events in the city, but this is not the proper way to express those grievances, however real, and we extend our deepest sympathies to the Pond family.

"Yet there is more to the story than was reported in the *Tribune* article. The *Tribune* has the habit—perhaps you've noticed—of leaving out what certain people in the community don't want you to know. When we return, we'll tell you *the rest of the story*."

He introduced another song, a male C and W artist this time, and the music, as before, faded from the room.

"The rest of the story?" Rachel said.

"Of course," Harlen assured her at once, "we're not saying you yourself are trying to hide anything, Miss Brandeis. You can't print what you don't know. Or perhaps you did know, and it was removed from your story."

"The story was printed as I wrote it. What are you talking about?"

"Patience."

This hugger-mugger annoyed her. She went back to an earlier topic. "You really think the FCC is interested in a tiny operation like this?"

"Oh, indeed I do. Come here, I'll show you." He beckoned and led the way up the stairs that Sparks had taken.

The lookout sat in a chair on the far side of what must have been a bedroom at one time, the room pitch-black except for the trace of nighttime light from outside. Rachel listened to the boards creaking and smelled the old-house decay as she and Harlen crossed over to the front window.

Through it, by following Sparks's directions and waiting until her eyes adjusted, she could just barely make out the silhouette of a car in the distance, a suggestion of a car, nothing but a scrap of unnatural sculpted shape, a darkness slightly darker than the rest.

"Who is it?" Her face was bathed in the drift of cold air coming from the glass.

"Don't know," Harlen said. "Been there for some time, before we left to get you. We went and returned by the back way, and the house is blacked out, nothing to see, but he knows there's somebody in here."

"Why don't you go out and ask?" she suggested and continued to peer through the window, trying to pick out more details in the landscape. "If it's the FCC," she asked, "why is he just sitting there?"

"Don't know that, either. Maybe waiting for his friends. The federales like to travel in packs. I'll tell you one thing, Miss Brandeis. You talk about the feds ignoring an operation like ours. We're exactly the people they go after. Grassroots movements like us. Illegal, they call us. Baloney. We're the real Americans. What you got here is free speech. It just galls the hell out of them that some little guy can get up a few hundred bucks, learn a little bit about transmitters and such, and presto, he's on the air." Rachel had often noticed that in darkness, perhaps because of the growing alertness of the other senses, people talked more softly and intimately.

"And what about interfering with other stations," she asked, "stations with licenses?"

"We don't interfere with anybody. This ain't Chicago. There's lots of dead space on the band. Ain't that right, Sparks?"

"Don't take but a few minutes to lock onto a dead frequency," Sparks said from his post.

"We've gotta get back downstairs," Harlen whispered, leaning closer. As they descended, he told her, "We're putting out information the people of Jackson have a right to know—the truth of this affirmative action business."

"Affirmative action?" Rachel asked. "Unless you know something that I don't, the city's done nothing that falls under the definition of affirmative action."

On the first floor, the last song was ending and Ray again leaning toward the mike.

"That was the immortal George Jones, folks, and 'These Days I Barely Get By.' And now…the rest of the story.

"It is a sad irony of this whole business that Mr. Johnny Pond was the target of these unfortunate young men. For you see, Mr. Pond is himself opposed to the plan to bring blacks to Jackson. He believes, as we do, as Mr. David Duke does, as all of you do, that people ought to be left free to make up their own minds. No one wants to start busing blacks into Jackson—nobody, that is, except a few misguided liberals..." Ray continued, inserting all the hot-button words into his editorial.

"Affirmative action was a bad idea from the beginning, but now, here in Jackson, it has run totally amok. People must be allowed to choose. You know that. Mr. Pond knows that. But a few people have decided to ram this thing down our throats. And now Mr. Pond has had to pay the price."

Harlen leaned very close to Rachel and whispered, "Using city money to attract blacks to Jackson, that's affirmative action, what-ever they try to call it. The black contractor down there at the dog track, that too. I'm talking about the spirit of the thing, not some narrow legalism. I'm talking about favoring one group over another rather than doing it the right way by letting every individual Amer-ican, whatever his color, compete on an equal basis. That's what Mr. Duke stands for. Give every man a chance to compete on an equal footing."

"What about women?"

"Of course, women, too. Everyone. An equal chance, that's all we want."

The fellow was determined to give her nothing but vanilla quotes. He possessed the smooth manner of a veteran Duke opera-tive, one for whom every question has an answer designed to sand another rough edge from the Duke persona.

"How is it you happen to know that Johnny Pond is against attracting black families to the city?" she asked.

"You'd be surprised. Anyway, if you'll pardon me saying it, you're the one, Miss Brandeis, that appears to be a little short of information here."

Ray was still on the air, talking to his invisible audience, telling them, "But you don't want to hear this from me. You'd far rather hear it from Mr. David Duke himself, who's going to be right here in Jackson next Monday, folks, at noon, speaking from the steps of city hall, in person. David has been misrepresented so often by the mass media that it's important that you hear his message from his own lips. So go on down. Monday, noon, city hall plaza.

"And now, as a foretaste, here's a recent speech by the man himself. His own words. A little sample of what you can hear for yourself at city hall on Monday. Go on down. Show the city council and their fellow travelers what the people of Jackson really think." And Ray powered up his tape deck and a voice that had grown familiar over the previous week began to speak and, as he moved the slide on his mixer, faded away. David Duke, the soul of reasonableness, David Duke, the apostle of equal opportunity. Rachel had had enough.

"Duke preaches white supremacy, Harlen. He's a Klansman. He's a neo-Nazi."

"Whoa, there. Watch it. Mr. Duke has never been a neo-Nazi. True, he once belonged to the Klan, but that was a long time ago."

"I'm sorry, but he is a neo-Nazi. He's a Holocaust denier."

"That's a lie. Look, Miss Brandeis...," he said, speaking intensely now. There were footsteps, Sparks coming rapidly down the stairs. "You're a Jew, right? Brandeis, that's a Jewish name. David has no problem at all with you making your career as a journalist." Suddenly, it was no longer Mr. Duke, it was David.

Sparks appeared.

"Second car."

"Are they coming?"

"Not yet."

"Damn."

"Shall we shut her down?" Ray asked, his hand hovering just above the mixer.

"No," Harlen said, "want to stay on long as we can. Owe the people that much. I'll take Miss Brandeis back. Sparks." With this single word, Sparks disappeared back into the room with the generator. "If it looks like they're coming," Harlen told Ray, "get out, forget the equipment."

"Gotcha."

"As for you, Miss Brandeis, the end of the interview I'm afraid."

"Why don't we stay," she suggested, "and see who it is?"

"As much fun as that might be, I don't think so. We can continue the conversation in the car."

Later she would regret the choice she made, but in the moment, thinking the old reporter's adage, don't become part of the story, she allowed herself to be hustled through the back room and then another room, the kitchen probably, impossible to tell in the gloom, and out the back door, where a car idled, only the parking lights lit. Harlen pulled at her with increasing urgency. In a few moments, they were in the car and bouncing wildly away from the pirate station.

❧

Sparks had lied when he said there was a second car. From the sentry post in the upper window, the scene hadn't changed, containing only the one car Rachel had spotted earlier. But as she and Sparks and Harlen skittered away down the gravel drive, the parking lights of this solitary vehicle flipped on, and it started up and slowly approached the dark house, making no effort to follow the others.

It rolled to a stop a few feet from the front porch, and a single figure climbed out and moved cautiously up onto the porch and knocked once, then twice. Immediately, the door was flung open and the lights from inside illuminated the figure, no FCC agent, only Reiny Kopp, the director of the Jackson historic museum.

"You still on the air?" he asked Wild Bill, who was peeling off his ski mask.

"Yup."

"Good."

"How'd it go?"

"Okay, I guess." Wild Bill rubbed his head vigorously. The mask had smeared part of the fake birthmark. "You'll have to ask Hal when he gets back. You would've loved him. Son of a bitch couldn't have been more sincere if he'd actually believed all that crap."

"You were good, too. I heard," Reiny said, and then, imitating Bill as best he could, intoned, "*the rest of the story.* Fucking Paul Harvey couldn't have done it any better."

"Listening, huh?" Bill laughed. "You need a better taste in radio programs."

"Liked your choice of songs, too."

"Thought you would."

"'Making Believe'?"

Wild Bill smiled, unrepentant.

"Just don't get too cute, okay?"

The pranksters all had their personal agendas, Wild Bill intent on salting his broadcasts with puns and secret clues, songs like "I'm Not the Man You Think I Am" and "If You Only Knew," his way of flipping his listeners the bird. As employees, pranksters left something to be desired.

In thirty minutes, Hal and Timmy returned.

"Well?" Reiny asked Hal, his longtime movement friend. Hal got the door prize for coming the farthest, all the way from the West Coast. Everybody was imported, Bill down from Canada and Timmy up from Iowa City. All the old subversive spirit had gone out of the local activists.

"Like a charm," said Hal, who had chosen Harlen as his nom de guerre. "Man, she was on the case. A friggin' news hen on a story, snooping on the sly, looking for clues. You should've been here."

"He was listening on the radio," Wild Bill said.

"Oh, yeah. How was the signal?" This question from Tim Wheeler, their technical guy, aka Sparks. That was Timmy's agenda, putting out a strong, uncluttered signal. He'd rather get caught than put out a crummy one. Reiny could appreciate that.

"Nice and clean, Timmy. Expect they can hear us clear over in Waterloo."

Probably, Reiny thought, they should be broadcasting at something less than twenty watts, but they'd be closing up shop in a couple of days.

He told Ray and the others that they'd handled the business about the cross burning just right.

"Man, those cross burners were some dumb fucks," Wild Bill said. "What the hell did they think they were trying to accomplish? And why Pond? Isn't he the one friggin' black guy everybody in this burg actually likes?"

"I don't know why they did it, they're morons," Reiny told him, "but I can tell you why they picked Pond."

"Oh, yeah?"

"You're gonna like it. Pond was the only black whose address they could find."

Hal shook his head. What a bunch of dildos.

"Anyway," Reiny said, "I called Duke's office, told him about the incident. Better he hears it from me. I told him it was a perfect opportunity—come up here and say he understands people's pain but that cross burning is flat-out wrong and so forth and so on, all his usual neo-bullshit."

"Did he buy it?" Hal asked.

"Not sure. Maybe. He was pretty freaked."

"I say we go ahead anyway, Duke or no Duke. Everything's set up."

Wild Bill had to get back on the air, so Reiny and Hal took their conversation out on the porch, where Reiny said, "Not to worry, we're operational, but let's hope he comes. It'll be ever so much nicer with him here."

They chuckled. It would, indeed, be ever so much nicer if they could screw Duke while they were outing all the racists in Jackson, two for the price of one. But nailing the locals was first priority.

Hal said, "I need more bodies. We've got a ton of shit to accomplish on Monday."

"I'll see what I can do." Reiny had his doubts about rounding up extra help. Jerry the Zip was the only Jackson antiwar activist from the old days still primed for a little deviant fun. A couple of Timmy's hacker pals, young but with the right attitude, were coming up from Iowa City. But no way around it, they were gonna be mighty thin on the ground. "Hard to get reliable people for this type of work," Reiny said. "What about the license plate? Did Brandeis see it?" It wasn't actually a tag, but rather the kind of promotional placard a dealer inserts on his new cars, a little free advertising before the DMV sends the plates to the buyer.

"I left the blindfold off until we got to the car. Took her around by the back. Left the parking lights on. Did everything but point it out for her." Hal, who possessed a mighty low opinion of the press, had been plumping for something rather more blatant. That was the problem with Hal, he was always plumping for something rather more blatant. Reiny didn't know if he'd gotten more timid or Hal more wacked-out in their old age. At some point, a person became so demented that he was actually insane, and who the hell knew where the boundary was?

"She's in the print media, she reads," he assured his friend. "We'll get a nice story outta her."

He gave Hal the venerable black handshake they'd used since the sixties. "Keep up the good work."

Reiny took the front steps two at a time. Now, he thought, for the hard part.

CHAPTER 70

~

Father Mike asked Jack Kelley to wait so they could have a word in private. Only take a minute. Janelle said she and Kitty would be in the car.

Mike had taken advantage of the brief spell of almost decent weather, clear but cold and gusty, to go outside onto the small plaza in front of the entrance to St. Columbkille's where he greeted the parishioners leaving Sunday morning Mass. Stone steps descended on three sides, and Jack waited at the foot of these. In the bright but weak sunlight, he toed the granite of the lower step, studded with iridescent chips of blue feldspar. It reminded him of Lake Placid blue granite, although the stone must have come from someplace closer. A small mystery, the provenance of that stone, which he'd never had time to pursue.

Mike was greeting stragglers, happy to chatter, happy to delay the few moments he needed with Jack, as if waiting time didn't count. He had doffed his clerical garments except for the long black cassock, which fit him more sleekly since he'd lost weight. The wind pinned the narrow skirts of the garment against his calves.

Jack turned his attention to the building, another project left undone although nothing so pleasing as the prospect of tracing the source of the granite. He knew where the dolomite veneers on St. C's came from: Mankato, Minnesota. No mystery there. The only mystery was when the parish council would get off its collective duff and do something about making repairs. The last tuck-pointing had been who-knows-when. Jack rubbed a forefinger in the joint between two of the stones, the gritty mortar abrading easily. Winters like this one were tough on mortar. Of course, every institution let its facilities fall apart.

Finally, Mike turned to descend, coming down with a trace of awkwardness. Steps of public buildings seemed never at a width allowing a man to take them without breaking stride, although Mike's present unsteadiness appeared to arise mostly from some internal cause. His normal robust good health no longer burst forth, and this impression of mortality softened for a moment Jack's irritation at the priest's persistent impositions.

Mike gripped his forearm.

"Can you come over to the rectory at two o'clock?"

"Why?"

"If I tell you, you won't come."

"Something to do with Tony Vasconcellos, then."

Mike leaned even closer, his pallid skin dotted with red pustules so tiny they were only visible close at hand and in the bright, revelatory morning sun. "I'm asking you, Jack...for the sake of everything we've been through together...just come."

Jack, of course, couldn't refuse.

"And bring Janelle," the priest said, having gained his first objective.

This further request appalled Jack. It was bad enough that he was trapped between the priest and the Vasconcelloses. But Janelle?

"I know," Mike said, anticipating Jack's vehement protest or perhaps just reading the look of horror on his face, "but bring her if she'll come. It might help."

"You can't be serious." This was no time to pretend that the relationship between Mike and Janelle was hunky-dory, or her scorn for idiots measured.

What the priest said was this: "I accept everything, Jack. Whatever happens, I accept everything." The sun cast his face in pitiless light and deep shadow. He could have been an ascetic.

∾

Jack considered not mentioning any of this to Janelle. He didn't in the car. He didn't after they got home, either. But then, as two o'clock stalked nearer and his desire to act in a forthright manner overmastered his better judgment, he decided, what the hell, given her low opinion of Father Mike, Janelle was bound to turn her nose up at the prospect of spending any of her free time with him. A mistake. She accepted at once. Jack hastened to point out that it probably had something to do with Tony Vasconcellos and his dysfunctional family. Janelle was not deterred. What was worse, she even seemed interested, or perhaps *curious* was a better word, as in curious to observe these new exemplars of man's fallen nature. She even took it upon herself to ask Kitty along. Why not make it a family outing?

Jack brooded over the cost of forthrightness. Too late.

~

Sister Ursula, Mike's majordomo, ushered the three of them past the books displayed in the entry hall and into the west parlor, where chairs had been organized into an oval.

Mike seemed entirely unsurprised by Kitty's appearance, an extra chair already present, like the seat devout Catholic families left at the dinner table for the unexpected guest. He still wore his cassock, normal indoor clerical garb, but on Mike, who took every opportunity to dress in civilian clothes, a little odd. The point of the formality, however, was transparent enough, investing the get-together with the authority of his office.

Tony Vasconcellos sat in one of the chairs, as expected, and one seat away, his wife Angela, also no surprise. Two of their children had come as well. The other attendees were more interesting: Ed Ohnesorge, the director of Catholic Charities for the Archdiocese, and a woman whose name Jack didn't know, but whom he believed to be one of Ohney's people, a family counselor if he remembered rightly. The Otts, Doug and Marilyn, the wealthiest parishioners in St. C's, had also come. Jack had no idea why Ohney and his associate were there—aside from the fact that the Vasconcelloses probably needed all the family counseling they could get—but he guessed at once about the Otts. They had to be the source of the sixty thousand dollars that Vasconcellos had put up in lieu of the bid bond for the track contract. They sat on the far end of the oval, their matched expressions somber and slightly bemused. No one appeared pleased to be there.

Janelle and Kitty didn't sit at once, Kitty sticking close to her mother as Janelle gave the room the once-over with her interior decorator's eye, no doubt inspecting the premises for signs of sacri-lege committed by Mike upon her restoration work. Compared to the well-fed Vasconcelloses, the two women were keen and sharp-boned. Finally, Janelle took a seat, not looking at it as she sat, but continuing to inspect the room. Then she turned her judging eyes on the Vasconcelloses.

Father Mike sat down as well. All the seats were taken now. He thanked everyone for coming and said at once, "Let us pray," reaching out to take the hands of the two people on either side of him, Angela Vasconcellos and the woman from the chancery.

Jack barely listened to the words of the prayer, conscious of the hands he held, Kitty's firm grip on one side and Doug Ott's less certain grasp on the other.

After the prayer, Mike introduced the two Vasconcellos children, Gina, the eldest daughter, perhaps twenty, and Leo, a few years younger. The girl was pretty but badly overweight—shamelessly overweight was the way Jack put the matter to himself—and the boy sullen in the teenage manner. Both reflected their mother in details, but possessed their father's bulk. Lonny Vasconcellos hadn't come. A small blessing.

Mike paused and looked around the circle. When he began speaking, it was to the Otts and to Jack, Janelle, and Kitty. "I thought it was time, given the course of events, that we met face-to-face. We have all been involved in trying to help Angela and Tony and their family, a concerted effort, for which I want to thank you. The help has been appreciated, it really has…

"And I understand we all have our own individual lives. We're all busy, taken up with many things… I understand that… But it does seem, too often, that we don't really know each other anymore, just about each other. Still, we *are* a faith community, and everyone in this room is committed to the success of the parish…and of everyone in the parish family. I believe there comes a time and a situation when we can no longer perform our good works at a distance, without taking the time to become personally involved…"

As Father Mike spoke, and before he revealed the purpose of the gathering, Jack realized what had happened, what must have happened, and his attention shifted, coming to rest on Leo Vasconcellos, who was sitting, head down and hands clasped loosely together, between his parents.

Leo was the third cross burner.

Chapter 71

~

On Saturday morning, Sam Turner had heard on the radio what had happened to Johnny Pond and his family. He immediately got up from the kitchen table and turned the radio off and stood, head bowed, feeling emptied out. Then, not bothering with a coat, he went out to his car and got in and started to drive toward the Ponds' home.

For the first few blocks, he was not himself and drove aware only of the agitation roiling deep within his gut and, on the surface, the calmness bestowed by this decisive act of his, going to the Ponds.

But as he continued on, the side streets flicking by in his peripheral vision, the spontaneity began to thin and thoughts came, fragmentary at first. What would happen when he got there? What would he say to them?

He became aware of the car, the air cold and clammy and seeping through his clothing. At a stop sign, the old hatchback's faulty muffler brayed as he stepped on the gas, slowly gaining speed. The gas gauge stood on empty.

Sam knew Johnny, it was true; he knew Johnny, but not so well, hardly at all. Johnny had helped him, manipulating things behind the scenes so he got the promotion to the drafting room in city hall. Yes, help had been given, but only as one of the brothers helps another, out of a sense that in a place like Jackson they got to stick together. That was all.

And that was the way it should be, Johnny helping Sam and not the other way around. Nothing Sam could do for him, nothing he could say would make a bit of difference. Sam was a charity case, had no right thinking his presence might make things better for Johnny. Helping Johnny was a fantasy.

And what about Johnny's family, who Sam didn't know at all, who were total strangers to him?

He stopped for gas and to think, shifting the freezing pump nozzle from hand to hand because his gloves were in his coat and his coat thrown over a chair back in the house. The helmet of cold eased his hangover a little. He tried to imagine the scene at the Ponds'. The words. The emotional intensity required. It would've been okay if he'd just done it, turned off the radio and called them on the phone or something. But this delay, filled with thoughts... hacking away at his better impulses.

He pumped six dollars worth of gas because that was all the money he had, and when he started off again, he felt the poverty of it, as if he had nothing left, his money gone, his spontaneity gone, everything gone.

He turned into an alley with a vague sense that he would go back home, but this turning away immediately caused a turning in his thoughts, too. A new dissatisfaction.

For Johnny *had* helped Sam before, and now this other thing had happened, and Sam feared—this was the turning in his mind—that in some way he had been responsible, that if he'd never applied for the job in the drafting room this other thing wouldn't have happened, either. He didn't know why else some white boys would burn a cross on Johnny's lawn. Didn't make any sense. What had Johnny ever done to anybody?

Sam thought this, and then he thought, *White boys don't need an excuse.*

He swung around in a parking space behind a building and started back out toward the Ponds', thinking he wanted to see the expression on Johnny's face when Johnny saw him.

At the next corner, he turned away again. He couldn't go there just because *he* had a need. He was already pretty near nothing in Johnny's eye, just a brother somehow managed to end up in Jackson, Iowa, and couldn't get ahead on his own. If he went out of his own neediness, just to make sure Johnny was laying all this shit off on the whites, not on him, Johnny would sense it and despise him for it.

Sam turned at the next corner and then again at the next, and for a long time, he drove randomly through the maze of white neighborhoods, his old hatchback spewing noise, its course as erratic as his thoughts. His mind doubled back on itself or, with a sudden hopeful inspiration, took off in a new direction, only to slow and wind around and around and finally come back to where he'd begun.

He did recognize one thing. All this discomfort he was feeling wasn't about his responsibility for what had happened to Johnny and his family. Or just about that. It was mostly about the drafting tools still sitting untouched in his bedroom after all this time. It was about his own exhausted desires.

At last, needing to do something constructive, he drove down to the museum and went back to work on the remounting of the black exhibit, listening to all the chatter about Johnny Pond, but not saying much himself. The others took his silence for rage.

∾

He worked late, helping with the panels that the vandals had damaged, repairing some and painting new ones where the old were beyond salvaging. Back home, he ate standing up and told his two white roommates the cross burning was just the same old shit. He decided he wasn't going to get drunk that night, and instead went upstairs and sat down at the card table with his drafting stuff on it and opened the old drafting text he'd found the previous summer at a library sale and riffled through its reams of pages, chapter after chapter, waiting for something to catch his eye. The book, the fatness and earnestness of it, was like belief itself, a lifetime of effort. It required a conversion, and Sam just wasn't up to it. He had the impulse to sweep it all onto the floor—Fuck it! But in the end he couldn't do that, either, not even that. It just wasn't in him.

He spent the night reading his fantasy novel.

On Sunday, he went back down to the museum and lost himself in the details of a panel he had been given to repair.

It wasn't three o'clock yet when Reiny Kopp appeared and abruptly judged the exhibit finished and told the museum staffers and the volunteers to go home. When Sam started to leave, however, Reiny approached and put a hand on his sleeve and said, under his breath, "Wait a sec. We need to talk. After the others have left."

And so, wondering what it might be about, Sam hung around as Reiny attended to other matters.

Hard to believe, Sam thought, that Reiny had some special need only Sam could satisfy. He was flattered, but it didn't make sense. Something strange seemed to be going on. For one thing, the exhibit didn't look finished. For another, Reiny didn't seem nearly as pissed off as he had earlier about remounting the exhibit. On top of that, Sam couldn't imagine what Reiny might want him for. He had no special talents.

But he respected Reiny. He respected Reiny's competence and energy and certainty about things. He respected them without quite believing in them and was drawn to the man even as he shied away from him. For Reiny had been a badass activist back in the sixties, and Sam remembered the potluck down on his houseboat the month before with his old activist pals, and Reiny berating them 'cause they'd lost all their subversive ardor. But you could still see it in him, something about his skinny, disjointed, nothing-to-lose body and the way his words always seemed to be linked to things unseen. Best stay clear of a man like Reiny Kopp if you knew what was good for you. But Sam was flattered, too, that Reiny would send all the others home and keep only him behind. After Sam's failure to go visit the Ponds the day before, Reiny wanting to see him seemed almost like an opportunity to redeem himself.

As they walked between the two old Burlington Railroad buildings, station and freight warehouse, cutting back and forth past the mammoth embankments of snow, Sam asked if it was really true, was the exhibit finished? It sure didn't look as good as it had the first time.

"Good enough," Reiny said.

He unlocked the door to the former freight building, and they started up the steep stairway.

The museum's administrative area was quiet, everyone gone. Reiny closed the door to his private office and waved Sam to one of the director's chairs arranged in front of his desk. He didn't sit down himself. He grabbed part of a newspaper from the top of the desk and tossed it over, a section of the Sunday paper—"Seen this?"—and then moved deliberately to the picture window behind the desk and stood with his back to the room.

Sam looked at the paper, the front section, a follow-up story on the cross burning and another about the pirate radio station that David Duke's racist friends had set up somewhere in the city.

"Yeah."

From his post overlooking the harbor, Reiny said, "A wonderful institution, the press."

When he next spoke, it was to return briefly to the earlier topic. "The exhibit's good enough, Sam, for what I've got in mind."

Having said this, having added a note of mystery, he abandoned the subject.

Everyone knew that he'd wanted to reopen the trashed exhibit, show people the vandalism, and since they wouldn't let him, he'd pretty much turned his back on the whole thing. Or that seemed to be what had happened. Sam didn't quite believe it. He thought something else must be going on, although he had no idea what. Reiny was a secretive mother, no doubt about that.

The museum director was still standing with his back to Sam and looking down at the failing afternoon light and stray flakes of snow.

"What do you mean," Sam asked, "good enough for what you got in mind?"

Reiny didn't answer. He turned and sat in the chair at his desk. He seemed distracted.

"So," he said, looking around as if searching for something, smiling to himself. Reiny's smile always seemed to include the complexity lying beneath the surface. "So...the city's slashing the budget. Layoffs. Pretty much inevitable, wouldn't you say?"

"Suppose."

"You got enough seniority to go back to hauling trash?"

Sam took off his hat and began fiddling with the visor. "Cutting back to two-man crews," he told Reiny.

"Ah."

Reiny left off his search and rose again and sauntered over to the door, opening it only long enough to check the dim outer office, then closing it again and turning on the light, the hanging lamp fixtures overhead, like giant upended ice cube trays, flooding the place with light, leaving nothing in shadow. He sauntered back, detouring toward Sam, and stretched out in another of the director's chairs, very close, his skinny face completely taken up by his fleshy lips and prominent nose and black, gleaming eyes.

"Not only that," he said, laying out almost straight in the chair, hands clasped on his stomach, ankles crossed, "David Duke's coming. Maybe already here. Maybe already talking to people. You planning to do anything?"

"About Duke?"

"No, about Daffy Duck."

Sam said, "There's gonna be a demonstration."

"Plan to take part?"

"Yeah. I figure." Sam had pretty much decided he wouldn't do it, not being a demonstration kind of person, but at that moment, nervous about whatever crazy scheme Reiny had in mind, the idea of demonstrating suddenly looked a good deal more appealing.

Reiny had dipped his head forward and peered at Sam from beneath his eyebrows, where hairs arced like tiny fireworks.

"I see. Well, that's all right, then. Got to have demonstrations, I suppose. A piece of advice: don't get in an argument with Duke. He'll eat you alive."

"Duke talks nothing but shit."

"True. But he'll reason with you, and you'll end up screaming at him. Ain't about talking shit, Sam, it's about style points… Anyway, doesn't much matter, I suppose. After Duke leaves, the problem's still here. Right?"

As he spoke, he studied Sam, and his gaze was like a separate conversation, and Sam felt whittled down by it.

"Duke don't help," he said.

"No, I suppose he doesn't. Still…he comes, you demonstrate, he goes…what changes?"

"Nothin' changes."

Reiny nodded and looked off into the distance, clicking his thumbs together. He mostly yakked a lot, but sometimes he would sit and wait and only go on when he was good and ready.

The canvas backrest creaked against its wooden supports as Sam tried to get comfortable.

Finally, Reiny was good and ready. "And these demonstrations, they're not like the old days, are they? Not like Birmingham in '64—Bull Connor, police dogs, fire hoses." He paused again, briefly this time. "But then, it's not 1964 anymore. Laws are in place. Racism has gone underground… And demonstrations are, let's face it, a little bit like fighting the last war. Don't you think?"

Sam shrugged. "Suppose. Gotta do 'em, anyway."

Reiny ignored this weak counterpunch. "Tell me, Sam, you ever dream of extreme acts? You must, being a black man. Ever dream, for instance, of putting yourself in harm's way for the cause?"

Sam's mind worked furiously. What was going on? What was this mother getting at?

"You got something in mind?"

Reiny studied Sam. "I hesitate because…frankly, Sam, and nothing personal, you don't inspire a lot of confidence." Reiny began to dredge dirt out from underneath his nails.

Sam swallowed. Probably he should be mad or challenge Reiny or something, but all he could muster was, "Wha'd'ya mean?"

Reiny glanced at him and cocked his shoulders and sniffed. "Doesn't matter."

"Why you bring me up here, man, why ya dissing me, it doesn't matter?"

Reiny got heavily to his feet and began to move around his desk. For an instant, Sam had the flickering impression that this all might be part of some act Reiny was putting on, but Sam was too much taken up with his own discomfort at the moment to think about it.

Reiny sat now behind his desk, impassive.

A white man, Sam thought. *A motherfucking white man.*

After letting this renewed silence drag out, Reiny leaned back on one elbow and said, the words spoken as firmly as the setting of a hook, "So, tell me, Sam, you're a drinker, right?"

CHAPTER 72

~

A short time after she had left Johnny Pond, El unceremoniously threw off the pain from the confrontation and stored
it for later wearing. When she felt like herself, she could do that,
treat her emotions as if they were garments to be put on and off,
hung away from the sunlight where they wouldn't fade. A number
of times over the next two days, as she had campaigned house to
house and chanced to remember, the encounter had returned in all
its vividness, like a hitch in her breathing, and she wondered what
could possibly be done.

Late Sunday afternoon, she stopped down at the law enforcement center and had the watch commander catch her up on recent
developments (one of the older cross burners now out on bail, the
minor in the custody of his parents) and the status of preparations
for David Duke's appearance the following day (in place, all leaves
cancelled). She would call the chief when she got home. Whatever
else, she had no intention of letting David Duke turn her town
into a flagship for white bigots.

Finally, she went down to the museum to check progress on
the remounting of the vandalized exhibit. The converted train
station stood empty, a dark shadow against the failing daylight,
the only light in the museum complex in Reiny's office on the
second floor of the freight building. Two other cars were in the
parking lot, his Suburban and one she didn't recognize, an old
Toyota hatchback.

She hadn't called ahead, but Reiny obviously expected her
to show up, because he had Scotch-taped a brief message to the
stationmaster's door: "Exhibit ready to reopen. What say Tuesday
morning? R."

She let herself in and walked from room to room, turning on
the lights as she went. The damage had been cleaned up, the only

reminder of it being the panel of pictures, taken on the day of the vandalism, which Reiny had mounted in the former stationmaster's office as a memento, the first thing visitors to the revived exhibit would see. The exhibit should have been reopened already, against the coming of David Duke, but she supposed the day after he left would work, too.

In the Greenville room, with its re-creation of the Mississippi Delta, she stopped and looked about herself, disconsolate at the impoverished scene. The last two or three times she'd stopped by, Reiny had been nowhere to be found, his obvious indifference something else taxing her patience. When he lost interest in a project, he barely went through the motions. Though he claimed, when she had finally caught up to him on the phone two days earlier, that the exhibit was almost ready to go, she couldn't see it. She still couldn't see it. More mannequins had been found, panels repainted, the church with its amen corner patched, new items arranged in the keepsake trunk on the porch of the shotgun house, but still, the panorama seemed shriveled and threadbare. Going through the motions. Perhaps when the background sounds were added... Perhaps if she let him turn the heat up, to simulate a Delta summer... Perhaps, but something was still missing. Re-creations should be better than the original, not worse.

In the Jackson room, one last remembrance of the vandalism survived: the frame for Pearl Johnson's quilt. Reiny had wanted to leave the defaced quilt up for everyone to see, El had wanted to remove all trace of it, and they compromised on the empty frame.

She stopped and stood still and stared at this void and imagined the quilt as it had originally looked with its brightly stitched scenes from the Johnsons' ordinary lives.

In the four corners, Pearl Johnson had placed symbols emblematic of the black struggle for freedom. The other patches, depicting scenes around the city or homey incidents from the Johnsons' lives, had made a greater impression on El at the time, but now, in her mind's eye, those four corners stood out more vividly, although she could not clearly remember what each stood for. A star—meant to remind fleeing slaves to follow the polestar—that was one... She remembered another, too, a patch symbolizing a safe haven where slaves might find shelter on their journey. Quilts were hung as signals outside cabins.

El closed her eyes, trying to visualize the patch. She couldn't, nothing more than a vague massing of color at the center of the field. Strange what came back to you. She opened her eyes and continued to stare and suddenly remembered something else, not what the patch looked like, but what Pearl called it: The Log Cabin Quilt.

Those corners, the ones she could remember and the ones lost to memory, had acquired a moral heft, like the Johnsons themselves, like the everydayness of their lives, all of it invested with a powerful moral stature in the aftermath of the vandalism. Lives lived in the shadow of what could happen. Lives lived at the sufferance of others.

Johnny Pond, she thought. And the sharp pang returned, regret and helplessness, the vision of him blocking the doorway to his home, his violent words.

What *was* to be done?

Perhaps nothing. Certainly, for him, for Johnny, for his family, nothing. He'd let nothing be done. He would, like the Johnsons, withdraw. She was sure of it.

In his life in the city, he had asked little, had perhaps expected little. Another ordinary existence, really. Another attempt at an ordinary existence. His great bulk, his football heroics, his radio career—all these set him apart from other men—but nevertheless… She remembered his trick of seeming to be simultaneously engaged and disengaged, of walking a little apart from others, of letting silences build up on his radio call-in show…

Probably nothing, nothing to be done. She regretted… But doing nothing was so easy. Do nothing, and nothing happens.

She started back toward the entrance, turning off the lights as she went. With her, she carried the image of the quilt. She arrived back in the old stationmaster's office and saw the pictures of the vandalism, so ugly, depicting such a hateful act, seeming to shed that hatred into the very air of the room.

And all at once, seeing those pictures and remembering the quilt, she had an idea. Why not find a Log Cabin Quilt to hang at the beginning of the exhibit? Or make one if they had to. Yes! Reiny would have to put his pictures somewhere else. The quilt simply must be the first thing people saw. Here would be a safe haven, a place away from the world outside. Here people could come, black, white, it made no difference, and spend a few minutes and wander at their ease, without fear. Here, in this small space, Jackson would be the city it ought to be.

Outside, she thought she'd go immediately over to the freight building and inform Reiny of her decision, but his office was now dark and her car the only one left in the parking lot.

CHAPTER 73

~

On the drive home, Janelle had grilled Jack as to why Marilyn and Doug Ott were involved with the Vasconcelloses, and he explained (leaving out his own sorry role in the business) that Tony Vasconcellos had been unable to get a bid bond for the track work and that Father Mike had gone to the Otts for a loan which Tony might put up in lieu of the bond.

"How much?"

"Sixty grand."

"You mean to tell me Doug Ott gave Tony Vasconcellos sixty thousand dollars?"

"Apparently."

"Umph."

"No doubt Vasconcellos had to pledge everything he owns, his business, his house, his cars." Jack still remembered with annoyance all the vehicles in Tony's driveway.

"The Otts wouldn't put anybody out on the street," Kitty said from the back seat.

"But they could lose sixty thousand, and it'd all be your friend Mike's doing," Janelle observed archly.

Janelle kept on saying your friend Mike this and your friend Mike that. In exchanges with her, he always felt he had to defend himself, even when it wasn't about him, so he was pleased to be able to tell her, "Doug and Marilyn will get their money back. The city won't take it, no matter how bad Tony's performance is. I've seen contractors stop work entirely on a project and the owner still refuse to go to the bonding company. Nobody wants to put a guy out of business."

"So you say. But they *could* take the money." Janelle had done the moral calculus and made up her mind, and once she made up her mind, the Pope could forget about changing it.

"But they won't," he said and let it go at that.

$\sim$

The Kelleys worked. They had always been a family that worked, seven days a week, fifty-two weeks a year. Sometimes they speculated about the possibility of taking a vacation, but the idea didn't sit well. Vacations seemed arbitrary, cut too precisely out of the work year, requiring planning and thus vaguely unnatural. Humans had, after all, been kicked out of the Garden of Eden, and God didn't just do it. He'd had something in mind. So the Kelleys worked, all of them. And after they got home from the meeting at the rectory, Kitty donned her whites and went off to the hospital, Janelle spread her remodeling paraphernalia over the dining room table in preparation for getting on the horn with one of her clients, and Jack dealt with the track paperwork that he had no time for during the week.

But before he went upstairs, he dug out the newspapers from the last couple of days and reread the stories about the cross burning, concentrating on references to the third member of the unholy triumvirate, name withheld because of age. Leo had tried to make a run for it, but didn't get far. A dumb, senseless act. Nothing in the stories shed much light on the situation, beyond the obvious. So he tossed the papers aside and headed for the stairs.

At supper, Janelle made her last pronouncements on the matter of Father Mike and the Vasconcelloses.

She had fixed a chicken sandwich for Jack and cleared places for them both at the dining room table. "I've got a question for you," she began. In the center of her own small clearing sat the carcass of the bird, which she was further dismantling with a paring knife, eating with her fingers. "Just why is it that Mike Daugherty is bending over backwards to help Angela Vasconcellos and her family?"

Jack smelled a trap.

"I don't know."

"What do you mean, you don't know? How could you not know?"

"Mike's a priest. He's out to do good in the world." In point of fact, Jack had never asked Mike exactly why he was helping Vasconcellos, at least not in the blunt way Janelle put the question. Mike could be counted on to come up with some sort of noble rationale that would put Jack's own foot-dragging in an even worse light.

Janelle had broken off and was gnawing one of the bird's lesser bones. She spoke around the edges of it. "This is more than doing good in the world, Jack. This is not healthy."

"I've never felt right about it," Jack agreed, as if he and Janelle were, of course, in complete accord on this matter. The problem was that his views were never as strong as hers. His anger became her outrage, his outrage her whatever came after outrage.

"If you don't feel right about it," she asked, "then why are you helping him?"

That was another thing about Janelle: her everlasting bluntness.

"I'm helping him...," Jack started and stopped and started again. "I'm helping him because he's my parish priest." This answer was without substance. Any answer with substance, even if he'd happened to have one, would accomplish nothing, not now.

"Hmm." She put down the bone and with her greasy fingers turned the carcass this way and that, searching for any scrap of meat she had overlooked. Janelle was thorough. "You know why I think he's doing it?"

"Why?"

"Guilt."

"What do you mean?"

"Don't be obtuse." *Obtuse* was one of Janelle's favorite words.

"He's done something?"

"Yes."

"What?"

"You tell me."

Jack paused, as if trying to figure out what she could possibly mean, although he knew perfectly well.

"Angela and Mike?" Jack had considered this possibility. Angela was an attractive woman.

"No, I wasn't thinking of her," Janelle said. "I was thinking of the priesthood. I was thinking...you know."

"The boys?" he interpreted, shocked, although, in truth, he had considered this possibility, too. With priests, you just never knew anymore.

"It happens," Janelle said placidly. "Of course, Mike's your big buddy, he could never do such a thing."

"No, that's right." Whatever his doubts, Jack would defend Mike.

"You'd be surprised," she said, abandoning the chicken, "at what goes on in the world."

"No, I wouldn't."

"Oh?"

It was the tone in which she delivered her pronouncements as much as their content which got Jack's goat, Janelle so very casual in her condemnations, matter-of-fact even, even interested, like a dog smelling another dog's shit. Her confidence in her own opinions and in his naiveté just drove Jack up the wall.

She ended the exchange by saying, "You can do whatever you want. But if Mike Daugherty thinks Kitty and I are going to cozy up to that woman and her children, he's got another think coming."

∽

It was well after nine when Jack returned to the rectory, impelled by the question he had never asked, determined to have it out with Mike once and for all.

In the dimness of the entryway, the books atop their lecterns were visible only as shadowy witnesses. Jack could smell the liquor on the priest's breath.

A single lamp burned in the parlor, the chairs back in their usual places.

"Drink?" Mike asked.

Jack shook his head, and the priest said, "You never accept a drink from me anymore, Jack."

They sat down, Mike settling back in the chair next to the book he had apparently been reading, saying nothing, waiting, letting the game come to him, and Jack, elbows on knees, massaging his hands, suddenly reluctant to begin. Priests had always been authority figures in his life. Even Mike, even after all this time. Jack had grown up before Vatican II, and some of the old-style deference still clung to him. With priests, you went so far, and no farther.

He couldn't remember the last time they'd been together this late at night, just the two of them. At the occasional public function was all. By rights, Mike should have been upstairs saying the divine office before he got ready to go to bed. Come to think of it, Jack couldn't remember when he'd ever seen him with a breviary in his hand. The book next to his chair looked to be a novel.

Mike waited. He wore slacks and a baggy sweatshirt. The single light left his face mostly in shadow, and a trace of dissoluteness and despair had been added to the asceticism that Jack had noted earlier in the day. All merely hints, visible to Jack only because he knew the priest so well. Or not visible at all, only imagined.

"You can forget about Janelle becoming entangled with the Vasconcelloses."

Mike nodded slowly. "Janelle is a sensible woman."

Even his criticism of her would be cast in the form of praise. Jack didn't quite know where to go from here, but now that they had begun, it turned out there was something on Mike's mind, too.

"Did you tell Lonny Vasconcellos that you hoped he wasn't attending Mass?"

Oh, shit, Jack thought.

"Got that from Tony, did you?"

"You shouldn't have said that, Jack."

Jack looked down at his hands, thumb kneading palm. "I was mad. Lonny was threatening the black contractor we've got down on the job site. If he *is* going to Mass, he isn't getting much out of it."

"You think that makes any difference? All Catholics have a grave obligation to take part in the Eucharist. You know that. A grave obligation, Jack."

"I was mad."

"That doesn't justify it."

Jack knew he was in the wrong, but at the moment to concede anything felt like conceding everything. He'd been at a disadvantage with Janelle, and now here he was at a disadvantage with Mike. He'd come over here to have it out, and look what was happening. He tried to change the subject.

"I noticed that Lonny wasn't there this afternoon. Where do you suppose Leo got the idea for his little stunt?"

Mike would not be put off so easily. "I don't know. At the moment, I don't care… The question is, Jack, do you really want to add the sin of failing to hear the Mass to the others that Lonny Vasconcellos must answer for? Do you?"

"No, of course not."

Mike seemed to relax. His voice became more coaxing. "I'm sure you don't. It was just a bad moment. I know that, Jack. I mean, consider yourself. You never miss. You're scrupulous… And this even though you're burdened with your own doubts." He left a long pause before continuing. "Are you not? Your own fear that your faith might be slipping. Your own spiritual travail… You see, I know, Jack. I know what it is that you've wanted to talk to me about all these months, but never been willing to." Mike spoke conversationally now, as a man will who's simply determined to make a point. But the words were obviously an invitation, as well.

And a shock. Mike had known all along. Of course he had. *But what a time*, Jack thought, *to bring it up*. The wrong time. Always the wrong time.

When he didn't respond, Mike answered the original question, "I got it from Angela. Angela is very upset with you."

"Everybody's mad at everybody." Jack saw his opening. "If you'd stayed out of it in the first place, none of this would've happened."

Now it was Mike's turn to say nothing.

"Why, Mike?"

"Why what?"

"Why are you involved with the Vasconcellos family? What's the real reason?"

"The *real* reason?"

"Yes."

"The Vasconcelloses are my parishioners. Why shouldn't I be?"

"I'm sorry, that's not good enough."

"I don't see why not."

"Janelle thinks Doug Ott is going to lose his sixty thousand."

"Might he?" Mike asked.

"Probably not," Jack conceded.

"I didn't think so." Mike spoke with assurance, as confident of his own judgments as Janelle was of hers. "Although," the priest continued, "even if he did… Doug Ott would rather lose the money than get involved. Worse than you are. 'Course, money doesn't mean anything to Doug. Inherited it, got plenty more where that came from."

"It's nice to know somebody's worse than I am," Jack said.

"He'd never come here late at night to confront me, either."

"I'm sure he wouldn't."

Jack mentioned Janelle again. He didn't exactly mean to invoke her opinions, didn't enjoy bringing her into the conversation at all, but Mike was more than a match for Jack's own weak sallies. He needed a stouter battering ram. "Janelle thinks Doug might lose the money. Whether he will or not is beside the point. You lose credibility. She thinks you're way over the line. She thinks there must be a reason."

"Janelle, as we know, is a woman of strong opinions."

"Yes. And, believe me, you don't want to know what they are."

Jack watched as Mike considered what it was that he didn't want to know.

"She thinks...perhaps...Angela and me?"

Jack started to say, "No. Worse," but stopped himself. It was bad enough that he was using Janelle in this assault upon Mike's battlements.

"No," he said instead, "that's what I think."

"And Janelle?"

"For that, you'll have to ask her."

Jack watched as the priest gathered in the implications of all this—what Jack thought and what Janelle thought, probably worse, and what worse amounted to.

"I see. Well..." He pressed his lips together and shook his head, clearly upset, unprepared for the brutality of it. "You can tell Janelle she's got nothing to worry about."

"And me?"

"You, either."

"I'm sorry." And Jack was. Some things should be left unsaid. And he didn't mean to make Janelle and Mike more enemies than they already were. But he was relieved, too, believing Mike's denials, although Janelle, no doubt, would not.

"But why, then, Mike? What is it about the Vasconcellos family? Why are you so involved?"

Mike frowned, his lower jaw stuck slightly forward. Acts had consequences, and whatever Jack's relief over the matter of sex, the protestations of innocence that he had exacted from Mike had raised a barrier between them. Just how high Jack was about to find out.

"There are worse sins than the ones you and Janelle are so fixated on," Mike told him. "Not more grotesque, I'll grant you, but worse nonetheless. I suppose we could talk about them. Someday perhaps we will... The trouble is, Jack, it requires a level of trust that you and I don't have. You want me to be honest with you, but you're not willing to be honest with me. You sneak off to Mass in the Cathedral Parish. You talk to me about everything but what's really on your mind. It won't do, Jack. It won't do at all. As for the Vasconcellos family, well, that's not a matter I'm willing to discuss. I help them because they're in my parish and they need help. That's all you have to know. If you and Janelle don't want to add your support, then don't. It's your choice."

Mike showed him out. At the door, he said, "Until you allow me to be your priest, Jack, you're going to continue to blame me. Me or Tony Vasconcellos or anybody but yourself."

As Jack walked away, he carried Mike's powerful criticisms with him, and, except for the liquor on the priest's breath, he might have accepted them. It seemed impossible that they should ever talk about those other matters. Somewhere along the way, they'd committed themselves to the relationship they now must suffer to continue...and abrade away until, like the mortar between the stones of the church, nothing remained.

CHAPTER 74

~

Johnny Pond wasn't sure when he was going to bring Chloe and the children back. Maybe never. He got up and went to work on Monday morning. No reason not to. At the radio station, he turned the photographs of his family around on his desk so that only he could see them. The joy he felt while chasing the cross burners had long since evaporated, no substance to it. He closed the iron grate against the furnace of his rage.

On the hour and the half hour, he did the morning news, among the items one about plans to arraign the cross burners. He read this with the newsman's practiced modulations, as if the matter had nothing to do with him. A second piece dealt with the arrival in town of David Duke. In a few hours, Duke would be standing, full of his Klan logic and self-righteousness, on the steps of city hall. Johnny read this story as he read the first.

The station manager wanted him to take a few days off, to go on home, as if he might find something there to comfort him instead of just the opposite. The other employees let him be after they'd offered their sympathies. Sympathies were of no use to him.

At 8:20, the receptionist called from the front and said that Sam Turner had come to see him. Johnny had little time to see Sam, or interest in seeing him, either, but Sam was entitled and so Johnny went up and brought him back to his office and told him to close the door behind him.

Sam did what he was bid and sat down and took off his hat, some sort of a cross between a baseball and a hunting cap, with a bill and earflaps. He propped it on his knee.

"Heard Duke's been in town a couple days," he began. "Goin' around meeting with people. You hear that?"

Johnny had sat back down behind his desk. "He flew in last night."

"That right?"

"I only got a couple of minutes, brother. What's on your mind?"

"Yeah, okay." Sam clasped the tops of his thighs, his hands small for his body, his body nothing to brag on, either, fragile boned, narrow at the shoulders. He had shaved his head, something unmathematical about the arcs and plains, as if bits of it had been chipped away. Johnny guessed he had done it more to hide the baldness beginning to creep in than from any proclamation of black manhood. He had a drinker's eyes. Narrow nose, thin lips. There were some Caucasians in the Turner family woodpile.

His expression managed a certain severity at rest, as if he might assert himself, but broke apart as soon as he began to speak, exposing crooked teeth. He had trouble getting his words out.

"I jus' wanted to say, man...you know...I'm sorry about what happened."

"Yeah. Okay." Johnny didn't want Sam's condolences any more than anyone else's. "Just like the good ol' days."

"Been thinking about it all weekend."

Sam had grabbed his hybrid cap and begun slapping it nervously against his leg. Johnny tried to imagine why he had come. Just to commiserate? Or perhaps he felt some responsibility here.

"It's none of your doing, Sam, if that's what you're thinking."

The cap came to rest. "I don't know, man. If I hadn't've bid on the job... I mean, I feel real bad."

The words couldn't undo anything and meant little to Johnny, but Sam had a need and Johnny remained mindful of his obligation to a brother.

"Listen, Sam, hardly anybody even knows I was involved in that. All done behind the scenes. This other thing—it's got nothing to do with you."

Sam didn't seize on this idea, as Johnny expected. Instead he started slapping his cap against his leg again, more agitated now, as if he didn't accept but couldn't refute what Johnny had said.

Johnny watched him struggling within himself and then said, "I haven't got time for this, brother. I've gotta be on the air. You've got nothing to feel bad about. This is white man's shit."

Sam ducked his head, a kind of twitching motion. "I know." He was dressed in the unconscious, fitting-in way of most Jacksonians, only his shaved skull un-Jacksonian.

Johnny glanced at the clock. 8:24.

"Aren't you supposed to be at work?" he asked.

"Yeah. But I wanted to…you know…"

"How you doing in the drafting room?"

"Okay." Sam's body language didn't say okay, though.

Johnny inspected him. He had helped get the job for Turner and expected him to perform. "You working on your own? At home? Brushing up your skills?"

Sam hesitated and then said, "Yeah, sure."

"You gotta do that, man. They're not gonna hand you a thing, not anymore. You've gotta work for it. You understand?"

Sam didn't say anything, having withdrawn and become passive under this sudden, unexpected assault.

"Let me tell you something, Sam. If anything good's gonna come out of all this, it's gotta be you." Johnny understood that by saying this, he was, in a way, blaming Sam. He didn't mean to, but it couldn't be helped. Sam was the only one who might benefit from all this. Nobody else was gonna get anything but grief. "You got that job. You moved on up. That's good, man, that's good. None of this other shit is your fault. It just shows what can come down. We make a little gain, and all hell breaks loose. Ain't your fault. But now you gotta perform, brother. Understand what I'm saying?"

"I don't know." Sam managed to stir himself slightly, but he sure didn't present an encouraging picture. "Seems like, you know, it's a pretty bullshit job. Got me doing nothin' but rinky-dink shit."

This statement raised the trapdoor on a snake pit of possibilities, but Johnny didn't have the time.

"What you telling me, Sam? You gonna lay down on me?"

Sam swung his head unhappily from side to side.

"Nah." He looked up, his expression suddenly keener. "But these motherfuckers, they'll never change, man. Sometimes you gotta just say, 'Fuck it, fuck the job, fuck everything.'"

Great, Johnny thought, just what he needed. "You say 'Fuck it,' my friend, but let me tell you, the only one who's gonna get fucked is you."

"This place never gonna change. You know that. These honkies'll never accept us." Sam started rocking from side to side, in a slow pantomime of a fighter ducking punches. "Sometimes you just gotta *do it*, man. You gotta rub their noses in their own shit."

Sam's agitation alarmed Johnny, totally unlike what he knew of the man. *Oh, shit*, he thought, *here's another motherfucking nigger about to lose it.*

"Rub their noses in what? What are you talking about?"

Sam waggled his head, cap teetering on his knee, his fists tapping the insides of his thighs, one and then the other, in a ragged rhythm. If he was going over the edge, he wasn't doing it with any style.

"What is it?" Johnny demanded. "What's goin' down?"

But as quickly as Sam had opened up, he began to close down. His hands became still. He sagged back in his chair.

"Ah…you know…Reiny…"

"Reiny Kopp? What about him?"

"Nothin'. I just…"

"What about Reiny Kopp?" Johnny didn't trust Kopp.

"Nothin', man," Sam said, backtracking as fast as he could, his voice dropping almost to a mumble. "He's just, you know, remounting the exhibit and all. Looking to—"

"The museum exhibit?"

"Yeah, but forget about it, brother, okay? Just forget about it."

"What about the exhibit? What have you got yourself into?"

"Forget it, man."

Something was on. Johnny wondered if there was any point in a talk with Kopp. Probably not. He peered closely at Sam, sitting crumpled up in the chair.

"Okay. The exhibit, there's something about the exhibit. Anything else?"

"No, that's all." The denial lacked all conviction.

"What?"

"No, man. That's all. Forget about it. I just wanted to come and see you and, you know, apologize. I feel bad about what happened is all." He spoke sullenly.

Kopp must have something planned for David Duke, Johnny decided. Well, okay, that was all right. Johnny didn't really give a shit what Kopp did. He could do anything made him happy. But Sam Turner wasn't built for the kind of games Kopp liked to play. Sam would get nothing but screwed.

"I don't care what Reiny's got in mind, Sam. You keep out of it."

Sam didn't respond.

"You hear me? Stay out of it… Look, you've got a good job. Worry about that. Forget about anything else. You've got your chance, brother. Don't fuck it up."

Something ticked at the back of Johnny's mind, and he looked at the clock again. Time was up.

Sam dipped his head, hangdog again, the person Johnny had always known.

"Get good, Sam, make yourself the best goddamn draftsman in the city. It ain't easy, it's hard, you better believe it. And expect no help, brother. You do it, you'll do it on your own. Understand? Do it for all the other brothers would kill for a job like that. Okay? And one more thing. You don't, there's not a damn thing anybody can do to save your sorry ass."

Sam moved restlessly in his chair.

"I can't talk about this anymore." Johnny had already opened the door. People passed in the corridor. "Go to work," he ordered.

As Johnny crossed toward the studio, he decided that Sam owed him an apology after all.

CHAPTER 75

~

Dexter Walcott laid the plans open on top of the gang box, and he and Mustafa, his foreman, reviewed the work. They were starting in the paddock building, where the dogs would be brought for weighing and drug testing and whatnot before the races, but which was now nothing more than a shell, columns and beams and trusswork, the roof and siding on, window and door openings cut and covered with translucent plastic sheeting, illuminating the space in a dim washed-out light. The white crews were working up on the deck of the grandstand or out at the kennels, so Dex and Mustafa had the place to themselves. Just as well.

"We'll need jigs here and here." Dex pointed. "Here, too. Be sure you don't toss any scrap." He warned Mustafa about this all the time, about ending up with too many useless odds and ends. Dex pissed his foreman off with the repetition of it. Couldn't be helped. Mustafa was a good worker, but he was sloppy if Dex didn't keep his eye on him, sloppy like a fox, for Mustafa didn't mind taking these "leftovers" home for the small projects he ran on the side.

"Ain't no profit in rework," Dex would tell him. "Plan your cuts so that scrap material can be used somewheres else." Mustafa listened, annoyed, maybe recalculating just how much he could get away with. But he was a good worker, worth more than he cost.

Dex finished reviewing the plans, and walked around the interior of the space and got his foreman lined out. Mustafa would be doing the same for the other crewmembers as they began to come onto the site. Dex figured he'd build up the crew slow, let the whites get used to seeing a few black faces at a time, so for the moment it was just him and Mustafa, doing work the carpenters would do later.

They snapped the chalk lines and then set to work on the bottom plate for the first of the interior walls. Dex cut the plates and spliced them together and lay them along the wall line, and Mustafa followed along, shooting them down using the nail set.

They continued to talk for a brief time, discussing who to bring on site first, how long they could delay beginning work over at the grandstand. Afterwards, the two of them being of different generations and different temperaments, they fell silent except for the brief exchanges required by the work. Mustafa turned on his boom box, but Dex told him to keep it down. If he wanted to listen to rap on this job, it'd be a private concert. No need to go agitating the natives.

They heard footsteps outside and the corner of the plastic on one of the doors was peeled up, and Chuck Fellows stepped through. He was not alone. With him came a little boy, a smaller version of himself.

Fellows had a certain way of entering a space. He looked at Mustafa, at Dexter, at the plate in Dexter's hand. Reminded Dexter of a flashlight beam.

Fellows nodded and they exchanged pleasantries.

"Everything going okay?" Fellows wanted to know.

Dexter took his time, thinking he ought to let Fellows do the talking, but then deciding he might mention Kelley. "Jack's been over."

"Looking out for you, is he?"

Dexter said, "Looking out for someone."

The low rap music in the background sounded more like grumbling resentments than proud assertions. Dexter listened for a few moments, then shook his head and turned his attention back to Fellows, who said, "Anything I can do?" and with a jittery energy grabbed one of the plates and hefted it and held it up so he could sight along the channel of the metal. He gave the impression of a man unaccountably ill at ease.

A short distance away, Mustafa continued to shoot down the sticks of bottom plate.

"Rather work with wood, had my choice," Dex said.

"Um," Fellows nodded. He seemed distracted. The boy, a solidly built little tyke, had taken off his hardhat and was struggling to cinch down the headband so it would fit better. Dexter didn't think a construction site was any place for a child.

"'Course," Dex added, "you want work nowadays, you can't afford to be too picky. That's what I tell all my boys. Flexibility's the key. I can work with metal. Done it for years. Has its virtues, too."

Fellows said, "That's right."

His son had begun to sidle away, his interest captured by something. He paid attention with the same frankness as the father.

Dex reached out, and Fellows handed him the plate. Dex inserted it beneath the end of the one Mustafa was nailing to the concrete.

"So what is it about Kelley?" Fellows asked after a silence. "He giving you a hard time?" Dexter, his back turned as he worked, listened to the tone of the questions, flat, matter-of-fact.

"Nope." Dexter had been over on the deck, checking the plans and doing some preliminary layout. The other trades had stocked material wherever they wanted. Getting them to move it was gonna be a hassle. But this wasn't the sort of thing he'd complain to Fellows about. Best try to work it out with the other contractors, go to Kelley if he absolutely had to.

"When you bringing your people on site?" Fellows asked.

"Pretty quick now."

"Are they commuting or are you putting them up locally?"

"Use car pools, I expect. Though it makes a mighty long day."

"What about staying in town?"

"At a motel or something? Thought about it. Too expensive. Might be we could find some local families willing to take a few in. Don't know."

Fellows had nothing to say to this, so they lapsed back into silence.

In the background, Mustafa's sullenness seemed as substantial a thing as the sharp reports of his nail set. Dex had no contacts in the local black community. He was reluctant, Jackson having the reputation it did, but it was probably something he should look into.

Finally, Fellows said, "If there's anything I can do…"

Dex rather liked Fellows. He supposed he might use him to get Jack Kelley off his back, if it came to that. Kelley was likely to be over there every two minutes—wanting to see Dex's material list, wanting to see his purchase orders, wanting to see his confirmed delivery dates, wanting to see his layout of the work—everything a CM would be interested in who didn't trust his contractor. Dex understood. He was an unknown as far as Kelley was concerned. Dex understood, but he didn't like it. It would undermine his authority with his own people.

He looked across at Mustafa, working on kneepads, moving slowly along the runner he was laying down, pressing the nail set firmly into the shallow metal channel, squeezing the trigger, his arm tensing as the fastener was driven home. They'd never worked a job in quite such a hostile setting as this. And come right down to it, Dex didn't know about Mustafa, what might happen. A good worker, sure, but as for the rest, Dex just didn't know. Or about some of his other people, either, the young ones particularly. They respected and disrespected in a way different from Dex.

So, yeah, it'd be good if Jack Kelley backed off, just let Dex do the job. Jack had no appreciation of Dex's situation. You could look at the man and tell right off he got only half the story. Chuck Fellows, too. Whites were like that. You just looked at them and you knew.

But Jack, for all his shortcomings, had one thing right: focus on the work.

"Much obliged," he told Fellows. "Keep it in mind."

"Good," Fellows said. "You know where you can find me."

"I thank you."

"In the meantime, I've got a small favor to ask."

A favor? "What might that be?"

"I got a meeting over at the construction trailer. You mind watching my son while I'm over there?"

This request, totally unexpected, did not please Dex. Nothing in the contract documents said anything about babysitting. "Perhaps it'd be best if you kept him with you."

"I'm concerned about the language, just as soon not expose him to that," Fellows said. "I'd appreciate it. I'd consider it a real favor." A note of anxiety had crept into Fellows's tone that was completely unlike the man.

If you were worried about the language, Dex thought, *why'd you bring him down here in the first place?* Still, Dex didn't see he had much choice in the matter. No call to alienate the man paying the bills.

"You all right with that, son, staying here with Mustafa and me for a bit?" Dex asked the boy, who merely shrugged.

"Thanks," Fellows said. "Be back soon as I can. As for you, Todd, you do whatever Mr. Walcott says."

Watching as Fellows stalked briskly away, in his don't-tread-on-me way, Dex wondered for the thousandth, for the five thousandth time at the oddness of human beings.

He looked at the son. "Anybody stays with me gets put to work."

From beneath his oversized helmet, the boy longingly stared at the plastic through which his father had disappeared, but resisted whatever urge he had to run after him. He seemed a sturdy lad, that much at least, not the kind to let fear get the best of him.

"How old are you? Todd, is it?"

"Yes, sir. I'm eight."

"Eight. Ripe old age. Well, let's see what we can find for you to do."

∼

Chuck circled the rim of the sand plateau atop which the construction was proceeding, looked down on the low sections of the island, and talked about the coming high water with Jack Kelley and Mitch Mitchell, the contractor doing the site work.

"The problem," Jack was saying, "is gonna be keeping the job open."

Kelley, of course, was only interested in the project schedule. They were standing on the western lip of the low mesa, the slope dipping down to the parking area, or what one day would be the parking area, once the dredge sand had been placed and built up to the finish grade and seal coated. Now a snowfield capped the old city dump and continued on to the water-ski club in the distance, shuttered for the winter, at the upper end of the slough separating the island from the mainland. Directly to the west, a thicket of trees shielded the slough, the boles of the trees reddish, their crowns hazy with swelling buds.

Kelley wasn't looking at any of this. His glance swept the length of the access road to the southwest, the nonunion entrance, which dipped down from the uncompleted, stubbed-off main entrance road out near the highway and looped for a couple of hundred yards across the surface of the island before climbing up onto the job site. Assuming the river stage rose to twenty-five feet, as the Corps of Engineers now prophesied, the island would be flooded, including the low stretch of road. The construction site would remain above the floodwaters but be encircled—an island on the island—the only access by boat.

Mitch Mitchell cantilevered out as far as he could over the edge of the sand and unreeled his tape measure, playing it down to the approximate height of the predicted crest.

"Eight feet."

"I suppose," Chuck said, just to pull Jack's chain, "when the time comes, we could simply close the project down for a while." A good long while. The Mississippi wasn't flashy. It didn't rise and fall in quick time, like some piddly-assed backwater. It moved in and took over the floodplain, like the dispossessed come to reclaim its patrimony. If they shut the operation down, it'd stay shut down. Jack, anyway, didn't react, and Chuck noticed that he didn't take much pleasure in the gibe himself. Whatever else he thought about the man, Kelley wasn't the sort to turn his back and walk away.

"You got two choices," Mitchell said, reeling his tape back in, "protect the access road as is or raise her up."

"Raise her up," Chuck told him.

"What about fill? Truck it in?" Mitch, of course, would be happy to do that, and get the benefit of a change order. He was dumpy and unphysical and pale, an indoor sort of guy, and when you looked at him, you wondered how he ever got into the grading business. He resembled a junior high school teacher or assistant vice president of some podunk bank. Anyway, he had the mind of a contractor, change orders being the next best thing to sex.

"We're gonna use sand out of the river," Chuck told him.

Jack roused himself from his reverie. "Oh? Steal from Peter to pay Paul?"

"No. We leave the sand already placed alone. I'm gonna start running my operation around the clock. We'll stockpile over near the water. If we don't have to pump so far, we can pump more. We'll use a scraper to move it around."

"Expect I can help there," Mitch said.

"Maybe. We'll talk about it."

"You sure you can provide enough sand?" Jack asked skeptically. Chuck's dredging operation was considered a joke, of course, all the work he'd put into it for the pissy little dribble of sand he'd managed to place so far. Pretty damn funny when you thought about it.

Kelley made his case. "The road will be at an angle to the flow of water, for all intents and purposes a dam, depending on how it crosses the island. Anyway, we need to build it like a dam. If the Corps is wrong about the crest, if it's even higher, you could end up with a helluva lot of pressure against the thing."

Chuck resisted the impulse to reassure Jack that he had everything under control, and instead told him the truth. "You're right, stupid to build the thing if we don't build it right. Can I pump enough sand? I don't know. We're just gonna have to adapt to the situation as we go along."

"I see," Jack said and seemed on the point of adding something else, but changed his mind. As Chuck had honed his reasons for disrespecting Kelley, he'd added to the bill of particulars this tendency of Kelley's to hold things back, to reveal only a corner of what was on his mind.

Mitchell, for his part, had been scratching his chin and listening. "Of course," he put in now, "sand—even the hydraulic stuff out of the river—ain't your ideal material for this sort of situation."

"No, that's right," Chuck agreed at once. "But then again, it was stupid to build the track out here in the first place." Chuck never kidded himself that any of this made a whole helluva lot of sense. "I figure it's the domino theory, one fucked up decision leading to the next. But the sand is usable. It might not be ideal, but it's usable."

"Yes," Jack agreed, "I suppose that's right. And we might as well forget about ideal solutions. We've got sand everywhere else to keep from liquefying and washing away. What's this but more of the same?" He squinted at Chuck, and seemed inclined to say some more, but, once again, didn't.

The discussion went on to the matter of accelerating the schedule for placing the riprap and what sorts of other remediation might retard infiltration of the sand by the floodwaters.

After Mitchell had gone away and as the two of them were walking back toward the construction trailer, Jack said, "Don't get all heroic on me, Chuck. If you can't pump the sand, tell me." He paused a beat. "I do care about finishing this job on time, even if you don't."

This bluntness didn't bother Chuck. It was refreshing, and Chuck took his time responding. If he'd changed any over the years, it had been to acquire a keener understanding that truth-telling wasn't as easy as it looked. Half-truths, therefore, being inevitable, he'd decided long ago that he'd err on the side of overemphasizing his self-interest in a matter.

"You're right, Jack, I don't care about the project. But the city needs the income from it. If they don't get it, they'll be paying off the track bonds out of general revenue money. That's my money, my damn taxes. And that I do care about."

They stopped to watch the work up among the beams and trusses, where ironworkers were just beginning to install the standing-seam roof, wheeling into place the forty-foot-long sheets, resembling the wings of giant prehistoric birds coming to roost.

Chuck's response had apparently alleviated for the moment whatever doubts Jack had concerning the dredge, for when he spoke next, it was on another matter. "Do you know who the third cross burner was, the underage one?"

"No."

"Another Vasconcellos heard from—Leo this time, Tony's son, Lonny's younger brother."

"Is that right?" Chuck found this idea...pleasing. "Who told you?"

"They're in my parish."

"I know."

"Oh?"

"My wife's been talking to your daughter."

"So Kitty tells me. Apparently they find our relationship, yours and mine, an amusing topic."

Chuck laughed. "I'm glad somebody does."

As they resumed their course back toward the construction trailer, Jack asked, "Do you suppose there's something we can do about it?"

"About our relationship?" This sudden invitation to discuss the matter, to thrash things out, to become pals, didn't much impress Chuck, and he said at once, "I dunno, Jack, you tell me." Chuck spent his days talking and being talked at, but he distrusted language. Language was a confidence game.

Jack didn't pursue the matter, instead referring back to the fact that he and Vasconcellos were in the same parish. "I suppose you think the fix is in, then."

"It had occurred to me." Diane had learned from Jack's daughter that some sort of long-standing animosity existed between Jack and Tony Vasconcellos, but Chuck assumed that wouldn't necessarily get in the way of lending a hand to a fellow Catholic.

Jack said, "My priest is trying to...I don't know what he's trying to do, but he's taken the Vasconcellos family under his wing."

Jack related the history of the triangular relationship among himself, his priest and Tony Vasconcellos.

"Anyway," he said when he was done, "I'm through trying to manipulate Tony. I've told him if he interferes with Dexter Walcott, Walcott wins, Walcott comes out looking like the good guy. The only way Tony wins is by putting out superior work. If Walcott's people put in ten-hour days, Tony's got to put in twelve. If Walcott's got twenty guys on the site, Tony's got to have twenty-five. If Walcott's gung ho, Tony's got to be super gung ho. That's the only way he wins. I've told Tony, and I plan to tell the other contractors, too. Put them all on notice."

Chuck said, "And Dexter, you're telling him, too?"

"I suppose. Hadn't really thought about it. He's not the problem."

"I can do it," Chuck suggested, since he was heading in that direction.

"No, let me. But you're right. If it's a game, Walcott deserves to know he's one of the players."

As he prepared to leave, Chuck said, "After all, Jack, it might make him work harder, too. You'd like that, wouldn't you?"

Having recovered some of his old irascibility for the moment, Chuck strode toward the paddock building to collect Todd. Outside, he heard the reports of the nail set, Dexter's man still shooting down bottom plates. Except that, when he entered, it wasn't the construction worker holding the gun but Todd, gripping it with both hands, the device recoiling as he set another pin through a bottom plate and into the concrete floor.

As soon as he saw Chuck he leaped up—the nail set rescued by Dexter's man before it crashed to the floor—and came over bubbling and trying to tell Chuck everything he'd been doing, the words bumping up against each other as they rushed forward.

Over the top of his head, Chuck said, "Thanks, Dex. I appreciate it." Walcott nodded.

Todd pulled Chuck across the floor and showed him a chalk line he had made. "You pull the string tight, it's all covered with chalk and you, you know, pick it up in the middle, like a bow and arrow, and let go, and—bwang!—it goes like that, against the floor. Isn't it neat, Daddy? I did it!"

Chuck hadn't expected this much and he thanked Dex again and said to him, "By the way, I've been thinking. If you do decide to find places for your people to stay in town, might be I can help. I'll talk to my wife. Perhaps we could put somebody up."

Dexter looked surprised, then nodded and said he'd remember. "Expect your wife might have other ideas."

"I'll let you know."

Back outside, Todd raced ahead a few steps and then turned around and skipped backwards. "Mustafa…Amin…al-Umana."

"What?"

"That's the name of the other man. He told me. It means…I forget what it means. Can I come back, Daddy, can I, can I?"

"We'll see."

"Neat!" And Todd was off and racing ahead again.

Chuck smiled at his son's enthusiasm. He was satisfied.

CHAPTER 76

~

After 10:00 a.m., his relief took over the newscasts and Johnny Pond had some time before *Sound Off* at 12:30. First he called Chloe to check on her and the kids, then a local realtor to begin the process of putting his house on the market. That done, he went up to city hall looking for Chuck Fellows to see about a matter one of the *Sound Off* callers had raised back on Friday. Back in Johnny's other life.

Fellows, working several jobs, was almost impossible to track down anymore, so Johnny ended up dealing with Seth Brunel, the assistant city engineer. When they had finished, Johnny asked what else was going on, and Brunel told him about the Corps of Engineers' prediction for the spring rise. Johnny went back to KJAX thinking that a biblical flood wasn't such a bad idea.

At noon, he returned to city hall and listened to the first few minutes of David Duke's speech. Not a particularly big crowd. Looked to be more counterdemonstrators and cops and press and gawkers than Duke supporters. Johnny, not there in an official capacity, moved among the others at his leisure, greeting those he knew, accepting sympathy for the cross burning, letting himself be seen. He spotted Sam Turner in among the demonstrators, but Sam moved slightly away, avoiding his gaze, and Johnny wondered once more just what it was Sam had gotten himself into.

Duke exhorted the mostly passive crowd. Johnny paid little attention. He'd heard it all before. He wasn't surprised at the anemic turnout despite the pirate radio station's nonstop ads for the event. For all his pseudo-sophistication, Duke was an anachronism. Jacksonians had moved on. Their racism was of a different sort.

Duke was a good-looking fellow in a college frat sort of way, a ginger-colored forelock snapping in the breeze, and word was he liked the women, so Johnny figured that that was what he was really about, came right down to it—out to get as much poontang as he could, all the rest nothing but tactics. Johnny wouldn't have minded rearranging his face for him. Permanently. See how much lovin' he got then.

A few minutes after twelve, Duke just getting wound up, Johnny left and went back to the station to prepare for *Sound Off*. Among his messages was a return call from the realtor. He made a quick callback, but got the machine.

In the studio, squeezed into the too-small swivel chair at the mixer, headphones on, he waited for the commercial break at the half hour to end, the lights on two of the phone lines already lit.

The wrong time to be selling a house. The local economy hurting, the market glutted, they'd never get their money out of the place, but made no difference, Johnny was determined to get rid of it. He'd take nobody's advice but his own. He knew the impression of cowardice that selling gave, as if he was running away. People could think what they wanted; he had no respect for their opinions. Selling had to do with his daughters, not him, what leaving or staying meant for them. He'd made up his mind. Better to grow up among their own kind, where they could learn to value themselves in a proper manner.

Sound Off began. He dispensed with his usual topical comments and went straight to the phones—the first caller a woman irate at what had been done to him and his family.

"Whatever we happen to think about this whole business, there was no excuse for that. Those young men were just plain ignorant. They don't know the harm they do… And your poor family, your poor little girls. I just feel heartsick for them."

Johnny thanked her and asked what she thought about "this whole business" and why she supposed the cross burners were ignorant. He listened to her responses, speaking only briefly himself, confining himself to a question or two more.

The next caller picked up the theme, for callers were usually listeners, too, and shows often became serial discussions. When a call got repetitive, Johnny would deflect it slightly, probing, seeking a new angle. But no new angles today, no surprises for him on this subject. His mind wandered.

Selling the house wasn't the only problem. Getting another job would be even trickier. There were lots of ex-jocks out there, too old and maimed to suit up anymore, looking for work in the media. Over the weekend, he'd started canvassing the people he knew in the business. He'd not go anywhere until he had a job. Had to have a job. One thing he'd promised himself—take care of the family, whatever else happened, take care of Chloe and the kids. He'd never become one of those poor damn niggers couldn't find employment and ended up a drunken wife-beater.

More people called with their condolences. *Condolences,* he decided, wasn't quite the right word. In his hostility to these well-meaning attempts to express sympathy, Johnny struggled to find the right label so that he could reject them. *Compassion, pity, charity...* Racism that dare not speak its name.

The conversations drifted. It was inevitable that someone would bring up the claim that had been made on the pirate station that Johnny opposed the plan to bring black families to Jackson.

"Can't say I'm surprised," the caller who did it said. "You've always been a sensible fellow, not the sort who toes the liberal line just because most of your people do."

Johnny didn't respond. Instead he let the silence drag out until the caller, anxiety mounting in his voice, blurted, "That is what you think, ain't it, a man oughta be able to choose for himself? City's got no right going out and using the people's money to recruit blacks to come here."

"As a matter of principle?"

"Of course, a matter of principle. If a man chooses, of his own free will and whatnot, to move here, well, that's fine, that's his business."

"I see. Then again," Johnny said, "we live in a democracy. Suppose the voters decided the city ought to go out and advertise for black families to move here..."

"It's wrong. People oughta be able to choose. That's bad enough, but you know what really ticks me off?"

"I have no idea."

"It's when people just assume you're a racist. Just because I'm against this thing, I'm a racist. It's like my wife, you know, always claiming she knows what I'm thinking all the time. You got a wife, you know what I mean. Right? Well, that's the way it is with this thing about going out and rounding up some blacks and bringing them here because El Plowman and people like her have decided we don't have the proper quota. I got nothing against blacks. I wish 'em the best. But just because I'm against this harebrained scheme of the mayor's, people think I'm prejudiced."

"But you're not."

"No, sir, I am not."

"Okay," Johnny said, "I can accept that. Anyway, as you say, no man can look into another man's soul and see what's truly there." He had to pause for a moment to adjust his tone of voice, for as he'd listened to the fellow, it had occurred to Johnny that he'd heard this particular line of bullshit, this stock-in-trade denial of closet racists everywhere, just one motherfucking time too many. "Let me ask you this," he began when he felt ready to continue, "do you suppose it's possible for a man to have no prejudice in him, none at all, and yet…despite all that, still be a racist? You think that's possible?"

The question dissipated like vapor, as if the caller lacked the necessary receptors. "Like you said, you can't tell what a man's thinking. I'm just telling you I got no animosity at all for the black man, I wish him the best. But it's flat wrong to go out recruiting people to—"

"I've got to move on," Johnny said and cut the man off. He could have pushed the point, but he had no intention of instructing these natural born fools in the true desire of their hearts.

And that was another problem, worse, much worse than the business about selling the house and finding another job. Johnny must now attend upon the need to suppress his anger. A black man couldn't afford to show his anger. A black man's anger could not become a social thing. No trace could linger on the surface, no insignificant peak remain visible for whites to see and suspect the vastness unseen, upon which their little ships might founder. Best if Johnny didn't even know about it himself, best if he turned the energy of it into getting ahead. Showing the world no emotions at all. Shuck and jive. Whatever it took.

Wasn't about him. None of it was about him. Was about his little daughters. Nobody else.

CHAPTER 77

~

When the car dipped down into the low area between the two rows of little houses, Todd Fellows let himself go loosey-goosey because he liked the feeling of his body getting jounced this way and that.

"I've never been here before," he told his dad.

"It's called Little Wales."

"Why?"

"Back in the nineteenth century when there were lots of lead mines in the area—you know about those—many of the miners came from Wales. They lived around here. Do you know where Wales is?"

"No."

As his dad explained, they approached the very last house on the street. Clothes were hanging on a clothesline. Todd knew about clotheslines. He'd seen buckskinners use them at rendezvous. Out in the yard was a sign saying, "Smoked walleyes and sauger." He knew what they were, too, some kind of fish.

His dad pulled into the driveway and pointed toward the big buildings out beyond the houses. "You see that area, how flat it is? That's fill. Millions of tons of rocks and sand and gravel were put there so they could build the industrial park. If we were here thirty years ago, that wouldn't have existed. You know what we would've been looking at? A slough, a backwater of the Mississippi. These houses used to be on the bank of the river then. And across from them would have been an island covered with trees. This place would have been just completely different from what it looks like today."

Todd, however, wasn't paying attention anymore. He was studying the clothesline, for the objects hanging from it were not clothes.

"What are those?" he asked. "Over there?"

His dad didn't answer immediately, like he usually did. The things were shaped a little bit like his sister's snowsuit, but smaller and not bright-colored, more like scroungy brown.

"Muskrat pelts, I expect."

"Do I know about them?"

"Probably not. I'll show you a picture when we get home. They're a little bit like beaver." He started to get out of the truck. "You stay here. I've got to go inside for a minute."

"Aw," Todd said, and then stopped himself, remembering the tone of voice that sometimes worked with his father. "Why can't I come?"

His dad kind of grimaced, a little like when he was on the point of getting fed up with Todd's pestering or something. Todd figured, given that look, no way he'd be allowed to tag along. But he was wrong.

"Okay, but stay close to me."

"Neat!"

Todd pushed the door open and hopped out and they walked through the packed-down snow toward the screened-in porch. The house seemed to be backwards, its front where its rear should have been. Todd checked out the muskrats as they passed nearby. If they were like beavers, maybe the man who lived there had trapped them, just like the buckskinners used to do.

"What's that, Dad? Is it a bathroom?"

"A privy? No. Probably it's Turcotte's smokehouse. I'll explain later."

The porch was lined with ice chests, like the one his mother packed for them to take on picnics. But they only had one. Here he counted fourteen and was still counting as his father knocked on the inside door and someone came and the door opened.

Boy, thought Todd, *this place isn't anything like home.*

The first thing he saw was the man's belt buckle, not the kind you'd buy in a store, more like something made in a crafts class or something, made out of metal and like a tiny little backbone and claws, the claws gripping the backbone. He looked up into the man's face, and what he noticed was his nose hair, sticking out in clumps, and white because he was very old.

"This is my boy," his dad said, and the man looked down at Todd without bending his head, just his eyes moving, and then turned and went back inside and Todd's dad followed and then Todd, into the darkness and strange smell.

The house was dirty with stuff thrown all over the place. At first, he couldn't see much. He sensed some movement and turned and saw the tail of a cat flick and disappear behind a chair.

His father and the man didn't sit down. They stood in the middle of the room talking about the dredge. Todd didn't care about the dredge. He thought it was pretty neat the first couple of times his dad took him, but then it got boring.

He saw another cat and followed it to where it crouched under a table. Todd scrunched down until he was more on the cat's level. They looked at each other. Todd edged a little closer, walking like a duck walks. The cat, yellow and brown and pretty scrawny, hunched itself up. "Kitty, kitty." Todd advanced another duck step, and the animal hunched itself up higher and hissed.

"Watch it there, sonny," the man said, "he ain't used to people."

Todd could tell by its eyes that the cat wasn't kidding, so he gave up the idea of trying to pet it and got up and started to wander around the room, to see what else there was to see. A hanging lamp cast a yellowish light down on a big table in the dining room, or what Todd supposed would have been the dining room if it had been a regular house. All the inside walls had been removed and the ceiling propped up with metal posts. He could see old kitchen appliances in one corner. Daylight came in through a window without a curtain, and an orangey glow came through other windows where curtains hung which were dingy and faded. All these colors, yellow and white and orange, mixed together to make a kind of muddy glow that was good enough to see by. The smell in the room didn't seem like a single thing either, but a bunch of different smells all jumbled up.

Almost at once, he spotted two more cats and then a third. He considered the possibility of trying to make friends with one of these, but decided that maybe they weren't used to people, either. Anyway, there was a lot of other stuff to check out. Coffee cans. He'd never seen so many coffee cans in his whole life—in rows and clusters and all by themselves, on tables and chairs and the floor. He looked in some. Mostly they were empty, although some contained metal and plastic stuff Todd didn't know the names of.

His dad was talking to the man in his explaining voice. The man wasn't saying anything.

A couch and a TV stood in the part that would have been the living room. The couch seemed sort of broken down and with a cloth like a bedspread thrown over it, and on top of it was another cat, this one asleep, so Todd sat down and patted it. A coffee can on the floor had ashes in it and the soggy-looking chomped-up ends of cigars, and he could smell the ashes as he peeked in.

Lots of videos were stacked next to the TV. The man didn't have just one of anything; he had zillions—ice chests, coffee cans, cats. Todd could imagine what his mother would say if she saw all this stuff. But he liked it. When you got to be a grown-up, you could do anything you wanted.

He got up and went over to see what kinds of movies the man liked to watch. On the edges of the videos were tiny pictures of naked ladies. Todd wasn't supposed to look at pictures of naked ladies, but he knew all about them. His dad had told him. He decided he'd better not be caught staring at them, though, and so he started to walk around again, sort of back and forth, as if the naked ladies were nothing to him.

Back and forth, until behind the door he found something even more interesting than naked ladies. These new things were lined up, because like with everything else, the man didn't have just one. At first, Todd couldn't tell what they were—a little bit like his snowshoes but made out of metal and with lots of parts. Then, squatting down, he smelled the kind of bad smell coming from them and saw the teeth and levers and springs, and he thought of the muskrats hanging from the clothesline.

And he remembered the beavers, too, that muskrats were like beavers. And this place seemed—except for the naked ladies—just the sort of place a real buckskinner would own, a *real* real buckskinner. So he went over to where the man and his father were talking.

"Excuse me, mister," he said, and the man looked down at him without bending his head. "Are you a buckskinner?" It'd be real neat if he was, Todd thought, something he could tell all his friends.

But the man just sniffed and sort of frowned and said, "I don't think so, sonny." He seemed awfully satisfied about something.

Todd felt his father's hand on the top of his head. "It's time to go, sport."

They went outside without anybody saying good-bye or anything, and when Todd asked about the smokehouse again, his dad said, "Later," and in the car just sort of sagged behind the steering wheel, looking funny, not the way he usually looked.

"Are you all right, Daddy?"

"Yeah, I'm fine, sport." His father sat up straight, and all at once he looked like himself again. "What say we go to Ames? We'll stop and get something good to eat on the way."

Todd didn't know where Ames was, or why they had to go there, but he knew what "something good to eat" meant: something Mommy wouldn't approve of.

"Neat!" This was turning into the best day ever. And off they went.

Chapter 78

~

Sam Turner imagined himself too weak ever to be a truly happy man, but at that moment, faced with the dangerous act he had let Reiny talk him into, the long string of commonplace events making up his life rose before him, filled with unrecognized pleasures, as a sick man remembers his health although a healthy man feels nothing. Sam would gladly have been anywhere else, sitting bored at his drawing board on the third floor of city hall or at home reading some half-assed fantasy novel or even back at the radio station being reamed out by Johnny Pond. Anywhere but next to that redneck bar.

He had parked in the tavern's lot, angled up to the side of the building, his right front bumper nuzzled close to the clapboards, which were rodent-colored in the glare of his headlights. Not many other cars in the lot, it being the supper hour on a Monday. A sign, "CC's Tap," hung off the corner of the building, the *T* fluttering in the darkness. In a month or two, it'd be light at this time of the day.

Sam had started out toward his regular hangout, to have a couple first, a little fortification before he put himself through the changes, but then decided different, figuring he'd better not give them any excuse not to serve him, and turned around and stone sober drove back down here to the flats, a neighborhood he'd always been told to stay away from.

Maybe nothing would happen. "You're not looking for trouble," Reiny had said. "Be reasonable. Be polite. See if you can get the bartender talking, see what sort of shit comes out of his mouth. Whatever. But insist on your rights. That's the key thing. You want a drink. This is a public establishment. If he refuses, then you leave. You got what you came for." It sounded so easy when Reiny explained it.

Sam looked at his watch, just after six. The other guy was probably inside already, the guy who was supposed to be his witness.

"They might serve you. Could happen. If it does, then that's that. Drink up and get the hell out of there," Reiny had told him.

"What if they decide to fuck with me?" Sam asked.

"If there's any rough stuff, the other guy we've got in there will call the cops. Whatever happens, Sam, we've got you covered." Reiny thought of everything. Except how long it'd take the cops to get there.

It being Monday night, Sam figured he might catch a break. On the other hand, CC's Tap had a real bad rep. Monday might be an improvement over Saturday, but it wasn't like hard-core motherfuckers checked out the calendar before they went drinking and working themselves up into a state of belligerence.

Abruptly, he opened the door and climbed out, thinking he'd get it over with. The flickering letter made a tzzz-tzzzt sound, like a short circuit…or like the sound of somebody frying in the electric chair. Sam's stomach fluttered in sympathy. He decided he wasn't quite ready.

Maybe a walk would help. Nice night for a walk, although the neighborhood had a rep, too, not just the bar.

Nobody seemed to be about. And the cold air felt good, like it could clear a man's head, settle his stomach.

Sam cut away from the building and down a deserted, treeless side street where the houses bellied up to the sidewalk. Porch lights lit or already off, working class people living by their schedules, Sam thought enviously. White people living their unconscious lives. Except when someone like him showed up.

He walked slowly and at the next intersection turned left with the vague idea that he'd go around the block until he came back to where he'd begun, and by then he'd have his nerve up.

In some places, the sidewalk had been scraped clean, in others the snow just packed down, and the sound of his footsteps came and went. He felt the lightness of his stomach, as if it had come untethered and was floating up against his rib cage.

Just why, he asked himself again, for the umpteenth time, was he gonna do this thing? What did he *really* want, beyond what Reiny Kopp wanted, beyond even his own worthless desire to become somebody in other people's eyes?

Sam's mind resisted these questions, and at the next intersection he continued on straight instead of turning left again. The character of the neighborhood altered slightly, the lots bigger and houses smaller, of single stories, set farther back, shabbier. He felt more exposed.

And alone. Or more alone, for he always felt alone, his aloneness for him a complex, fundamental thing. He often thought about it. He was a kind of expert at being alone. Didn't just come from being a black man in a place like Jackson. He'd been alone in the projects, too. He was alone in company. He was alone in time, too, come right down to it, the past and future things he'd never have the experience of, any more than he'd ever go to the South Pole or inside some sheikh's harem. This life, his life, here and now, this was the only thing he got to work with and he was fucking it up.

At the next block, he continued on although he was getting farther away from his car and had a sense of increasing danger. His mind seemed to have smacked up hard against its limits.

He concentrated on his surroundings, which had changed again, become more like an imaginary neighborhood, more like neighborhoods in movies, with trees and neat front lawns, even the snow neat and unmarked, even a picket fence here and there, a place where a man ought to feel as safe as in church.

Nobody out. People lived indoors nowadays. Looking at these houses was like looking at a white man and wondering what he was thinking.

Sam stopped at an empty lot, illuminated by a streetlight. The snow sagged in places, pools of shadow scattered across it. Along one side, a row of sticks poked up. Maybe the tops of tomato stakes, he thought, maybe a garden under there. He envisioned the place in the fall, the vegetables mostly picked, leaves and vines matted down and discolored. It reminded him of his old job hauling trash.

A car passed, slowing, and Sam figured he'd better keep on moving. At the next block, he turned left, back toward the main street, CC's Tap so far away now that entering it seemed not such a hard thing to do. Probably they'd serve him. Probably he'd have his drink and then get the hell out of there. But maybe they wouldn't. Maybe it'd turn out just the way Reiny wanted it to. Sam could picture the place, with its license hanging behind the bar. He could hear the bartender saying, "Fuck off, nigger. We don't serve your kind." The motherfucker would think he was safe, his word against Sam's, but he wouldn't know about the witness. Reiny was right. Most of the time, nothing you could do, but every once in a while...

Sam started to walk faster.

He was headed toward the city bus barn in the distance, out on the main drag, the houses behind him, empty storefronts on either side of the street. He passed a store with a large "For Lease" sign plastered across the display window and, nearing the recessed entryway, he slowed again and edged over to the curb, feeling the presence of someone else.

The thing of it was, he thought as he checked around the corner, trying to separate figures from shadow, the thing of it was that a man could change all at once, he was sure of it. All Sam's life seemed to him like a preparation, a waiting on just the right moment, when he would push his old self aside and become the person he was meant to be.

A voice came out of the dark.

"Hey, you! What the fuck you think you're lookin' at?"

Sam could see nothing. He remembered how far away his car was and, in the moments still left, had time to regret that he hadn't gone into CC's Tap when he'd had the chance.

CHAPTER 79

~

El Plowman's car phone was ringing as she returned with the pamphlets she had left over from her canvass of a street of tract homes off Kennedy. In the darkness, she fumbled with her keys, expecting the ringing to stop at any moment. When it didn't, the worry that she wouldn't answer in time became the worry that the call would announce some new calamity.

Finally, she got the door open and leaned over and grabbed the phone out of its cradle.

"Yes?"

"El!" The voice seemed far away and was breaking up.

"Who is this?"

"Luther!"

"Where are you?"

"I'm flying my plane...Des Moines! Got legislative commit... meetings...next...days!"

Luther Muller, she thought. *Oh, dear*. Her fears were confirmed. Luther never contacted her unless something had gone wrong.

El didn't ask what was bothering him. Luther didn't require any prompting.

Instead she settled herself in the driver's seat and closed the door and, to gain time, inquired as to just what he was going to be doing in the state capital and, since he was down there, would he mind checking on the status of a couple of senate files the city was concerned about. She always tried to put conversations with Luther to some good use, before the inevitable.

But the inevitable could be put off only so long.

His voice continued to break up so that she only heard parts of words. "...my under...the museum ex...reopen...tonight. Are... ware...that?" he asked.

"The exhibit reopens tomorrow, tomorrow morning at ten," she said.

"Not...I've...told." In the background, she could hear the plane's engine.

"Who told you?"

He mentioned one of the people who was on the museum board along with her and Luther.

"He's been wrong before."

"...seemed pretty sure. I wouldn't...past Reiny Kopp to pull some...Would you?"

She wouldn't. And as soon as Luther had mentioned the museum, El had thought, *Reiny*. And she remembered how little effort he had been putting into the remounting of the black history exhibit. She'd wondered why. She still wondered why.

"Okay, Luther, I'll check it out," she told Muller.

"Give me...call, will you? I want to know...going on. I'll... Regency Suites."

El hung up and started her car and turned on the heater, for she suddenly felt quite cold.

With David Duke in town, the day had been quite bad enough already. She didn't need anything else to go wrong, thank you very much. Perhaps Luther's information was erroneous. After all, what could Reiny possibly have in mind? She didn't know. But how could she know? She didn't think like Reiny. Almost no one did.

She sighed and put the car in gear and headed down to Ice Harbor Place and the museum.

∾

Media vehicles filled the museum parking lot.

El parked where she could find a place and got out. Near the entrance to the exhibit stood a decommissioned UPS truck with Illinois tags and the company logo painted out, and in its place, in elaborate gothic script: Signifyin', Inc.

She hurried into the stationmaster's old office—empty, the ticket seller's table deserted, the pictures of the vandalism still mounted. The room appeared unchanged from her last visit. She'd meant to come down earlier in the day. She'd been meaning to spend more time down there for weeks. If it hadn't been for the stupid mayor's race she'd gotten herself mixed up in... She knew Reiny couldn't be trusted. She knew! Damn!

At the closed door to the Mississippi Delta room, she stopped and listened, but could hear nothing, her mounting irritation edged with a kind of nervous energy.

Cautiously, she entered. The day before, the room had been a mock-up of a Mississippi Delta panorama. Now it stood entirely altered, or not altered at all, for it had been transformed back into the railroad waiting room it had been for so many years, and for an instant, El had the impression that the exhibit had merely been disassembled. The oak benches were back, the ashtrays atop their tall black canisters, an old wooden telephone booth in the corner, the "Greenville, Mississippi" sign that had been hung above the ticket office grille replaced with "Jackson, Iowa"—a worn, utilitarian, impersonal, and slightly oppressive space. But this initial sense passed at once, for it was populated by Reiny's mannequins, arranged in various attitudes and now dressed in 1940s-era traveling outfits.

Almost at once this second impression itself began to erode, the mannequins assuming a more lifelike appearance, suggesting street performers adept at holding poses for long periods. El's glance fell on a pair dressed as an elderly man and woman and sitting on one of the benches. With a start, she realized that she recognized them: Emma and Pete Breitbach, the longtime local political activists. As she stared, they started to talk to each other, as if picking up a conversation previously left off.

What the...?

El looked at the others. More real people. Each time she let her gaze linger on a figure, it came to life, pacing or buying a ticket or going to make a phone call. She recognized a few, a couple by name, some only by sight. Most were strangers. A young black man, the only black in the room, stood near the entrance from the station platform, dressed in a snappy, mint-green suit and dark green fedora, a long black topcoat thrown over one arm, a good-looking man, smiling with a confidence that seemed part of the costume he wore. When she looked at him, he started to advance into the room. This was the apparent signal for everyone to come alive, as actors begin to move when a curtain rises. But then, El realized as she watched the scene, this *was* a stage and these *were* actors. She was beginning to understand.

With upright carriage and crisp steps, like a dancer's progress toward his mark just before the tune begins, the young black man approached the Breitbachs and asked for directions. They pointedly ignored him. He looked down with a kind of superior mien on this rudeness, as if it was to be expected, and then executed a turn and approached someone else, with no better luck. All at once, from behind El, came a brusque masculine voice.

"Hey, you, boy!"

A figure in a police uniform, whom El hadn't noticed earlier, strode past her and intercepted the black man.

The scene continued. El, who had been too startled to attempt to intervene at first, now found intervention unnecessary. She glanced at the sign above the ticket office and at the 1940s costumes and remembered a story from that time in the city's history—or a myth, part myth, for she'd heard it repeated in more than one form.

The actors paid no attention to her, treating her like an audience member who had somehow managed to wander up onto the stage and was, like a balky prop or backstage noise, to be simply ignored. She moved around to where she could read the name on the cop's badge.

Then, abruptly, she left, going out on the platform and stopping and noting, almost with satisfaction, the silence that descended in her wake, the scene she had been watching aborted as soon as she had closed the door behind her.

She considered the situation. The Pullman coach, part of the original exhibit, stood on the far side of the platform, sealed up, irrelevant to Reiny's present purposes. He'd wanted to mount an exhibit on racism in the city, he wanted to rub the noses of the people of Jackson in their hypocrisy. He wanted them to see it, and he wanted the world to see it. She'd told him no, but what was a no to Reiny?

Yet, she had to admit, it was all so very, very clever of him, this turning of the exhibit into a setting to dramatize one of the most shameful acts in the city's history—although there were many who claimed it had never happened. And after the cross burning and David Duke's appearance, she might almost have applauded his antics. The people of the city had not risen up with one voice to condemn the cross burning and to repudiate the likes of David Duke. The hearts of too many of them were soiled with their dislike of blacks. Didn't they deserve this?

Staying close to the building, she moved along to the large sliding door of the former baggage room. Inside she found the media people who belonged to the vehicles parked outside. They clustered around a scene taking place in the middle of the room, their backs to her and their camera lights tenting the area with a bright dome.

El squeezed through until she could get a good look, a living room filled with 1940s memorabilia. Several black actors, two men and a woman, were performing.

"Who knows what happened to that boy by now?" the woman was saying intensely.

"I'll go," one of the men, the older of the two, said. "I ain't afraid to go."

"I want you should both go," the woman told him. She was gazing at the younger man, the gaze intense with conflicting emotions—entreaty, command, fear, love.

Like the actors in the earlier scene, these wore retro clothing, a calf-length housedress, full cut trousers, woolen shirts with wide lapels—working class people, etched in sharp light and shadow by the floods of the camera crews. Reporters stood around with their microphones and notepads. Off to the side, a museum staffer operated a video camera. Other staffers mulled around, as well as a couple of the museum board members, members who were, she noted, particular friends of Reiny, including the one who had talked to Luther Muller. A staffer spotted her and quickly looked away.

El hunted for Reiny and found him recessed in a kind of open pocket in the midst of the journalists, attending to the performance with an intensity that suggested that he, too, had spotted her. No doubt he'd been waiting for her arrival, expected it despite his attempt to keep her ignorant of the event. *Tribune* reporter Rachel Brandeis stood familiarly at his elbow, as if they were in collusion.

El turned her attention back to the drama. Certainly, as head of the museum board, she could put an end to it then and there, but equally certainly, that would merely add to the story.

She edged her way around to the board member who had blabbed, a retiree and history buff, famous for never disagreeing.

"Did you know Reiny was doing this, Karl?" she whispered.

"Something, ain't it?"

El repeated her question.

Karl shook his head. "But you know Reiny. Always got something up his sleeve." He didn't seem annoyed. It didn't seem to make any difference that he was on the museum board and the board had been bamboozled.

"What's the play?" she asked, although she already knew.

"Remember back in '48, black man arrived in town, from somewhere down south there?"

"The bridge?"

Karl pressed his lips together and nodded.

"Of course," she reminded him, "nobody really knows what happened." All they knew was the urban legend that had grown up and been reshaped over the years: a black man arrives in town, a good-looking fellow reputed to have relatives locally, but never identified, and to have a preference for white girls, also never verified. Events unfolded as they would in a tale of this sort. The cop in the other room had been real enough, named Hogan, Francis Hogan, who in the thirties and forties had told blacks getting off the train that the sun better not set on them in Jackson; Hogan was dead now, but still had family in town.

For the rest of the performance, El hung back, keeping an eye on Reiny. The matter would unravel as he intended. Perhaps it was for the best. She wished the museum board had given him permission to go ahead with something on racism. They would have had some control then. She'd tried to convince them, Luther Muller and the others, but no, they wouldn't hear of it. And now this.

The size of the press corps dismayed her, reporters everywhere, network people with all their fancy, high-tech gear, who had come for the David Duke rally and stayed on for the aftermath, all the good copy to be had in a city where the underbelly of racial animosities had been exposed to the daylight. The locals were there, too, of course, including Johnny Pond. El particularly noticed Johnny, wearing his new grim demeanor. They had nothing to say to each other. After the scene at his house, the first move was his, although El wouldn't wait forever.

While most of the actors were black, the ominous voices of whites issued from speakers hung on the walls between the sets, rumblings as of a crowd on the point of becoming a mob.

The room was large, and the observers moved from scene to scene, finally arriving in a far corner, the deepest recess of the old railroad station, where behind a baffle of screens stood a single panel. On it had been mounted the grainy photo of the corpse of a black man, hanging from the lower cord of a truss bridge. Just the picture, nothing else, no caption, nothing.

El waited. Reiny made no attempt to skip out on her, no attempt to approach her. At the end of the performance, the actors and media people mingled around a table set up with coffee and cookies. The actors ignored her, perhaps having been forewarned. El guessed that this was a one-time-only performance. Reiny probably planned to set up monitors in the rooms to show tapes, assuming the exhibit continued to be open to the public, as it undoubtedly would be. Probably he didn't much care one way or the other. What he cared about was today, all the reporters still in town, the timing of the performance anything but an accident. As if, she lamented, the reputation of the city hadn't sunk far enough already.

The reporters began to approach her. She volunteered no opinions, only saying that if there were questions to be answered, Reiny Kopp was the one to answer them. Then Rachel Brandeis came up, with a different question.

"An interesting exhibit, El," she said, "but tell me, wasn't Reiny supposed to remount the old one?"

El hadn't given a thought as to what her public response might be to this particular inquiry. Did she want to say anything?

"Much has changed over the past few days, Rachel," she temporized and then began to recount recent events in the city as if to imply, without actually stating it, that whatever Reiny had been expected to do no longer necessarily applied.

As she talked around the matter in this way, El noticed that one of Reiny's old antiwar buddies had entered the room and sought him out, clearly agitated. His name was Terry or Larry, something like that, and he dressed as if the sixties had never ended.

"What?" Reiny said, the word reaching halfway across the room.

Rachel was persisting, asking her question in a slightly different way.

"Excuse me," El said.

She walked across to Reiny. "What's going on?"

"Nothing." He turned away and started out of the room. El hurried to keep up. Behind her, she could hear the reporters, sensing that something else had happened, coming in pursuit.

"What is it?" she demanded at Reiny's back.

"Somebody beat Sam Turner up," Terry or Larry said.

They were out on the platform now.

"How badly?"

"Pretty bad, Mayor."

"Where have they taken him?"

"St. Luke's."

What was this Larry or Terry person doing, El wondered, bringing such news to Reiny?

They were moving at a dogtrot through the waiting room, the actors there in sudden confusion and scattering to let them pass. El got as close to Reiny as she could and lowered her voice.

"What's this got to do with you?"

But all he said was, "Fuck," and increased his pace, through the stationmaster's office and out into the parking lot, faster and faster still, until El could no longer keep up.

∽

That night, a rash of minor acts of vandalism occurred—racist slogans and swastikas painted by taggers, a Confederate flag left hanging from a bridge overpass, billboards defaced. Toward dawn, someone entered the dog track construction site and broke into the gang box of the black contractor working on the project, stealing several thousand dollars worth of tools.

David Duke condemned these acts at a hastily called news conference in Louisiana, where he had returned immediately following his speech.

CHAPTER 80

～

Consciousness came and went. Sam couldn't breathe except through his mouth. Pain welled up behind his eyes and flowed through his skull and pulsed. He tried to get more comfortable, but something had happened to his chest, every movement an agony, an ice pick driven through his ribs. People came and went, he didn't know who, didn't care. Whispering. The lights turned down low.

The pain increased, sharp brightness strangling the black center of his vision, and then nothing.

～

Somebody was hovering over the bed. Sam opened his eyes, then closed them and breathed through his mouth.

"Sam? Sam? You awake?"

Sam opened one eye partway. In the half-light of the room, the face hovered over him, high bony cheeks, eyes buried in shadow.

"Reiny?"

The face moved closer, scanning. "You okay?"

"Feel awful." Sam's words, nasal sounding, seemed trapped inside his skull.

"Look, man, I'm sorry." Reiny spoke softly. Behind the outline of his head, a ghostly light played across the ceiling. Sam felt nauseous and closed his eye and tried not to move.

"Where am I?"

"St. Luke's. Intensive care."

"What happened?"

"Some guys beat you up."

Sam remembered nothing. Why would somebody beat him up? He was always nice to people.

"Oh, man," he managed.

Reiny was leaning close. "What the hell were you doing? Why didn't you go into the bar?"

Sam lay back, his mouth open, gasping for air. Bar? He was supposed to go into some bar? "What time is it?"

"Almost seven."

"Night?"

"Morning."

"How long I been here?"

"Since early last night. When you didn't show up, the guy I had waiting in CC's went out looking for you."

CC's. That sounded familiar. Must be CC's Tap. There was something he should know about CC's Tap. Last thing he remembered was being in his car, driving somewhere.

He was hooked up to intravenous pouches, hanging from a stand. The thin tubes reaching down toward his arm glowed in the dimness, as if filling his veins with pure light. He felt nauseous again and closed his eyes. The place was quiet. Nobody seemed to be around.

"How you get in here?" he asked Reiny.

"Told 'em I was your brother."

Sam had a sense that this was funny. They weren't even the same color. He tried to laugh, but the ice pick put an end to that.

"Half brother," Reiny said.

When Sam opened his eyes again, Reiny was inspecting him, this way and that, toting up the damage, looked like. "They really did a job on you."

"Who?"

"Don't know. When my guy found you, they were gone. Why didn't you go into CC's?"

CC's again. What was he doing down that part of town? No place for a black man in his right mind.

"I was supposed to go in there?"

"Yeah."

"Sorry, man," Sam said, although he didn't know what he was apologizing for.

"Don't worry about it."

"What was I supposed to do?"

"We'll talk later. Just keep your mouth shut, okay?"

Sam moved and felt the pain in his chest. The glowing tubes wavered. His nausea returned, and he closed his eyes, lifting his chin and opening his mouth wider to ease his breathing. "Feel awful."

"You got a right. They really messed you up. And shit, man, I am sorry. It shouldn't have come down this way."

The nausea eased for a moment. It came like waves breaking.

Reiny was staring toward the open area of the room. When he noticed that Sam had opened his eyes again, he leaned even closer. "Just don't say anything, okay?"

"Can't remember."

"You will."

"I screwed up?"

"Don't worry about it."

It was easier for Sam to talk if he made his sentences very short. He'd screwed up? Made sense. He did it all the time. He tried to remember. "David Duke."

"He's gone."

"Good."

"Yes, good."

"What you got me in, man?"

"Nothing. Don't worry about it. When they ask you what you were doing down there, say you don't remember."

"Don't."

"You will. Just don't say anything."

People would think he was a damn fool showing his face in that part of town. Hell, he was a damn fool, whatever Reiny had him doing. And he couldn't even remember. Probably best not to. "Oh, man."

"You did your bit, my friend. Tried to. Worked out okay, except for this. Now it's over, okay? It's over, and it's time for all of us to lie doggo. Okay?"

Best just say okay, and be done with it. So Sam did.

"Get well," Reiny said, "that's all you have to do." Reiny was too complex for his own good.

Sam said, "You're something else."

"Let people think whatever they want."

"Don't give a shit what anybody thinks," Sam said, which was a lie. Even in all that pain, he knew the lie.

He tried not to move. Or remember.

Chapter 81

~

Three weeks later, during a break in a city council meeting, El Plowman approached Johnny Pond and asked for a private word. Johnny, mindful of their recent encounters, looked away and wondered what another conversation with El could possibly accomplish, but nevertheless he turned back and nodded.

He'd begun to talk to El again, no longer so pissed off about all her do-gooder interference that had led to the cross burning and the rest. Decent people should have a better world to be decent in. But she should have known. First you do no harm.

As she led him down the corridor away from the council chamber, Johnny said, "I heard that the people at Ultima Thule changed their mind about moving their operation here."

"We don't know that yet. Off the record, they haven't been responding to our calls."

He asked another question about the matter, but El just shook her head. Made no difference. The city had become radioactive. No way the company would ever move there now.

El had stopped near the city manager's office.

"Have you found someone to buy your place yet?" she asked.

A few people had looked, but no offers. The realtor said you can always find a buyer, for the right price, but Johnny would be damned before he'd take a pittance and give some white boy the satisfaction of practically stealing the place. The job situation in other parts of the country didn't look any better. He'd brought Chloe and the kids back to Jackson while he looked. He didn't want to do it, but he didn't want to be away from them any longer, either. Families break up for all sorts of reasons.

To El, he merely said, "No. Not yet."

"I hope you don't. I hope you'll reconsider and stay." She moved closer and laid a hand on his forearm. "I've got a favor to ask."

Johnny registered her words, and then said, "Why would I want to be doing anything for you?"

She looked at him, frowning and shaking her head. "It's not for me."

"Who then?"

"When was the last time you talked to Sam Turner?"

This was not a name Johnny was pleased to hear. If it had been months since he'd seen Sam, if Sam had left the city entirely, that would have suited Johnny just fine. Unfortunately… "Saw him yesterday. At the Jesse Jackson demonstration."

"You did? I looked for him. Did you speak to him?"

"Not hardly. He was inside city hall, up on the third floor, looking out the window."

"Is that right? He didn't come down? How odd. Why, do you suppose?"

Johnny chose not to offer an interpretation.

"Have you talked to him recently?" El asked.

"Not since the beating. He's been avoiding me."

"He has?"

"I told him to get his ass in gear, to forget about Reiny Kopp and whatever Kopp had in mind, to concentrate on his work in the drafting room. That's what I told him. Apparently not words he was particularly anxious to hear."

"He's in danger of getting laid off."

"Not surprised." Johnny changed the subject. "Tell me, what's gonna happen to Kopp?" Reiny had been a very busy fellow.

"Off the record? Well, you can imagine. People on the museum board are perfectly livid. He was ordered to remount the old exhibit. He was told and told. But no, he wouldn't listen…talk about people not listening." She pursed her lips and shook her head several times.

"And, of course, there was everything else that happened."

"Yes," she acceded glumly, "he was no doubt involved in some of that, too."

"Some?"

"Some. A lot. I'm not sure. What about you and your family, what happened to you?" The quiet and hesitant way she said this acknowledged her own culpability in the matter.

"No, I don't believe he had anything to do with that," Johnny said. "But just about everything else."

"I don't know. Frankly, I don't want to know. Even if you're right, I doubt it'll ever be proved. Any more than the stuff he did in the sixties was ever laid at his doorstep."

"Reiny's a clever fellow."

"Yes, he is. And if he *is* responsible, I hope it doesn't come out. It'd give comfort to the wrong people."

She was being willfully ignorant here, but about this last she was correct. No point to give comfort. Best let David Duke take the credit.

"Anyway," she had gone on, "I'll do what I can for Reiny. For all his faults, he's very good at museum work, it won't be easy to replace him—but I don't know. There's a lot of anger."

Johnny nodded. El hadn't told him anything he didn't already know. More than likely, Kopp could start looking for other employment. Except for the added publicity that would have resulted, he'd have been fired on the spot. Johnny was of two minds. On the one hand, he approved of Kopp rubbing the noses of the locals in their racism. On the other, Kopp was just acting out.

El moved the conversation back to Turner.

"At the moment, I'm worried about Sam, not Reiny. Why don't you go talk to him, find out how he's coming along? Maybe he's buckling down now. Maybe after what happened. Maybe that's why he stayed up in the drafting room during the rally."

"If he is, fine," Johnny said. "Nothing more I can do."

"If he's laid off, he'll need recommendations. He has to start putting in more of an effort."

Johnny took up a position with his feet comfortably spaced, his hands thrust into his pockets, and his shoulders back. "Seems to me, Eleanor, you need to get out of the business of bringing racial harmony to Jackson."

El glanced around as she spoke, as if to make sure the others hadn't wandered too close.

"This isn't about that. It's about Sam. You need to talk to him."

"I do?"

"We got him into this, you and me."

That much was true. But finally irrelevant, something else she didn't, with her best of intentions, understand.

"Whatever we did, El, now it's up to him." For many blacks, it wasn't simply a matter of deficient skills. Many lacked drive, too, and that often wasn't their fault, either. A hard fact of life. "If Sam's gonna fail," he told Plowman, "not a blessed thing you or I can do to stop it. There's lots of Sams in this world. You help them out, and they fail anyway. Just the way it is. You gotta give them a chance. You gotta do that much. But if you expect them to succeed, too, if you think you can solve the thing without the suffering part, then you don't understand the nature of the problem. You can't. I don't care what you do, people are gonna fail, they're gonna suffer, and it's young black men gonna suffer the most. Just the way it is."

"And so you stop trying?" she challenged him, obviously stung by his words and not a woman to give up.

"Did I say that?" he told her sharply. "When the next young man comes along, you give him a chance, too. You see what I'm saying? You don't give up on him just because the last one failed. And the one before that. And the one before that. There'll be many failures, El, but you've gotta keep on trying."

Like Johnny himself, El had a way of puffing up when she was mad. He understood that about her. "So you won't go see him."

"That's right, I won't go see him."

He watched her walk away, done arguing, and couldn't help but admire the woman despite all her wrongheaded ideas about what it was possible to accomplish in this world.

⌇

El detached herself from Johnny's aura, his big man's heat, and returned to the meeting. Indeed, she was angry, but conscious at that moment more of his anger than her own. Once, he'd been playful. Even his hostility had had a staged quality about it, something mounted for the purpose of a demonstration. Now, since the cross burning, the playfulness had fallen away, and she felt the deeper, truer anger lying beneath.

It had been that kind of year in Jackson, a year for surface niceties to fall away and the bedrock to be exposed.

The meeting resumed. El sat in the mayor's chair and listened to the matters being discussed and thought about her misconceptions. Everything about Johnny Pond had changed—his expression, his manner of moving and speaking, even his clothing, all somber and guarded now. But then again, nothing about him had changed. She had made the mistake of thinking that because they shared a sense of justice that they therefore shared an understanding, but it simply wasn't true. Johnny's complexity wasn't hers.

The meeting wore on. The palms of El's hands were cool, and she pressed one, then the other, against her forehead. It was also no doubt true that Ultima Thule would never move to Jackson. And Reiny would have to be fired, and Sam laid off. Johnny and his family would leave. And what had she accomplished?

She remembered only too vividly standing on the steps of the post office and looking out over Washington Park and Johnny telling her she hadn't been elected to save Jackson from itself. Any business the city lost, he had said, was honestly lost.

It was true. It was true.

Everything had been honestly lost.

Acknowledgments

~

A s much as anything else portrayed in The Loss of Certainty series, the issue of race unites all Americans, our version of the larger human struggle of different peoples to live together in harmony. The events in *The Gamble* were partially inspired by events in Dubuque, Iowa, where most of the research for the novel was conducted. The narrative, however, is quite distinct from those events, and any resemblance between characters in the novel and real people is purely coincidental.

As with the other volumes in the trilogy, it would not have been possible to write *The Gamble* without the help of a great many people, more than I can possibly thank in this brief note. For aid in specific sections of the present work, I am grateful to Bob Blondin, Jim Brady, Ed Cawley, Ed Coleman, Jerry Enzler, Ken Gearhart, Jim Gonyier, Tim Heller, Paul Horsfall, George Kapparos, Gordie Kilgore, Mark Kisting, John Klostermann, Steve Kraft, Barry Lindahl, Matt Lorenz, Andy Marshall, John Mauss, Sandy and Armie McDowell, Frank Murray, Pat Ostrander, Ernie Roarig, Jim Schute, John Taylor, Don Thilmany, Don Vogt, Marv Vosberg, and Jim Westmark.

For expertise on the art of dredging, I spent time aboard the US Dredge *William A. Thompson*, witnessing a decidedly more impressive and complicated operation than that mounted using the small, dilapidated dredge in The Loss of Certainty. I want to express my appreciation to skipper Ed Sing and the crew of the *Thompson* for demonstrating the proper method of dredging. I also wish to thank Charles Robers, of Robers Dredge, who discussed cold weather dredging with me.

As in the other technical fields discussed in the trilogy, the errors are all mine.

Bill Banbury, the construction manager of the Dubuque dog track project, who made it possible for me to spend many hours on the construction site, has, over the years since, never flagged in his enthusiasm for my project or willingness to answer yet one more question.

For matters relating to the negotiations between the city and its unions, I am particularly indebted to Dubuque personnel director Randy Peck, who made it possible for me to sit in on negotiations between the City of Dubuque and its unions. Also generous with their assistance in the matter of union negotiations were Dubuque County Administrator Jan Hess, along with Bob Flannery and other union members.

Bart Jones, John North, and Bill Jungblut led me through the intricacies of the treatment process at the Dubuque water plant. By spending shifts at the plant, as well as in other city departments, I got a feel for the jobs that I could not have acquired otherwise.

For the scenes involving the Catholic Church, I am indebted to Deacon Tim LoBianco, who kindly spent many hours helping me understand the religious community in Dubuque, as well as touring the local motherhouses with me.

During my time in Dubuque, as worker or fly on the wall of city departments or poking into other aspects of life in the city, I spent many interesting hours with a wide diversity of people. So, to a certain extent, the people mentioned above are also stand-ins for all the others who helped me gather the information which formed the basis of The Loss of Certainty. To each and every one them, I say, thank you.

Questions for Discussion

~

1. Was it true, as El Plowman said at the end of *The Gamble*, that everything had been "honestly lost"?

2. Do you think the author approved of what Reiny Kopp did? Identify the moral heart of the novel.

3. Should El Plowman have abandoned the attempt to get black families to move to Jackson in the face of Johnny Pond and Fritz Goetzinger's opposition to the idea?

4. Johnny Pond asked a *Sound Off* caller, "[D]o you suppose it's possible for a man to have no prejudice in him, none at all, and yet...despite all that, still be a racist?" What do you think Pond meant?

5. Aggie Klauer, in one of her walks with El Plowman, tells her that to bridge the gap between the races, it's not good enough for them to live together. They've got to work together, too. Can you think of an instance where this actually happened in the novel?

6. What would you do "after all the laws are in place but the racism still remains"?

7. Deuce Goetzinger seems to face an impossible task when it comes to getting the city to accept his idea of participatory democracy, as it's not an issue the city is required to negotiate over. What's the point, then, of his continuing to push the idea? What can he possibly achieve?

8. Why do you suppose Deuce's idea is so threatening to Paul Cutler, the city manager? After all, he'll have a veto over whatever the committee recommends, and it might be a source of good ideas, a way of skirting around the normal bottlenecks in a hierarchical organization.

9. Compare El Plowman's proposal to bring black families to Jackson with Deuce Goetzinger's proposal that a committee without instructions be created as part of the union agreement with the city.

10. Compare the idea of change represented by the dog track construction with that represented by the other narratives in the book.

11. How are Chuck Fellows and Jack Kelley similar and distinct? How would you describe "the tasks" with which life has presented them?

12. In *Jackson*, Volume One of The Loss of Certainty trilogy, the employee buyout effort was led by Homer Budge, the union head, and Skip Peterson, the CEO of the meatpacking company. In *The Gamble*, Deuce Goetzinger attempts to make city hall into a participatory democracy, and El Plowman, to attract middle-class black families to the city. If you have read both novels, are there qualities that are shared by these four characters that suggest why they have attempted such ambitious undertakings?

13. And finally, compare *Jackson* and *The Gamble*. What are the themes that tie these two books together?